Spirit Song Prequel

DESULTI

An Epic Fantasy

ROSS HIGHTOWER & DEB HEIM

Black Rose Writing | Texas

ISBN: 978-1-68513-510-2
PUBLISHED BY BLACK ROSE WRITING
www.blackrosewriting.com

Printed in the United States of America
Suggested Retail Price (SRP) $24.95

Desulti is printed in Andalus

*As a planet-friendly publisher, Black Rose Writing does its best to eliminate unnecessary waste to reduce paper usage and energy costs, while never compromising the reading experience. As a result, the final word count vs. page count may not meet common expectations.

Praise for
Desulti

"This story is more than just epic fantasy. It's a powerful exploration of women's rights and the fight for independence, which is intricately woven through the plot, making it all the more impactful. With exceptional writing skills, Hightower and Heim weave a beguiling tale of intrigue, betrayal, romance, and action."
–Sublime Book Review

"I'm a huge fan of Ross Hightower's writing. The *Spirit Sight* series takes place in a masterfully built world, as rich and complex as George R.R. Martin's *Song of Ice and Fire*, but with even more heart. And *Desulti* is the best one yet. This book centers around dynamic women, each one powerful in her own way. The plot is twisty and the intrigue is intense, but the characters are who will keep you up at night, turning the pages to find out what happens next!"
–Carrie Newberry, author of ***Wolf is a Four-Letter Word*** and ***Pick Your Teeth with My Bones***

"Hightower and Heim have built a politically volatile world similar to "House of Cards." Desulti's leaders put personal gain above their people, leaving the fate of Argren on one woman's shoulders...and she's not even a player."
–Cam Torrens, award–winning author of the ***Tyler Zahn*** series

"Too much epic fantasy is geared to teenage fanboys. This book is not for them. Women are the core of this story. They are the heroines and villains, and the authors avoid easy tropes and simple answers. Looking forward to the next installment."
–Wayne Turmel, author of the ***Johnny Lycan, Werewolf PI*** series

"This is a world I can't wait to explore further. Richly developed and meticulously crafted to a Tolkien-like level of detail, these pages are living and breathing—Desulti, Alle'Oss, Murtair—the classes reflect an all too familiar world. We find pieces of ourselves in these characters, no matter how different their lives or situations may same. This is indeed epic adventure woven into epic fantasy that is sure to delight and illuminate."

–Jacob Hostetler, author of *Around Curiosity's Edge, Hidden Meridians*

Thank you, Annette, for your unwavering support,
insightful suggestions, and undying friendship!

Maps

You can find maps, comprehensive character lists for the Spirit Song world and more at https://rosshightower.com/argren

Books in the Spirit Song Saga

Prequels

Argren Blue

Desulti

Oss'stera (Coming Soon)

Spirit Song Trilogy

Spirit Sight Volumes One and Two

Spirit Light Volume One

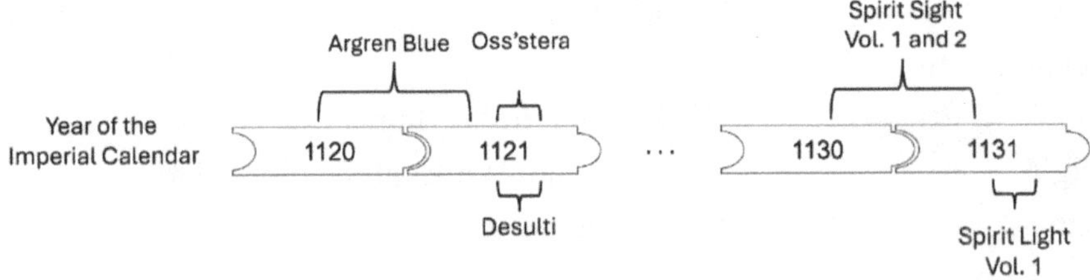

Characters

Desulti

Gabra Caste

Lyssa	Chief Executive of the Inner Council
Siofra (she off ra)	Chief Financial Officer of the Inner Council
Tilla	Chair of the Ruling Council
Elois	Governor Adelbart's daughter, partner of Brie

Angus Caste

Nessa	Head of the Murtair on the Inner Council
Cara	Lyssa's assistant
Eithne (eth knee)	Siofra's assistant
Orla	Plays a prank on Tove
Tish	Lyssa's thug

Burne Caste

Danu	Works at the fulling hut
Brigid	Danu's friend. Works at the dining hall
Cianna	Tove's counselor

Baird Caste

Gwynna	Tove's guide at the beginning

Brochen Caste

Tove	The first *Alle'oss* Desulti

Murtair

Brie (brē)	Brings Tove to the Desulti
Laoise (lehr sha)	Cianna's partner
Eirin (ear in)	Siofra's escort
Tara	Arrives with Siofra
Aedion (ā don)	Arrives with Siofra
Caedan (kā don)	Arrives with Siofra

Alle'oss

Hela (hell ah)	Works for the Order's quartermaster, Tove's friend
Meya (may ah)	Assigned as Tove's servant

Tye (tie)	Cook at the Boar's Head
Shia (shee ah)	Owner of the Boar's Head
Seele (seal)	Works at the fulling hut
Frey	Works at the fulling hut
Jens (yens)	Asked Brigid to dance at the Boar's Head
Garth	Confronted Tove her first time at the Boar's Head
Balder	Nessa's gardener
Aron	Ragan's companion
Eriu (err you)	A young witch

Others

| Ragan   (ray gun) | Former Seidi novice |

The Order

The Desulti Inner Council

Responsible for day-to-day operations of the Order

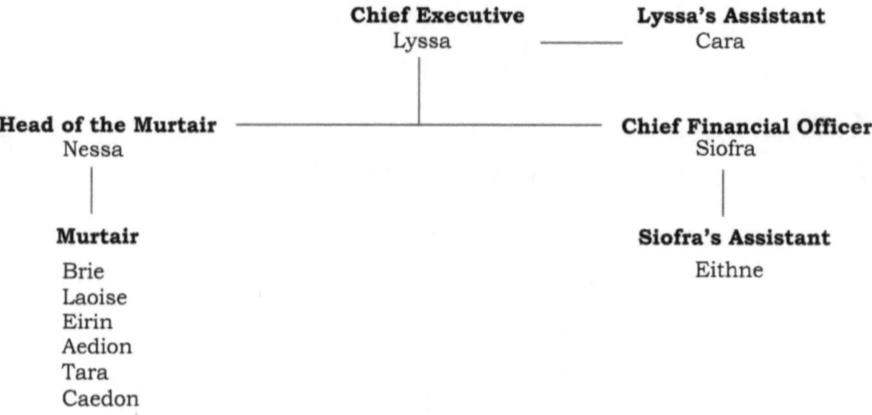

The Desulti Ruling Council

Responsible for setting policy for the Order and for appointing the members of the Inner Council

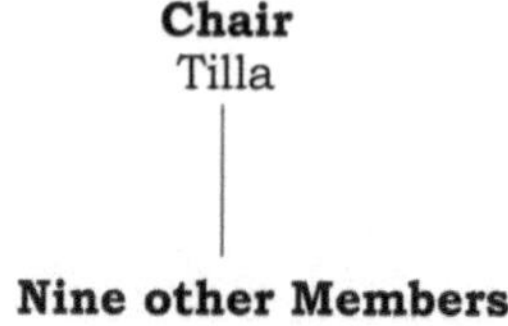

"After many months enduring the torment of the soul spirits' visions, I finally glimpsed a future in which the Alle'oss win their freedom. All my efforts have been in nudging events this way and that in an attempt to bring about that future. I now know that is a fool's errand. The possibilities are too numerous, the effects of my interventions too unpredictable. All my meddling only brought me to the edge of despair.

Yet, in my wanderings in the soul spirits' bleak realm, I sensed other presences, presences that could only be the gods. And when I had nearly given up hope, they showed me the way forward. The great sweep of the future is wrought by a few people. People with the charisma, strength of character, determination, moral certitude, and the ineffable qualities required to bend events to their will. To bring about the future I seek, I need to find those people, people who seek the same future I do, put them in the right place, and nudge them down the right path. Then I must step out of the way, place the world's fate in their hands, and pray the gods have not led me astray.

To my great surprise I discovered the rebel Tove is one such person, a fulcrum on which the fate of Empires pivot. As she travels from Richeleau toward the tangled web the Desulti have become, I fear the fate of Argren depends on whether I can set her on the proper course."

From the Book of the Witch, Ragan Hunter

DESULTI

Prologue

"Tell me a story," the boy said.

The old monk smiled down at the little boy. "What would you like to hear?"

"Tell me how Tove became a Desulti."

"Ah," the monk said. "I haven't told you that one in a long time."

"No, you haven't," the boy said, his voice taking on an aggrieved petulance.

"Do I ever deny you a story?" the old man said.

The boy's brow smoothed. His head tipped to the side, and he gazed up at the monk with wide, placid eyes. "Last week," he said finally.

The monk laughed. "Yes, indeed, I did say no, didn't I? However, I would think the preparation of supper an adequate excuse. No?"

The boy sat on his narrow sleeping platform and gathered his quilt into his lap. "It was a good supper."

The monk smiled, sat, wrapped the boy in his quilt and pulled him into his lap. "Now, let's see. Tove."

"Yes."

"Tove had a very difficult childhood," the monk said. "She never knew her parents."

"Why?"

"Some say the Inquisition killed them, but the truth is no one knows," the monk said. "Not even Tove," he added, anticipating the boy's question when he saw his brow furrow. "The nuns of the Vollen Church raised her until she was old enough to escape, and then she grew up on the streets in Kartok on her own."

"Until Alar found her," the boy said, his worried expression clearing.

"That's right. She had just escaped the Inquisition herself and her ordeal left her scarred."

The boy drew his finger down his cheek from below his eye to the corner of his mouth. "On her face."

"Mm hmm." The monk knew the scar on her face was not the deepest scar she bore, but the visible scars were awful enough for the boy.

"But Alar gave her a home and a family," the boy said, reassuring himself.

"That's right. Alar was the leader of the rebels who called themselves *Oss'stera*. That means our struggle in the *Alle'oss* language."

The boy yawned and lay his head on the old monk's chest. "Why are the Desulti only women?"

"In the Empire, women have few choices and no power. Many years ago, some Imperial women ran away and hid in Argren near a village called Ka'tan. They knew the Empire would come looking for them, so they resolved to make themselves powerful."

"But not by fighting."

"That's right. They knew they could never defeat the emperor's armies, so they sought power through wealth. Now, they are richer than the emperor and that is how they protect the women who come to them."

"But the Murtair fight."

"Yes, the Murtair are Desulti who fight when they have to. But even the Murtair prefer to resort to less violent means."

The boy's face screwed up.

"They would rather not fight if they don't have to," the monk explained, "but they can fight if they need to."

The boy's face relaxed. His eyes drooped, then he roused himself. "But how did Tove become Desulti?"

"*Oss'stera* recovered some stolen art, art that the Imperial governor —"

"Adelbart."

"Art that Governor Adelbart was using to pay the Desulti money he owed them."

"Then Brie came looking for the art. She was Murtair."

"I thought I was telling the story," the monk said with a chuckle.

"I'm helping," the boy said.

When the monk's laughter died, he said, "Now, where was I?"

"Brie came to get the art and Alar fought her."

"Yes. They didn't know one another yet, and they fought."

"How could Alar beat a murtair?"

"Alar is a realm walker. He can enter *annen'heim*, the land of the dead, and return. When he's in *annen'heim*, it appears to him as if time in our realm stops."

The little boy's head tipped back, and he frowned up at the monk.

"He can move very fast. So fast he could defeat Brie."

The boy returned his head to the monk's chest. "But then they became friends."

The monk waggled his head. "Yes, eventually, they became friends."

"But the Union came and stole the paintings from *Oss'stera*."

The monk was familiar with this ritual. The boy had heard the stories so many times, he knew them by heart. Though the old man would start the story, the boy would finish it, his version reflecting what was most important to a four-year-old. "Oh no," he said. "What happened?"

"The Union took Brie and Tove to the prison," the boy said.

"But Alar rescued them," the monk said.

The boy nodded. "He could do it because he was a realm walker. And he rescued the governor's daughter. Her name was Elois. The Union put her in prison, too."

The monk had long decided the boy didn't need to know Elois ended up in prison because of her father's personal peccadilloes. "Did they get the art back?"

"Yes. *Oss'stera* defeated the Union and got the art back."

"But how did Tove become Desulti?" the monk asked.

The boy yawned. "You tell it. I'm too sleepy."

The old man smiled, gazing at the stone wall of the small sleeping chamber and listening to the boy's breaths lengthen. It was just as well he fell asleep. Someday he would know the complicated series of events that followed were part of his own story. But for now, they were beyond a four-year-old's understanding.

Still, the sound of his voice helped the boy sleep, so gazing at the wall and rocking gently, he said, "Ragan, a witch with the gift of prophecy, told Alar he would never free his people hiding in the forest. She told him to follow the Desulti's example and make *Oss'stera* rich." He looked down at the sleeping boy. "Now, most men wouldn't have known what to do, but Alar is greater than most men."

"To satisfy the governor's debt with the Desulti, he made a deal that allowed the Desulti to sell the precious pigments produced by the *Alle'oss* in the Ishien River Valley." His eyes were drawn to the small painting on the wall above the boy's bed. It depicted a man and woman standing on a sun-washed balcony. The woman's dress was painted in the blue called Argren Blue, a pigment more valuable than gold. His gazed lingered on the painting while he rocked. The love evident in the couple's expressions always caused the old man to contemplate the life he might have had. But only fleetingly.

He looked down at the boy and mumbled, "Now, where was I? Oh, yes. Then Alar made a deal with the governor that allowed *Oss'stera* to export *Alle'oss* products from Argen free of Imperial taxes and regulations. Adelbart was grateful to Alar for rescuing his daughter, so he agreed. Alar and his fellow rebels, Scilla and Ukrit, went to the Imperial city of Lachton to make their fortune."

He stood and lay the boy on his sleeping platform. Gazing down at him, he said, "But how did Tove become Desulti? Well, Alar made a deal with Brie to allow Tove into the Desulti. He hoped Tove would help *Oss'stera* form valuable connections, and he hoped Tove would find peace there. But Imperials have a deep-seated prejudice against the *Alle'oss,* and there had never been a Desulti who wasn't Imperial before. Tove knew it would be difficult, but she hoped to find a place she felt safe. She didn't know there were people who would use her for their own ends."

The full story is told in *Argren Blue: A Spirit Song Story* by Ross Hightower and Deb Heim.

Chapter 1

Sanctuary

Tove lifted her gaze from the small fire to watch Brie and Elois through a veil of smoke. When the three of them set out from Richeleau weeks before, Tove tried to ignore their whispered conversations. But after three weeks being a reluctant voyeur to their flirting, she decided if they wanted privacy, they should exchange their sweet nothings out of her earshot. Elois finally caught her eye and had the good graces to look embarrassed. But she returned her attention to Brie, anyway. That wasn't new. Outside Brie's daily lectures on what awaited Tove, the two women ignored her.

Tove looked up at the star filled sky, refusing to let the tears that gathered in her eyes wet her cheeks. She missed the people she left behind, the members of their small rebel group, *Oss'stera*. They were the only family she ever knew. But it was Alar, their leader, who she missed the most. Alar, who rescued her from the streets of Kartok, who gave her a reason to live after the Inquisition stole her life. It was Alar who struck the deal with Brie that made Tove's entry into the Desulti possible. She was thrilled at the time, but three weeks on the road being ignored by this cooing couple left her profoundly homesick.

Of course, her acceptance into the Desulti wasn't certain. Not yet. She and Brie would have to convince the leadership to accept an *Alle'oss* woman. As Brie reminded her every day, the Desulti didn't accept women who weren't of the Volloch caste, and the *Alle'oss* were considered Brochen — the broken caste. If Tove was as cynical as most people believed her to be, she would assume Brie was trying to chase her away before they arrived.

If that was her goal, she would be disappointed. As much as Tove missed her fellow rebels, the idea of joining the Desulti consumed her. The Desulti, or the Order, as Brie called it, were women who fled the Empire. Women from the upper caste, the Volloch, had little say over their lives in the patriarchal Empire. Some Desulti came to the Order to escape arranged marriages, others sought shelter from abusive spouses or parents. Some simply sought opportunities denied them in the Empire. In the Order, a woman's fate depended on her own talents and initiative, not the men who ruled their lives.

And they could be Murtair, like Brie. The Murtair were the elite. In the Empire, they were called assassins, but it was more correct to call them fixers. They fixed the Desulti's problems. Assassination was a last resort. More often, they applied pressure. Reluctant business partners, delinquent debtors, nosy gendarmes, recalcitrant Imperial officials. All could be swayed to the Desulti way of thinking by a visit from a masked Murtair.

Finally, noticing Tove watching her, Brie whispered to Elois. Elois rose and set about arranging her bedroll. Brie watched her with a soft smile on her face. When she sat up and looked at Tove, the smile fell away. "We arrive tomorrow."

This was news. Tove hadn't been this far into the mountains before, and Brie had given no indication where they were before this moment. When they left Richeleau, Tove would have greeted this news meekly, but two weeks of Brie's lectures and the couple's icy disregard wore away Tove's dewy-eyed fawning on the murtair.

"Are you going to lecture me on how difficult my life will be again?" Tove asked.

Brie's expression didn't change, but she studied Tove for long moments before saying, "If you are as flippant tomorrow, you will never be Desulti. It will be difficult enough getting them to accept you without you offending the members of the Inner Council."

Tove fought the instinct to drop her eyes. To hide her face. Instead, she rubbed the scar that ran from her left eye to the corner of her mouth, then pressed her hands to her thighs to prevent them from betraying her nervousness. "Don't worry. I remember what you told me to do."

"See that you do," Brie said. "They'll insult you and the *Alle'oss*. They'll call you *I'oss*."

Tove's face warmed at the slur, but she didn't respond.

"You must not rise to it. You must bury your temper." Brie pursed her lips. "If you can. I will paint you as a woman who has suffered horribly at the hands of Imperial men." Her eyes flicked to Tove's scar. "I'm guessing that's not far from the truth."

Tove couldn't stop herself from lowering her eyes. Noticing her fingers digging into her knees, she forced her gaze up and pressed her lips together.

"But I will also tell Nessa you have potential. She's the leader of the Murtair."

Tove's breath caught.

"I've seen enough to believe it might not be a lie," Brie said.

"I can become Murtair?" Tove asked, unable to hide her desire.

Instead of answering, Brie said, "If she believes me, she will vote to admit you. Lyssa is the Chief Executive, the head of the Inner Council. She will never vote to admit you. Nessa will have to maneuver Siofra into agreeing

. Siofra is the Order's Chief Financial Officer, in charge of the Order's commercial interests. She's less... prejudiced than most Volloch. But admitting a Brochen woman into the Order is bound to be disruptive. She may decide it isn't worth it." She paused, then said, "Even if they allow you into the Order, many will object. They will make your life miserable and will look for any means to rid the Order of the *l'oss* stain."

Tove knew the insult was deliberate, meant to test her, but she couldn't hold her tongue. "Having second thoughts about the deal you made with Alar?" She knew the scar on her face stood out against her darkening skin, but she didn't care. "Want me to slink away so they won't hold you responsible for *staining* your precious Order?"

Again, Brie's stoic exterior didn't crack. "That anger will stand you in good stead in the months to come. If you can control it. If you can't, you'll be on your way home tomorrow. Assuming they let you go."

"You didn't answer my question," Tove said. After weeks of indifference, she needed someone to care, even if it was only the taciturn murtair.

"I would not have agreed to the deal if I didn't believe in it," Brie said. For the first time, her eyes left Tove's and something of her inner thoughts troubled her expression for a moment before it was gone. "I... I have my own reasons for wishing you success. I need to make sure you are serious. That you understand what you will face. I will do what I can to get you in. After that..." She shrugged.

When she fell silent, Tove held her breath. What reasons could this dangerous woman have for wanting Tove to be Desulti?

But instead of explaining, Brie gave her head a shake and retrieved her bedroll. Before retreating into the shadows where Elois had gone, she said, "For Daga's sake, keep your temper under control."

***

Ka'tan was an *Alle'oss* city, high in the mountains of Argren. The first women who banded together to found the Desulti fled the Empire and decided Ka'tan was remote enough for them to be safe. They established the first Desulti community in a valley southeast of the Ka'tan. They called it Téama, an ancient Vollen word that meant refuge. From its humble beginnings, it grew and was now larger than most *Alle'oss* villages.

Knowing they could never defend themselves against the Empire's armies, the first Desulti determined to make themselves powerful through their own enterprise. Now, the Desulti's commercial interests extended throughout the known world. They were rich beyond imagining and were not shy about exerting their influence through whatever means they thought necessary.

While they waited in Richeleau for the snows in the mountains to recede, Alar and Tove learned as much about the Desulti as they could. It wasn't much, but it was clear the Desulti inspired as much fear among the Volloch elite as the Inquisition did among the lower castes. Tove watched Brie swaying in the saddle ahead of her. Before she left, Alar told her, "Be careful. The last thing people who anger the Desulti see is a woman wearing Murtair blacks."

He meant it as a warning, but it fired Tove's imagination. Her fingers came up and traced the familiar path of her scar. She'd seen Brie fight. The murtair was a small woman, like Tove, but she doubted Brie ever *felt* small. Not like Tove did. Small and vulnerable. Brie may have had doubts about Tove, but Tove would swallow her anger, suffer any insult, do anything it took to not feel afraid anymore. The Desulti would have to do a lot worse to her than call her names.

They finally topped the pass they had been climbing all morning to reveal the village of Ka'tan to the north. When the first Desulti arrived, the village was a small collection of modest buildings. But due to the Desulti's prosperity and discovery of coal in the surrounding mountains, Ka'tan grew into the third largest city in Argren.

Brie pointed to the east. "Téama is beyond those hills, a league from Ka'tan. Another two hours." She twisted in her saddle and looked down the narrow path they climbed to get to the top of the pass. "Last chance to back out. They're watching us now. They know we're coming. If you descend to the bottom of the valley floor, they won't let you go without asking who you are and what you're doing here." Though it was late spring, her breath misted in the cool mountain air.

Tove nodded. "I'm ready."

Brie studied her face, then said, "Let's go," and urged her mount into motion.

***

Brie described Téama as they approach it, but Tove was still impressed by the Desulti community. It was larger than she thought it would be, nearly as large as Ka'tan. Having lived in both of the larger cities in Argren, Kartok and Richeleau, she decided Téama was an odd mix of Imperial Kartok and *Alle'oss* Richeleau. The streets followed the Imperial grid pattern, and there were buildings constructed in the staid Imperial style, but there was more green space than in Imperial cities and many buildings adhered to a more eclectic *Alle'oss* aesthetic.

From the attention Brie received, Tove guessed it wasn't often a murtair arrived. Many of the Desulti women waved and followed them through the streets. The Desulti were easy to identify because they had the black hair almost all Imperials shared. Some of them wore white robes, but most were indistinguishable from Volloch women elsewhere in the Empire. She saw one other murtair, wearing the tight black clothes all murtair wore. Unlike Brie, whose scalp was shaved, this woman had short hair. The woman exchanged a nod with Brie, then fixed an intense gaze on Tove. Tove glanced back after they passed and found the murtair still watching her.

Outside of the unnerving attention of the murtair, no other Volloch seemed to notice her. After Brie's repeated lectures about how unwelcome she would be, Tove imagined hostile crowds pelting her with rotten vegetables as soon as she arrived.

Besides the Desulti, there was also a surprising number of *Alle'oss*, identifiable by the many hues of red or blond hair. In contrast to the Desulti, many of the *Alle'oss* peered at her, pointed and broke into conversations as she passed. Even though Ka'tan was a large town, they recognized her as a stranger.

She caught up to Brie and asked about the presence of so many of her countrymen.

"Most of the Desulti in Téama are involved in running the Order's affairs," Brie said. She held Tove's gaze and said, "The *Alle'oss* provide the services too menial for women in the Order."

Tove barely pulled her retort back before it escaped her lips. Instead, she asked, "Are they slaves?"

Brie laughed. "No. They're paid for their services, and they're free to leave if they want to." She looked away so that Tove barely heard her say, "As long as they follow our rules."

Tove studied Brie's profile, fighting to hold her tongue. She wouldn't make it very far if she rose to such mild provocations.

They stopped at the edge of a large paved plaza surrounded by the imposing stone buildings common in Imperial cities. The only difference between these and most Imperial buildings was the absence of the friezes and statues that glorified the Empire's history. Brie pointed to the largest building across the plaza. "That's the Great Hall," she said. "They know we're here and they'll be waiting for us. You ready?"

"The Inner Council," Tove said. When Brie nodded, Tove said, "I'm ready."

As they approached the plaza, the Desulti women following Brie noticed Tove, but only stared curiously. Now, as it became apparent they were heading toward the Great Hall, curiosity shifted into uncertainty and disbelief. News spread quickly, and the numbers swelled. By the time Brie called an *Alle'oss* man over to tend to their horses, the crowd had guessed Brie intended to take Tove into the Great Hall. While the mood wasn't openly hostile, there was an edge that sharpened as the three of them mounted the steps.

Brie led them into a large room she identified as the reception hall. It was as large as the ballroom in the governor's mansion in Richeleau, but it was much more spartan than that grandiose chamber. The walls were bare, unadorned stone. A row of columns along each side left darkened alleys along the walls. Light from windows high on the walls lit the ceiling, but had little effect on the rest of the room. A rectangle of sunlight from the immense doors illuminated the center space, and small braziers set at intervals along the sides pushed the shadows back into the spaces between the columns.

The room was empty when they entered, save for three women standing on a dais at the far end. Tove, Brie and Elois were followed by the crowd that gathered as they crossed the plaza. They poured into the dark spaces on both sides of the room and filled the large open space behind Tove.

Brie told her to keep her eyes downcast when they met the Inner Council, but Tove couldn't help studying the three women, trying to match them to Brie's descriptions. The woman on the left, wearing the blacks of the Murtair, must be Nessa. She gave Brie a small smile before turning a speculative gaze on Tove. On the right was Siofra, wearing the kind of stylish dress Tove often saw elite Volloch women wear in Kartok. Siofra ignored Tove but cast a disapproving frown at the crowd. The woman wearing a white robe standing between the other two, giving Tove an icy stare, must be Lyssa.

Without taking her gaze from Tove, Lyssa said, "Brie. You've returned." The murmurs of the crowd quieted.

Brie only gave her a brief nod.

"We've had word from Richeleau," Lyssa said, her eyes leaving Tove for the first time. "Governor Adelbart is in very good health."

"He was when I left him," Brie said.

"I assume, despite evidence to the contrary, you've managed to secure payment of his debt."

"We worked out a payment plan."

"Who authorized you to propose such a plan?"

Nessa cleared her throat. "Lyssa," she said. "You know the Murtair have broad discretion when in the field. Let us hear the details of this plan before we pass judgment."

Only a slight tightening of the muscles around her mouth revealed Lyssa's irritation. "Of course," she said. "I look forward to hearing your explanation." She looked past Brie. "And who is this?"

Brie turned and gestured to Elois. "This is Elois, Governor Adelbart's daughter. She has already been accepted into the Order in Richeleau." Brie waved Tove forward. "And this is Tove —"

"She's *Alle'oss*," Lyssa said.

Tove felt the pressure of the crowd's response to this statement on her back.

Brie gave Tove a small nod.

Tove licked her lips. The words seemed so simple when Brie had her rehearse them. Now, they fled her mind. She opened her mouth and hesitated before they came to her. "I request sanctuary," she said, fumbling over the last word.

Brie explained the varying personalities and motivations of the three women of the Inner Council and how they might respond, but their reaction to Tove's simple statement was identical — shock.

And then the room erupted.

Chapter 2

Deals

Tove whirled to face a roiling sea of anger and disbelief. Retreating from the surging crowd, she crouched and raised her fists. Someone shoved her from behind, nearly throwing her to the floor. And then Brie appeared before her. The murtair's back was to Tove. She stood relaxed, arms loose at her sides, but the women in the crowd recoiled, uncertainty and fear wiping the anger from their expressions.

"Clear the room!" someone behind Tove shouted. Moments later, women wearing uniforms similar to the gendarmes Tove was familiar with from Richeleau appeared and herded the crowd toward the exit.

Tove straightened, breath coming in ragged pants, heart thumping. She forced herself to meet the glares that reappeared as the women receded from the murtair. Brie warned her. She shouldn't have been surprised, but the suddenness of the outburst, the intensity of the anger, shocked her.

As the gendarmes pushed the immense doors closed, the slice of the city and blue sky beyond narrowed, leaving the room lit only by the braziers and the feeble light filtering down from the windows. Tove's legs twitched before she controlled the impulse to flee, to squeeze through the gap of the closing doors and escape. But then the doors banged shut. The sound, echoing hollowly in the immense room, unlocked buried memories. Memories of other doors, of darkness and men whose icy indifference was far more terrifying than these women's anger. To keep the dark at bay, she focused on a brazier.

When Brie turned and stepped between Tove and the flame, Tove was in control again. The murtair hesitated, searching Tove's face, before brushing past her. Tove focused on the fire for a moment more, then turned to face the women of the Inner Council.

All three women were watching her, but each one's reaction was entirely different from the others. The shock that was her initial reaction still held Siofra frozen. She stared at Tove as if she couldn't decide if she really heard Tove say the words. Lyssa glared, fists clenched at her sides, anger and disgust vying for their place on her porcelain face. But it was Nessa's expression that was the most curious. The corners of her mouth quivered, as if she were fighting a smile. Their eyes met for a moment. Then Lyssa's angry retort, echoing in the nearly empty room, broke the spell.

"Is this a joke?!"

Then all three women were speaking at once.

The words spoken, Tove's part in the drama was over. She only needed to control her temper while the debate raged.

Elois watched, open-mouthed, as the women argued. When she noticed Tove looking at her, she grimaced and looked away. Brie waited impassively until the women ran out of steam. In the pause, Nessa said to Brie, "Explain yourself."

"It's true that Tove is *Alle'oss,*" Brie said. Lyssa started to speak, but Nessa put a hand on her arm to forestall her. "We are all women, and we are Desulti because we suffered at the hands of Imperial men or because we seek opportunities the men of the Empire deny us." She turned her head and looked at Tove. "Few of us have suffered more than this young woman." She paused, allowing the women on the dais to examine Tove, Brie's words undoubtedly bringing their attention to her mangled face. "Her induction into the Order is part of the deal I struck to settle Adelbart's debt."

"If you think we would accept this *Voss* into the order for mere financial gain —"

"We agreed to hear the details of this deal," Siofra said in an even voice. "Let us listen to Brie's proposal before we dismiss the idea."

Lyssa turned a horrified expression on the other woman. "What could she possibly say that would induce us to accept this Brochen filth into the Order?"

Suddenly hot, despite the cool air, Tove opened her mouth before Elois's hand on her arm got her attention. She dropped her gaze and pinched her leg, letting the sharp pain distract her.

Motion in the corner of her eye drew her attention. While Lyssa and Siofra argued, Brie's hand, hanging by her thigh, was gesturing. Tove peeked up at the dais. Nessa watched Brie's hand intently. When her eyes found Tove's, Tove lifted her chin and forced herself to hold her gaze, willing the woman to see into her heart.

Long moments passed, then Nessa seemed to come to a decision. She gave Brie a small nod, then stood quietly, waiting for a pause in the argument. When it came, she said, "Let us retire to chambers to discuss this in private." Her voice wasn't loud, but the other women fell silent at once.

Her pale face blotchy with anger, Lyssa glared at Tove as she said, "I can't think of anything anyone can say that would justify this travesty."

"Nessa has asked to retire to chambers," Siofra said. "We must honor her request."

"Very well," Lyssa spat, and turned away. "Let's get this over with."

As the three women filed out a door at the back of the dais, Nessa frowned at Brie and made several quick hand gestures.

After they were gone, Brie sagged. She took a deep breath and blew it out, then turned toward Tove and favored her with a rare smile. "You did well."

"What's next?" Tove asked.

"Nessa has agreed to take up your case. She only has one vote, but there is hope. Siofra hasn't dismissed your request out of hand."

"What do I do?"

"Nothing. I'll have someone take you to your room where you can wait," Brie said. She rested a hand on Tove's shoulder. "For Daga's sake, don't do anything. Stay in your room. Don't talk to anyone. No matter how long you have to wait."

Tove nodded. "Of course." Brie led her to the exit and pushed open a small wicket door embedded in one of the immense doors. The crowd, which spread out across the plaza, fell silent when Brie appeared. The other murtair Tove saw earlier stood at the top of the steps. She glanced back when they emerged, nodded to Brie, then resumed gazing across the plaza.

Brie signaled to a young Desulti and instructed her to arrange a room for Tove. "Stay out of sight," she said to Tove before entering the Great Hall.

Weak with relief, Tove looked out over the plaza. She thought of Alar and whispered *Oss'stera's* battle cry, "*Otsuna.*" She grinned in the face of the sea of hostility, imagining how proud Alar would be that she made it this far. The Desulti would learn to respect the *Alle'oss.* She would make sure of it.

*****

The three women of the Inner Council were already seated when Brie entered the council room. Lyssa sat at the head of the council table, Nessa and Siofra flanking her. Unlike the austere reception hall, intended to intimidate visitors, this room was intimate and comfortable, the lavish decor reflecting the Order's wealth. And it was blessedly warm from a fire in the hearth.

Brie took her position at the far end of the table, hands clasped behind her back. She stared at a spot above Lyssa's head and readied herself.

"Explain," Lyssa said.

Brie rehearsed this moment repeatedly as they made their way into the mountains. She let her gaze drop and took in the expectant faces. She would give her report to all three, but she was only speaking to one of them. Lyssa would never vote to allow a Brochen woman into the Order. The arguments she rehearsed were for Siofra.

Despite being born into privilege, Siofra was one of the most caste blind women Brie had ever known. She judged women by the value they brought to the Order, regardless of caste. Her vote wouldn't be biased by her prejudices. The question was whether she understood the turmoil Tove's entry into the Order would bring. She remained aloof during the events that roiled the Order in recent years. Was she truly oblivious, or did she simply want to keep her hands clean? Nessa and Brie were gambling that it was the former. They hoped Siofra, a creature of her ledgers, contracts, and the give and take of commerce, would be intrigued enough by the deal tied to Tove's presence that she would vote yes.

Brie gave her report, breezing past the complex details of her mission to recover Governor Adelbart's debt and emphasizing her poor assessment of the governor. He was not a worthy partner for the Desulti. She explained Elois's capture by Union mercenaries and the role Tove and Alar played in her rescue. She explained *Oss'stera's* ambush of an Imperial supply caravan, optimistically painting them as a force to be reckoned with. And only after establishing Alar, Tove and *Oss'stera* as worthy of the Desulti's respect, she explained the deals she struck with Alar and the governor, tying Tove's request for refuge to the deals.

Having finished her narrative, Brie stood motionless, face impassive despite her roiling emotions and racing heart. If they voted to deny Tove immediately, all her and Nessa's plans would fall to ruin. They would not get a second chance.

"Well, that is quite the story," Lyssa said. "I'm —"

"I suggest we take the issues one at a time," Siofra said, before Lyssa could gain momentum.

Brie had to clench her thighs as relief weakened her legs.

"First, there is the issue of this Alar," Siofra said over Lyssa's protests. "You say he can disappear and reappear at a distance in an instant?"

"That's correct," Brie said with a brisk nod. "He dispatched four Union mercenaries patrolling the different sides of the alure atop the fortress wall in Richeleau in less than a minute." After witnessing that feat, Brie told Alar shared secrets were the basis of relationships. But secrets were also the currency the Murtair dealt in and she would spend that currency now. She needed the Inner Council to respect Alar, *Oss'stera*, and, by extension, Tove.

"A *l'oss* killed four Union mercenaries?" Lyssa scoffed. "By himself?"

Having already related the relevant facts, Brie didn't bother answering.

Siofra asked Nessa, "Have you ever heard of such a thing?"

"Perhaps," Nessa said. "It was said long ago there were sisters of the Seidi called realm walkers who could enter the Otherworld and return. While they were in that realm, time seemed to stop in our realm. It would appear as if they crossed a distance in an instant. That sounds very much like what Brie described."

"But they were Seidi *sisters*," Siofra said. "There were no male realm walkers?"

"Not that I've heard," Nessa said. "But it was long ago. Perhaps the accounts of male realm walkers have been lost." She chuckled. "Or suppressed. You know how jealous the witches in the Seidi are of their glory."

"We should deal with him," Lyssa said. "At the very least, he should not be allowed to breed. If this man is indeed a realm walker, we would not want this ability to proliferate among the *l'oss*. They would become quite unmanageable."

That brought the conversation to a halt as each woman considered the implications.

Finally, Nessa said, "What kind of man is Alar?"

"He is a true believer in his cause; freeing the *Alle'oss* from the Empire," Brie said. "He is a visionary, but also pragmatic, willing to listen to reason. I believe he is a man of his word." She paused, then said, "We can work with him."

Lyssa scowled and was about to speak when Siofra cut her off again. "Before we decide what to do about Alar, let's take up the issue of this plan to repay the governor's debt. It seems a good deal to me. There is a passionate demand for *Alle'oss* pigments far beyond the Empire's borders. And it says much about Alar that he offered to pay Adelbart's debt from *their* share. Very pragmatic. It supports Brie's judgment of his character." Her eyes cut to Lyssa. "But I'm even more intrigued by this black market arrangement between the *Alle'oss* and the governor."

"How do we benefit from that?" Lyssa asked.

"I'm not sure," Siofra said. "Yet. However, having a conduit out of Argren free of Imperial regulations and taxes… It shows unexpected foresight for an *Alle'oss* to include this in the bargain. This Alar is ambitious. It might behoove us to seek a relationship with him. We will have to determine the details of this arrangement with the citizens of the Ishien River Valley, of course. The demon is always in the details. But I vote we pursue this opportunity."

"I agree," Nessa said, before Lyssa could comment. "And that settles the question of what to do about the realm walker."

"Correct," Siofra said. "We watch him, determine if Brie's evaluation is correct. For now."

Lyssa didn't look entirely convinced, but even she could see the value of the deal. And she was impatient to move on to what she considered the critical issue.

"Before we get to the last issue," Nessa said. "I believe Brie is to be commended for how she handled a complex situation."

Lyssa's lips pursed, but before she could speak, Siofra said, "Agreed."

"She brought a *l'oss* into the Great Hall to request sanctuary," Lyssa spat. "Whatever good she has done is eclipsed by that affront." She focused on Brie. "What could you possibly be thinking, bringing this woman here?"

"Her admittance into the Order is part and parcel to the deal," Brie said. "Alar required *Alle'oss* representation in the Order." That wasn't entirely a lie. It *was* the reason he gave, but though she only knew Alar for a brief time, he struck her as a man with unusual foresight. She didn't know what he had in mind, but she was sure his plans benefited from Tove's presence in the Order.

Brie stared straight ahead as the women debated, but her attention was on Siofra. It was clear she was wavering. Nessa skillfully intervened whenever she seemed to lean toward Lyssa's point of view, but if she decided to vote with Lyssa right now, there was little Brie, or Nessa could do. An hour later, when the three women finally ran out of words, Brie held her breath.

"It's clear we will not be able to decide tonight," Nessa said. "I suggest we sleep on it. We'll reconvene in the morning to vote."

Siofra looked from Nessa to Brie, a thoughtful expression on her face. "I suppose that is wise."

"What could possibly happen tonight to change our minds?" Lyssa asked.

"Perhaps a night's sleep will cool tempers," Nessa said. "And I would like to speak to this young woman."

Lyssa sniffed and rose abruptly. "Do what you want. We can meet tomorrow morning to vote, but I will not debate the issue any longer. If you want to debate, I'll call the Ruling Council. You can try to convince them."

After Lyssa exited the room, Siofra studied Brie. "I'm sure you and Nessa have much to discuss, but I would like to see you in my chambers when you finish here."

"Of course," Brie said.

Siofra nodded to Nessa, rose, and glided from the room.

When the door closed, Brie sagged, let her chin drop to her chest and wiped her hand across the stubble on her scalp.

"That went about as well as could be expected," Nessa said. Brie looked up. "Are you sure about this woman?"

"Yes," Brie said. "She's everything we discussed." She better be.

"And you've told her nothing?"

"No. She's pristine."

"Let us hope you are correct about her," Nessa said, as she rose. "We will not get a second chance. Make sure she stays out of sight tonight. Lyssa would never stoop to meet her, but we don't want Siofra talking to her. Bring her to my quarters after first bell."

Chapter 3

Tove in the Dark

Word of what happened in the Great Hall spread. The intense anger that erupted when she requested sanctuary ebbed, but as Tove looked out across the plaza, she saw a lot of hostility. The woman Brie instructed to lead her to her room descended the stairs. Before following, Tove glanced at the murtair keeping watch.

The black-clad woman appeared completely indifferent to the drama unfolding around her. She stood at ease, thumbs hooked in her belt, gazing out over the crowd. Tove wasn't fooled. Though her posture appeared relaxed, her stillness belied a coiled readiness. As Tove set off after her guide, the murtair's eyes followed her progress. Tove doubted she was there to protect anyone in the crowd from Tove. She was there to ensure nothing happened to her.

Tove forced her chin up, focused on her chaperone's swaying black curls and ignored the whispered insults thrown her way. No one accosted her. They moved aside, clearing a path, but she felt their disapproval.

They crossed the plaza, leaving the crowd behind as they entered a narrow lane beside a plain, one-story stone building. Halfway to the other end, the woman led her inside into a long hall that extended the length of the building. Boarded-up windows along one side left the hall illuminated only by sunlight entering the door through which they entered. The woman opened one of the doors on the opposite wall and stepped aside.

Tove peered into the dark room. Like the windows in the hall, the window on the opposite wall was boarded up.

"There's a lamp on the table beside the bed," the woman said.

Tove swallowed and nodded.

"There's a privy through that door."

"What is this place?" Tove asked, looking at the row of closed doors in the hall.

"One of the original dormitories. It's slated for refurbishment. No one lives here now."

Tove stood in the doorway, unable to force herself into the confined space. She glanced at the woman, whose expression revealed impatience. To give herself time, she asked, "What's your name?"

The woman looked as if she wouldn't answer at first, but then she said, "Gwynna." She looked down the hall past Tove. A handful of women had followed them into the hall and were watching quietly from a distance. "Is it true you requested sanctuary?" she whispered.

Tove nodded absently, gazing into the dark room.

"They'll never let you in."

"Why?" Tove asked.

"Why… because you're *l'oss*," Gwynna said, as if Tove was stupid. She shook her head. "Even if they let you in, they'll make your life miserable. Why would you volunteer for that?"

"They?" Tove asked, her eyes flicking up to Gwynna's black hair.

Gwynna's cheeks reddened. Her eyes went to the women at the far end of the hall, but she didn't answer.

"*They* are women," Tove said, returning her gaze to the prison cell. "*They* offer refuge to women abused by Imperial men." She took a deep breath, let it sigh out, and wiped her palms on her shirt. "Thank you, Gwynna." She gathered herself, sucked in a breath, and stepped across the threshold.

She was halfway across the room when she looked over her shoulder, heart thudding, and said, "Wait until I light —"

A sullen expression on her face, Gwynna pulled the door shut, leaving Tove in the pitch black room.

Hot, prickly sweat sprung up on Tove's skin. "This is not —" she said through gritted teeth. "I'm safe here." But she was not safe from her memories. Terror, agony, rough stones slick with blood, the stench of fear. And screams. Hers, others. She lost the ability to discern the difference in the dark.

She dropped to her knees, swallowing a scream. Despite the utter silence in the room, she clamped her hands over her ears against the screams echoing hollowly in her mind. The walls closed in, becoming the coffin-like cell they threw her in each time they finished with her.

Light! With a force of will, she scrambled across the floor until she collided with the table on which she saw the lamp. The lamp teetered and almost fell before she caught it. She lifted the glass chimney with shaking hands and set it rattling on the tabletop. With one finger on the small strike plate beside the wick, she felt for the flint.

The small stone slipped through sweat slicked fingers and fell to the floor. "Nooo!" In a panic, she felt on the floor for the small stone, her breath coming in low grunts. She couldn't find it.

Lurching to her feet, she stumbled blindly toward the door, arms extended in front of her. Her hand was on the latch when Brie's admonishment penetrated her panic. *For Daga's sake, don't do anything. Stay in your room. Don't talk to anyone. No matter how long you have to wait.*

Did she come all this way, just to throw Alar's trust away in the first hours? She remembered the hope she felt when she learned there was an order of women. Women like her. Women who escaped abuse, who rejected men's right to rule their lives. Women with the strength and power to walk unafraid wherever they wished. Despite the hostility she encountered since she arrived, she wasn't willing to give up that hope. She couldn't face that. Still, with the pressure of the dark pressing in on all sides, she opened the door a crack. Voices. The women who followed her and Gwynna. She couldn't let them see her like this. Easing the door shut, she sank to the floor, crawled into a corner, pressed her hands to her ears, and wept.

***

Siofra's assistant rose and led Brie into her mistress's inner office. "Siofra's waiting in her chambers," the woman said over her shoulder as she led Brie across the immense office to a door behind the desk. She knocked once. When a voice answered from within, she opened the door and stepped back.

Of the members of the Desulti Inner Council, Siofra enjoyed the fruits of the Order's great wealth the most. Unlike Lyssa, who clung to Imperial tastes despite being a Desulti since she was twelve, Siofra's rooms reflected the exotic and far-flung cultures the Order dealt with. Both women's quarters were in stark contrast to Nessa's austere rooms.

Siofra stood at a large window, gazing toward the snowcapped mountains north of the city. Brie stopped in the center of the room and waited beside a settee imported from Tsada. Siofra told her once the elegant images of snow cranes on the lush fabric were hand-painted. In Brie's opinion, if you were going to spend so much on a small couch, it should at least be more comfortable than the stone bench in her quarters. She kept that thought to herself.

"Have a glass of wine, Brie," Siofra said, without turning around.

Brie glanced at an elaborately carved table beside the settee where a wine chiller contained an open bottle of white wine. A glass had already been poured for her. She hesitated, then picked it up by its delicate stem with fingers hardened by callouses.

"It's *Alle'oss*," Siofra said, still talking to the window. "The wine. Really quite wonderful. Delicate, fruity, surprisingly complex. Nothing like heavy Imperial whites."

Brie looked down at the pale yellow liquid. She wasn't a drinker. Murtair couldn't afford to indulge in anything that affected their discipline. She took an experimental sip and decided she would have to take Siofra's word for the wine's qualities.

"Of course, its quality owes much to Argren. The mountains, the soil, the climate," Siofra said. She turned to face Brie, a half-empty glass in her hand. She had changed into an elaborately embroidered silk house coat. "But I believe it's more than that."

When she didn't continue, Brie felt obligated to ask, "What do you think it is?"

"The *Alle'oss,*" she said with a small shrug. "They have the souls of artists. In many things. Wine." She lifted the glass to eye level and gazed at the swirling liquid. "Food. Music. Art…" She looked past the glass at Brie. "Like the new school artists. The men and women who produced the paintings you allowed to slip through your grasp." When Brie didn't respond, Siofra sipped her wine and said. "Though, I suppose a murtair couldn't be expected to appreciate the significance of such exquisite art."

"It was a complicated situation," Brie said.

"Yes, I gathered that."

Brie glanced down at the wine in her hand, placed it on the table and clasped her hands behind her back. She knew exactly how significant the art she *allowed* the *Alle'oss* to keep was.

Siofra looked at the glass Brie discarded. "Still, this deal with the *Alle'oss* has potential, and perhaps in the long run, it will be better for the Order. If we are forced to choose."

Brie noted the slight emphasis on the word forced.

"Come join me," Siofra said. She turned toward the window and waited for Brie to step up beside her.

"I understand your decision on the art. As you said, it was a complex situation, and you made a choice." She shrugged one shoulder and sipped her wine. "What I don't understand is why you and Nessa are so interested in the *Alle'oss* woman."

This was what Brie was waiting for. She and Nessa discussed what Brie should say. She prepared to launch into her explanation, but the other woman interrupted her.

"Oh, I know you said it was part of the deal," she said, a distant note in her voice, as if she were deep in thought.

Brie almost bulled ahead, but the doubt behind Siofra's words gave her pause. "You don't believe me?"

Siofra cupped the elbow of the arm holding the wine in one hand, tapped her lips with the rim of the glass, and gazed out the window. "Oh, I believe this Alar may have asked for this condition. But there is something else going on here. Nessa was too interested in prolonging the discussion. Despite the risks this woman presents. I don't like it when I don't understand something."

Surprised by Siofra's admission, Brie studied her. She didn't know the Order's Chief Financial Officer well beyond their official interactions. She only knew what Nessa told her. But, gazing at the woman's thoughtful expression, Brie realized Nessa was wrong about Siofra. She wasn't oblivious to the implications of Tove's entrance into the Order. She knew perfectly well what it meant, and she sensed their conspiracy. It was all Brie could do to hide her astonishment. Siofra was intrigued.

"Admitting this woman will change the Order forever," Siofra said quietly. Almost as if she were speaking to herself. "But of course, you and Nessa know that. So, what are you trying to achieve?" She turned from the window and studied Brie's face.

This was the moment. Brie knew her limitations. Unlike Nessa, she was a warrior, not a politician. She learned from hard experience what Siofra could glean from the smallest slip of the tongue. She needed to play on Siofra's curiosity without giving anything away. Allowing her lips to twist, she dipped her head, then let her eyes flick to the side. Her lips parted, but then she pressed her mouth closed and pulled an impassive mask over her face. If she were anyone else, Siofra might dismiss it as nervous fidgeting. But Brie was Murtair. It was as close to admitting she had something to hide as if she spoke the words.

After long moments, something like irritation flickered across Siofra's face, and she broke their gaze.

Was it enough? "Can I ask which way you will vote?" Brie asked.

"No. You may not." Siofra sipped her wine and said, "You may see yourself out."

Without another word, Brie turned and left Siofra gazing at mountains turned purple by the setting sun.

***

Brie found Tove huddled in a corner in the dark. In a flash, she saw her and Nessa's plans falling to ruin. Fueled by adrenaline, she thrust her lamp at Gwynna, crossed the small room, and jerked Tove roughly to her feet. "Why are you sitting on the floor, weeping in the dark?" Though the tears dried, the tracks on Tove's face were evidence of their passing.

Tove pointed toward the table beside the bed. "I… the flint fell."

Brie glanced at Gwynna standing in the doorway, then put her face close to Tove's and murmured, "You need to pull yourself together." She gave Tove a shake. "Look at me!"

Tove startled, focused on Brie's face and fought free of the murtair's grip. "I just need… I need to get outside." She pushed past Brie and made for the door.

Brie caught her and pulled her to a stop before she slipped past Gwynna. She pinched Tove's chin between two fingers made iron by callouses and peered into her eyes. Tove jerked her head free.

"Wash her face," Brie said and shoved Tove toward Gwynna.

Gwynna took Tove's arm and led her down the now deserted hall to a room that contained the baths. Brie's mind raced, searching for a way out. What was she thinking, hitching her and Nessa's plans to this damaged woman? But it was too late. It was either Tove or they would have to abandon everything.

When Gwynna returned with Tove in tow, Brie got Tove's attention and pointed into the dark room. "Whatever that was," she growled. "You need to hide it where no one will see it. Do you understand?" When Tove nodded absently, Brie glared at Gwynna.

"I understand," Gwynna said, nodding vigorously.

Brie dabbed at the moisture on Tove's face with her sleeve.

Tove stepped back and pushed Brie's arm away from her face. "I got it," she said. "I just… *Zhot ti* in Kartok… small spaces… the dark." She started panting, and a hand came up to press her scar.

Brie slapped her. Not hard enough to leave a mark, but enough to get Tove's attention. She tapped Tove hard on the chest with two stiff fingers. "You're here because I saw something in you. That's what everyone else must see from now on."

"I said, I got it!" Tove said, a scowl chasing the lost puppy expression from her face.

Brie studied her. "That's more like it."

"Am I in?" Tove asked, rubbing her chest.

"They haven't voted yet. They'll decide tomorrow. We're going to meet Nessa. Make sure she sees the woman I saw in Richeleau and not whatever that was."

"What woman? What did you see? Tell me what I need to say. What I need to do."

A surge of the same compassion Brie felt for this young woman in Richeleau stopped her retort. She and Tove shared the prison cell together, knowing they would likely be dead before the following morning. It was Tove's steadfast refusal to give into despair that convinced Brie the young woman was the one she was looking for. Her voice softened when she said, "Just be yourself, Tove." She hesitated, wanting to say more, to offer some encouragement that meant something. Instead, she said, "Let's go," turned and walked down the hall.

Chapter 4

She's Perfect

Tove followed Brie outside, leaving Gwynna at the exit to the dormitory. They returned to the plaza in front of the Great Hall, stopping at the corner to peer into the plaza.

Outside, underneath a familiar spring star field, Tove's panic faded, leaving shame in its wake to warm her skin. "I'm sor —"

"Shhh!" Brie looked back at her. Fortunately, shadows cloaked the murtair's expression. "Come on," she said and led Tove across the silent plaza.

Tove assumed they were returning to the Great Hall, but as they passed the fountain in the center of the plaza, Brie veered to the left and entered the street that ran along the west side of the Great Hall. Eventually, they came to a short road lined with the kind of houses common in the wealthy Imperial neighborhoods in Richeleau.

Brie stopped in front of the gate in a wall that surrounded the smallest house on the street. "You ready?"

"Ready for what?" Tove asked.

"To meet the leader of the Murtair," Brie said.

"Nessa."

"Yes."

Desperate to regain this woman's confidence, Tove's words tumbled over one another as she rushed to say, "The woman you were signing to in the Great Hall."

Brie hesitated and studied Tove's face. "Welcome back."

"You going to tell me what's going on?" Tove asked, grateful the dark hid her blush.

"I hoped you could figure that out on your own," Brie said and opened the gate.

She led Tove up the walkway and knocked on the wide double doors. A moment later, one of the doors opened a crack and a woman, whose black hair had gone mostly to gray, peered out at them. No words were spoken, but when the woman saw Brie, she pulled the door open and ushered them inside.

Tove fought to keep from lowering her face when the woman focused on her scar.

"She's waiting in her office," the woman said.

Brie led Tove down a short hall that ended in a closed door. She glanced back before pulling the door open.

The room was much larger than Tove expected. Nessa sat behind a desk that was dwarfed by the mostly empty space. The desk was centered on the back wall, which was covered with floor to ceiling bookshelves. An arrangement of comfortable looking chairs sat to one side of the room in front of a hearth in which a low fire warmed the room. The golden glow of the fire and a lamp on Nessa's desk provided dim illumination that barely touched the high ceiling. In the day, the room would be awash in light from tall windows that filled an entire wall.

Tove came to a stop beside Brie in front of the desk.

Nessa ignored them. Head down, she wrote on a single sheet of paper on her empty desk. It was so quiet Tove could hear the scratches of the quill between the ticks of the pendulum clock on the wall opposite the windows. Tove's nervousness eventually gave way to annoyance. She glanced at Brie and found the murtair staring expressionless at the bookshelves. Taking a deep breath, Tove blew it out in a rush.

The progress of the quill across the page stopped. Slowly, Nessa placed the quill in its stand beside the inkwell. She sat back and stared at Tove. When Tove didn't look away, Nessa said, "Patience isn't one of the *Poss's* virtues, apparently."

Tove's hands, hanging at her side, twitched involuntarily, but she managed to keep her face blank. Though she assumed the comment was meant for Brie, the murtair didn't respond. Nessa studied Tove, as if she were trying to determine something. Catching herself chewing her lower lip, Tove pressed her mouth closed and let her eyes drift to the bookshelves behind Nessa.

"How did you get that scar?" Nessa asked.

Tove froze. Her hands twitched again, but she stopped her instinctive need to cover her disfigurement. Most people fought their desire to stare. Their eyes darted to the scar, then returned to her eyes, checking to see if she noticed. She was used to people's fascination with her scar. She understood it, and preferred people who were up front about it. They were quicker to get beyond their curiosity.

But the flat, uncaring tone in this woman's voice caught her off guard. And when the initial shock ebbed, an old anger reasserted itself. Her face, and her many scars which were not visible, were a testament to Imperial arrogance and cruelty. When Tove first heard of the Desulti, she allowed herself to imagine a place where women, free of male aggression, lived in a mutually supportive utopia. Even the short time since she arrived was enough to disabuse her of that dream. This woman was an Imperial. She might not wield the same instruments of torture as the Inquisition, but Tove saw the same dismissive arrogance in her expression.

Feeling as if she were leaping from a cliff, she asked, "Does my face offend you?" Ignoring Brie's small cough, she continued, "Am I not pretty enough to join your Order?"

"I asked you how you got it?" Nessa asked, not rising to Tove's vitriol.

"An inquisitor gave me this when I tried to cut his balls off."

Brie made a small, choking sound. A small grin appeared on Nessa's face, but Tove barely noticed. The small part of her mind still clinging to the dream cried out in despair and the room faded from consciousness.

"You may wait outside," Nessa said, more dismissal in her tone than in the words.

Tove didn't react at first. When Nessa sat forward, retrieved her quill and bent over her desk, Tove glanced at Brie. Brie nodded to the door. With one more glance at Nessa, Tove spun around, pushed through the door, and slammed it behind her. Heart hammering, she made sure the old woman who admitted them to the house was absent, then slumped against the wall, dropped her head and rubbed furiously at her scar. Anger and despair fought for their share of her thoughts. But a shameful part of her felt relief. She missed Alar, Scilla, Lief and even Ukrit. She wanted to go home. Why did she volunteer for this abuse?

***

"She's perfect," Brie said with more confidence than she felt after finding Tove weeping in the dark.

"Her temper will get her killed," Nessa said.

"That's the fire we were looking for," Brie responded. "She'll need that if she hopes to survive."

"You've forced our hand," Nessa said, with an irritated shake of her head. "I had hoped to meet the woman you chose before she requested sanctuary. I'm not sure this woman is who I would have chosen." Nessa gazed past Brie to the door. "It's not too late. If she were to run away tonight, disappear…"

"It's Tove or no one. Our only hope is the rush of events overwhelms Siofra's caution. If she's given time to consider…"

"What do you see in Tove that I don't?"

Brie described how Tove stood up to Union mercenaries alone when she and Brie were captured. How she freed them from their bindings and wounded a hulking mercenary, giving Alar time to rescue them. She finished with, "She's resourceful, determined, and behind her rough exterior, there is a keen intelligence." Nessa's gaze shifted to the far end of the room. "Most importantly, the rebels in her group are devoted to her. For your plan to work, she must win people over, be someone worth bringing the Order to the brink of civil war."

Nessa chuckled. "My plan?"

"Yes, Mistress," Brie said. She had noticed Nessa's willingness to claim credit tracked her momentary confidence in the plan.

"We have to hope you're right. But none of that matters if Siofra votes no," Nessa said. "How did your meeting with her go?"

"I didn't offer the justifications we discussed. Siofra didn't ask anything directly, but she was probing. She knows we're up to something, and she's curious. I… piqued her curiosity."

Nessa gazed at Brie. After a moment, she nodded and her eyes lost focus. "I would have thought it unwise to arouse her suspicion on purpose, but this may turn out better than we hoped. Siofra has never been able to resist a puzzle."

Brie remained silent.

"What do you think she will do?" Nessa asked.

"She's not as oblivious to the turmoil Tove would cause as we believed. Still, she has no ingrained hostility toward the *Alle'oss*. She won't reject Tove out of bigotry. She sees the value in the deal with the *Alle'oss* and she's curious." Brie shrugged. "I'd make it fifty fifty."

Nessa made a dismissive gesture. "The deal is immaterial. But her curiosity might get the better of her, might be enough for her to vote yes if only to find out what we're planning." She was silent for a moment, then she said, "I hope."

"What if she votes no?"

"Then all is lost."

"Will you go to war?" Brie asked.

"We don't have to make that decision." Nessa looked to the door beyond which Brie hoped Tove was waiting. "Not yet."

Chapter 5

Siofra Gets a Hint

Siofra tipped her glass, bringing the wine perilously close to the rim, and gazed at the fire in her hearth through the golden prism. She sat on the floor, her legs tucked beneath her, her back to the settee. Though she would never admit it, the settee she spent so much to bring back from Tsada was more comfortable as a backrest than a place to sit. She really only bought it to complement the rug on which she sat.

She brushed her fingertips across the rug's rich weave. It was the colors that drew her eye when she saw it in the bazaar in the Tsadan capital. Gold thread wound its way through the intricate designs, glinting in the firelight. Rich reds, deep blacks, just enough of the bright yellows to pop without being garish.

And blue. She rested a fingertip on the blue highlights in the wings of a bird the Tsadans called birds of paradise. The small splashes of blue caught the eye, but it was nowhere near as deep and pure as Argren Blue. Though all the *Alle'oss* pigments were valuable, the real prize was Argren Blue. What would the Tsadan rug weavers pay for even an ounce of that brilliant pigment?

Lyssa and Nessa were unaware of Siofra's extensive intelligence network in Argren. Or at least, she assumed so. Lyssa dismissed the

Alle'oss as unworthy of notice. It was hard to tell what Nessa thought most of the time. Officially, the Murtair was the Order's intelligence apparatus, but Siofra didn't trust Nessa. Besides, what interested Siofra wasn't always a priority for the Murtair. So, at great expense, Siofra developed her own sources.

Siofra learned of Governor Adelbart's extortion of the *Alle'oss* in the Ishien River Valley long before the Murtair. In exchange for his *protection,* the governor demanded the lion's share of the revenue they earned from the pigments. Siofra always judged Adelbart a feckless twit, but that one-sided deal was worthy of the powerful crime syndicates that operated in the Empire.

It intrigued Siofra so much, she investigated and was stunned to discover what people outside the Empire were willing to pay for *Alle'oss* pigments. It was Siofra who issued the contract that sent Brie to collect the governor's debt. She knew he couldn't pay and fully expected Brie to deal with him. Killing an Imperial governor was no small matter, but the Desulti had their rules and he was only the governor of Argren, after all. The storm would pass, and others who would cross the Order would learn a valuable lesson; no one was beyond their reach. With the governor out of the way, all she needed to do was make an offer to the citizens of the Ishien River Valley they couldn't refuse. It would even be a better deal than the governor forced on them.

Then Brie returned, leaving the governor alive and offering the Order exactly the deal Siofra was contemplating.

Normally, that would have thrilled her, but Brie also brought what would almost certainly be a poison pill for the deal; the *Alle'oss* woman who requested sanctuary. Siofra would normally vote no, refuse to allow the woman into the Order. She could still make the deal she originally contemplated. She didn't need the *Alle'oss* rebel leader, Alar. It may take a bit more to convince the *Alle'oss* where their interests lay, but they would see reason. Eventually.

But the question of what Nessa and Brie were up to wouldn't leave her alone. She was curious, but was she curious enough to risk the upheaval this woman would bring? The question had been on her mind since the murtair left her.

The door to her rooms opened after a small knock. That would be her assistant, Eithne.

"Would there be anything else, Mistress?"

Siofra gestured to the wine glass Brie discarded and said, "Have a glass of wine and sit, Eithne." She patted the rug beside herself. When her assistant was settled, Siofra asked, "What do you know of Brie?"

Eithne gazed at Siofra for a moment, then looked at the fire. "I don't know her personally." She sipped her wine. "But who knows any of the murtair well?"

"What have you heard?"

"She must be very good," Eithne said.

"Why?"

"You and Lyssa request her more than any of the others."

Siofra nodded. She knew that, of course. But the riddle of what she was up to brought home how little she knew about Brie, the woman. Her assistant made a small noise. When Siofra looked at her, she could tell she wanted to say something. "Yes?"

"It's just… You remember when you sent her to Lord Brucker's estate?"

Siofra's eyes unfocused for a moment. "Horses for the Imperial Cavalry," she said. "Maybe five months ago?"

"Six months," Eithne said. "Lord Brucker refused to pay the contracted price. He claimed the horses didn't meet the cavalry's standards."

"Yes," Siofra said. "Brie's report said Brucker was right. She allowed him to amend the contract."

"That *is* what the report said," Eithne said, and took another sip.

"But…"

"Well, the only people who see the original report are the murtair who writes it and the clerks in the records' office. They transcribe them and distributed one copy to the owner of the contract and one to Nessa. The originals are stored in the records office."

"Yes, I know this."

"Nessa requested the original a week after it was filed."

Siofra stared at her. "How do you know?"

"My partner works in the records' office. She mentioned it only because it's a bit odd. Almost no one requests the original reports, especially so soon after they're filed." Eithne gave a small shrug. "We assumed she had a question about an error in transcription."

"Why is this significant?"

"The report was missing," Eithne said. "The original. Nessa was furious, but they never found it."

"Why have I not heard of this?" Siofra asked. "This should have been reported to the Council."

"Has it not? I would assume Nessa reported it."

Siofra shook her head and returned her gaze to the fire.

After a short pause, Eithne asked, "Did you learn anything from Brie about the *l'oss* woman who requested sanctuary?"

"Heard about that, have you?"

"Who hasn't?" Eithne asked. "It's all anyone is talking about." When Siofra didn't respond, Eithne's brow furrowed. "The Council won't let her in, will they? I mean, they can't."

Siofra sipped her wine.

"Why would Brie think they would?"

"Yes," Siofra said. "That is the question. What are they hoping to accomplish?"

"You mean Nessa and Brie?"

Siofra nodded.

"So, Brie didn't explain herself? When she was here earlier?"

"No," Siofra said. "But I wouldn't expect her to if she were acting under Nessa's instructions. Brie would never betray Nessa. I was only hoping Brie would reveal something inadvertently." They listened to the soft sounds of the fire. "That report that Brie filed," Siofra said.

"Yes?"

Siofra sat up and turned to face her assistant. "There is something you can do for me before you leave for the night."

"Mistress?"

"Bring me the records of the Murtair contracts for the last two years."

"Of course." Eithne rose, set the glass on the end table, and left the room. Minutes later, she returned with a large ledger book. The book recorded every Murtair contract anyone in the Order issued. Most people in the Empire assumed if a murtair showed up, it meant someone's death, but assassination was a relatively rare goal of a contract. Most of the time, the murtair was only ensuring the Order's interests were served. Whether that required murder was up to the Council or the murtair. Eithne knelt on the floor beside Siofra, laid the ledger on the rug and flipped through the pages to the date of Brie's contract with Brucker.

Siofra set her glass aside and rose to her knees. She and her assistant knelt, side by side and perused the lines in the ledger.

"What are we looking for?" Eithne asked.

Siofra found the contract they discussed, tapped the column that identified the murtair assigned, written in her assistant's precise script. She ran her finger along the line until she reached the column that summarized the outcome. "Brie agreed to amend the contract."

"Yes," Eithne said. "That was what the report said."

The tiniest note of reproach in her assistant's voice brought a small smile to Siofra's face. She flipped pages, running her finger along the summary column, until she reached the most recent contract which was Brie's trip to recover the governor's debt. There was no summary on that line, of course, because Brie hadn't had time to file her report.

She sat on her heels and retrieved her wine. "Fifteen," she said and took a sip.

"Fifteen?"

"Since Brie's trip to visit Lord Brucker, fifteen contracts have resulted in the murtair siding with the target of the contract."

"Is that high?"

"Very high. The Council doesn't send a murtair unless we are sure it is required. I hadn't noticed because so few were mine." She retrieved her wine and settled back against the settee.

"You don't think this is related to Brie and the *l'oss* woman, do you?" Eithne asked as she stood and bent to retrieve the ledger.

"It's hard to see how," Siofra said. "It could be a coincidence, but coincidences often mask hidden truths."

Alone again, Siofra gazed into the fire. Regardless what she told her assistant, the anomalous contracts confirmed to Siofra that Nessa and Brie were involved in a conspiracy. The fact that Nessa didn't make an issue of Brie's missing report was too unlikely to dismiss. She let her eyes unfocus, allowing herself to sift through the possibilities.

Long moments later she snapped back to the present, her eyes focusing. "Oh!" she whispered. "No, it couldn't be." It would explain everything. But it was too much to hope for.

Chapter 6

Initiation

By the time Brie emerged from Nessa's office and led them without a word into the village, Tove, still simmering, had decided to leave at her first opportunity. But the walk across the peaceful village in the crisp night air cooled her anger. Brie waited in the doorway of her small room while Tove lit the lamp. Before Tove closed the door, she met Brie's gaze and hesitated, surprised to see something other than the usual inscrutable mask on her face. Fear or worry. With half her face in shadow, Tove couldn't tell which. But the idea that this woman was capable of either shocked her.

When Brie turned away, Tove came to a decision. She would not slink away in the night. She would force them to deny her entrance into their Order. Show the world who they really were. She would walk out of the Great Hall with her head high. Then, at least, she could tell Alar she gave it her best shot. Assuming they let her go.

Laying on her side on her small bed, she gazed at the flame and wondered what Alar and the other rebels were doing at that moment. Sleeping, undoubtedly, but where? Alar, Scilla and Ukrit were on their way to an uncertain future in Lachton. Were Alar and Scilla in one another's arms? She hoped so. Alar deserved some happiness.

A surprisingly short time later, her door opened after a knock. Though her face was obscured, Tove recognized Brie. Was it dawn already?

"Time," Brie said and retreated into the hall.

Tove groaned as she stood. She hadn't slept a wink. "I'll be home in two, three weeks at the most," she mumbled. Running her fingers through her short hair, she splashed chilly water from a basin onto her face and followed Brie.

***

"Did you sleep at all?" Eithne asked Siofra.

"It shows, huh?" Siofra asked. She did her best to cover the signs of her fatigue, but there was little she could do about her bloodshot eyes.

"No, not at all," Eithne said with a straight face.

"You're very sweet. But you're a terrible liar." Giving up on her hair, Siofra turned away from her assistant and said, "Help me with this. A simple braid will do."

Eithne set to arranging Siofra's hair. "Have you decided how you'll vote?"

Eithne had been Siofra's assistant since before Siofra became the Order's Chief Financial Officer. They weren't friends, but in all that time, her assistant never expressed doubts about Siofra's decisions. The subtle rebuke behind Eithne's question was a preview of the turmoil the *Alle'oss* woman's petition portended.

"I haven't." Catching Eithne's pursed lips in the mirror, Siofra said, "Whatever I decide, I expect you to support that decision, regardless."

"Yes, Mistress. Of course." Finishing the braid, Eithne stepped back and clasped her hands at her waist.

Siofra turned to face her. They gazed at one another for a long moment, then Eithne said, "It's time to go."

***

Brie led Tove across the plaza to the Great Hall. Dawn wasn't an hour past, but a crowd already gathered to learn of her fate. She searched the faces turned to watch her pass and wasn't surprised to find them overwhelmingly hostile. She had the feeling that were she not accompanied by a murtair, they would not have let her pass. Brie stared down the few whose angry words rose above the mutters.

When they entered the Great Hall, Tove was surprised to find the reception hall empty and lit only by gray light leaking through the windows high on the walls. Brie led her through a door at the back of the hall into a smaller, more opulent room. The three women who held her fate in their hands sat at the far end of a long table.

Brie came to a stop and stood with her hands clasped behind her back. She glanced at Tove and nodded to a spot beside her.

Tove spent the night telling herself the vote didn't matter. That she would be happy to rejoin *Oss'stera.* She almost believed it. But as she stepped up beside Brie, she had to lock her knees in place to steady her trembling legs. The fire in the hearth warmed the room, but it didn't account for the sweat trickling down her ribs. She let her lips part and took slow breaths to tame her racing heart. Nessa and Siofra looked as if they had as little sleep as she had, though Siofra obviously tried to hide the signs of her fatigue with expertly applied makeup. Lyssa was the only one in the room who appeared well rested. And confident.

"Before we vote on this trav —" Lyssa started.

"We agreed there would be no more debate," Nessa said.

Tove was grateful. If she had to listen to them debate the value of the *Alle'oss* again, she might lose it. Besides, she wanted an early start heading home.

Lyssa pursed her lips. "Indeed, we did," she said sourly. "I vote no."

"I vote yes," Nessa said immediately.

Lyssa's mouth dropped open. She twisted in her seat and stared at Nessa.

"Why are you surprised?" Nessa asked. "I thought my sentiments were clear yesterday."

"I assumed you were just being obstinate," Lyssa said. "What are you thinking? How can you possibly vote to allow this woman into the Order?"

"Need I read from the Charter?" Nessa said. "We are a refuge for women who have suffered from the Imperial patriarchy." She paused and gave Lyssa a small smile. "This woman has suffered far more than *many* who are in the Order."

Tove couldn't help chuckling at Lyssa's shocked reaction. Whatever hidden meaning Nessa's statement carried, it was a dart to Lyssa's heart. Tove watched the two women bickering, the last of her idealistic illusions about the Order falling away.

Hearing Tove chuckle, Brie glanced at her, brow furrowed. Tove smirked and shrugged. Fortunately, Nessa and Lyssa, distracted by their own drama, didn't notice. She glanced at Siofra and found her watching her. When their eyes met, one corner of Siofra's mouth turned up.

Lyssa and Nessa finally fell silent. Once Lyssa composed herself, she said to Siofra, "So, Siofra, you have the deciding vote. Let's get this over with."

Siofra gazed at Tove.

Tove glanced at the other women. Lyssa was surprisingly relaxed, apparently sure of the verdict, but Nessa's tension was clear despite her attempt to hide it. When Tove returned her gaze to Siofra, the small smile reappeared on the woman's face.

She looked at Lyssa and said, "I vote yes."

There was shocked silence, as everyone in the room, aside from Siofra, reassured themselves what they heard. Then Lyssa erupted, standing so quickly her chair clattered to the floor.

Tove chuckled, then laughed as Brie grasped her arm and pulled her from the room. The door closing cut off the raised voices.

Tove attempted to pull her arm free, but Brie's vice like grip held her fast as she guided her across the reception hall, their footsteps echoing in the empty room.

They stopped before the doors and Brie finally released her.

Massaging her arm, Tove said, "I'm in."

"Welcome to the Order," Brie said grimly. "Daga save us."

"Please, stop. You're making me all teary."

"I'm leaving," Brie said. The small flick of her eyes to the side was so uncharacteristically furtive for her, she might as well have shouted her unease.

Tove stared at her, then looked at the doors behind which the hostile crowd awaited the verdict.

"Normally, newcomers are given some time to… recover from whatever trauma they fled. Ease into their new life," Brie said. When Tove returned her gaze to her, she said, "I'm not sure you will have that luxury."

"Where are you going?" Tove asked numbly. She started at the sound of a shoe scuffing the stone floor behind her, but she didn't take her eyes off Brie's face.

Brie looked over Tove's shoulder and said, "Don't take her back to her room until after the ceremony. Make sure she is taken care of."

Turning her attention back to Tove, Brie's hand came up and hovered awkwardly before coming to rest on Tove's shoulder. "I told you it would be difficult, and that I wouldn't be able to protect you." She gave Tove's shoulder a squeeze, then let her hand drop to her side. "Be strong. I believe you are the kind of woman who will find alli — friends. People on your side." She nodded to the person standing behind Tove, but before she turned away, she said, "Don't forget who you are, Tove."

"Who do you think I am?"

"A woman, an *Alle'oss* woman. Someone who has seen more cruelty, has earned this sanctuary as much as any woman here." Her mouth tightened. She gave Tove a small nod, then she turned and walked deeper into the Great Hall.

Tove watched her go until she lost her in the shadows on the far side of the cavernous room. With a sigh, she gathered herself and turned to find Gwynna watching her.

Without a word, Gwynna turned and walked away. Tove followed her through a side door, then down a darkened hall. Gwynna stopped at a door at the end of the hall and turned toward Tove. "The initiation ceremony," she said.

"Now?"

"They'll come for you when they're ready," Gwynna said with a shake of her head. "It should be soon."

Before Tove could ask one of the other questions that popped into her head, Gwynna pulled the door open. She gestured for Tove to enter. It was a small room lit by two lamps mounted on the opposite wall on each side of another door. The only furnishing was a bench along one wall.

Tove turned in time to catch a glimpse of Gwynna before she pushed the door shut. The door closed with a snick, leaving a silence so deep Tove imagined she could hear the tiny flames in the lamps. Alar's smiling face came unbidden into her mind and with it, a powerful wave of emotion robbed her legs of their strength, sending her to her knees.

Hot, prickly tears pooled in her eyes. "No!" she growled. They could do what they wanted to her, but she would not let them see her weakness. She wiped the one tear that escaped her eyes from her scarred cheek and thrust herself to her feet.

Glancing at the door, she mumbled, "Why is that woman always closing me into small rooms?" She dropped onto the bench, leaned forward, and rested her elbows on her knees. She thought about Alar and the others she left behind, but this time she was ready, and a small smile curved her lips. Alar would be proud of her. It had only been a few weeks since she saw them, but it wouldn't surprise her if they were well on their way to the riches they hoped would sustain the rebel's efforts.

****

Tove wasn't sure how long they made her wait in the small room. At first, she expected them to come for her any moment. Gwynna implied that would be the case. She almost decided they forgot about her until Gwynna appeared with a tray that held bread, a clay pitcher full of water, and a clay cup. Her vague answers to Tove's questions were not helpful and left Tove with the impression she was as baffled by the delay as Tove was.

"Lyssa's trying to figure a way out," Tove muttered to herself after Gwynna left.

Famished, she finished the bread immediately, but, conscious of the fact there was no privy, after slaking her thirst, she only sipped the water. She fell asleep, sitting on the bench for a time, and woke in a panic, afraid they came and left without her when they found her sleeping. To remain alert and ease her boredom, she paced.

Sometime later, she stopped pacing and stood in the center of the room, wondering if she should just leave. There was no way to tell the time in the small room, but based on the pressure on her bladder, she guessed it was approaching the evening. Before she could decide, the door between the two lamps opened behind her. She turned and found a woman she didn't know, wearing a long white robe, gazing at her.

"It's time," the woman said, then disappeared down a hallway.

"About time," Tove muttered as she followed. The woman was waiting beside another open door a few paces down the hall. Tove stopped and peered into the room. It was a quarter the size of the reception hall. Lamps glimmered at intervals on the bare stone walls and dozens of candles on tall stands provided sufficient light to see the faces of women watching her from tiered benches along the sides of the room. The only familiar faces were Nessa and Siofra. Their noncommittal expressions were an oasis in the desert of stony stares. On the opposite end of the room, Lyssa stood on a small raised platform, the icy disapproval in her expression illuminated by two braziers on tall stands. All the women wore the same white robes. All except a woman who stood in front of the platform, to one side, facing away from Tove.

The woman who retrieved Tove made a small, impatient sound. When Tove looked at her, her eyes narrowed. "Well?"

Tove entered the room. Lyssa pointed to a spot on her left, beside the woman facing Lyssa. When Tove stopped, the other woman looked at her. It was Elois, the governor's daughter. They were to be initiated together. Tove smiled, but Elois looked away without returning it.

"Today, you begin your life as Desulti," Lyssa intoned. "Kneel."

Elois dropped to rest her knees on a small pillow. Tove looked down at her feet and saw only the stone floor. It was so petty, she shook her head and couldn't help chuckling as she knelt. A murmur went through the spectators. When she heard someone step up behind her, she almost leapt up, but out of the corner of her eye, she noticed another woman standing behind Elois.

"You shed your hair, as you shed your previous life," Lyssa said. "And as your hair regrows, you grow into your new life."

The person behind Tove took a handful of her short hair and pulled it taut until Tove winced. Dull scissors sawed at her hair until it finally parted, then her barber dropped the hair so it fell across her face. Without pause, another handful of her hair was pulled painfully tight, hewn, and dropped it onto her face.

Lyssa's eyes never left Tove, but now that Tove knew their game, she wouldn't allow Lyssa the satisfaction of seeing her wince. When the scissors were finally withdrawn, she noticed the woman behind Elois applying a cream to Elois's scalp. She waited, but no one applied the cream to her head. Just as she caught the glint of a straight razor beside Elois's ear, someone took a hold of her head and pulled it roughly to the side.

The blade dragged across her scalp had not been whetted. One pass was not sufficient to remove all of her hair, forcing her tormentor to scrape repeatedly over the same spot. Tove yelped the first time the blade nicked her scalp, and though the woman paused, she didn't apologize. On and on it went, long after the sharp blade removed all of Elois's hair. When it finally ended, she straightened her neck, feeling rivulets of blood trickling past her ears.

The tortuous ordeal ending only brought the pain in her knees to the forefront. She ground her teeth, forcing a blank expression onto her face as the woman behind Elois washed her naked scalp with a wet towel, dried it and applied something that produced a soft moan from Elois.

Noticing Lyssa still watching her, Tove smiled, wiping the sneer from Lyssa's face.

Lyssa turned her attention on Elois, clasped her hands at her waist and gave the woman a warm smile, "Now we are all sisters for life." She lifted the arm on Elois's side and said, "Welcome to the Order. Rise and begin your new life."

As the woman behind Elois helped her to her feet, the women seated around the room rose, came forward, gathered around Elois and murmured welcoming words. Still on her knees, Tove was buffeted and forced to her hands and knees. Pressed on all sides, her knees aching and stiff, she couldn't get her feet under herself. Gritting her teeth, she crawled through the sea of white robes until she made it to the side of the room and could pull herself up to sit on the lowest bench.

She wiped her cheek and gazed at the blood on her hand. Looking up, she watched the women usher Elois out the door. In the silence that followed, tears threatened again to betray her anguish. She squeezed her hand into a fist and pressed blood smeared fingers against her lips, feeling ridiculous. Such small cruelties. After what she'd already experienced in her life, it was laughable. Then why did it hurt so much?

It was the pressure on her bladder that saved her from weeping. She forced herself to stand and hobbled on stiff legs toward the door. Just before she made it, Gwynna appeared in the doorway, a lamp in one hand. Despite the woman's cool demeanor, the familiar face forced a small sound from Tove's throat.

Gwynna turned without speaking and disappeared down the hall.

With a sigh, Tove followed. Gwynna led her out into the plaza in front of the Great Hall. Looking up at the stars, she found the answer to how long she waited in the small room. It was near midnight. The late hour was a blessing. Tove expected to have to run a gauntlet of abuse, but the plaza was deserted.

Another younger woman, an *Alle'oss* woman, slouched against the wall outside her room. When they appeared, she straightened and eyed Tove.

Gwynna gestured to the woman and said, "This is Meya. She will be your servant."

"Servant?" Tove asked with a frown.

"Yes," Gwynna said. "You didn't think I would be the one shepherding you around, did you?"

Tove stared at her. "What is it with you Volloch? Are you all cruel from birth, or is it something they teach you?" Gwynna flinched, but before she could reply, Tove said, "I've gotten along my whole life, not once needing a *servant.* I think I'll be fine. Just show me where to go and what to do."

"You may not *wish* to have a servant," Gwynna said. "Nevertheless, Meya has been assigned to you. You may use her or choose not to use her as you wish." She said to Meya. "Return in the morning."

Meya dipped in a small curtsy and squeezed past Tove. As she passed, she gave Tove an enigmatic look.

Gwynna opened the door and gestured for Tove to enter. Tove hurried to cross the room to the table on which the lamp rested. She fumbled the flint through shaking fingers again but managed to light the lamp on the second try. When she turned around, Gwynna still stood in the door. She hesitated, then closed the door. Did she wait to allow Tove time to light the lamp? If she did, it was the first kindness any Desulti other than Brie had shown her. She hurried to the privy.

Chapter 7

Not What I Imagined

Siofra kept her silence as she made her way from the initiation chamber to her office. Normally, she would join the others, welcoming the new members, but she didn't trust herself to speak. Her assistant, Eithne, sensing her mood, followed quietly.

She strode through her office and entered her private rooms. Not until Eithne shut the door did Siofra vent her anger.

"How dare they desecrate our most sacred ceremony!" She snatched up a wineglass from the end table where she left it, eyed the wine remaining in it, then flung it at the fireplace.

"Mistress!"

Siofra whirled on her assistant, searching for a target for her anger. "What?!"

Shock struck Eithne dumb.

Seeing her fear and hurt, Siofra shut her eyes and squeezed her hands into fists, struggling to gain control of herself. After a long moment, she let the tension go, placed a hand on her chest, and opened her eyes. "I'm sorry, Eithne," she said. "It's not your fault."

"Fault? For what?" Eithne asked. "What has you so angry?"

Her anger roaring up again, Siofra threw out a hand. "That — Did you not witness that ceremony?"

Eithne blinked. "Yes, Mistress." A note of rebuke entered her voice. "The *l'oss* got what she deserved, didn't she?"

Siofra's mouth dropped open. She stared at her assistant, seeing something in her she never saw before. She heard Eithne use the *l'oss* slur before, but it never occurred to her such hateful bigotry lurked behind its use. Siofra lifted a hand and used it to emphasize her words. "Eithne, regardless of what you think of the *Alle'oss*, regardless what you think about this woman being in the Order, the fact is she *is* Desulti. To desecrate our initiation ceremony with such… petty… adolescent meanness demeans us all."

"Mistress, I —"

"Get out," Siofra said, but seeing the hurt return to her assistant's face, she took a step toward her and said, "It's been a trying few days. I'm exhausted." Reaching out, she squeezed Eithne's arm and forced a small smile onto her face. "We have much to do before I leave for the wedding. Come back, bright and early."

"Yes, Mistress," Eithne said. She dipped her head and hurried from the room.

Watching her go, Siofra wondered if she might have made a mistake voting to allow the *Alle'oss* woman into the Order. If a woman as gentle as Eithne could condone such demeaning treatment of Tove, what would other more outspoken women do? With a deep sense of foreboding, she turned and made her way to her bedroom. "I'm sure it won't be the last time I have occasion to regret what happened today."

Later, she sat on the edge of her bed, gazing at a sliver of moon over the mountains. She fanned her gossamer nightgown out around her and brushed her fingertips across the silky fabric. Despite what Lyssa and Nessa believed, Siofra wasn't oblivious to what was happening to the Order. They assumed she was too absorbed in the Order's business affairs to pay attention to their machinations. But she recognized what was happening when Lyssa orchestrated her coup.

She watched Lyssa pack the Ruling Council with her own people. She kept her mouth shut because she knew the opportunity it represented for herself. The Ruling Council set policy and elected the Inner Council. The Inner Council was responsible for the day-to-day affairs of the Order, which included the normally routine task of accepting new members. When the new Ruling Council voted Siofra Chief Financial Officer, a position she coveted since she became Desulti, Lyssa thought she bought Siofra's acquiescence. And she was right.

Siofra loved what she did. Growing up, she wasn't allowed to attend the same schools as her brothers. She learned business at her father's knee. She followed him as he worked, hung on his every word, dug into his ledgers, read his contracts, and asked an endless stream of questions. He tolerated her interest when she was young, but as she neared the age of *consent,* he grew exasperated.

"Your husband will not be so patient as I am," he told her.

When she told him she had no intention of marrying, he threw up his hands and stalked away. It had irrevocably altered their relationship, but it hadn't quenched Siofra's thirst for knowledge.

The night he announced he made a match for her, he told her, "Now, you must put all thoughts of business out of your mind. You must put your energies into being a good wife and mother."

Siofra hadn't left that night, but the die was cast. There was a Desulti house near her home. Her family rode past it in their carriage on their way to attend services in the Vollen cathedral. Ironically, it was her brothers' obscene gibes about the Desulti that alerted Siofra to the Order's existence. From the age of eight, Siofra peered out the carriage window at the walled compound as they passed, imagining a place where she could make of herself what her desires and talents allowed.

She left late the night she met her intended. He wasn't an unkind man, and it was obvious he felt lucky for the match. Siofra knew she would dominate the marriage and would soon be running his business affairs from behind the scenes. But he was a man. And, more importantly, Siofra was not one to hide her brilliance behind another.

So she ran away and entered the Order. Her eyes watered at the memory of her initiation. When the women embraced her at the end of the ceremony, she knew she found her home.

Coming back from her memories, she focused on the moon. There was much about Tove's initiation to lament, but it was the desecration of what Siofra regarded as a sacred ceremony that brought her growing unease about what Lyssa was doing to the Order into stark relief. Tove was of the lowest caste, but that shouldn't make a difference. If a woman deserved to be Desulti, she deserved the same respect as everyone else. Her heart thumped at the memory of the young *Alle'oss* woman on her knees while what should be her sisters stepped over her.

But what could she do about it? Siofra had considerable sway within the Order, but she had little influence on the makeup of the Ruling Council. Without a means to influence policy, she was powerless to change anything. If she protested too vigorously, they would replace her. She stood aside as Lyssa took control, and now she would have to accept the consequences of that choice.

Unless she was right about what Brie and Nessa intended.

She lay down beneath her covers and stared at the ceiling, resigning herself to another fitful night.

***

After welcoming Elois to the Order, Lyssa returned to her drawing room, accompanied by her assistant, Cara, and Tilla, the Chair of the Ruling Council. She sloshed brandy into a snifter and approached the hearth, turning her back on the other women. Only a rigid hold on her roiling emotions allowed her to maintain an air of calm. It was Tilla's idea to humiliate the *l'oss*. In the grips of an unreasoning anger after the vote, Lyssa agreed. She gulped brandy and coughed at the burn. But it wasn't only anger she felt now. What was it?

"She laughed!" Cara shouted behind her. "Did you see?" She paused, then grumbled, "But what would you expect of a *l'oss?*"

Lyssa stared into the fire in the hearth. That was it. It was shame she felt. She wanted the *l'oss* to grovel. To be so grateful they allowed her into the Order, she would debase herself, put up with any humiliation for the privilege. But the Brochen woman laughed at them and somehow elevated herself above her betters. The memory of Tove's mangled face smirking up at her cleansed her anger of the taint of shame.

"It was a mistake," Cara said. "We looked small and petty. What were you thinking?"

Lyssa slammed her snifter on the mantelpiece and whirled around, but before she could vent her anger on Cara, Tilla interrupted her.

"It was perfect."

Stunned, Lyssa and Cara gaped at her.

"How could you possibly say that?" Cara asked.

"You saw how everyone ignored the *l'oss* during the embrace," Tilla said.

Cara threw her hand out. "Did you happen to notice Siofra and Nessa's faces?" She said to Lyssa, "They won't forget —"

Lyssa put a hand up to silence her and said to Tilla, "Explain."

"We gave everyone permission," Tilla said with a firm nod. She made a cutting gesture with her hand. "The Inner Council voted to allow this woman into the Order. We can't do anything about that. Not legally, anyway. But the initiation ceremony let everyone know she doesn't deserve respect." She looked from Cara to Lyssa. "You should hear the way people are talking about her. We just have to wait. They'll make it so unpleasant, she'll leave on her own."

Lyssa hesitated, but Cara wasn't willing to admit defeat. "We can't just let her leave. Couldn't we..." When Lyssa looked at her expectantly, she shrugged and said, "A murtair in the night."

Lyssa considered the tempting possibility, then shook her head. "If something were to happen to her now, everyone would point the finger at us." She frowned. "Besides, to take the life of one of our own, even a *l'oss*... It sets a terrible precedent. Even if Nessa agrees with us about her presence, there's no telling how she'll react to that. Her murtair are loyal to her." The thought of a dozen angry murtair sent shivers through her.

"What was she thinking? Nessa?" Cara asked. "She's been so… cooperative with everything we've done so far."

Lyssa shook her head in dismissal. "After the vote, she told me she was just supporting Brie. She never imagined Siofra would vote yes."

"It was Siofra," Cara said, finally finding the culprit. Putting a hint of accusation in her voice, she said, "You were so sure you knew her."

Lyssa met her eyes and held them until Cara looked away. "Siofra is always thinking about profit. Brie was clever to tie this woman to her deal with the *l'oss.*" She frowned. "Still, it's unlike Siofra to be so obtuse. She had to understand what she was doing to the Order. What is she thinking?"

"What did she tell you?" Tilla asked.

Lyssa waved a hand. "She just said the woman suffered abuse, blah, blah, blah, and deserved to be in the Order. What one would expect her to say. But…" She shook her head. "She's not an idiot. She must have something else in mind."

"Get rid of her," Cara said emphatically.

Lyssa gazed past her. The women on the Ruling Council were loyal to her. She could simply have them dispose of Nessa or Siofra, if necessary. But she would rather not lose Siofra. The woman had an uncanny grasp of commerce. Lyssa's plans relied heavily on Siofra's management of the Order's finances. Besides, the next few months were going to be challenging enough without the turmoil that would result from such a drastic move. "We are at a delicate stage," she said. "The last thing we need is for this silly situation to render those two less predictable."

"So, should we let this *l'oss* stay in the Order?" Cara asked.

"Of course not!" Lyssa spat.

"Then what do we do?"

"We wait and see what happens," Tilla said firmly. "She's not actually hurting anything. So what if a *l'oss* calls herself Desulti for a while? It's not going to stop us from making the changes we want to make. Once we get through that, then we'll see."

"That's right," Lyssa said. "And if it becomes so unpleasant, she leaves, she'll have to make her way through the mountains alone. We won't need the Murtair to take care of her and no one need know what happened." She retrieved her brandy. "We proceed with our plans. Keep an eye on the *l'oss*. And on Siofra. We can always solve both problems after we move the Council to Kartok."

***

"She actually laughed," Nessa said with a chuckle. She dropped into the chair behind her desk and looked up at Brie. "You might be right about this woman."

"The whole thing was embarrassing," Brie said. "What was Lyssa thinking?"

"Yes, that *is* surprising," Nessa said. "She's been so methodical until now. But if she has a tender spot, it is for the sanctity of social standing." She sat back and fixed Brie with a speculative gaze. "It was you who pointed that out to me. That's why you said your plan would work. Don't you remember?" When Brie nodded, Nessa gave her head a shake and smiled. "In any case, this sort of irrational outburst plays right into our hands. We can use this."

"Maybe," Brie said. "You don't… you don't think Lyssa would stoop to killing her?"

Nessa pursed her lips. It was as she feared. Brie was developing feelings for the *l'oss*. "Hopefully, not too soon," she said slowly, watching Brie's expression carefully. She sat forward. "You aren't becoming fond of this woman, are you?"

"I don't know her history, have only had glimpses of what she's suffered," Brie said. "But I suspect she deserves sanctuary more than most of the women in the Order." She paused. "You said it yourself."

Nessa waved a hand dismissively. "That was just to goad Lyssa."

"And yet…"

Nessa's eyes narrowed slightly. It was Brie who discovered Lyssa was amending the agreements the murtair negotiated with recalcitrant Volloch. Always against the Order's interests. It wasn't so much the financial considerations that Nessa found objectionable. It was that Lyssa was undermining the Murtair. If outsiders discovered the Murtair could be circumvented, they would lose their fear and that would be disastrous for the Order. Besides, Nessa didn't appreciate Lyssa undermining her authority. So, Nessa investigated, and what she found shook her to her core.

Lyssa only came to the Desulti when she was twelve out of loyalty to an older sister. Having never suffered the way many women in the Order had, she retained misty rose-tinted memories of elite Volloch society. Balls, banquets, afternoon tea, genteel gossip – all the ephemera which were Volloch women's favorite pastimes. And most important to Lyssa; she missed the privilege her elevated status afforded her. The Order was good to her, offering her opportunities she never would have had in the Empire. But she never lost her resentment at being denied what she regarded as her birthright.

After Lyssa became the Chief Executive, an opportunity fell into her lap that would allow her to take her place in Volloch society. The details of the deal were complex, but the gist of it was that the Order would become a legal entity in the Empire, on a par with the powerful guilds that controlled commerce. Lyssa would move the Council to Kartok, the heart of imperial influence in Argren, where she could live out her society fantasies.

The changes would shatter the Order. The Order's business dealings would be subject to Imperial legalities. Worse, Lyssa agreed to the emperor's demand to eliminate the hated Murtair. Without their fear of the Murtair, the Volloch elite would capitalize on decades of resentment to eviscerate the Order in the Imperial courts they owned.

Lyssa thought the Order's wealth would insulate them, but that was foolish. Volloch men would take advantage of the Murtair's absence to exact their revenge. Men who were forced by the Murtair to treat the Order fairly, men whose wives, mistresses, sisters, or mothers sought sanctuary in the Order. Nessa wasn't sure what Lyssa was thinking, but she wasn't willing to find out. Lyssa had to go. Nessa considered going to Siofra. But the Order's CFO owed her elevation to Lyssa, and she was far too secretive for Nessa to trust her. Besides, Lyssa owned the Ruling Council. If she realized Nessa and Siofra were conspiring against her, she would simply have them removed.

Assassination risked open warfare within the Order, but Nessa had almost concluded it was necessary when Brie offered a means to remove Lyssa using the Order's own Charter. It would be traumatic for the Order, but they would survive and if she played it right, Nessa would be able to make the changes she thought necessary.

Returning from her thoughts, Nessa considered Brie, who waited patiently while Nessa ruminated. Brie's plan was brilliant, but Nessa's plans went far beyond what Brie intended. Besides, Nessa had no intention of allowing a *l'oss* to remain in the Order. After she dealt with Lyssa, she would find a way to deal with Tove. She didn't need Brie's growing fondness for the woman to complicate matters.

Nessa glanced at the dark windows, her voice taking on a casual tone when she said, "You're leaving in the morning."

"Yes," Brie said. "Siofra owns the contract. It was sudden. Wasn't even brought to the Council."

"I approved it," Nessa said. She reached for her quill and pulled a stack of paper into the center of her desk. Without looking up, she said, "You may enjoy this contract more than most. I've heard the Ishien River Valley is quite beautiful this time of year."

***

An hour later, Nessa sat in one of the comfortable chairs in front of her hearth. Waiting. The clock struck the second bell when the tap came on the door. Her housekeeper opened the door, then stepped aside to allow the visitor to enter.

"Good evening," Nessa said and gestured to one of the other chairs. The woman made herself comfortable, sitting back and crossing her legs. When she settled, she gave Nessa a wide grin. "The ceremony was an embarrassment," Nessa said.

"Thank you!" the woman said. She smiled widely and stretched her arms languidly over her head before letting them rest on the armrests. "My idea, actually. Lyssa was so furious with Siofra, she wasn't going to hold the ceremony at all. Not until Cara reminded her of Elois." Her tone took on a playful lilt when she said, "The governor's daughter." With a small shrug, she said, "The rest was my idea. No pillow. Dull razor. All that."

"It was perfect," Nessa said. "What was Lyssa's reaction?"

"She was furious," the woman said with tinkling laughter. "You should have seen her."

"What does she intend to do about Tove?"

"Nothing," the woman said and flipped her hands over and back on the chair's armrests. "I talked her into letting the women in the Order take care of the problem. She's worried about disruptions derailing her plans for the move." She drummed her fingers and let her gaze drift to the bookcase. "If it's still a problem after the move, she'll take care of it then."

That was the best possible outcome for Nessa's plans. "Anything else?"

"She doesn't trust Siofra," the woman said. "Thinks there has to be some hidden reason for her vote."

"Thank you, Tilla," Nessa said. "That will be all."

Tilla hesitated and gazed speculatively at Nessa. "So, why did you want this woman in the Order?" she asked. "You said it's to foil Lyssa's plans, but how does it help?"

"Just keep an eye on Lyssa. Let me know if her plans change."

Tilla pushed her bottom lip out and stood. "Okay. You're not going to tell me what this is all about."

"In due time," Nessa said. "I'll need you to play a very important part soon. Just keep an eye on Lyssa and be ready when the time comes."

***

Tove lay in her bed, staring at the lamp, quietly letting the tears she kept at bay all day fall. She was a Desulti. She chuckled softly. "Not what I imagined," she said into the silent room.

She replayed the initiation ceremony, forcing herself to linger over the horrible moments so she wouldn't forget. Compared to what she already experienced at the hands of the Inquisition, the Desulti's petty cruelties were pathetic. With a little distance, she realized it was only painful because she expected to find a welcoming haven. A place where she could dismantle the walls she erected to keep herself safe.

But, as dispiriting and humiliating as the ceremony was, it only had the opposite effect they intended. Most of the brothers of the Inquisition who deserved her retribution were beyond her reach, but the Desulti were not. They didn't deserve to die, but Tove would make sure they regretted the way they treated her. It was one of the hard lessons she learned as a child. If you didn't respond to bullies, the predators learned you were an easy mark. They had no idea what trouble they brought themselves this day.

She let her fingertips play across her tender scalp. The blood from the many nicks dried, but her skin felt raw.

There was a light tap on the door.

Tove lurched upright. It couldn't be her servant already. She crossed the room, rested her hand on the latch, and gathered herself before pulling the door open. It was Gwynna.

The Volloch woman held a large bowl under one arm, a lamp in her other hand, and a towel over her shoulder. When Tove didn't move or say anything, Gwynna cocked an eyebrow and said, "Back up."

Tove allowed her to enter. Gwynna set the lamp and bowl down on the desk, pulled the desk chair into the middle of the room, and gestured for Tove to sit.

Tove kept an eye on her until she was forced to look away when she sat. She waited, listening to Gwynna moving about. Then a warm cloth pressed against her scalp. She sat rigid as Gwynna swabbed her tender skin, carefully brushing the dried blood away. The wet rag disappeared and was replaced by a soft dry towel. Gwynna patted her head gently and dried the stray droplets which escaped down her cheeks and neck.

When the towel disappeared, Gwynna spoke for the first time. "The salve will sting at first, but it will settle in."

Tove gave a quick nod. A moment later, Gwynna applied the cool cream to her scalp. She winced when the salve first encountered the small cuts in her scalp, but as Gwynna's gentle fingers massaged her scalp, the pain receded. Tove moaned involuntarily and let her eyes close. "Bless the Mother," she murmured. "That's wonderful."

Too soon, Gwynna finished. She appeared in Tove's vision, carrying the lamp and set it on the bedside table next to the other one which had began to gutter as the oil ran low. Tove stood when Gwynna turned around.

"Meya can make sure you have oil for your lamp," she said. She gathered the bowl, but left the small crock of salve. "You should apply this again tomorrow." Then she walked past Tove and opened the door.

Before she disappeared, Tove said, "*Tok.*" When Gwynna frowned at her, Tove said, "Thank you."

Gwynna nodded, then pulled the door shut without speaking.

Chapter 8

Fear Not the Night

Brie paused at the top of the pass that led out of the valley that contained Ka'tan and Téama. She turned her horse so she could watch the rising sun reveal the valley and let her thoughts drift to what this new day would bring to the Order.

After consoling Elois for the travesty of an initiation ceremony, she dropped in on her sister to say goodbye. Danu was waiting for her, primed to tell her what everyone was saying about Tove. Brie sat quietly and let her go on until she ran out of steam. Listening to her sister's words tripping over one another in her excitement, it struck Brie how similar her shy sister was to Tove. It wasn't obvious at first glance. Tove was all rough edges and the subtle warning signs of a feral cat. Danu was as gentle and vulnerable as a kitten. But behind the superficialities, they were two awkward peas in a pod.

Tove's fumbling attempts to learn about Brie's relationship with Elois suggested the idea of two women together came as a revelation. Not that the *Alle'oss* cared who a person loved, but Tove obviously had a difficult life, one devoid of healthy relationships to emulate. So, when Danu eventually got around to the questions everyone wanted her to ask Brie, Brie shushed her and told her about Tove. About her bravery. About her tragic past. About their conversations while in the dungeon waiting to die. And, most of all, about Tove's fascination with her and Elois.

Danu grew quiet as Brie talked, her eyes taking on the faraway look that meant she was deep in her inner world. When Brie hugged her sister as she left, Danu patted her absently on the back and mumbled vague goodbyes. Brie had to wave her hand in front of her face to bring out her smile.

Brie learned long ago she couldn't push Danu, but she hoped knowing Tove's secrets would give her sister the courage to take matters into her own hands. Watching the sun emerge from behind the mountains, Brie couldn't help smiling, imagining Tove and Danu's first meeting. If they could find a way to navigate the barriers they erected, they would be perfect for one another.

It was for her sister that Brie suggested her plan to Nessa. Being Murtair shielded Brie from the humiliations other lower caste women suffered. But she watched what her sister had to put up with in dismay. Danu was smart, funny and too kind for her own good. She had a difficult enough time navigating the world without extra burdens. Brie brought Danu to the Desulti thinking she would find a safe space to blossom. The Order was not that place. Not anymore. But she and Danu left her family and all they knew for the promise of a better life, and Brie would see that promise fulfilled.

The problem was in finding the proper motivation for Nessa to go along with the plan. The head of the Murtair wasn't as virulently prejudiced as women like Lyssa, but her casual disregard of the lower castes was just as harmful. Nessa was unmoved when Brie brought to her attention Lyssa's imposing the Empire's rigid caste system in the Order. It wasn't until Brie informed Nessa that Lyssa was amending the murtairs' contracts that Nessa chose to act.

Brie got a sense of how the plan was working when she visited the archives to research the Ishien River Valley. She'd had to use her most intimidating Murtair aura to interrupt the argument between the two women working the desk. What surprised Brie was that neither of the women were among those she groomed to agitate for Tove.

So it appeared the plan was working, but Brie was beginning to have her doubts about Nessa's intentions. It was clear she cared little for Tove's fate after she served her purpose. Worse, Brie suspected Nessa agreed to send her to the Ishien River Valley to get her out of the way. She had plans she didn't want Brie to know about. Brie needed to complete this contract and return as quickly as possible.

***

Tove woke to someone hammering on the door. As a member of *Oss'stera*, she was used to sleeping wherever she could find shelter and would often wake up with no idea where she was. Not this time. The many nicks in her scalp bled while she slept and glued her head to the fabric. The pain brought back the previous evening in sharp relief.

She slid out from beneath the thin blanket, sat on the edge of her bed, and searched for the resolve that coalesced in her after the ceremony. It fled during a night filled with troubled dreams, leaving her with a deep dread for what was to come. Today would be bad.

When she could put it off no longer, she stood and shouted, "Come in, already!" As she crossed the chilly room to the desk where the crock of salve sat, the door opened to reveal Meya. When her servant saw Tove in her small clothes, she hesitated before entering and closing the door.

"*Lorna*, Meya," Tove said. She picked up the still damp blood-stained towel and wiped it gingerly across her scalp. "*Sheoda*, that's cold."

"Mistress," Meya said. "You only have a half hour to finish breakfast before the cart leaves to take you to your job."

"Job?" Tove set the towel down, retrieved the crock, dug her fingers into the salve and raised a brow to Meya. "Who gave me a job?"

"I don't know who gave you a job, Mistress," Meya said. "They just told me to get you there." She paused, eying Tove's hand, working the salve into her scalp. "On time. In a half hour."

"Does every new person get a job?"

Meya looked at Tove as if she wasn't sure if she was joking. "No. Not everyone."

"So, why am I so lucky?"

"I wouldn't know," Meya said. "I'm just a servant."

"What types of people get jobs?" Tove asked. Seeing the frustration in Meya's face, Tove cut her off. "I know. You don't know. You're just a servant." She set the crock down and began sifting through the clothes she discarded the night before. She'd never had anything resembling a job in her life, though she was familiar with the concept. "They pay me for this job?" she asked as she tugged on her pants.

"Yes, Mistress. A little, so you have some spending money."

"I don't need money for food, clothing and other necessaries?"

"Since you are in the Order," Meya paused the smallest amount before continuing, "Mistress. You can eat in the dining hall for free. Anything else you need, tell me and I'll see if it can be procured."

Tove settled her shirt on her shoulders, then set to buckling the belt that held her shirt tight at her waist. "What's with the mistress? They tell you to say that?"

"It's the proper way for a servant to address a Desulti."

Tove noticed the slight emphasis on the words servant and Desulti. "We're both *Alle'oss*," she said, sitting to pull her boots on.

"You're Desulti," Meya said, her eyes flicking up to Tove's naked scalp.

"I've been *Alle'oss* since I was born. Desulti for less than a day."

Meya didn't reply.

Tove threw a cloak over her shoulders. "I'll need some changes of clothes, oil for the lamp." She glanced at the cold woodstove in the corner. "Wood for the stove, a thicker blanket…" Taking in Meya's impatient frown, she said, "Let's start with that." She waved toward the door, then followed Meya out into the hall.

Meya led her hurriedly across the plaza, angling to the right of the Great Hall. It was still dark, but the morning star was just peeking between two mountain peaks in the east. The dining hall turned out to be a long, one-story stone building, a block from the square. Meya pulled the door open and stepped out of the way to allow Tove to enter.

"You're not eating?" Tove asked.

"Servants aren't allowed," Meya said.

"To eat?"

Ignoring Tove's sarcasm, Meya pointed across the room. "Pick up a plate on this end. The women behind the counter will serve you. When you have everything you want, you can take any seat at the tables." She met Tove's eye.

"I know. I have twenty minutes," Tove said.

"Fifteen. Hurry, we're letting the heat out."

Meya pushed the door closed, and Tove turned to find a sea of faces pointed her way. Every table was full, though, she noted, few women had plates in front of them. She hadn't noticed how quiet the room became while she was talking to Meya. An expectant hush. "*Lorna,*" she said loudly, then made her way past a fireplace where a fire poured forth warmth. She gave the two women behind the counter a smile and picked up a plate. Holding it out, she said, "Whatever you have, and plenty of it."

The closest woman snatched the plate from Tove's hand, piled eggs, bacon, potatoes and beans on it. Then she hocked loudly, spat on it and held it out with a wide smile on her face.

Tove ignored the laughter and conversations that broke out behind her. She studied the woman's face, committing it to memory, then she picked up a small loaf of black bread from a basket at the end of the counter, turned and returned the way she came. Taking a bite, she walked slowly and gazed at the women watching her and laughing.

Meya was waiting for her outside. "Did you get enough to eat?"

Tove took another bite of the bread and studied the woman's face, noting the slight lift at the corners of her mouth. She took a moment to finish chewing, then swallowed and said, "You knew they were going to do that."

"Yes, Mistress," she said, fighting her grin. "I heard them mention it."

Tove studied her. After the previous night, she wasn't surprised by the behavior of the women in the dining hall. But receiving the same treatment from this *Alle'oss* woman… Suddenly, the loneliness she'd been fighting since she left Richeleau surged. It never occurred to her becoming Desulti would alienate her from her own people. How was she going to survive this? Meya watched her expectantly, obviously expecting some reaction.

But Tove wouldn't give her the satisfaction. Emotions revealed vulnerability, exposed weaknesses that could be exploited. She didn't know the source of this woman's hostility, but until she did, she would keep her armor intact. Waving a hand, she said, "Lead on. Let's see what other horrors they have in store for me."

A small furrow appeared between Meya's brows as she turned away. Tove took a step, then drew in a sharp breath as the anguish she bottled up threatened to overtop her defenses. Trailing behind her servant, she muttered the lines from a poem that became a mantra when she was locked in the Inquisition dungeon. She had no idea where it came from, or when she learned it. It emerged fully formed into her mind in the endless night of her cell. She murmured it in the dark, repeatedly, marking the time and clinging to the small comfort the words dredged from forgotten memories.

Hanar bilat, pat offar notte
Luwar Wattana en fail'and
Se honuok dywir hirte
Satamar varol-lan'and

She didn't know what it meant until she and Alar found an old woman to help them translated it.

So sleep small one, fear not the night
But seek Wattana's fairy lights
And shelter from the shadows long
Embrace the lan'and's aching song

She took it as one of life's mysteries that it applied so perfectly to her circumstances. The familiar ritual calmed her, reminding her she survived far worse than she was likely to experience at the hands of the Desulti. She just needed to make it through this day. One day. Then she would worry about the next.

Meya led Tove farther from the plaza until they reached the eastern edge of the village. The sun was making its imminent arrival known when they turned onto a road that led out of the village and a wagon came into view. An *Alle'oss* man glowered at them from the driver's bench.

"About time," he growled, and jerked his thumb over his shoulder. "Hop in."

Tove took one look at the bed of the wagon, then climbed up onto the driver's bench and wedged herself in beside the man, forcing him to scoot over.

"No one rides up here with me," he said.

"*Lehasa*," Tove said, returning his scowl with a grin. "Good thing I'm not 'no one'. *Ērtsa* Tove."

The man's face smoothed. He glanced up at her bald scalp. "The *Alle'oss* Desulti. Thought they were putting me on." He looked past Tove to Meya, then said to Tove, "*Ali somi tsila somata sheoda tikan aju ma'ama* (They did a shit job shaving your head)." He flicked the reins, setting the single mule into motion.

Tove twisted around to look at Meya. Her servant watched them with a frown on her face, but when she saw Tove looking, she spun around and walked away. Facing forward, Tove peeked at the man out of the corner of her eye. His shoulder length hair was blond, but gray in a patchy beard and smile lines at the corners of his eyes were evidence of his age. His frown gave the impression he was angry, but she didn't feel any tension coming from him.

"*Ērtsa* Tye," he said.

The simple utterance was so unexpectedly free of hostility, it nearly brought tears to Tove's eyes. "*Lorna*, Tye," she said, embarrassed by the husk in her voice.

His eyes flicked her way. "Not sure what you're thinking, becoming a Desulti, but I expect they're not making it easy."

"No," was all Tove trusted herself to say. He nodded, but didn't say anything else. Tove swallowed. "I thought it would —" Clamping her mouth shut, she gave her head a firm shake and said in a firmer voice. "What really hurts is being treated the same way by Meya."

"Yeah, I expect so," he said. "Opinions are divided."

"Whose?"

"Up in Ka'tan," he said, nodding his head in the direction of the town. "Some think you're joining the enemy. They see it as a betrayal, an *Alle'oss* joining the Order."

Tove stared at his profile. The thought never occurred to her, but how could it not? Some of her fellow rebels considered it a betrayal when *Alle'oss* made any concessions to fit in with Imperials. She let her gaze fall to her knees. Somehow she focused only on the fact the Order were all women. It never occurred to her women who fled the Empire's paternalistic restrictions would still be considered Imperial by the *Alle'oss*. But the difference between what she experienced here and in Kartok was only a matter of degree. She traced the scar on her face with one fingertip.

Tye, perhaps sensing her mood, remained quiet, until she turned to look at him again, then he said, "Some think you're getting above your raising, thinking you're Imperial."

Tove stared at him, then snorted. The idea that any *Alle'oss* thought becoming Imperial was somehow above being *Alle'oss* was ridiculous.

"I agree with you," he said with a small smile. "It seems more stooping to me."

They rode in silence for a few moments, then Tove asked, "Are there any on my side?"

"Not sure it's on *your* side, but there's some who feel allowing *Alle'oss* in the Order might make it less…" He waved a hand.

"Imperial?"

"Yeah. That."

"What do *you* think?" Tove asked, surprised to find her heart racing. Perhaps because so few had shown her even a glimmer of kindness since she left Richeleau, she needed him to be on her side.

He looked at her for the first time. "I wasn't sure. Was thinking I'd wait and see, like some others." He faced forward again. "You seem like a decent sort. Whatever you're thinking, doing this…" He shrugged and gave her a small smile. "Now that I met you, I find myself rooting for you."

Tove felt tension she'd been carrying since she arrived in Téama ebb away. They sat in silence for a time, then she said, "That's enough. For now."

"Might do to let others get to know you."

A half hour later, Tye nodded to a curve in the road and said, "It's around this bend."

"What awful job do they have me doing?" Tove asked, though she caught the odor on the light breeze sometime before and had a bad feeling she knew what it was. The sour stench reminded her of the tanneries relegated to the far outskirts of Richeleau.

"Fulling," he said with a wide smile.

That was not what she was expecting, but the odor, which grew stronger as they neared their destination, suggested fulling wouldn't be any better than the tanneries. "What's fulling?"

"One of the things we have a lot around here is sheep."

"I've heard that."

His eyebrows rose for a moment, and he looked at her. When she nodded, he said, "Well, when you first weave the wool, it produces a low-grade cloth. Oily and the weave is loose. To make it into the high-quality cloth we're known for, you put it through a process called fulling."

"And that's a stinky process."

"I see you noticed."

"Hard not to."

"Yeah, well, that's why it's done way out here," he said. "What they do is they collect urine —"

"Urine?!"

"Yeah. They let it sit and ferment for a bit. Then they immerse the low-grade cloth in it and sort of… swish it around." His eyebrows lifted again.

Tove had an unpleasant feeling she wasn't going to like the answer, but she asked anyway, "How do they swish it around in the pee?"

He didn't explain, but he winked and said, "Just remember, it won't kill you. It's just unpleasant."

The sun had risen above the mountains when they rounded the curve and a long, one-story timber framed building came into view. The roof extended out over long stone troughs in which *Alle'oss* men and women seemed to be marching back and forth. They wore long tunics that hung to the middle of their thighs, leaving their lower legs bare.

"Bless the Father," Tove whispered, earning a chuckle from Tye.

When the wagon appeared, the *Alle'oss* stopped and watched them approach. A small group of Volloch women standing beside the troughs, Desulti, Tove assumed, also watched.

When the wagon came to a stop, Tye said, "I'll be back to pick everyone up at the end of the day."

"*Tok,*" Tove said, "*Aka… mealetha* (Thank you. For… everything)." She climbed down, hesitated while she returned the gazes of the *Alle'oss.* On their faces, she saw the range of opinions Tye mentioned. Hostility, contempt, but also curiosity.

While the cart made a wide turn, Tove crossed the narrow space between herself and the Desulti women. She smiled at the woman standing in the front and said, "*Lehasa.*"

"We don't speak that language here," the woman said coolly.

Tove gestured to the *Alle'oss* watching from the troughs and said, "I was talking to them." She didn't take her eyes off the woman standing in front of her, but she heard one of the *Alle'oss* snicker.

"Nevertheless," the woman said, "we don't speak illegal languages here."

"Illegal?" Tove asked.

"Speaking Brochen languages like *I'oss* is illegal," one of the women standing at the back of the group said.

Tove frowned at her and pursed her lips. "Maybe it's because I'm new, but I'm having trouble understanding," she said. "You run away from the Empire because they treat you like property and worse, but you still follow their rules?"

"It's our rule!" the woman in front of her snapped.

"Which you borrowed from the Empire," Tove said. She let her gaze drift across the faces of the Desulti until she met the eyes of a woman standing at the back. She couldn't read her expression, but there was something other than contempt she saw on the other faces. Returning her attention to the leader, she said, "Odd that you live in Argren but don't allow anyone to speak *Alle'oss*. I must have missed the orientation." That brought more than one snicker from the *Alle'oss*.

Before the woman could respond, Tove said, "I'm Tove, by the way. Can I have your name?"

"I am Orla. You may address me as mistress."

"Well, *Orla*, I was told I have a job here. What sort of job is it?" Orla's smile raised hairs on the back of Tove's neck.

"You will be helping your countrymen," she said and gestured to the troughs.

"Helping them do what?"

"Walking in pee," one of the Desulti in the back said.

Tove turned to look at the *Alle'oss*, seeing something different in their expressions than she saw when she arrived. She faced Orla again and said, "I see only *Alle'oss* walking in the pee." She waved a hand toward the women standing behind Orla and asked, "What is it you lot do?"

"We're in charge."

"So, the Desulti don't walk in the pee?"

Orla's smile widened. "No."

Tove took a step to close the distance and punched her in the jaw. She dropped in a heap and lay moaning in the grass. There were gasps from everyone present, then stunned silence. "I'm Desulti you *nā minu*," Tove said. "Whether you like it or not." Most of the Desulti rushed to gather around their fallen leader. All except the woman standing in back. When she looked up, Tove caught a small grin on her face before she hid it behind a blank mask.

Tove turned toward the *Alle'oss* and said, "But I'm also *Alle'oss.*" She dropped her cloak and belt to the ground, stripped off her boots and pants, climbed into the trough and asked a man gaping at her, "So, what do we do, just walk around?"

Chapter 9

A Boiling Cauldron

"Fulling?" Siofra asked.

"Yes, Mistress," Eithne said.

"For Daga's sake, why?"

"I couldn't tell you, Mistress."

Siofra gaped at her. Noticing the ledger in her hands, she lay it on her desk and tried to formulate a meaningful question. She considered for a moment that the young woman chose the job on her own, then rejected the idea.

"There's more, Mistress."

"Yes?"

"The details aren't clear, but apparently the *I'o* — Tove assaulted Orla."

"Orla? Is she okay?"

"Yes, Mistress."

"Why, pray tell, was Orla there?"

"I couldn't say, but there was apparently a small crowd who witnessed it."

"A crowd? At the fulling hut?" Siofra massaged the back of her neck. She slept all of an hour the previous night and woke with a crick.

"Usually, it's hard to get any of the people *assigned* to that operation to spend any time there." When Eithne merely shrugged, she asked, "And you have no idea *why* Tove felt she was supposed to be there?"

"No, Mistress."

"Lyssa," Siofra said. When she saw the uncertainty on Eithne's face, she asked, "You don't agree?"

Her assistant gestured with one hand. "It's just... it seems so clumsy. The initiation ceremony, then humiliating her by assigning her to the fulling operation with the other... *Alle'oss.*" She gave her head a shake. "Lyssa isn't usually so obvious."

Siofra chuckled. "She can be obvious enough when she wants to send a message." When Eithne started to speak, Siofra said, "But you're right. She might want to send the message that this woman isn't welcome, but these acts seem so..." She waved a hand, grasping after the right word.

"Petty."

It was the word Siofra used the night before. "Yes," she said. "And as you say, it's also clumsy. Not at all like Lyssa." She settled into her desk chair.

"Maybe Orla and some of the others took it on themselves," Eithne said. "There are enough people angry enough." She paused, then said carefully, "Are you sure you should be leaving tomorrow?"

Siofra sat back and gazed at the mountains through her windows. She was to attend the wedding of her friend, Violette Bergamot, in Lachton. The trip would take weeks. But she would hate to miss that long-awaited event. It was rare that so many influential Imperials would be gathered in one place. She already scheduled meetings with several powerful lords. She also planned to pay her respects to Governor Adelbart on the way.

"Probably not," she said softly. "But I'm afraid it can't be avoided."

"Yes, Mistress."

"Thank you, Eithne," Siofra said. Once she was alone, Siofra gazed at the forgotten ledger, but that tedious work had lost its appeal. Rising, she crossed to her credenza and poured herself a glass of wine.

"It's almost midday, after all," she mumbled. Gazing out her window at the mountain peaks. The Order might have irrevocably changed when she returned from the wedding. Hopefully, it would be for the better.

***

"Fulling?!" Lyssa asked.

Cara gave Lyssa a sly smile. "And she punched Orla."

"Punched —" Lyssa let her gaze drift. "What kind of animal is this *l'oss?*" When she focused on her assistant again, she asked, "What happened after that?"

"Nothing. The *l'oss* got in the troughs and — Well, you know…" Cara shrugged. "They took Orla to the infirmary. She's as mad as a wet hen, but she'll be fine."

"Did she *choose* that job? The *l'oss.*"

"I don't see how she even knew it was a possibility," Cara said. "She's been here all of two days, and the fulling hut is well outside the village limits. Who could have told her it was there? She hasn't spoken to a counselor."

When women entered the Order, they were given time to get settled into their new life, but no Desulti was allowed to idle for long. The Order assigned a counselor to help them adjust to their new life and find where they best fit within the Order's vast organization. Lyssa would have to remember to instruct the counselor's office not to assign a counselor to Tove.

"You know what Orla is like. I think it was her idea to play a prank on the *l'oss,*" Cara said with a wide smile. "This is what we hoped would happen, right?"

"But Tove obviously knew what they were doing. Why else punch Orla? Why didn't she just walk away instead of walking in…" Lyssa gaped at Cara. "Why not just leave?"

"She said something about being Desulti and being *Alle'oss,*" Cara said. "Maybe she was making a point."

Lyssa couldn't imagine it. What point could she hope to make by walking in urine? She gave her head a small shake. "Has Tove had contact with anyone in the Order since she arrived?"

"Gwynna," Cara said. "I suppose it's possible she said something to her. Brie had Gwynna escort Tove around and she visited Tove after the initiation and was alone with her for a half hour."

"Alone?" Lyssa asked. When Cara nodded, she said, "I want to talk to Gwynna."

When she was alone again, Lyssa rose from her desk and crossed the room to gaze out the window. She didn't want to have anything to do with this Tove. She expected her to fade meekly into the background, like the subservient *Alle'oss* who cleaned their homes and served their meals. But this incident filled her with a deep foreboding.

***

"She assaulted Orla?" Nessa asked, not even trying to hide her glee.

"Dropped her with one punch," Laoise said, with no hint of humor. "Orla apparently insulted the *Alle'oss* who work in the troughs." Laoise was one of the few murtair who never shaved her scalp, preferring to keep her hair short in the style of Imperial men.

"Insulted… What happened after that?"

"She declared herself Desulti and *Alle'oss,* then climbed into the trough."

"What did the other Desulti do?"

"Nothing," Laoise said with a shrug. "They tended to Orla. All except Danu."

"Danu. Good," Nessa said. "And Lyssa and Siofra?"

"They have been informed."

Nessa settled back in her chair. When she didn't speak again, Laoise asked, "Do you want me to keep watching her?"

"Yes," Nessa said. "Let me know any interaction she has with members of the Order. Who, what they talk about."

"And if Orla or anyone else becomes aggressive?"

Nessa doubted it would come to that so soon. Not without further agitation. Violence was almost unheard of in Téama. It was more likely there would be other incidents like the one at the fulling hut. But, it wouldn't do to have something happen to Tove so soon. "Intervene if you judge she is in any real danger."

Laoise gave her a crisp nod, then turned to go.

When she was alone, Nessa said to her empty office, "You were right about this woman, Brie." It was time to set things in motion.

***

Nessa had known the woman standing before her since Shailey began training for the Murtair four years before. She had difficulties with the physical demands of the program and dropped out after a year. But she impressed Nessa as someone she could trust with tasks for which she couldn't use a murtair. The problem with using the murtair was that every contract was reviewed by the Inner Council. There were times when Nessa preferred to avoid that scrutiny.

When Brie brought her plan to Nessa, she immediately thought of Shailey as the woman to organize the agitators who would fan the flames. Brie had her own ideas about who to use, but Nessa wanted someone who owed her loyalty to her. Someone with a reliable ruthlessness.

Shailey waited patiently, her eyes roaming Nessa's office.

"You remember what we discussed?" Nessa asked.

Shailey turned her attention on Nessa, gazing at her from beneath heavy brows. "Stir the pot," she said. "Won't be hard. The village is a boiling cauldron as it is."

Nessa's brows rose.

"The elites are already agitating against her," Shailey said. "The usual lackeys and hangers-on are following their lead." She paused, then shrugged. "There's plenty with differing opinions, but recent events and Lyssa's reforms have taught them caution. We just need to give them the courage to speak out." She chuckled. "The *Ioss* is doing what she can. A lot of people wouldn't mind punching Orla. I'd take a swing at her myself if the opportunity arose."

Nessa chuckled. "Yes. Tove couldn't have made a more perfect entrance into the Order if we scripted it."

Shailey didn't respond.

"You know what to do," Nessa said. When Shailey nodded, she said, "I expect regular reports."

"You think you have the votes when the time comes?"

Nessa frowned at her, not expecting her to have guessed what she intended.

Shailey shrugged. "Wasn't hard to figure out. I'm just curious what you're thinking. If you want to take over the Council like Lyssa did, you're going to need the votes, and I'd put the odds of you coming out on top at fifty fifty." She glanced up and to the right, then amended her assessment. "At best." She gazed at Nessa for a moment and said, "Not like you to leave it to chance."

Nessa was too shocked to respond immediately. Shailey had proved to be a loyal and effective operative, but Nessa would never have suspected her of such insight. The idea of getting rid of her flitted through her mind, but she banished it with a shake of her head. She had no one else she would trust with this task.

"You don't need to worry about the details," she said firmly. "I haven't left anything to chance. You just do your part, and I'll make sure you're rewarded."

Chapter 10

Stranger in the Mirror

Alone in her room, Gwynna closed her eyes, enjoying the feel of the stiff brush bristles against her scalp. The sensuousness of it brought to mind a dark room, her fingers massaging a woman's scalp, a moan of pleasure. She couldn't explain why she did it. The memory left her confused and vaguely ashamed, though she couldn't say why. Everyone peppered her with questions about the new Desulti, but she hadn't confessed to anyone about her moments with Tove after the initiation. She'd also kept her promise to Brie and hadn't told anyone about Tove's reaction to the dark.

She set the brush down and gazed at her reflection in the mirror. Pale skin, soft contours, large dark eyes, curly black hair. Her mother's face. Her face. Yet the woman in the mirror was a stranger to her. She let her eyes unfocus, blurring the image of the stranger and bringing memories of the girl she once was into sharp clarity. That frightened girl, her face bruised and battered, was who she was. Still. Not the stranger in the mirror.

Before she fled her home, she would sneak into the hallway when her father and brother were out working their small family farm and gaze at her reflection in her mother's mirror. It wasn't that she was fascinated with her own appearance. It was that the mirror was the last relic of her mother's nurturing presence in the ramshackle house.

She remembered the girl's black hair, dulled by filth, chopped short by her father with a dull knife. "No one'll think you're pretty now," he would snarl.

In the present, the hand of the stranger in the mirror came up, fingers caressing soft, glossy curls.

The girl's sallow skin pulled taut across cheeks hollowed by want.

Gwynna watched the stranger in the mirror caress the supple skin of her cheek.

But were those superficial differences the only ones? What of the woman within? Why, after all this time, did she still feel like that frightened girl? The stranger in the mirror had no answer for her.

It was a neighbor who told her about the Desulti. She dragged Gwynna aside at the winter festival, fingers digging painfully into her arm, and told her if she didn't leave home, her father would eventually kill her. Like he did her mother. They were poison, those words. She couldn't say she was happy before she heard them, but not knowing there was an alternative, she got on with things. Afterwards, all she could think about was how desperately unhappy she was.

They were of the Volloch caste, which her father explained meant they were better than everyone else in their small farming community. He would watch the wagons of more prosperous farmers carrying their goods to the market in the nearby city and say, "At least we're not them stigs." He was fond of that derogatory term for Styrians. To Gwynna, the people he referred to as stigs seemed much better off than their family. Being Volloch didn't seem to amount to much that made a difference as far as she could see. But it meant everything to her father and her brother. It wasn't until her neighbor told her the Desulti accepted only Volloch that it meant anything to her.

She let her eyes unfocus again as she remembered the fateful day when she escaped. She woke early to do her chores as she always did. But this morning, as she was carrying the slop bucket out to the pigs, she caught sight of herself in her mother's mirror. She froze, thinking for a moment it was her mother somehow. It was the bruises that fooled her. Her father and brother would be sleeping their drunk off for hours, so she set the slop bucket down and tiptoed over to the mirror. The sight of her battered face terrified her.

Returning from her memory for a moment, Gwynna watched a fingertip in the mirror tracing the scar above the stranger's eyebrow.

If her neighbor hadn't planted her poison, she would have counted herself lucky he didn't damage her eye. She would have picked up the bucket and got on with her chores, promising herself she wouldn't provoke him next time.

But as she stood in the hall, staring at her reflection, her breaths shortened and thinned until she was panting. She had a choice. *She* had a choice. Before she knew she made a choice, she was creeping down the hall to her father's bedroom, choosing her steps carefully to avoid the loose boards. She pressed her ear to the door and listened to her father's snores. Gwynna couldn't recall how long she remained there working up her courage, but eventually it occurred to her the worse that would happen if he caught her was he would beat her to death. Another kind of freedom.

The stranger in the mirror stared back at Gwynna with round eyes, chest rising and falling in shallow gasps, remembering easing the door open. She peered through the crack at the dresser on the opposite wall. Her father didn't know she knew he hid his coin pouch in the bottom drawer.

Somehow, the girl made it across her father's bedroom, picking her way through the debris that cluttered the floor. The small pouch wasn't as heavy as she hoped. She hesitated, the hand with the pouch hovering over its hiding place. It wouldn't be enough. But it was too late to back out now. She clutched the pouch against her stomach to prevent it from jingling and escaped into the hall. Once she eased the door shut, she clamped a hand over her mouth to smother giddy laughter. She was really doing it!

The stranger in the mirror smiled at the memory.

She hurried to the bedroom she shared with her brother to pack some essentials. She had her hand on the latch when she heard him stir. He never abused her the way their father did, but he never defended her either. She hovered outside the room, undecided. Would he try to stop her? Raise the alarm and wake their father? Deciding it was too risky, she ran on tiptoe to the kitchen, grabbed a loaf of day old bread and fled into a misty rain as her bedroom door opened.

The neighbor told her the nearest Desulti house was in the city of Maintz. She said all Gwynna needed to do was to get there and they would take her in. No questions asked. They wouldn't care about her family's desperate circumstances. All they would care about was that she was Volloch.

She ran, clutching the pouch and the bread to her breast. She hoped her brother was just getting up to go to the privy and would assume she was out doing her chores. That would give her time to get far away before they missed her. But she left the slop bucket in the hall. They came after her before she was a hundred paces from home.

When she heard them hollering her name, she dropped the bread and the pouch, hoping it would be enough for them to let her go. It wasn't. The rain made the road a quagmire and the sticky mud sucked at her bare feet and ankles. Leaving the road, she cut across an open field. But she had forgotten about the Orn River. She never learned to swim, so she ran along the bank, searching for a place to hide. The flat terrain offered no refuge. Desperate, she wondered how long it would last if she lay still and let him vent his anger on her.

Spotting a Volloch man in one of the small fishing vessels that plied the river, she ran along the shore, screaming and waving her arms. He merely glanced her way, then tacked away from the shore.

Her father would have caught her if it wasn't for a Styrian family passing in a small flat-bottomed boat. When they saw her running frantically along the river bank, they veered toward her. Her father was charging across the field when she plunged into the water up to her waist. They pulled her onto the boat, then heaved on long poles to push the boat out of her father's reach. She lay on the deck, sobbing hysterically, watching her father keeping pace with the boat, bellowing incomprehensible threats.

Still drunk from the previous night, he quickly fell behind. When the family's father tried to help her to her feet, she skittered across the deck and would have leapt into the water if the mother hadn't intercepted her. The older woman cradled Gwynna's head against her breast while Gwynna sobbed.

When she could speak, she told them where she wanted to go. They took her to the Desulti house in Maintz. She had no way to thank them. She hoped her joyful tears when the mistress of the house welcomed her were enough.

Her neighbor was right about the Desulti. They took her in without question. A month later, she underwent the initiation ceremony in Téama and became Desulti. She was safe here. Safe from her father and every other man. The girl she was became the woman who would never again have to cower in the face of a man's brutality.

But her neighbor wasn't right about everything.

She assumed being Volloch was enough. That all women in the Desulti were equal. But it didn't take her long to discover that even here, the circumstances of one's birth mattered. It came as a shock to discover not all Volloch were the same. Lower level Volloch were relegated to the jobs no elite would have and made aware on a daily basis where they stood.

The stranger in the mirror looked back at her and muttered, "But at least you're not one of them *l'oss.*"

***

Gwynna sat stiffly in Lyssa's outer office. The Chief Executive had never spoken to her before. Gwynna didn't even know how the woman knew she was alive. When two gendarmes appeared at her door early in the morning, she had been shocked when they told her Lyssa wanted to talk to her.

While she waited in Lyssa's outer office, she wracked her brain for what the head of the Desulti Inner Council might want with her. The only thing she could think of was what she did for Tove after the initiation. Everyone knew what Lyssa thought of the *Foss*. Why did she do it?

She had been trying to decide that since she left Tove's room that night. At first, she tried to convince herself it was just an impulse. That it didn't mean anything. A onetime thing that she could forget about. But it wouldn't leave her alone. What possessed her to go to Tove's room that night? Why did it leave her so confused?

The door to Lyssa's office opened, and her assistant appeared. She stepped back and held the door open. "Lyssa will see you now, Gwynna."

Gwynna got stiffly to her feet and followed her into the office, glancing up occasionally but keeping her eyes on her feet. Lyssa sat behind her desk, smiling as Gwynna approached.

"Good morning, Mistress," Gwynna said and tried a small curtsy.

"Please, have a seat, Gwynna," Lyssa said and gestured to a chair in front of her desk.

Gwynna perched on the edge of the chair. She lifted her eyes to Lyssa and tried to force herself to meet the older woman's eyes, but had to look down at her hands in her lap.

"Gwynna," Lyssa said. "I understand you work in the laundry."

"Yes, Mistress."

"Do you enjoy it?"

"It's… I'm happy to contribute to the Order," Gwynna said. In truth, she hated the laundry.

"Yes," Lyssa said. "We all have to contribute, and though some jobs are more glamorous than others, they are all important." She paused and said, "Though I wonder if we might find a way for you to use your talents in a more rewarding way."

Gwynna looked up. "Is there a problem with my work?"

"No, of course not," Lyssa said. "In fact, I've been told you are a very diligent worker." She stood, came around her desk, and sat in the chair next to Gwynna. "You've been at the laundry for some time, after all. I'm sure we can find something more interesting for someone as diligent as you."

Gwynna hardly dared think this was why Lyssa wanted to see her, but the possibility of getting out of that dreary job encouraged her to say, "I would like that, Mistress." She peeked up at Lyssa with a small smile.

Lyssa turned to her assistant. "See that Gwynna is assigned a counselor. Make sure she knows we want Gwynna to have a job that makes better use of her talents."

Gwynna's heart fell, remembering her first embarrassing encounter with her counselor. When the woman asked her to list all her skills and talents, Gwynna's mind went blank. What skills and talents did she have? After all, how much skill did it take to pour slop into a pig's trough?

Lyssa must have guessed the thoughts playing out on Gwynna's face, because she said, "Don't worry, dear. I'm sure we can find something better than the laundry."

"Thank you, Mistress," Gwynna said, trying on a smile. "Is that why you asked to see me?"

"No," Lyssa said. "I asked you here because you have had more contact with our most recent member than anyone else." When Gwynna gave her a worried frown, Lyssa gave her a reassuring smile. "Don't worry. I know Brie asked you to *guide* her when she arrived. You aren't in trouble."

"Thank you, Mistress."

"These *l'oss*," Lyssa said with a flourish. "I'm sure you agree. The way they think is a mystery. They're different from you and I. You understand."

"Yes, Mistress."

"I asked to speak with you because I would like your insights into what kind of person this Tove is."

When she fell silent, Gwynna looked up and found Lyssa watching her expectantly. "Um…" she started, feeling her face warm. "She's like anyone else. Quieter than most." When she noticed the disapproval in Lyssa's expression, she cast about for something she might want to hear. She had her mouth open, ready to tell Lyssa about Tove's reaction to being in the dark room, when she remembered the promise she made to Brie.

"Dear?" Lyssa asked. "You were going to say something more?"

Gwynna shook her head. "She's just… what you would expect from… a *l'oss.*" She looked up hopefully, but Lyssa only frowned.

"You went to her room," Lyssa said, her tone firmer. "After the initiation. You were there for a half hour. You brought her salve for her scalp."

Gwynna felt the blood drain from her face. "She… the cuts on her scalp. I just… It was like the piglets back home I had to take care of when they were sick."

"Piglets?"

Gwynna nodded vigorously. "I don't know why I did it. She was just so… like the sick piglets." She clenched her fists and shook her head. "I've regretted it ever since."

"Of course, dear. We've all felt the pull of our maternal instincts. It happens."

When Gwynna looked up, a smile appeared suddenly on Lyssa's face.

"What did you talk about while you were with her?"

"We didn't talk," Gwynna said. "I told her how to apply the salve. She said thank you. Or at least, I think she said thank you. She said it in *l'oss.*"

Lyssa looked up at the ceiling, disappointment in her face.

Worried the tantalizing possibility of escaping the laundry was fading, Gwynna found herself saying, "There is one thing."

Lyssa looked at her, "Yes?"

"I promised I wouldn't tell."

Lyssa sat forward. "Who did you promise?"

"The murtair. Brie."

Lyssa's eyes flashed. Her body tensed and she leaned forward. "What we say in this room is just between the two of us." She glanced at her assistant hovering behind Gwynna. "The three of us. No one else will ever know what you tell me, Gwynna."

"She… Tove is afraid of the dark," Gwynna said.

Lyssa stared blankly at her. "The dark? You mean like a child?"

Gwynna shook her head vigorously. "No. It's much worse than that. When I first took her to her room, I closed the door before she could light the lamp. When Brie found her later, she was huddled in the corner, weeping. She was terrified." Gwynna looked at Lyssa. "She said something about Kartok and something called zhotee, or something like that. She's got that scar on her face. I thought she might have been tortured."

Lyssa sat back and gazed over Gwynna's head. "Very interesting," she said. Her eyes found Gwynna's again, and the smile reappeared. "Poor dear. One wouldn't wish something like that on anyone, even a *l'oss.* Right?" She reached out and touched Gwynna's shoulder. "Your maternal need to protect this woman is perfectly understandable, given what you saw."

Gwynna gave her a tremulous smile.

Lyssa stood abruptly. "Now," she said. "We both have jobs we must get to. Thank you so much, Gwynna, and remember, your secrets are safe with me."

"Will the counselor come find me?" Gwynna asked.

Lyssa's face went slack for a moment, then she smiled and said, "Of course, dear."

***

Lyssa hadn't really expected to learn anything useful from Gwynna, but she struck gold. She wasn't sure, yet, how she could use the information, but knowing an enemy's vulnerabilities was always useful.

What was more interesting was the news that Brie made Gwynna promise to hide Tove's reaction to the dark. Why was Brie so invested in this woman? She considered Brie might be in love with the *l'oss,* but Cara told her Brie and Elois were together. If it wasn't love, then there had to be a more devious reason. She couldn't imagine the usually solid, efficient Brie causing such mischief on her own. That only left the possibility she was acting on Nessa's behalf. But what did the head of the Murtair hope to gain?

Her assistant returned from escorting Gwynna out with Tilla, the Chair of the Ruling Council, trailing behind her and said, "That was interesting."

"What was interesting?" Tilla asked.

Ignoring her, Lyssa said, "Yes, it was."

"Is it useful?"

"What are you talking about?" Tilla tried again.

"I don't know yet," Lyssa said to Cara. "But it *is* very interesting." She paused, then asked, "Do we have anymore information on how Tove ended up at the fulling hut?"

"Orla says it was just a prank," Cara said. "The women who were there concocted it together. No one told them to do it."

Lyssa nodded. "This is what we hoped would happen. The women of the Order making it so uncomfortable for Tove, she decides to leave on her own."

"It is, Mistress."

"You might not be so sure after what I have to tell you," Tilla said, apparently abandoning her efforts to find out what Lyssa and Cara found so interesting.

"What is it?" Lyssa asked, acknowledging the woman for the first time.

"Orla and the other women involved in the prank were… gloating in the Blue Hen tavern last night and apparently, there were some who objected to what they did. There were words exchanged, an argument started and… fists were thrown."

"An actual fight?" Lyssa asked, aghast. Violence of any kind was almost unheard of in Téama. It was why they had so few gendarmes.

"Yes. Apparently, the gendarmes were required to break it up."

Lyssa stared at Tilla, then gazed out the window. "Someone *defended* the *l'oss?*" She focused on Tilla. "Other *l'oss?*"

"Desulti," Tilla said.

"Were they arrested? Do we have names?"

"The gendarmes decided it was enough to send everyone home," Tilla said. "Apparently, when they got everyone calmed down, it came out that it was Orla who threw the first punch. They couldn't very well arrest the hero of the day. Besides, it's not like they have to deal with this sort of thing very often."

Lyssa drummed her fingers on her desk. "This is something we need to keep a lid on. Tell the Gendarmerie Director I want the perpetrators arrested if it happens again."

"Yes, Mistress," Cara said.

As her assistant was turning away, Lyssa said, "Make sure she understands who to arrest."

Chapter 11

Making Friends

Tove knew the fulling job was only a prank. She didn't need to stay. But Tye told her to let others get to know her, and her tormentors had unwittingly given her the best introduction to her coworkers possible.

The confrontation melted their initial hostility faster than anything else could have. Though she could tell they weren't quite sure what to make of her at first, something subtle changed when she puked over the side of the trough. Everyone stopped and watched her wiping her mouth with the back of her hand. When she resumed trudging through the foul liquid, shuffling her feet to ensure the cloth was thoroughly steeped, she noticed them exchanging looks. It seemed to be a test or rite of passage. She didn't know whether it was something everyone had to pass, or it was just because she was Desulti. Whatever the case, some of them began speaking to her as the morning wore on.

But it was during the midday break, the first day when she followed the others to a nearby stream, that the ice truly broke. Something about washing their legs in the frigid glacier fed stream, squealing and laughing like children breached the last barriers. After that, they treated her like everyone else. To a point. She sensed their curiosity, but no one asked the question they all wanted to. Until the fourth day.

***

"Here." Frey said, holding out a chunk of cheese and a slice of bread. His smile deepened the wrinkles at the corners of his eyes. Most of her coworkers were older and Frey was the oldest. He more shuffled than walked, and though he still had a full head of hair, it was white as snow.

"*Tok*," Tove said. She'd seen little of the Desulti from that first day. She wasn't sure why she hadn't been arrested, but she wasn't about to complain. Meya barely spoke to her, but Tove caught her servant watching her when she brought the items Tove requested. The women in the dining hall continued to find ways to make her meals unappetizing, so her coworkers took it in turn to bring her food. It was enough for a midday meal and a little extra for the evening.

"So, how came you to join the Order?" Frey asked. His voice had a practiced casualness about it.

Tove looked up, sensing the sudden interest from the others. They climbed a high hill for their midday meal, searching for a breeze which would carry the stench away. Not always successfully. Today the breeze was just right, fresh and chilly, the spring sun blunting its bite. Gesturing to her full mouth, she chewed and gazed down at the fulling hut, where she could see the Desulti woman who smiled when she punched Orla. Her coworkers told Tove her name was Danu. While Tove watched, Danu lifted the cloth from a trough with tongs, peered at it, then made notes on a slate. Tove couldn't help wondering how she got that job.

Swallowing, she returned her attention to her coworkers, who watched her expectantly. "It's complicated," she said.

"I expect it is," Frey said. "There's a lot of us confused on the subject." He gestured around and said, "You've got us willing to listen, anyway. Try to explain."

"I grew up on the streets of Kartok," she said, then had to stop for a moment. "I don't remember much about my early life. Don't remember my parents." She gestured vaguely, raised her gaze and met the old man's eyes. "Don't want to talk about the details, but somewhere along the way, I ran afoul of the Inquisition. Was an inquisitor who cut my face." She pressed her index finger against her scar, then let her hand drop. Giving her head a shake, she said, "There were other men…" She took a bite and chewed, gazing at the mountain peaks north of Ka'tan. "I don't hate all men. It was a man who found me when I was about to give up. His name was Alar. He brought me into *Oss'stera*. Saved my life. Gave me a reason to live."

"Our struggle?" one of the oldest women asked.

Tove nodded and said, "We… want to make things better for the *Alle'oss*."

"Better?" a woman asked. "Better than what?"

"Our struggle," a man named Seele said slowly. His eyes narrowed. "What are you, some kind of rebels?"

When Tove didn't answer, he took it as confirmation.

"That's foolish!" he said, scowling at the others, looking for support.

Tove watched the others, gauging their sentiments. Most of them agreed with Seele, but not all.

"The only thing that happens when you resist," Seele said, "is you stir up trouble. There's consequences, and the people who cause the trouble aren't the only ones who suffer."

"So, you're saying we just lay down and take whatever they do to us?" a woman whose name Tove hadn't learned asked.

"That's better than getting killed or forced to starve because a few deluded idiots think they can fight the Empire," someone else said.

Tove watched them argue. She already knew all the points they made, had heard the same arguments for years, and wasn't interested in changing their minds.

Eventually, Frey shouted everyone down, turned to Tove and said, "You're awfully quiet on the subject. What do you think?"

She stuffed the cheese into a pocket of her cloak, sat up and wiped her hands on her tunic. "I never said we were rebels. But… You think you can stay safe, keep your family safe if you stay meek. But you step out of line even a little bit, or they think you did, they'll come for you and there's nothing you can do about it." She gestured to Danu, who was standing beside the trough, her face to the sun. "They're sure they're better than us. Call us *l'oss.* That's not okay."

Seele started to speak, but Tove waved him down.

"I ain't arguing with you. I already heard it all. Alar, he thinks the same as you. He says we won't get rid of the Empire capturing supply caravans or killing Imps. There will always be more Imps."

"What does he think we should do?" the woman who defended the rebels asked.

Tove shrugged and gestured around to the group. "Well, not all of us, but he wants to make *Oss'stera* as rich and powerful as the Desulti."

Mouths dropped open. Incredulous looks were exchanged. "But they're Imperial," Seele said.

"Yeah?" Tove asked, staring blankly at him.

He lifted a hand toward the fulling hut and said, "They're already rich."

"No," Tove said. "They're rich now, but these women run away from the Empire and left their wealth behind. They *made* themselves rich." She paused and gazed around. "If they can do it, so can we. Least that's Alar's plan."

"So, whoever is in this *Oss'stera* will be okay," Seele scoffed. "The rest of us just have to deal."

"No," Tove said, shaking her head. "One day there will be a war. *Oss'stera* will be ready. We're going to become strong and rich. When the war comes, we'll be able to fight, and we'll be rich enough to help everyone." She looked around, inviting anyone to argue, but they looked thoughtfully back at her. She thought Alar mad when he explained it to her, but as she climbed into the mountains with Brie and Elois, she decided if anyone could do it, it would be Alar. "Alar wanted us to have someone on the inside, someone who can learn what they do." She dropped her gaze.

"So, that's why you joined the Order?" Frey asked.

Tove looked up. "Part. For me… When I heard there was this order of women who did their own thing. With no men." She almost stopped, but the woman she focused on gave her an encouraging smile. "I thought I would be safe here. I thought being a woman was more important than being Imperial." She almost mentioned her desire to be Murtair, but decided that would make her sound foolish. Instead, she dropped her gaze, expecting someone to rebuke her for her stupidity, but no one spoke. "It hasn't turned out to be what I expected it to be. Obviously. I guess you think I'm pretty stupid."

"No," Frey said. "Not stupid. Naïve, maybe."

"Maybe not," an older woman said. "Not about that last part, anyway. The Desulti used to be different. Better, anyway. They weren't so…"

"Hateful," Frey said.

"Bigoted," someone else offered.

"Imperial," several people said.

There were some chuckles at that, allowing everyone to relax.

"It all took a turn for the worse when that Lyssa took over," Seele said and several people nodded.

"You going to stick around?" Frey asked Tove. "I don't imagine they're going to let you go unscathed after…" He gestured down to the fulling hut. "Especially, you being *Alle'oss*. You could go back to this *Oss'stera*."

Tove laughed. "I ain't leaving. The Desulti might not be what I expected, or wanted, them to be, but they got me mad now." She took a bite of bread and grinned. "They're going to be sorry about that."

***

Tove was in her room, getting ready to go to work, when someone knocked. She opened the door, expecting Meya's surly countenance, but she was surprised to find a Volloch woman waiting for her.

"My name is Cianna," she said with a bright smile. "I have been assigned to determine your place in the Order."

"My place?" Tove asked.

Cianna looked past Tove into her small room and said, "Perhaps we could go for a stroll. It is a lovely spring day."

"Um, okay," Tove said. It didn't escape her that the woman didn't answer her question, but whatever she had in mind, it would delay her trip to the fulling hut, so she didn't argue. It might be a lovely spring day, but for someone who spent her entire life at Argren's lower altitudes, Tove found the Desulti village chilly. Throwing her cloak over her shoulders, she stepped out into the hall, closed her door, and followed Cianna.

Apparently, whatever Cianna intended, she wasn't in a hurry. She strolled through the sun washed plaza, holding her satchel in front of herself with both hands. She took dainty steps, her face turned to the sun, a small smile on her face. Tove was used to ignoring the looks she received from nearly everyone, Desulti and *Alle'oss* alike, but she was surprised that Cianna seemed indifferent to the hostility. Tove was about to prompt her when she spoke.

"No one is allowed to remain idle in the Order," she said and gave Tove a bright smile. "After a suitable adjustment period, every woman is expected to contribute in a manner best suited to their temperament and abilities."

There was a cheerful lilt to her voice that Tove found appealing. She shoved her hands in her pockets, matched Cianna's pace, and returned her smile. "You mean I have to have a job?" she asked.

Cianna cocked her head, pursed her lips, and said, "Try not to think of it as a job. We want to help you find your *passion*. To put you in position so you feel you are contributing to *our* Order."

"I already have a job," Tove said. She watched Cianna, curious how she would take this news.

For the first time, Cianna frowned, an expression Tove found even more distracting than her smile. "Excuse me?"

"I've been working at the fulling hut."

Cianna stopped walking and faced Tove. "Fulling?"

Tove nodded.

Cianna gazed at her, her lips parted slightly, then her head tilted, and a brow rose. "I had heard rumors to that effect. Some sort of mean-spirited prank. But why on earth are you still working there? Is this something you want to do?"

Tove snorted. "Not especially, but it's the only way I can eat."

Cianna stared at her.

"The women in the dining hall aren't happy with my presence."

"Well, this is quite extraordinary," she said. "I will have to look into this." The smile returned, and she said, "I can assure you that if you don't wish to walk in… urine simply to eat, you do not have to. I will find a place for you more suited to your talents."

Her smile widened, and Tove found herself liking the woman.

Cianna started walking again. "Now, I assume you have skills beyond walking in urine." She gave Tove a conspiratorial smile.

"Some," Tove said.

Cianna gestured to a bench at the edge of the plaza. When they were seated, she pulled a sheet of paper and stylus from her satchel, rested the paper and satchel on her knees, and looked at Tove expectantly.

"Oh, uh," Tove said. "I'm a fair bowyer —"

"Bowyer?"

"I can make bows," Tove said. She waited while Cianna made far more notes than she thought that fact deserved, then she said, "I can shoot, hunt, forage. I'm fair dab cooking. Stews, soups, that kind of thing."

Cianna made more notes. "Anything else?"

Tove gazed at her, trying to decide how much to tell this woman. "I can handle a knife and I'm good in a scrap." She smiled to herself when Cianna simply bent over her paper without comment.

"Anything else?"

"That's about it," Tove said, feeling a little embarrassed.

"Can you read?" Cianna asked.

"I'm a little slow, but yes," Tove said, grateful that Alar insisted she learn. "I'm sorry," she said when Cianna looked at her again. "It doesn't sound like much."

Cianna returned the paper to her satchel. "Oh, you would be surprised." She leaned toward Tove and whispered, "Some of these elite Volloch women are simply hopeless." Sitting up, she waved a hand and spoke in a normal voice. "They can read and write, do some embroidery, play an instrument…" She stopped speaking for a moment, her mouth still open, then she said, "They have all these skills, but frankly how many people do you need who can do needlepoint?" She leaned close enough that Tove caught a whiff of her flowery perfume and whispered, "I've never had anyone tell me they could do any of the things you can do." She straightened and gave Tove an incredulous look. "Never!" Giving Tove's knee a pat, she said, "You are unique, Tove." She winked and added, "In many ways, apparently." She rose and said, "I'll be by anon to offer you some options. Good day!"

As she was turning to leave, Tove asked, "So, I don't have to go to my job anymore." When Cianna gave her a blank look, Tove said, "Fulling."

"Do you *want* to?" Cianna asked with a horrified grimace.

Tove would be happy if she never had to walk in pee again, but it was the only way she could get a meal. "I do like to eat," she said. "I worked four days. Can I get paid for that?"

"Yes, of course," Cianna said. She sat, pulled a fresh sheet of paper from her satchel, wrote on it, then handed it to Tove. "Take this to the bank." She rose and pointed to a large building across the plaza. "They will pay you."

"*Tok,*" Tove said, taking the paper. When Cianna lifted an uncertain brow, Tove said, "Thank you. For everything."

"*Alle'oss?*"

"*Da,*" Tove said.

"How do you say you're welcome?"

"*Aurina sha.*"

"*Aurina sha,* Tove," Cianna said, twirled and walked briskly across the plaza.

Tove watched her, marveling at the turn her day took. Other than the half hour she spent with Gwynna after the initiation, this was the only pleasant interaction she had with another member of the Order. It left her feeling soft and buoyant. She sat on the bench enjoying the sun and ignoring the glowers of passing pedestrians.

Chapter 12

So I Don't Forget

Tove exited the bank and gazed down at the coins in her palm, angling her hand so they glinted in the late afternoon sun. The bits of metal amounted to more money than she ever had at any one time in her life. If Cianna could find her a job that paid anything close to fulling, she would count herself rich.

She held her pocket open and dropped the coins in, one at a time, enjoying their soft clink, then gazed around the plaza. Now what? After Cianna left her, she explored the village. Her first impressions were confirmed. It was an eclectic mix of Imperial and *Alle'oss*. The one thing that seemed a bit odd was that there didn't seem to be enough people for such a large village. There were many buildings, like her dormitory, that didn't appear to be in use. Maybe the Order was so wealthy, they just threw up a new building whenever they got tired of the old one.

Her grumbling stomach reminded her the only thing she'd eaten all day was some cheese the *Alle'oss* gave her the previous day. Having coin now, she considered going to one of the cafes or taverns she saw in the village, but decided against it. In the dining hall, she could at least see if someone spit in her food. There was no telling what would happen out of her sight in a cafe.

Noting her long shadow on the cobbles of the plaza, she realized it was almost time for her fellow pee walkers to return, so she set off across the plaza. When she arrived at the outskirts of the village, a familiar carriage approached. It ferried the Desulti to and from the fulling hut. She moved to the side of the road to allow it to pass.

To her surprise, the carriage stopped. When the door opened, she tensed, wondering if Orla finally found her courage. But Danu emerged, the woman who smiled when Tove punched Orla. Tove was ready to fight a moment before, but Danu's appearance unsettled her. She shoved her hands in her pockets and fought the urge to turn her head to show only the unmarred side of her face.

Danu knocked on the side of the carriage and the driver flicked the reins, setting it in motion. She watched it go until it was out of sight, then she turned to look at Tove with an unreadable expression.

During the long, tedious hours marching back and forth in the troughs, the appearance of any Desulti was a distraction. Tove found this quiet woman particularly distracting, though she wasn't sure why. In the four days she worked, she didn't know if she heard Danu speak more than ten words. She often caught the woman smiling to herself, but if she became aware that anyone noticed, the smile fled behind a watchful mask. She always wore the same shapeless tunic and loose pants, as if she were trying to hide in plain sight. Her short hair reminded Tove of a patch of blackberry bushes; tufty and unruly, and too short to fall into her eyes. Even so, she had a habit of swiping at her forehead, as if brushing bangs from her eyes. A habit Tove found fascinating for some reason. After studying her whenever she appeared, Tove decided there was enough of a resemblance with Brie that they might be sisters.

"You weren't at work today," Danu said. Her hand came up to brush at her forehead.

"No," Tove said, feeling inexplicably foolish.

"Why?" A small furrow appeared between Danu's brows.

"You didn't have enough *Alle'oss* to humiliate today?" Tove's skin flushed hot. Her hand twitched, but she stopped it before it came up to rub her scar.

Danu's lips twisted, and her hand came up to her forehead again, but she remained silent.

"I wasn't supposed to be working there," Tove said, trying a lighter tone.

"Then why were you?" Danu asked, her brows drawing together. "You could have left the first day."

"It's complicated." Danu nodded, but the frown remained. "My counselor came by today and promised to find another job for me." Tove watched a range of emotions vying for a place in Danu's expression as she processed this news. "Haven't seen Orla since that first day. She okay?"

Danu snorted. "She'll live," she said and gifted Tove with a quick grin.

Tove caught herself staring, then cleared her throat and asked, "She don't work there? Usually?" She felt her face warm again. Of course, Orla didn't work at the fulling hut.

Danu shook her head, the mask returning. "Fella and I are the only women in the Order who work there on a regular basis."

"How did you get that job? Your counselor recommend that to you?"

"Someone has to do it," Danu said defensively.

"Someone in the Order?" Tove asked, regretting her anger but unable to stop herself. "You don't trust the *Alle'oss* to manage it?"

"Listen," Danu said, anger edging her voice. "I just stopped to apologize for what happened. I don't — Sorry," she said and turned away.

"Thank you," Tove said desperately. When Danu stopped, Tove said, "For the kindness. Way I see it, it wasn't your fault. You don't need to apologize to me."

The wagon that transported the *Alle'oss* appeared around a bend in the road. Danu, who had been about to speak, looked past Tove to the wagon. "Goodbye," she said, turned and strode toward the village.

Tove watched her walking away, disappointed she didn't look back. Taking a deep breath, she whooshed it out and wiped damp palms on her shirt. "That was… I don't know what that was," she said to herself. She turned to greet the wagon and waved at Tye.

"You decide fulling isn't for you?" the driver asked with a scowl.

"You going to Ka'tan?" Tove asked, returning the greetings of her former coworkers.

"You slumming?" Tye asked.

Tove climbed into the driver's seat. She patted her pocket and said, "Got paid. Want a proper *Alle'oss* ale and a meal ain't been spit in."

"I can take you," he said. "But you got to find your own way back."

"I can walk," Tove said.

"Be dark soon. It's an hour walk. Gets cold up this way."

"The woman said she can walk, Tye," Frey said. "Let's go."

As they trundled around the outskirts of Téama, Tove told them about her conversations with Cianna and Danu.

"They tried to humiliate you," Tye said, referring to her first day at the fulling hut. "They tell you to do this *sheoda* job, then they make sure there's an audience to spread the word."

"Their mistake was in thinking I can be humiliated," Tove said with a grin.

"No," Tye said. "Their mistake was in not sending a murtair instead of Orla." That caused a few laughs.

"That's why there haven't been consequences for punching her," Frey said. "Whoever set you up doesn't want to advertise the fact."

Tove considered the implications. "So, you don't think it's all of them? The ones that set me up?"

"They present this front to the world that they're all one. It's the Order against the world," he said. "But there's infighting, power struggles. Especially lately. That encounter with Danu… probably more like her, too afraid to speak up."

"What do you mean?"

"They used to be a more harmonious lot," he said. "Or more so than now. Not sure what's going on. They keep their secrets, but you hear whispers."

"Who's whispering?" Tove asked.

"They use a lot of folks from Ka'tan as servants," Frey said. "Some of these Desulti seem to think the people working for them are part of the furniture. They say things. Let things slip."

Tove twisted around in her seat so she could see his face.

He gave her a knowing smile and said, "If someone had a grudge against the Order, wanted to make them sorry for how they treated her, she should get to know those people work for them."

"Course," Tye said, "you got to get them, the *Alle'oss*, on your side first." He nodded to her coworkers, who crowded forward to listen. "You made friends here, but there's still those with an opposing opinion."

Tove thought of Meya, who became even surlier after the incident with Orla.

They rode in silence until the outer buildings of Ka'tan came into view. "You know a good tavern?" Tove asked. This prompted laughter from everyone. "What?"

Tye pulled the reins, bringing the wagon to a stop, then gestured to the building on Tove's side of the road. The sign above the door had a picture of the head of a boar with an apple in its mouth. She heard music that increased in volume when the door opened as a couple exited.

"The Boar's Head?" Tove asked. "It's a tavern." They grinned at her. "What's so funny?"

"This is Tye's tavern," Frey said. "Or, more properly, his wife's tavern. Tye just works there."

Tove pointed at it and gave Tye a questioning look.

"Yep."

"Then why are you driving the wagon every day?"

"Can't have these folks walking all that way. They're old," he said. "Especially as they have to walk in pee all day." He waved a hand and said, "Everyone out." When they started to comply, he said, "Frey, take our young Desulti in and introduce her around a bit. I'll buy your ale."

"You'll buy my ale and a meal," he said.

Tye laughed and urged the mule into motion.

Frey stopped Tove on the porch. "I'll introduce you to Shia. That's Tye's missus. If people see her acceptin you… well, it'll go a long way. Not going to make friends with everyone tonight, so don't try. Just be agreeable." He started to turn away, then hesitated. "And, uh, don't punch anyone."

Tove nodded solemnly. "Not making any promises, but I'll count to ten before I do."

He gazed uncertainly at her, until she grinned, then he gave his head a shake and reached for the door.

Their coworkers apparently warned everyone in the tavern, because when Tove entered, the room was quiet and everyone was staring at her. She stopped inside the door and gazed around. They didn't all look angry, which Tove took as a good sign. "*Lehasa*," she called.

After an awkward silence, a woman standing at the end of the bar shouted, "Sif, I'm not paying you to stand around gawking. Play!"

The fiddle player standing on a small stage in the corner, put his fiddle to his chin and started sawing out a sprightly tune, prompting the other patrons to return to their meals and drinks.

Tove heard Frey mumble, "So far, so good," as he set off around the side of the room to the bar. "Two Ales and two bowls," he shouted over the music to the bartender, then he led Tove toward the end of the bar where the woman who spoke to the fiddler sat on a stool.

Before he could speak, the woman asked, "This her then?"

"Shia, let me introduce Tove, our *Alle'oss* Desulti," Frey said.

The woman gave Tove the impression she was considering buying her, the way she looked her up and down.

She motioned Tove forward, leaned in, and said, "I don't allow fights in my tavern."

When she pulled back, she gave Tove a look. Tove nodded. "No one starts anything, I'm as peaceful as a kitten."

The woman studied her, then gave her a nod and said, "Good enough." She lifted a hand and signaled the bartender, who set two tankards on the bar. A serving girl set two bowls on the bar, staring frankly at Tove as she turned away.

Tove stared at the bowl until Shia leaned in and said, "No one would do anything to your food here."

She turned her head to look the woman in the eye. Then she took hold of the tankard in one hand and the bowl in the other and nodded to Frey.

He led her across the tavern to a table against the wall occupied by their coworkers. Halfway across, a man suddenly leaned back in his chair, stretched his arms, hands behind his head, and extended his legs into the aisle. Tove stopped, foot hovering, then put it down. The other people at his table were watching her expectantly. "Really?" she asked.

His companions laughed. He grinned, withdrew his legs, and made an elaborate gesture for her to continue.

Tove set her bowl and tankard down next to Frey's as the music ended. "Shia doesn't seem like a bad sort."

"She's a pillar of the community," Frey said. He gestured with a spoon toward the bar. "That, there, went a long way." He touched the side of his nose with his index finger and winked. "You keep your nose clean tonight, the whole town will be talking a different tune tomorrow." He lifted a spoonful of stew, before adding, "Just, you know, don't —"

"Punch anyone," Tove said, rolling her eyes. "I got it. You punch one person." She scooped up a spoonful of stew and shoved it into her mouth. "Oh, bless the Mother!" she moaned. She could put it down to the fact she had almost nothing to eat all day. But that wasn't all of it. There were the familiar *Alle'oss* herbs and spices, but there was something she didn't recognize, something that added a tanginess that complimented the sweet, nutty flavor of the boar.

"Tye's recipe," Seele, the man who was angry about rebels, said with a grin.

Tove pointed at the bowl with her spoon, brows rising. "That old grouch?"

"He says the only reason Shia married him was for his wild boar stew," Frey said. "That's the reason it's called the Boar's Head."

"Head?" Tove asked, brows rising.

"Just the name. I think."

Tove shrugged and took another spoonful. "Whatever it's got in it, it's the best thing I ever put in my mouth." She looked up at the twitters from some of the others. "What?" When no one answered, she returned her attention to the stew.

Two hours later, Tove peered into her tankard. It was only her second ale, but her head swam alarmingly. Not surprising, as it was only the third ale she ever drank. The first was at the Black Husky in Richeleau, the night Ukrit came looking for *Oss'stera*.

She and Seele sat at the table alone, their coworkers having called it a night. Despite his negative reaction to the idea of rebels, he seemed quite interested in *Oss'stera*. Alar's relentless lectures on the subject of security in mind, Tove gave guarded answers that didn't seem to satisfy his curiosity. After a while, he fell silent and now they sat quietly. Tove gazed at the crowded room, wondering how Alar and the others were getting along.

She looked down at her tankard, then pushed it away. When she looked up, she saw Meya looking back at her from across the room.

Their eyes locked, but before Tove could read her enigmatic expression, someone stepped in front of her, blocking her view. She looked up as the man who tried to trip her earlier, rested his hands on the table, leaned toward her and said, "I'm surprised a traitor like you would stoop to frequenting a *l'oss* tavern." Tove could smell the alcohol on his breath from across the table.

"Go away, Garth," Seele said. "You don't know what you're talking about."

"Shut up, Seele," Garth said. "I'll deal with you later."

Tove didn't move. "I promised I wouldn't fight."

He straightened and gestured to the exit. "Well, we can just step outside. That way, you don't have to break any *promises*. Wouldn't want you to besmirch your *honor.*"

"You're drunk, Garth," Seele said. "She'll kick your ass."

Tove glanced at Seele. She didn't need any help picking a fight. Especially, as she wasn't sure she was any less drunk than Garth.

"Leave her alone," a woman sitting at a neighboring table said and was joined by others.

"Why does she get to come here?" someone else shouted. "She's Desulti. They got their own places."

"She's *Alle'oss,*" Seele shouted back.

Tove couldn't help a half smile.

"She *chose* to be Desulti," several people shouted back.

Tove stood abruptly, prompting Garth to take an unsteady step back. She took a moment to make sure of her balance, then looked out at the patrons in the tavern.

"*Ērtsa Alle'oss!*" she shouted, jabbing her chest with her thumb. She pointed to the scar on her face. "Was an inquisitor in *Zhot ti* in Kartok gave me this, so I don't forget." She glared at Garth. "You don't know me. Don't know anything about me." She waved a hand toward the Desulti village. "There's a lot of those Desulti think they know you. Call you *l'oss.* Think they're better than you because of who your parents were." She gestured across the tavern. "Is that who you are? You no better than them? Judge a person before you know what they are?" She paused, chest rising and falling, swallowing a wave of nausea. "I got my reasons for what I've done, but none of you care about that." She focused on Garth again. "I came here tonight to be with friends and to be among my people. *My* people!"

The tavern was silent. Shia appeared at Garth's side and said, "You best go home, Garth." When he looked at her, she said, "In fact, I don't allow fighting in my tavern, nor instigators. You're no longer welcome here."

When the words finally registered, his mouth dropped open in outrage. He threw a hand toward Tove. "You banning me because of her?"

"No. I'm banning you because you were picking a fight." Tye appeared behind her wearing an apron and carrying a heavy ladle. "Now, are you going to leave, or do we have to throw you out?"

"Leave, Garth," the woman at the next table who defended Tove said and was joined by others.

Garth hesitated, scowling at Tove, then turned and stumbled between the tables and threw the door open. Before the door blocked her view of him, Tove saw him turn and glower at her.

Shia glanced around and waved a hand. "Show's over," she said. "You best be finishing up. This is last call." This was greeted by moans, then laughter. Shia put a hand on Tove's shoulder and eased her down into her seat. "I appreciate you not rising to Garth's bait."

"Gentle as a kitten," Tove said, hot, thready breaths arresting her attempted smile.

"Hmm," Shia said. She took Tove's half full tankard and lifted a brow at her before turning to leave.

Tye took her place and smiled down at her.

"What?" Tove asked.

He sat, nudging Tove over on the bench.

"That didn't help, did it?" Tove asked.

"That was perfect," he said. When Tove gave him an incredulous look, he said, "You'll never convince people like Garth. Imps arrested his son a while back." He nodded at her look, then continued, "But your fulling coworkers have been talking, and there's a lot of people wanted to find out what kind of person you are. You showed them you won't be intimidated and you're proud to be *Alle'oss.* That'll get them thinking. It's a start." He gave her a wink and said, "And that bit about *Zhot ti* was a nice touch."

She glowered at him. "Was true."

"I believe you." he stood, lifted his hands, palms out. "But you showed them you got as much right as anyone to hate the Empire. They'll want to know more about you." He looked down at her. "You sure you're able to walk home?"

Tove stood, swayed for a moment, then said, "Whoa." Steadying herself, she said, "Fresh air will be good for me."

A half hour later, Tove was halfway to the Desulti village, staring up at a star filled sky. The walk and the cold cleared her head. She was replaying her impromptu speech in her head again, remembering the thoughtful faces turned her way when she finished. Maybe it would make a difference. "Alar would be proud," she said to the night.

"Then Alar must be a lying traitor, too."

Tove whirled toward the side of the road. Garth appeared out of the forest, a club dangling from his hand.

Tove's heart thudded against her ribs. She took a step back. Memories of other men appearing out of the dark flooded up from where they hid, waiting to remind her she was a small woman, helpless against stronger men. She turned, ready to flee, then stopped. She was done running. She may be small, but she was not helpless.

Peering warily at Garth, she noticed him swaying precariously on top of the low embankment next to the road. He must have had more to drink after leaving the tavern. Unbuttoning her cloak, she let it fall. She recognized the expression on his face. It would do no good to try talking to him. He stepped off the low embankment. While he was still in the air, Tove sprung forward.

Surprised, he swung the club as his feet hit the gully beside the road. The club missed, but the hand wrapped around the handle struck her cheek. She drove her shoulder into his abdomen. The air left his lungs in a whoosh and he fell, sitting with his back against the embankment. Gasping, he lifted the club, waving it blearily toward Tove, then he heaved, and vomit oozed from his mouth and ran down his chin. Tove kicked him in the head with the inside of her boot. He rolled over onto his side and lay still.

Looking down at him, she explored her cheek with her fingers. It was going to swell. *"Zut,"* she muttered. She bent down and pressed her fingers to the side of his neck. He was alive, but if she left him out here, he might die of hypothermia. She stood and glanced around. The prospect of returning to Ka'tan wasn't very appealing. She was exhausted and the tavern would likely be deserted by the time she got there. She had no idea who to talk to in Téama about this sort of thing. Would they even care that an *Alle'oss* was injured?

With a sigh, she picked up her cloak and emptied the pockets, threw it over Garth, then knelt and tucked it in. Rising to her feet, she gave him one last look, then turned and continued walking. Maybe Meya could get her a new cloak.

Chapter 13

An Offer Hard to Refuse

Before Brie left Téama, she read what little the Desulti recorded about the Ishien River Valley and studied maps, but it didn't prepare her for her first view from the top of a pass in the northern end of the valley. Even this late in the season, snow capped the highest peaks ringing the valley. The northern end was a patchwork of green meadows and evergreens. Dense forests that climbed the lower slopes of the surrounding mountains carpeted the rest of the valley floor. A large sapphire blue lake, glinting in morning sunlight, dominated the center. The ribbon of the Ishien River emerged from the lake and wound its way to the valley entrance in the south.

Wood smoke rose from at least three villages. Lirantok, her destination, nestled up against the southwest shore of the lake. After allowing herself time to enjoy the view, she nudged her horse forward and descended the pass.

When she reached the road that wound around the perimeter of the valley floor, she paused to allow a buckboard to pass, nodding to the man and woman who gaped at her. The woman swiveled around to keep Brie in view until the buckboard disappeared around a bend. Brie grinned, imagining the conversation they must be having. If the

Ishien River Valley was anything like other *Alle'oss* communities, news of the odd woman they met on the road would spread throughout the valley before the sun set.

As she urged her horse into motion, she put her hand on her scalp. It had been months since she let her hair grow and she found it difficult to leave the soft fuzz alone. The murtair shaved their head when they entered the program to symbolize shedding their old life, just as they did when they joined the Desulti. And just as any woman was free to do as they wished after their initiation in the Order, the murtair were free to regrow their hair. One of the reasons most murtair remained hairless was because it set them apart. It was a way to create a sense of sisterhood among women who usually operated alone.

But there were a host of practical reasons for the murtair to keep their scalp clean. It was easier to maintain during the grueling training regimen and on long missions when opportunities for bathing were rare. The linen they wrapped around their heads and the wigs they sometimes wore to disguise themselves fit better without hair. More importantly, a bald scalp made them instantly recognizable. Fear was their greatest asset. It did no good to create the mythology surrounding the Murtair if no one recognized them. When a woman wearing black, with linen wraps or a bald scalp, appeared, there was no mistaking who they were. Powerful lords sometimes fainted at their mere appearance.

But that terrifying reputation was problematic for her current mission. Siofra made it clear she was merely to negotiate with the citizens of the Ishien River Valley. She was not to use any of the tactics they used to bully and intimidate. But Brie wasn't fooled. Why send a murtair if not to intimidate? Siofra was offering a steel fist in a velvet glove. She wanted to offer the *Alle'oss* an opportunity, but remind them what could happen if they declined.

So Brie compromised. She wore her blacks, but she softened her appearance by growing her hair and eschewing the face wraps. That was enough for most people to recognize her as Murtair. And if they didn't, it probably wouldn't matter. Brie had always had a way of intimidating people. It was why the Gabra boys in her hometown who tormented her sister left her alone.

Wanting to arrive in the village in the late afternoon, she took her time, riding slowly and enjoying the cool summer day. Her appearance in the outskirts of Lirantok was noticed almost immediately. A group of children gathered and paced her horse as she neared the town square. By the time she entered the square in the center of the village, everyone knew she was coming. Although Lirantok retained some of the eclectic charm of other *Alle'oss* villages, it was obviously more prosperous than most. The buildings bordering the cobbled square were constructed primarily of brick. There were a variety of businesses, suggesting most of the citizens had coin to spend rather than goods to barter. A plank wharf and two docks bordered one side of the square. A pair of small sloops were tied up to the dock, their crews unloading their catch. One of them glanced up at the sound of her horse's hooves on the cobbles, then got the others' attention and pointed.

She reined her mount to a stop and surveyed the square. It was a busy scene, people out shopping before heading home to prepare evening meals. Shopkeepers tidying up before closing for the day. Children playing. And everyone staring at her. She walked her horse over to a group of men sitting in front of what looked like a tavern, dismounted, and tied the reins to a hitching post. The men watched her warily as she approached.

"Looking for Old Jep," she said.

"Found him," a man with long white hair and an unlikely red beard said.

Brie noticed the stir her statement caused in the group. The rumor mill being primed. She allowed her amusement to show on her face when she asked, "Mind if we have a word in private?"

She saw recognition when Jep's eyes flicked to her black clothes and short hair. He knew what she was.

"Well, now," he said. "I just had a seat before you arrived. Was going to share an ale with these gentlemen." He lifted his tankard. "You're welcome to join us." He gazed at her for a moment. "Plenty of time to talk later. Unless you're in a rush."

Brie looked up at the sky. The sun was already behind the tops of the buildings. She had been sleeping under the stars for days and wouldn't mind a night in a bed indoors. "You got an inn in town?"

Jep nodded toward the southern side of the square. "Best inn in the valley. But you're welcome to my guest room. Give us a chance to talk. In private."

If Brie were like most women, a line like that would set off alarm bells. But Brie was not like most women.

The man sitting to Old Jep's left shifted down a chair and shouted through the open door. "Need an ale out here, Shep!"

Brie sat and gazed across the lake at the mountains. Much of the valley was in dusk, but the snow that capped the mountains across the lake gleamed in sunlight. Old Jep tipped his chair, resting his back on the bricks of the tavern. A man wearing an apron appeared with a tankard. He opened his mouth to speak, but when he saw Brie, he hesitated.

"Just hand that to…" Jep said and lifted a brow.

"Brie," Brie said, taking the tankard. "*Tok*," she said, and grinned at their reactions.

"*Kisu Alle'oss da?*" Jep asked, his brows rising.

Brie shook her head and took a sip. "A few words here and there." She didn't normally drink, but she enjoyed an *Alle'oss* ale now and then, especially when she was trying to fit in. She lifted the tankard toward Shep and gave him a satisfied grin. Shep glanced at the door, then reluctantly entered the tavern.

"Tama!" Jep shouted to a boy crossing the square. The boy angled over and Jep said, "Take care of Brie's horse for her."

The boy frowned and eyed Brie. Brie dug into a pocket and tossed him a coin. When he opened his palm and gazed down at it, his eyes widened and his face broke into a grin.

As Tama led the horse away, the men and Brie sat in silence, sipping their ales. Brie glimpsed the men talking when she entered the square, so she knew the silence was because of her. "Nice place you have here," she said.

"*Tok*," several of the men said.

Brie gestured to the boats tied up at the dock. "What do they catch? Trout?"

"Mostly," Jep said. "Some pike."

"Don't usually have many fish in mountain lakes." Brie said.

"That's true," the man who made way for her said.

When he didn't elaborate, Brie grinned at Jep and sipped her ale.

An old man with one eye on the other side of Jep leaned out and asked her, "You came up the valley road?"

Brie pointed to the road she entered the village on and raised a brow.

"Yup," he said.

She stared at him. Surely, he saw her appear in the square from that road, but he only returned her gaze until she nodded.

"You see any sheep?" he asked.

"Sheep?" she asked. When he nodded, she said, "No, no sheep."

He nodded, a satisfied grin on his face, and sat back. The news produced a round of approval.

Jep grinned at her and said, "That means they've all moved up to the high pastures. A little late this year."

"It's them Olgren boys!" the one eye man exclaimed. "Useless as three-legged mules."

"Just the older one," the man on her left said. "Got his head in the clouds, that one."

"Ayup," several people agreed.

Brie smiled and sipped her ale, listening to the conversation bounce from topic to topic.

The sun was truly down when Jep said, "Well, I best be getting back."

"Your offer still good?" Brie asked.

"Ayuh," he said as he stood. He gestured with a shrug of his shoulder and set off across the square.

Brie jumped up and looked for a place to put her empty tankard.

"Here," said the one eyed man. "I'll get that."

She caught up with Jep as he was exiting the square. "You Desulti?" he asked.

"You've met Desulti before?" Brie asked.

Jep shook his head. "Suspected it when I saw the hair, though I heard you lot shaved it all off. Knew for sure when I recognize the name."

"Alar tell you about me?"

Jep shook his head again. "Ukrit and Scilla. They told me about the deals they made with the governor and the Desulti. They also warned me to keep an eye out for someone like you sniffing around."

"Not very trusting," Brie said.

"Well, I'd say they had the right of it," Jep said, looking down at her. "Not sure why you're here, but I suspect it's not in their favor."

"But it might be in yours and the rest of the valley," Brie said.

"You breaking the deal with the pigments?"

Brie shook her head. "No, that's a good deal for everyone."

"Then what is it?"

"It's the deal with the governor to bypass Imperial attention on exports from Argren."

Jep gazed at her. "You want to be part of it." When she pressed her lips together, he said, "You want to take it over."

Brie didn't answer right away. She waited as they left the tightly packed center of the village and climbed a forested hill on which more widely spaced cottages rested. Jep led her to one of these, opened the unlocked door and entered. He gestured to the table, then lit a lamp. Brie sat and watched him organize a small meal. Setting a platter on the table with a soft cheese, bread, and slices of apple, he sat opposite her and said, "Let's hear it."

"This Alar… and Ukrit and Scilla are… surprisingly canny, considering…" She took a slice of bread and spread cheese on it. "Considering they have no experience in commerce." She took a bite and chewed, letting the pause emphasize the last point. "I have to admit to underestimating their… fighting skills and determination. But fighting experience doesn't translate to commerce."

"And you Desulti have this experience," Jep said. He smeared cheese on an apple slice and popped it into this mouth.

Brie watched him chew, then put the bread she was holding down and picked up an apple slice. Spreading cheese on it, she said, "The Desulti have been in the business of making money for a long time. We already have access to markets where your products will be in high demand. Most people outside Argren won't even do business with the *Alle'oss*, especially *Alle'oss* without a… reputation. We'll take over shipping, distribution, security. All you need to do is provide the merchandise. We'll take care of everything else."

"And take most of the profit." Jep took a bite of apple.

"We'll take our share, but there'll be plenty to go around." Brie shrugged. "A small percentage of what the Desulti can provide is a lot more than you'll get with… others."

"You want me to cut out Ukrit and Scilla."

"I came to you because I heard you have a lot of respect in the valley, but I assume it's not just your decision." Before Jep could respond, she said, "If you're worried about Ukrit and Scilla, we'll hire them. They'll make some coin and learn the business. Consider it an apprenticeship. Siofra was quite impressed that they put this deal together with the governor. Someday, when they've learned, they can run their own operation."

"Siofra?"

"She's in charge of the Desulti's business interests," Brie said. "She's very good at her job. And she's fair. If you reach an agreement with her, you can expect her to keep it."

Jep chewed thoughtfully. "I need time to think on this. Consult some others. You stick around for a week?"

"I expected as much," Brie said. "You want me to move into the inn?

"Not necessary."

Chapter 14

I Need a Knife

Tove opened the door to a knock and found Cianna waiting in the hallway. When the woman saw Tove's bruised cheek, her smile fell away.

"What happened to you?"

"Ran into a door," Tove said. She turned, looking for her cloak, then remembered she left it with Garth.

"A door?" Cianna asked with a frown.

Tove tried to step through the door, expecting Cianna to retreat to allow her through, but the woman didn't budge.

"Tove," she said. "We're not going anywhere until you tell me the truth." Tove started to respond, but Cianna held up a hand. "I took a risk coming to you. I was told you would not need a counselor, but I took it upon myself to defy those instructions." She clasped the handle of her satchel in both hands and said, "There was this incident with Orla and now… If you are in trouble, or if you are… causing trouble, I need to know."

After her conversation with Tye and Frey, the question of why the Order assigned Tove a counselor occurred to her. She half hoped it was a sign there were divisions in the Order and at least some of them had her best interests at heart. That Cianna took it on herself was disappointing. Still, seeing Cianna's earnest expression, Tove couldn't help but smile. This woman, at least, seemed to care for her welfare.

"Tell you what," she said. "Let's take a walk, and I'll tell you all about it."

Cianna's face cleared. She gave Tove a brisk nod and stepped back to allow her to enter the hall.

Tove remained silent until they were walking along the edge of the plaza. "Why do you suppose you were told I wouldn't need a counselor?" she asked.

Cianna cocked an eyebrow. "You were going to tell me how you got a bruised cheek."

"I'm getting there," Tove said, grinning at Cianna's disapproving frown.

The counselor's lips twisted, but then she waved a hand and said, "I hear what everyone is saying. They say you don't deserve to be Desulti because you are *Alle'oss.*"

"And you don't agree with that?"

"No, of course not," Cianna said.

"But why, when they told you I wouldn't be assigned one, did you take it on yourself to be my counselor?"

"We were supposed to be talking about you?"

Tove motioned to a bench in the sun. She sat back, resting one arm along the back of the bench. Cianna sat on the edge, half turned toward Tove, her satchel on her knees. She looked at Tove expectantly.

"The Desulti aren't the only ones angry about me joining the Order," Tove said.

A small furrow appeared between Cianna's brows, then her face cleared and she gave a small nod. "The *Alle'oss*," she said. "Was it your servant?"

"Meya?" Tove asked. "No."

"Someone else who works here?"

"No," Tove said. "I was feeling a little homesick last night, so I took a trip to Ka'tan."

"Oh," Cianna said. "And someone there attacked you."

"It was nothing. He was drunk. He has a reason to have a grudge against the Empire."

"He?" Cianna asked.

Tove nodded.

"Will there be any future… incidents?"

Tove held up both hands up. "Not looking for trouble." She dropped her hands and said, "But I'll go where I want, when I want." She returned Cianna's gaze. "You give into people like that, they think their hate's okay."

Cianna gazed out over the plaza. "You are a braver woman than I am."

Tove chuckled.

"What?" Cianna asked.

"You assigned yourself as my counselor when you were told not to," Tove said. "Anyone give you trouble for that?"

A quick grin flitted across Cianna's face as she extracted a sheet of paper from her satchel. After returning the satchel to her knees, she winked and said, "Not yet, but it's early." She handed the paper to Tove. "Good news! I found a job that is perfect for your unique skills."

Tove took the sheet and scanned it. "What's this?"

Cianna leaned over and tapped a wax seal on the bottom of the page. "It is a requisition for a bow and arrows," she said.

"Requisition?" Tove asked.

"You can take this to the quartermaster, and she will allow you to pick a bow and some arrows."

"Why?"

"You're our hunter," Cianna said with a wide smile.

"You have a hunter?"

Cianna waved a hand. "Well, not at the moment. We *had* a hunter, up until a year ago. She had a rather unfortunate accident up in the mountains. We've been purchasing game from *Alle'oss* hunters, but I suspect they are selective about what they choose to relinquish to the Order. And their prices are exorbitant. Everyone assumes the Order can afford whatever they ask." She leaned in confidentially. "You may have noticed the fare in the dining hall is rather monotonous."

"I don't eat in the dining hall," Tove said.

"Still," Cianna asked, brows rising.

"The women who work there keep finding ways to make my meals… unappetizing."

Cianna stared at her. "Then what are you eating?"

"My fulling coworkers brought me food. Not sure what I'll do now. That was one of the reasons I went to Ka'tan last night." Cianna looked away. "This job, being a hunter. Does it pay?"

"Hmmm? Oh. Yes. However, you are paid by the dining hall based on what you bring to them." Her lips twisted again. "An arrangement that is potentially problematic."

"Yeah," Tove said. When she saw the disappointment on Cianna's face, she smiled and said, "Hey, it's a start. Like you said, the menu has been monotonous. The possibility of a little variety might change some minds."

Cianna brightened. "Let us hope so," she said. She gave Tove directions to the quartermaster, then stood and gazed down at Tove thoughtfully. After glancing over her shoulder, she leaned closer and said, "There's a small park on the north end of the village." When Tove nodded, she said, "I sometimes like to have my midday meal there. It's usually deserted. I have plans today, but shall we say, around the eleventh hour tomorrow?"

"*Tok*, Cianna," Tove said. "That would be nice."

Cianna smiled and gave her a brisk nod. "*Aurina sha*," she said, turned and walked across the plaza.

***

The woman in the quartermaster's office examined the requisition Tove handed her suspiciously, as if she was sure Tove forged it. After studying the wax seal repeatedly, she sighed and said, "Follow me." Without waiting to make sure Tove followed, she turned and walked down a long hallway. She stopped at a door and held her hand up toward Tove, warding her off. Only when she was sure Tove wouldn't come closer, did she look through the door, hold up the requisition, and say, "Hela, I have a requisition for a bow and arrows."

Tove was surprised it was a man's name and the voice that answered was undoubtedly male. A moment later an *Alle'oss* man appeared. The beads in his blond braid represented Ka'tan and something else she didn't recognize. He had the lean, weathered look of someone used to the outdoors. He glanced at Tove and took the requisition. The woman eased past Tove, pressing herself against the wall so they didn't make contact.

Tove looked over her shoulder, watching her retreating down the hall. When she turned back, the man was studying her. "You'd think *Alle'oss* was a disease she could catch," she said.

He looked past Tove. "She's not the worst." His eyes returned to the requisition. "I think it's the *combination* of *Alle'oss* and Desulti that's got them all wound up."

Tove studied him, wondering which side of the issue he came down on. When he looked up, he met her eyes and held them for a moment, offering no clues.

"Says here you are to be issued a bow and arrows," he said. "What's this for?"

"My counselor got me a job as a hunter."

He looked her up and down. "You got any experience as a hunter?"

"Some," she said. She paused and said, "I got a lot of experience with a bow."

His eyebrows quivered. His eyes flicked instinctively to where her braid would be if she had hair. "Where are you from?"

"Kartok, originally," she said. "Did most of my hunting near Richeleau."

"Game is different up here in the mountains," he said.

"How so?"

"We got some deer in the summer, but mostly elk, moose."

"Boar?"

He nodded. "Plenty of boar, but they're bigger and meaner than in the lowlands. Plus, we got bears, lions, wolves."

"How about Imp rangers?"

He gazed at her, the corner of his lips wanting to grin. When she didn't look away, he said, "Come on." He turned and led her to a door at the back of the building. Outside, he led her to the middle of three long one-story buildings. Pulling the door open, he motioned Tove inside. Sunlight pushed the darkness toward the back of the building, leaving the far end dimly lit. He walked to a rack containing a variety of bows and lifted a longbow.

"Now," he said, "you only need one arrow to kill a man dead." He leaned toward her slightly and said, "Even an Imp ranger." Straightening, he said, "But you'd have to be extraordinarily lucky to kill one of the high mountain bears with one arrow." He pressed his index finger to his cheek, below his eye. "They have little beady eyes. Not a big target, but that's about the only place you might have a chance unless they're right on top of you."

Tove couldn't decide whether he was giving her advice or mocking her inexperience. "That how the last hunter died?"

He chuckled. He held the bow next to Tove. It was nearly a foot taller than she was. He returned the longbow to the rack and studied the other bows. "No," he said. "She fell off a cliff. That's what killed her. The animals had their share, but that was after she was dead. Probably." He winked, then pulled another bow from the rack.

It was unlike any bow Tove ever saw. Short with a pronounced arc, it looked as if it was constructed from materials other than wood. He offered it to her and said, "This is a compound bow."

Tove hefted it. "It's short."

"Right," he said. "And it's lighter than most long bows. Much easier to handle in rugged terrain."

"But will it take down something as big as an elk?" She grinned and asked, "Or a bear?"

He laughed. Moving to a cabinet beside the rack, he pulled a length of sinew from a drawer. He nodded to her to follow, picked up a quiver of arrows, and led her outside. They walked down the narrow space between two of the buildings, which Tove guessed were all warehouses.

Looping the quiver over his shoulder, he held out his hand and took the bow from her. Touching the back of the bow, he said, "This is ibex horn."

"How's it attached to the wood?"

"Glue."

"Hide glue?"

His brows lifted.

"I have some experience as a bowyer," she said, feeling unreasonably proud.

"Ah. Right. Anyway, the horn gives the bow more power. This bow will take down the largest game at two hundred paces." He winked. "If you're a good shot."

They emerged into a wide-open space. Fifty paces away, a target that had seen better days rested.

"Watch," he said. He retrieved the length of sinew and demonstrated how to string the bow. After plucking the string, he handed it to her.

She hefted the bow, then tugged on the string experimentally. Taking an arrow from him, she nocked it, lifted the bow, and drew the string back to her cheek. Taking aim, she breathed out and loosed. The arrow skipped off the top of the target and embedded in the embankment behind it. She stared at the bow.

He laughed. "Stronger than it looks," he said. "You'll get used to it." He handed her the quiver. "I'll leave you to it. When you're done practicing, come find me."

"*Tok*," she said.

***

Tove slipped out of the trees at the edge of Téama, paused and popped a blueberry into her mouth. Hela sat on a boulder beside the road twenty paces away. He waved, looking as if he expected her. After practicing with the bow and signing all the forms Hela produced, she took a trip into the forest north of the village. The sun was just visible above the mountains to the west as she approached him.

When she drew near, she said, "Was you who was following me."

"You noticed," he said, his brows rising slightly. When she didn't respond, he said, "You obviously have experience in the forest. You're quiet. You don't leave any trace you passed. Difficult to track. And that was a good shot with the squirrel."

Tove took another blueberry. She didn't expect to bring down any big game her first time. The reason she spent the day in the forest was to feed herself. She was gratified to find some of the same mushrooms that were staples for *Oss'stera* around Richeleau. The squirrel tasted the same as the dozens she had eaten the past few years. The familiarity of it brought back so many memories of Alar and the other rebels, she ate it with tears in her eyes. Lifting the pouch full of blueberries, she said, "Was just trying to feed myself today."

"You don't eat in the dining hall?"

"Me and those women don't see eye to eye," she said and tucked the rest of the blueberries into her pack for later.

He nodded. "Tell you what. I'll take you out, show you how to find game, how to avoid predators. Teach you what I know."

Tove glanced at the forest, then studied him. "You and me out there alone?"

"Ah," he said with a knowing smile. "I understand." He dropped from the boulder onto the road's surface and held a hand to his chest. "I can assure you, I am the paragon of virtue." When she only looked at him skeptically, he shrugged and said, "I'll be here at the sixth bell in two days. You got a bedroll?"

She nodded slowly.

"I'll bring the provisions and everything else we need."

"Why would you do that?"

He gave her a big smile and said, "Because you got all those Desulti spitting mad."

Tove let a small grin curve her lips. "You don't like the Desulti?"

He shrugged. "Some of them are decent enough. Let's just say it won't hurt to shake them up a bit. Bring them down to earth with the rest of us. I'll teach you everything I know about hunting game in the mountains, and you can tell me about hunting Imp rangers." He winked, turned and started walking, calling over his shoulder, "If you decide to trust me, meet me at the sixth bell in two days."

She watched him walking away, considering his offer. He was right; she knew very little about hunting anything larger than squirrels and rabbits. By the time *Oss'stera* had bows powerful enough to bring down deer, they became embroiled in battles with the rangers and Union mercenaries. She needed his help. Still, she would be alone with a man she didn't know. A man who was much larger than her, far from any potential help. She snorted and mumbled, "Not that anyone here in the Order would come if I needed them." As he approached the center of the village, he turned and disappeared down a side road. "I need a knife," she said to herself.

Chapter 15

Courage to Make a Change

When the small park Cianna told Tove about came into view, she was relieved to see Cianna sitting on a blanket spread on the grass in a patch of sunlight. Part of her worried her counselor would have bowed to pressure and wouldn't come. And besides, the blueberries Tove finished at breakfast were the only thing she'd eaten all day. She was famished.

"You came," Cianna said, her face lighting up. She patted the blanket, inviting Tove to sit, then knelt, opened the top of a basket and extracted the lunch she promised. There was cheese, grapes, bread and a small crock. Once she had it arranged, she set the basket aside and sat with her legs tucked beneath herself.

Tove sank to sit cross-legged across from her. "I gotta eat," she said with a smile.

"Is that the only reason?" Cianna asked with a mischievous grin.

Tove felt her cheeks warm. She held Cianna's gaze for a moment, then had to avert her eyes.

"Don't worry, Tove," Cianna said. "I have someone in my life."

"Oh, I wasn't..." Tove said, then she saw Cianna's grin and couldn't help smiling in return. After a moment, she dropped her eyes and plucked a grape from the bunch. "Do, uh, all the women here…" She popped the grape in her mouth and gestured to the village over her shoulder.

"Like women?" Cianna asked.

Tove looked up and held Cianna's gaze.

"Most do here," Cianna said. "But that's an anomaly."

"A what?"

Cianna tore off a chunk of bread and spread red jam on it from the crock. "Many women who come to the Desulti have suffered at the hands of men," she said and took a small bite. "It's easier for them to find comfort with other women. Others prefer the company of women because that's who they are." She gazed at a hawk making its way toward the mountains while she chewed. After she swallowed, she gestured with the bread and said, "Of course, there are many women in the Order who prefer men. Everyone's circumstances and history are different."

"And that's okay? The men?" Tove asked. "I mean with the Desulti."

"Well, any man who has a relationship with someone in the Order must meet very strict criteria." Cianna took a delicate bite of the bread and licked a bit of jam from her lip with the tip of her tongue. When she swallowed, she said, "It's made very clear to them what we expect."

"What happens if they… don't meet those expectations?"

"They're introduced to a murtair," Cianna said with a wide smile.

"You kill them?!"

"Oh no," Cianna said, shaking her head. "The murtair rarely kill. Their reputation is usually enough to get someone's attention."

"How…" Tove pressed her lips together. Before she could try again, Cianna guessed her question from her expression.

"How does one become Murtair?"

"Yes."

"Nessa must admit you to the program. So you either have to impress her in some way or you must be recommended by another murtair." Cianna set the slice of bread down and pulled some grapes off the bunch. "You already have some skills Nessa values, and you apparently made an impression on Brie. You never know. Of course, very few complete the program and become Murtair. It's very difficult."

They ate in silence for a time, until Tove asked, "So, some Desulti women are with men?"

"Oh yes," Cianna said.

"But no *Alle'oss* men." Tove said.

"No, I'm afraid most of the women who come here retain their prejudices. It would be frowned on. I suspect there are some… you know. In secret."

"I don't see many Volloch men here."

"There are a few. The woman who owns the Elkhorn tavern is married to a Volloch man. But you must remember, only a small percentage of the Desulti live here," Cianna said. "Most are out in the world taking care of the Order's business interests." She gestured with a piece of cheese. "The problem is women can't own property and aren't taken seriously in business in the Empire. So, women with male partners go out into the world. The men appear to be in charge, but they are not. It's part of the expectations for marrying a Desulti."

"There are businesses owned by women in Kartok. Volloch women," Tove said.

"Yes, well, here we come to a dirty little secret," Cianna said, putting the cheese down and brushing her hands together. "To outsiders, it may appear as if the Volloch are all the same. All a part of the privileged caste, but we have our own castes." She held a hand above her head. "Gabra. Like Lyssa. The elite." She lowered her hand until it was even with her eyes. "Angus. Like Nessa. Just below the elite." She lowered her hand to her chest. "Burne. Just above the lowest. Like Brie." She let her hand fall and picked up her bread. "And then there are Baird. The lowest of the low. Like Gwynna." Taking a small nibble of her jam coated bread, she said, "The names come from the original clans in the Vollen nation and reflect those clans' reputations." She made a flourish with the bread and smiled. "Abria was of the Gabran clan, of course."

Tove gazed toward the mountains, chewing a chunk of cheese. "Gwynna was really kind to me after the initiation."

Cianna brushed some crumbs from her skirt. "I heard. That *is* surprising. She had a very difficult childhood. Painfully awkward. Never lets anyone close." She sighed. "She always seems very sad to me."

Tove hadn't seen Gwynna since that night. She would have to look for her, to thank her. She took another grape and rolled it around in her palm. "I saw poor Volloch in Richeleau and Kartok. They were these…"

"Baird?" Cianna asked. "No, not necessarily. Being rich or poor is just a superficial difference. There are *Alle'oss*, maybe most *Alle'oss*, who are better off than many Volloch, but all Volloch consider even the Baird above the richest Brochen. What matters is your caste." She licked a dab of jam from her finger, her brows knitting. "My father was richer than the lord to whom we owed fealty, but it made little difference. That might be why he…" She gazed into the distance momentarily, then gave her head a small shake. "Did you know Brochen derives from the same word as broken in ancient Vollen? The Gabra are quick to point out to the Baird and Burne they may be low, but at least they are not broken." She emphasized the last words with the bread in her hand. When she noticed Tove's expression, she said, "Of course, not everyone believes such nonsense. But people can be very protective of their place in the world, regardless how lowly it is. You may not be able to improve your position, but at least you can look down on those below you." A chilly gust of wind raised goosebumps on her legs, and she brushed her skirt so that it covered her knees.

"How do they decide who's what?"

"Everyone just knows," Cianna said with a shrug. "It's part of who we are. It's who your family is." She gestured toward the village. "Of course, the existence of the Order is evidence that being in the upper castes isn't always enough. Just look at the number of Gabra and Angus women here. Not every woman who comes here has suffered abuse. Many of them are here to escape the expectations of their caste. Siofra, for example, is here because she has a good head for business and would have no opportunities anywhere else."

"So the Volloch women I saw in Kartok running businesses. They're… what?"

"Baird or Burne, more than likely. It's shameful for a woman to run a business. I mean, only a woman who can't find a capable man would stoop so low. But since no one expects the Baird or Burne to have self respect, they can get away with it." Cianna laughed at Tove's expression. "It's as silly as it sounds, but…" She shrugged. "It is what everyone believes. Or most everyone."

They ate in silence while Tove considered. "When Brie told me about the Desulti," she said, her eyes flicking up to Cianna, "I imagined a place where women could be safe. Where everyone would be…"

"Equal?"

"Yes. I mean, you all ran away from the Empire, for different reasons, but most of you left because you weren't treated fairly. Or worse." She looked up and said, "But you brought all that stuff with you. Or a lot of it, anyway."

Cianna gazed toward the mountains. "My mother brought me when I was six. We were Burne, so considered lower caste. It was different, then. I remember how much happier my mother was here. She had a head for math. That didn't matter in the town where I was born, but when the Order found out how good she was, they sent her to school. She was thrilled."

"Where is she?"

"Oh, she's in Tsada," Cianna said. "It's across the sea. She's in charge of the entire spice trade for the Order in Tsada." She chewed a bit of cheese, her gaze unfocused. "That wouldn't happen now. For the women who come here now, their caste is more important than their abilities. The counselors have guidelines now we're supposed to apply based on caste. The guidelines specify what jobs are possible." She focused on Tove. "The guidelines don't apply to you, of course, because the Brochen caste wasn't included. That was the excuse they gave me for why you weren't assigned a counselor."

"Why did it change? The Order?"

Cianna lifted her gaze to mountains. "I often imagine how difficult it must have been for those women who first came here. How brave they were. They had nothing." She gave Tove a confidential smile. "They only survived the first few years due to the generosity of your countrymen." The smile fell away, and she returned a faraway gaze to the mountains. "A fact most in the Order have forgotten. They knew if they were to survive, they would have to make the most of what every woman could contribute. As women appeared, sometimes one at a time, sometimes in small groups, they evaluated them all equally, and put them where they could contribute to the best of their abilities. No one cared who they were or where they came from." She turned a smile on Tove again. "A true sisterhood, bound together by shared need to protect themselves from a hostile world. And, slowly, they became wealthy, powerful. And dangerous." She shrugged and looked away. "The founders tried to maintain the same sense of togetherness and equality, but as their time passed, people forgot the hard times. I suppose you can say the change started when those women began to die. It's easy for women who arrive now to take the sanctuary the Order offers for granted. To ignore the sacrifices that made it possible." She leveled a gaze at Tove. "And to ignore how easily it can be taken away. And for some women, especially those who didn't escape desperate circumstances, it's tempting to wonder why the Order needs to exist at all."

"Like Lyssa."

"Like Lyssa." Cianna squared her shoulders and straightened her back. "The real change started when Lyssa became head of the Inner Council. There was a fire. A lot of people died, including many on the Ruling Council and two on the Inner Council. The Ruling Council used to be elected by all the women in the Order, then the Ruling Council elects the three women on the Inner Council. Lyssa was the surviving member of the previous Inner Council. She used an obscure provision in the Order's Charter to call an emergency election. The Charter was written when the Order was very young and all the Desulti were here, so this provision was written in a way that could be interpreted to say only the women in Téama could vote. It should have been rewritten long ago, but as I said, it was obscure and needed only in an unlikely emergency."

"No one protested because everyone agreed it was important to have a Council quickly. It can take months to collect votes from all corners of the world. So, the vote was held and by *coincidence*, everyone voted on the Council were Gabra. Nessa was put in charge of the Murtair, because she was the longest lived murtair, and happens to be Angus. Siofra, who is Gabra, was put in charge of the Order's business interests, because she is remarkably good at that." She gave Tove a sly grin. "A cynic might say the fact that both of those women rarely pay attention to anything outside their own affairs had something to do with their appointment."

"So, the Gabra on the Council changed everything."

Cianna nodded thoughtfully. "They cited how efficient it was to hold elections with only women in Téama as justification for changing the election rules. And they made a lot of other changes as well. The guidelines for counselors based on caste are just one example. Women who protested were posted elsewhere, so they had no say in future elections. Most of the women still in Téama are either upper caste who are loyal to Lyssa or lower caste who know their place." She paused. "You may have noticed how few people live here for how large Téama is."

Tove nodded thoughtfully, then said, "So, what the Order used to be is gone forever."

"Probably."

"Why did Nessa and Siofra vote to allow me into the Order if I'm lower than the Baird?"

"Yes," Cianna said. "That is curious, isn't it?"

"Maybe Nessa or Siofra were hoping to stir things up."

"Well, it certainly has done that," Cianna said. Her tinkling laughter filled the small park and coaxed a smile from Tove. "The Gabra and Angus are all of a same mind. They are trying to figure out how to get rid of you. But the lower castes are split. There are arguments, heated arguments, and some have been physical."

Tove glanced back at the seemingly peaceful village. "I ain't seen nothing like that. Mostly, what I see is people who don't want me here."

"It's mostly behind closed doors. For now. I'd be careful about going out alone, though."

Tove chuckled. "That's the only way I can go out." She eyed Cianna. "How about you? You said you assigned yourself to be my counselor. Anyone say anything about that?"

"I was sternly rebuked," she said with an exaggerated frown. Then she shrugged and said, "And reassigned to a clerical position."

"I didn't thank you enough for helping me," Tove said. "I'm sorry for the trouble it caused you."

"Don't worry about me. My partner is Murtair. The worst they can do is put me in a boring job."

"Least you aren't walking in pee," Tove said, returning her grin. She took a bite of bread with what turned out to be raspberry jam. When she swallowed, she asked, "You know Hela? He's the one gave me the bow."

Cianna nodded. "I know," she said. "I've been keeping track."

"Is he trustworthy?"

"Completely," Cianna said. "I told him to keep an eye out for you."

Tove nodded. That explained why he took such an interest in her. "Why are you helping me so much?"

Cianna shrugged. "It seemed unfair to me. I've been here longer than most. I've seen what it could be. We never had an *Alle'oss* join the Order before, but I've seen what being treated fairly for the first time in their life can do for a woman. Seen them arrive beaten down and watched them blossom." She replaced the lid on the crock of raspberry jam and returned it to the basket, then smiled at Tove. "For you, later." After returning the rest of the food to the basket, she closed the lid and said, "I'm not the only woman who doesn't like what has happened to the Order."

Setting the basket aside, she leaned back and let her head fall back, so the sun fell on her face. "You are in a unique position, Tove. Most of the Baird and Burne women don't like that they've been put back in the low position they thought they were escaping when they came here. But it *is* what they are used to. They grew up with it and they accept it as their lot in life. Most people don't have the courage to defy entrenched social conventions on their own. They need someone to show them change is necessary and possible. Someone to follow." She lowered her face and looked at Tove. "But the *Alle'oss* have *never* accepted the place the Volloch try to put them in. You're in the Order, so you can't be ignored as easily as other *Alle'oss*, but you don't fit within the Volloch *guidelines*. They can't figure out what to do with you. More importantly, the arguments among the lower castes are bringing uncomfortable questions into the light."

"Those women, the ones fighting about me. The ones taking my side. Do they have the courage to make a change?"

"Perhaps. If someone were to show them a way."

"Is there a way?"

"It's been a long time since I read the Charter," Cianna said with a small grin. "But maybe it's time I read it again."

Chapter 16

She's Crafty

Tove knelt on the edge of a cliff and gazed down at the wooded slope that rose across a lively mountain stream.

Hela knelt beside her and pointed. "This is a perfect place for elk. They like north-facing slopes. There's better forage for them, especially in spring when the leaves are tender." He pointed to a relatively still pool in the stream. "They'll come out of cover for water."

"It's a long shot from here."

"Right. I'd get a little lower." He pointed to a ledge that ran along the face of the ridge below them.

"Then just wait?" She glanced at him.

"You can try tracking them, but your best bet is to find a place like this and stake it out. They come back to places they like."

Tove let her gaze follow the course of the stream as it descended toward a narrow valley between towering, snow-capped peaks. There were mountains near Richeleau, but they were mere hills compared to these. In her short time in Téama, she had fallen in love with these mountains. There was a serene majesty to them, a sense of timelessness that appealed to her. But what she liked most was the solitude.

Her early years in the biggest city in Argren, Kartok, had been lonely and devoid of any tenderness. If she was born anywhere else but Kartok, another *Alle'oss* family would have taken her in when her parents died. But Kartok had become an Imperial city. Authorities condemned foundling *Alle'oss* children to an orphanage where nuns of the Vollen Church reeducated them. The priests told them the nuns would help them grow up to be ideal citizens of the Empire. Still Brochen, but happy with their place in society. It was a travesty. When the priests left, the nuns did the minimum required to keep the children alive and kept whatever funds they were allotted for themselves.

Her life didn't improve much after she escaped the orphanage, but at least her fate was her own. Until she ran afoul of the Inquisition. She swallowed and dropped her head, resisting the urge to rub her scar, unwilling to dredge up those memories.

Alar rescued her from that terrible life, but even among the family she found with *Oss'stera*, navigating social situations was taxing for her. The barriers she erected to keep herself safe weren't so easily dismantled. Even within the warm embrace of her fellow rebels, she often felt isolated, as if she were watching their happiness vicariously from a distance. She hoped the Desulti would be a refuge where she would feel safe enough to let the barriers down, but that obviously hadn't worked out the way she hoped.

Coming back from her memories, she studied Hela's profile. She was wary of him the first time they climbed into the mountains, keeping her distance during the day and sleeping with her knife in her hand. But Cianna was right about him. He was one of the good ones. An open book, he had no ulterior motives, as far as she could tell. He was willing to give her space when she needed it and never took offense. And he was a good teacher. Not only was he imparting to her all his woodcraft, he filled her in on Ka'tan's gossip. It wasn't long before she found herself enjoying his company.

"You know we're being followed," he murmured.

"Thought it was my imagination," Tove said, returning her gaze to the stream. "Whoever it is, they're good."

"I agree. Took me days to notice it," he said. "If I had to guess, I'd say they were Murtair. Seen glimpses of black."

Tove's head snapped around.

He met her gaze and nodded. "Someone's keeping an eye on you." He stood and looked toward the valley. "Not surprising, is it?"

Tove stood. "Guess not. You think it's Nessa?"

He shrugged. "Assuming they *are* Murtair, it could be any of the Inner Council. They can all issue a contract for a murtair." He thought for a minute. "Course, if it's a contract, they all know about it because two of the Inner Council have to approve it. If it's not a contract, then either it's Nessa or a murtair has thrown her lot in with either Siofra or Lyssa, and Nessa doesn't know about it." He frowned. "Or maybe a murtair is acting on her own."

Tove stared at him. "Place is a pit of vipers," she said and looked out at the mountains.

"Why do you think they allowed you in the Order?" he asked, an uncharacteristic hesitancy in his voice.

"Been wondering about that myself."

"I haven't heard anyone discussing what happened," he said, "but I'm guessing Lyssa was against it." He glanced at her and she nodded. "So, the others had to vote yes."

"Nessa," Tove said. "She was the one who argued for me. I assume it was because it was Brie made the deal with Alar to make me Desulti."

"And Siofra?"

"No idea," Tove said with a shrug. She looked up at him. "Those three playing some game. Not sure what it is, but I'm in the middle of it. Somehow."

***

It was nearly evening when Tove left Hela at the edge of the village. She tugged a pouch full of blackberries from her pack and munched on the tasty treat as she made her way to her room, choosing a route at random. The bow she was already fond of was tied to her pack with her quiver. They caught glimpses of elk and deer but were never close enough to waste an arrow. But she knew where game traveled now. It was just a matter of time.

The sun was below the buildings, leaving the street dusky and cool. Clambering through the mountains north of the village left her tired, but it was a pleasant fatigue. Still, she wasn't paying as much attention to her surroundings as she usually did. The scuff of a boot and a snippet of conversation brought her head up on the quiet street.

Two women slouched against the front of a shuttered bakery. Tove was about to give them a nod in greeting when they stepped away from the wall and moved to intercept her. She angled away, but they increased their pace to cut her off.

Coming to a stop, she eyed them. The one who stopped in front of her was slightly taller than she was, but much bulkier. The other one standing to the side was taller than Tove by half a foot and lanky. "Can I help you?" Tove asked.

"Yeah," the short one said, "you can go back to where you came from."

"Where you belong," the other one said.

Tove glanced up at the tall one. "I belong *here.* Your Inner Council said so. Or are you saying they don't speak for you?"

"Lyssa didn't vote for you," the short one said. "She's the head of the council."

"She's one of three. Least she was when they voted. You heard something different?"

The two women glanced at one another, looking confused, but before they could speak, Tove leaned toward the short one and said confidentially, "Got a murtair following me." She hooked her thumb over her shoulder. The women's expression became wary as they looked down the street. "You got business with me, you better get to it before she catches up."

The women glanced at one another again. Tove watched their faces, hoping they decided to leave her alone. But she was disappointed. When the taller one scowled and took a step toward her, Tove shot forward and punched the short woman in the breast. She stepped to the side, away from the tall one, but she underestimated the woman's reach. Her fist caught Tove in the cheekbone, just below her eye.

The woman followed her punch, lunging to grapple with Tove, but Tove stepped forward at an angle, putting the short woman between her and the taller woman. The short woman was bent over, her arms crossed over her chest. Tove kicked her behind the knee and shoved her toward the other woman. When the taller woman caught the falling woman, Tove jammed the pouch of blackberries in her face, ground it in, then turned and ran.

***

"Two gendarmes?" Nessa asked.

Laoise nodded. "Yes, Mistress. They weren't in uniform."

"You didn't intervene?"

"It was over quickly," Laoise said, not responding to the implied criticism. "I would have been there if it grew more serious."

"Tove handled two gendarmes that quickly?"

Laoise nodded. "She's crafty." When Nessa gazed out the windows of her study, Laoise said, "I'm pretty sure she knows I'm following her as well."

Nessa nodded. That wasn't surprising. It was hard even for a murtair to follow someone for days without being noticed.

"You want me to keep following her?"

"Yes," Nessa said.

"And if she is attacked again?"

Nessa focused on her. "Don't let them kill her."

Laoise hesitated. "How exactly am I supposed to determine when to intervene?"

"Use your best judgment."

"So, you don't mind if she's assaulted. You just don't want her to die," Laoise said doubtfully. "What if she dies?"

Nessa stood. "That would be unfortunate." It was as close to a rebuke as Nessa ever gave her murtair.

Laoise's expression was enigmatic. She gave Nessa a nod, turned, and left.

Nessa stared at the door. She doubted Brie told Laoise what they planned, but it would be surprising if Laoise didn't suspect something. She gave her head a shake. It didn't matter. Based on what she was hearing from Shailey, the situation was simmering and, with a little heat, would rise to a boil soon.

***

"Is there anything else?" Lyssa asked Cara.

Her assistant adjusted her glasses and said, "You asked me to keep on top of the unrest the *l'oss's* presence has caused."

Lyssa sighed. "Yes, of course."

"There have been two more fights. That I know of, though, there has been a dramatic increase in the number of women requesting new accommodations. It's mostly among the Baird and Burne."

Lyssa's brows knitted.

"It appears people are choosing sides," Cara said.

"How could this be happening? Surely, there couldn't be this many women supporting the *l'oss.*"

"They are a vocal minority, apparently."

"What of the woman, Tove?" Lyssa asked. "We hoped she would become uncomfortable enough to leave on her own."

"She has been…" Cara paused, searching for words. "She's usually alone. She goes to Ka'tan, or she's up in the mountains. Hunting, I presume." Cara shrugged. "She takes different routes, leaves at different times. She's wily. There is little opportunity for those who object to her presence to make her aware."

Lyssa stared at her assistant.

"There was one incident," Cara said.

"Yes?"

"Two women confronted her yesterday."

"What happened?"

"I'll let them tell you," Cara said, then retreated to the door.

The two women entered, their eyes roaming the office, but not finding Lyssa. They were gendarmes, though they weren't wearing their uniforms.

"What in Daga's name happened?" Lyssa asked.

They glanced at one another. "We wanted to show the *l'oss* she wasn't welcome."

"And?"

The shorter woman shrugged and gestured vaguely. "She…" Her voice trailed off and her eyes cut to the taller woman.

Lyssa gaped at them. "That slip of a girl got the best of you?"

"She punched me in the breast." The two women nodded, as if this scandalous news excused their shame.

"Get out," Lyssa said.

The two women were turning away when the shorter one paused. "She said she has a murtair following her." She said it defensively.

"Following her?" Lyssa asked. "Did you see the murtair?"

"Well… no."

Lyssa stood, approached her windows, and ignored them as they shuffled out the door.

Cara cleared her throat.

"Yes, Cara?" Lyssa asked.

"It looks as if we have underestimated the *l'oss* again."

"Yes, it appears so." Lyssa pursed her lips. "You think it's possible a murtair is keeping an eye on her?"

"That would mean Nessa is keeping an eye on her."

Lyssa turned abruptly. "What is that woman's interest in Tove?"

"You could simply have the gendarmes arrest Tove," Cara said. "I'm sure we can come up with some charge. Even if we couldn't make it stick, we could keep her in a nice, dark cell for a while."

"But there would be a trial," Lyssa said. "And it would further inflame emotions. We can't afford that. Not now. Unless… Didn't the last hunter die up in the mountains?"

Cara hesitated. "Yes, she did."

"If Tove were to suffer an accident up in the mountains, all alone… Problem solved. Who would be able to complain?"

Cara nodded slowly. "Yes. If it looked like an accident." She gave her head a shake. "It wouldn't work if there is a murtair keeping an eye on her."

"We just need to make sure the murtair is elsewhere."

Cara hesitated and cocked her head. "Laoise is the only murtair in Téama at the moment."

Lyssa nodded. "We issue a contract."

"But, Nessa —"

"If we designate it an emergency," Lyssa said, "we have two weeks to inform the Inner Council. Find Laoise."

***

It was almost midnight before Cara located Laoise. That it was not long after Tove retired to her room supported the idea she *was* keeping an eye on the *l'oss.* Lyssa awaited the murtair's appearance, her heart thumping a steady rhythm. Despite the difference in their positions, Lyssa had to steel herself every time she spoke to a murtair.

Her main problem with the murtair was they violated Daga's given social order. None of the reforms the Council imposed on the Order could rectify that blight. Unfortunately, very few women outside the Baird and Burne castes completed Murtair training. Nessa's predecessor, a Baird, arrogantly explained to Lyssa that Murtair training was a crucible that revealed a woman's quality. In Lyssa's mind, all this proved was that the baser human traits were sufficient for being Murtair. After all, dog could be trained to tear a man limb from limb. That the murtair thought they were entitled to equal standing in the Order was galling.

When Laoise suddenly appeared in her office door, Lyssa flinched involuntarily. She ground her teeth as Laoise stood quietly in the doorway, her eyes making a circuit of the office, ignoring her and Cara. When she deigned to enter the room, she came to stand in front of Lyssa's desk and met Lyssa's gaze. Lyssa bit back her rebuke, suppressing her anger and the shame which stoked it. The truth she would never admit to anyone was the murtair terrified her. Lyssa knew the belief they could read minds was a myth propagated by the Order, but she couldn't dismiss the feeling this woman sensed her fear.

"Mistress," Laoise said after an insultingly long pause.

Lyssa dug her fingernails into her palms. She was Gabra, the head of the Inner Council, for Daga's sake! This woman was beneath her. Taking a breath, she reminded herself it was only a matter of time before she could rid the Order of this stain. Forcing herself to sit forward, she cupped her hands on her desk and met the murtair's steady gaze.

"Laoise," she said. "I have a very important contract for a murtair. It's on a matter that requires the utmost haste and discretion. As you are the only murtair in Téama and the matter is urgent, it falls to you."

Laoise hesitated. Her eyes flicked to Cara, then returned to Lyssa. "I can leave as soon as I inform Nessa."

"That won't be necessary," Lyssa said. "I've designated this contract an emergency. You must leave immediately. As soon as you leave here. I will inform Nessa."

Laoise didn't react at first, then the muscles at the corners of her mouth tightened. "What is the contract?" She skimmed the document Cara handed her, then looked at Lyssa. "An importer shorting shipments is an emergency?"

The anger beneath Lyssa's fear flared. "You don't get to decide what is an emergency! You carry out the contracts we give you without question."

Laoise hesitated again, her eyes narrowing, then she said, "Of course, Mistress. Is that all?"

Cara intervened before Lyssa could erupt. She took a step forward and spoke in a rush, "Yes, Laoise, that is all. Though the contract appears inconsequential, we can assure you that it is of the utmost importance. You must leave immediately."

Laoise glanced at her, nodded to Lyssa, and said, "Mistress." Without another word, she turned and left.

Lyssa stood abruptly. "The unmitigated arrogance!" she said, as Cara rushed to close the door. She came around her desk and paced.

"Mistress, it worked."

Lyssa stopped and struggled to regain her composure. "Right," she said. "You're right." She pivoted around and returned Cara's smile. "She'll be gone by the morning. Now, who should we get to take care of the *l'oss?*"

"Tish," Cara said.

"Perfect!"

***

Cianna rose from her bed when she heard Laoise enter their apartment. She was late, but that wasn't unusual. Tove didn't keep to anything like a regular schedule. Cianna suspected it was by design. She found Laoise standing at the desk they shared in the study.

"You're late tonight," Cianna said, slipping her arms around Laoise's waist from behind, squeezing and thrilling at the tautness of her lover's body.

The murtair twisted around, took Cianna in her arms and met her seeking lips with her own. Their kiss lingered, but Cianna could tell something was bothering Laoise. She broke their kiss and said, "Something is wrong."

Laoise extricated herself from Cianna's arms and lifted a sheet of paper from the desk. "It's a contract. For Lyssa. She's made it an emergency. I'm to leave immediately."

Cianna held the document close to the lamp and read it, fingers of her other hand to her lips. Letting the contract hang in her hand, she stood and frowned at Laoise. "Shorting shipments?"

"That was my reaction."

Cianna hesitated, then reread the contract.

"What do we do?" Laoise asked. "Two gendarmes attacked Tove yesterday."

Cianna looked up abruptly. "Gendarmes?"

Laoise nodded. "Not in uniform."

"Were you involved?"

"Happened too fast," Laoise said.

"Is Tove okay?"

"She is. She took care of them on her own. I'm beginning to think Brie was right about her."

"Me too," Cianna said. "You think they were acting on Lyssa's orders?"

Laoise unbuckled the straps that held her blouse tight, lifted it over her head and dropped it to the floor. As she began unwrapping the linen strips that bound her breasts, Cianna saw her shake her head, though her attention was elsewhere. "Too clumsy," Laoise said. Dropping the cloth atop her blouse, she let her arms hang at her sides. "My guess is they took it on themselves, and it probably won't be the last time."

Cianna's eyes wandered up to Laoise's face. "What... what should we do? About the contract?"

"This is your show," Laoise said. "If I take the contract, Tove will be exposed. If I don't, there will be consequences for me if things don't go well." She took Cianna in her arms. "I could tell Nessa."

"No!" Cianna said.

"Then what should I do?"

"Ignore the contract," Cianna said. She put her fingers on Laoise's mouth to stop her nibbling her neck. "Keep out of sight and keep watching Tove."

"And if things go badly?" Laoise made it past Cianna's defenses and ran the tip of her tongue along Cianna's jaw.

"We'll… we'll deal with whatever comes. Together." She lifted up on her toes and found Laoise's mouth. When she broke the kiss, she asked, "We have a half hour, right?"

Laoise swept Cianna up and carried her to their bedroom.

Chapter 17

A Lost Little Boy

Tove dropped her spoon into her empty bowl and gazed across the tavern. She considered it progress that her arrival in the Boar's Head earlier was uneventful. There were some whispers and hostile glares, but most people only noted her arrival and returned to their conversations. Most of her fulling coworkers left earlier. Only Seele remained. He nursed an ale and gazed, half-lidded, at something Tove couldn't see.

"So, Seele," Tove said, pulling him from his thoughts. "What did you do before fulling? I assume you haven't always walked in pee."

He held her gaze for a moment, then let the back of his head rest on the wall and sipped his ale. "Sheep," he said.

"Sheep?"

"Ayuh," he said. "Merinos." He said it proudly.

"That a kind of sheep?"

"Best wool in Argren."

Tove grinned and asked, "How did you get from raising the wool to dousing it in pee?"

He cleared his throat, sucked in a breath, and blew it out. "Well, with my back the way it is, I can't do the heavy work anymore." He squinted at her. "You remember Garth's son, the one who was arrested by the Inquisition?" When Tove nodded, he said, "When the boy married my daughter, I gave them the farm to run."

Tove stared at him. "Garth's son is your son-in-law?" When he nodded, she asked, "Why didn't you tell me?"

He started to speak, hesitated, then said, "Family business."

Tove waited, but when there was no more explanation forthcoming, she asked, "So, your daughter is running the farm alone?"

"Her and my granddaughter." He gave his head an odd shake and said, "Garth… he's had some issues since his son got taken. He's got enough to deal with."

"I'm sorry."

He nodded.

They sat in silence for a time, then Tove asked, "But why does that explain you fulling?"

"When they took him away, people stepped in to help out." He gestured vaguely. "But, you know, people got their own lives to live." He sipped his ale. "So we hired a man."

"And he has to be paid."

She watched him nod quietly, then sat back and listened to the fiddle. When the fiddle player finished his set, she said, "So, you sell the wool to the Desulti, they make it into cloth and sell it outside Argren."

He nodded. "They make a mint too. Everyone knows Merino is the best wool."

"Why don't *you* sell the cloth? Why do you let the Desulti make all the coin?"

His head rotated to look at her. "Thought you said this *Oss'stera* was going to get rich in commerce."

She nodded, taken aback by his sarcastic tone.

"No one outside Argren is going to buy from the *Alle'oss*." He waved a hand toward Téama. "The Order has all the contacts.

Logistical know-how. They have the power to demand the price they want."

Tove stared at him until he looked away, then she settled back, wondering if Alar knew that.

An hour later, she exited the tavern and paused on the porch, breathing the crisp mountain air to revive herself before heading back to Téama. A man and a girl heading toward Ka'tan on the far side of the street drew her attention. It was their furtiveness and the fact that an obviously young girl was out so late.

As they neared, she felt it. Like her brain was twisting on itself. If she hadn't met Ecke, the witch Alar rescued from the Inquisition the previous year, she might not have recognized it. The girl was a witch. That was why the man shielded her behind himself and why he peered suspiciously at her as they passed.

"Hey!" she shouted and took off after them.

The man pulled the girl close and threw a glance back at Tove, his expression full of fear. When he took hold of the girl's arm and started running, she stumbled and fell, allowing Tove to catch up.

"Wait," Tove said, holding up her hands in a placating gesture. "I'm not going to turn her in."

He lifted the girl to her feet and eyed Tove cautiously. "What are you talking about?"

Tove took a step toward them, glanced down the road toward Ka'tan, then said to the girl, "*Lehasa*, my name is Tove." She smiled and the girl, peeking out from behind the man, glanced up at him, then tried a tremulous smile. Tove pointed to the trees and asked, "Do you see the spirits?" Only witches could see the small, luminous orbs that gave them their magical gifts. It was why the Inquisition hunted them down; to prevent the witches from growing old enough to weld their power.

"Leave us be!" the man said and pulled the girl into motion.

"Wait!" Tove said and ran to get in their way. She gestured to the girl. "She's a witch." When the man shrank from her, pulling the girl behind him, she hurried to say, "I'm not going to turn her in."

"Then what do you want?"

"Someone will figure it out. No matter how careful you are," Tove said. "Most people won't say anything, but it only takes one."

His face screwed up, revealing the anguish of a parent worried for his child. "What do you suggest we do?"

"There's a village down near Richeleau called *Honutok*. There's a man there named Alar. He'll make sure she's safe. He's done it before with others."

"Richeleau?! We came from down that way," he said. "I brought her here cause it's the farthest place from the Empire in Argren."

"No place is safe, and it's less safe here than other places. There's a cathedral of the Vollen Church in Ka'tan," Tove said. "Listen, Alar rescued a witch from the brothers. Her name is Ecke. She lives in *Honutok*." She reached out and took his arm to cut off his response. "They can teach her to hide herself." Witches were easy for the Inquisition to find because their presence caused pain in people nearby. Tove didn't understand it, but she had to grit her teeth being so close to the girl. Hope softened the hard edges of anger and despair in his expression. "No one will be able to feel her. No one will know she's a witch."

His hand rested on the shoulder of the blond girl peering up at Tove from behind him. "*Honutok*, you say?"

Tove nodded. "Ask for Alar or Ecke. Anyone there will take you in. She'll be safe." She gave him directions and made him promise to leave at first light. She offered to let them sleep in her room, but he claimed they had family nearby.

He extended a hand and Tove took his forearm. "*Tok*," he said.

"*Aurina sha.*"

As he turned away, he said to the girl, "Come on, Eriu. I'm plumb tuckered out."

"Thank you," the girl said to Tove over her shoulder.

Tove waved, feeling buoyant. Like she'd done something real against the Empire. Like Alar must have felt after rescuing Ecke.

Turning toward Téama, she set off down the misty road with a spring in her step.

When she neared Téama, she turned off the Ka'tan road so she could make her way through the village by a different route than she usually took. No one had openly threatened her since she encountered the two women, but being predictable grated on hard earned instincts instilled in her in Kartok.

On a whim, she wound her way through the empty streets until she stood in front of Nessa's dark house. "What you got in mind for me?" she murmured, her breath misting in the chilly air.

The clop of horses' hooves on cobbles sent her scrambling into the shadows at the base of the wall that surrounded Nessa's house. Five horses appeared from a side street a block away. The streetlights were dark this late, but the gibbous moon provided enough light to recognize the white uniforms of Inquisition brothers.

"*Sheoda,*" she breathed. What was the Inquisition doing in Téama? There could be no greater representative of what the Desulti fled than these men. Her instinct was to run, but she ignored it. She needed to find out if she recognized them.

The riders reined up in front of the largest house on the street. The men dismounted and two of them disappeared through the gate in the wall that surrounded the house.

She couldn't make out the faces of the three remaining on the street nor understand their low voices, but there was no way she could get closer without exposing herself. While she waited for the others to return, she considered the question of why they were here. Could it be because of the witch she saw earlier in Ka'tan? The Inquisition normally only sent an inquisitor and three regular brothers after a witch. But Ka'tan was deep in Argren. Maybe they sent more when they had to come this far. But why stop in Téama and who were they visiting?

She was considering making her way around the block so she could get closer when she heard the door to the house slam open. Three brothers appeared, postures stiffened by anger. One of them turned and spoke to someone who was out of sight through the gate. Tove strained to hear what he said, but despite his obvious anger, his voice was too low to understand. Then his voice rose. "Find him!"

Tove flinched involuntarily. Cold sweat slicked her body. Her muscles locked her in place, like prey in the presence of a predator. She knew that voice, heard it echoing in her nightmares. Inquisitor Hoerst. She couldn't see his face, but there was no mistaking his voice. Her hand pressed to her scar, the searing memories of the blade slicing her cheek, forcing her eyes shut.

But this was a chance she never expected to have. She couldn't let it slip away. Slowly, she rose to a crouch and pressed her back against the wall. She glanced at the knife, which found its way into her hand. It wouldn't be enough. Not against their swords. She needed her bow. Sheathing the knife, she sprinted across the street. No one shouted an alarm. They were too focused on their argument. She ran through the streets toward her room. Arriving in the dim hall, heart thundering in her chest, she yanked the door to her room open and froze.

"Tove," the woman sitting quietly on her bed said. "I've been expecting you."

It was Ragan, the former Imperial witch who had a habit of appearing at the most unexpected moments. Her presence alone might not have derailed Tove's burning need to kill the man who left her scarred, but the baby boy gazing placidly at her from Ragan's lap gave her pause. She stepped into the room, chest expanding and contracting like a bellows, and stared at the baby.

Whoever it was, he wasn't her problem. "Ragan," she said and crossed the room to retrieve her bow. "This isn't a coincidence, is it?"

"You won't need that," Ragan said. When Tove turned, Ragan nodded at the bow.

"How do you know what I need?" Tove asked. Alar told her Ragan could see the future. It was the only thing that explained the fact the woman seemed to know far more than she had any right to. But despite the fact the witch helped *Oss'stera* rescue Alar's beloved, Scilla, from an Inquisition prison the previous autumn, Tove found her creepy. She didn't trust her.

"They'll be gone before you get back," Ragan said.

Tove retrieved a piece of sinew and set about stringing her bow. "Oh, yeah?" she asked. "Where're they going?"

"Searching the road to Richeleau, more than likely."

"Searching for —" Hoerst had said, "Find him." Tove's eyes dropped to the boy who was still watching her, the fingers of one pudgy hand in his mouth. "They looking for him?"

Ragan only gave her the half-mocking smile Tove found so irritating.

"Who is it?" Tove asked. "The boy. He's not yours. You had a girl." Ragan's daughter was born in *Honutok* the previous winter. Tove watched, fascinated, as a deep sadness transformed Ragan's enigmatic grin.

The witch lowered her head and kissed the boy's head. When she looked up, lamplight glistened in her eyes. "He's lost. Just a lost little boy who doesn't deserve his fate."

"*Lika*," Tove said, mesmerized by the change in the intimidating woman.

Confusion crossed Ragan's face. "Excuse me?"

"*Lika*," Tove repeated and gave her a head shake. "It means lost in *Alle'oss*."

Ragan's eyes took on a distant look. "Lika," she murmured. The boy twisted around and craned his neck to peer up at her, perhaps noticing the odd tone in her voice.

Tove whirled at the sound of a footstep in the doorway. An *Alle'oss* boy of maybe ten summers, glanced at her, his eyes going to her scar, then he looked past her to Ragan. "They're gone," he said. "Three back to Richeleau and two to Ka'tan."

"Eriu!" Tove said. The two going to Ka'tan were after the witch she met earlier.

"They aren't looking for Eriu," Ragan said. She picked up a long shawl from the bed and rearranged the boy on her lap. "Aron," she said. "Can you help with this?"

"Sure," the boy said. Ragan stood and she and Aron worked together to bundle the baby against her chest.

"They don't know about Eriu, yet," Ragan said as Aron tied the ends of the shawl together at her shoulder.

"Yet?"

"You can't help her, Tove," Ragan said.

"They catch her?"

"She lives," was all Ragan said. She walked to the door, the baby's dark eyes looking up at Tove as she passed. "Don't worry, Tove. You'll have another opportunity with Hoerst."

"Another — What If I don't want to wait?"

"But I need you to," Ragan said. "I, you, all of Argren need Hoerst to live." She rested a hand on Tove's arm. "For now. Besides, you have enough to be about here."

"What —" Tove started, but Ragan disappeared down the hall.

"*Andustra,*" Aron said, then followed Ragan.

Tove stared at the open door, conscious of the bow hanging from her hand. Alar told her they could trust Ragan. No. That wasn't what he said. He said Ragan's goals aligned with *Oss'stera's*. For the most part. He also said to be wary if she asked Tove to do something for her.

She thought of that smug monster, Hoerst, escaping and took a step toward the door before reason prevailed. Even if she ignored the witch's desires, she would never catch them on foot. She stood, hand on the latch for a long moment, then closed the door, unstrung her bow and returned it to its place, then fell into bed.

Gazing at the lamp, she considered who the baby might be for a while, then thrust the riddle from her mind. She had enough to deal with without becoming entangled in that witch's business. Ragan was right about that, at least. Hoerst got away. But the truth was she was no worse off than she was before tonight, and it was strangely reassuring that Ragan told her she would have another chance at him. That was far more than she ever hoped for.

A more immediate question was who Hoerst was visiting and why that person would know anything about the baby boy? Her eyes unfocused, smearing the small flame across her vision. It wasn't her problem. Just another example of the Order's tangled politics. She had enough to deal with.

As she drifted at the edge of sleep, the significance of the witch telling her she had enough to do here occurred to her. It meant Ragan peered into the treacherous waters Tove was navigating. What did that mean? Deciding she would twist herself in knots if she worried about it, she chose to ignore it. Closing her eyes, she let a dreamless sleep take her.

***

Lyssa watched Hoerst and the other brothers ride away, careful to maintain her outward appearance of calm. The brother Hoerst left behind, turned and met her eyes, his feelings on the subject clear on his face. He was a replacement for the brother who let the baby be taken. Lyssa wasn't sure what that man's fate would be for failing so spectacularly, but she didn't care.

She whirled and strode up the walkway to her front door. She didn't tell Hoerst, but she knew who took the boy. It had to be that witch, Ragan. When the witch came to her months ago and told her Hoerst would be bringing the woman to have her baby, Lyssa assumed she was on official business for the Empire. After all, she had the tattoo of a Seidi witch at her left temple, and she had been right about Hoerst and the woman. It wasn't until much later she recognized the warning signs. The witch's tattoo was that of a novice, not a full sister. The Seidi would not entrust such an important task to a novice. Another suspicious sign was that she told Lyssa not to tell Hoerst she came to see her. Lyssa had been too blinded by the opportunity Ragan set in front of her to heed the warnings. It was the witch's hints that led Lyssa to demand the concessions that led to her deal with the emperor.

Lyssa entered her drawing room, trailed by the brother, and found the baby's mother staring into the fireplace. Soft golden light illuminated her face and glistened in the tears on her cheeks. The thought that the woman met the witch in her home without Lyssa's knowledge enraged her even more than Hoerst's condescending rebukes.

"What have you got to smile about?" Lyssa snapped. Addressing this woman without a title was the highest insult Lyssa could think of.

The woman startled. Her head turned slowly toward Lyssa. "He's safe. They'll never find him, now," she said. "All your plans are in ruin."

Lyssa barked a laugh. "Your deceit hasn't changed anything. Hoerst assured me the emperor will honor our agreement." The inquisitor told her the boy's disappearance changed nothing. The Order would still move to Kartok and be accepted as a legal entity in the Empire. Her triumphant smile faded when a wider smile chased the momentary surprise from the woman's face.

"Now, why would he do such a thing, do you think?" She returned her gaze to the fire, dismissing Lyssa.

It wasn't this woman's status in the Empire that stopped Lyssa from slapping her for her insolence. It was shock. She'd been too agitated to see it for herself. Why would the emperor honor the deal if Lyssa didn't do the one thing he required of her — keep the boy secure until Hoerst retrieved him?

Lyssa shook her doubts away. Because the emperor saw the value of having the Order within the Empire. To his coffers, if nothing else. That was why. She needed to organize the search, but before she left the drawing room she said, "Yes, the witch took your half-breed spawn, but the Inquisition will be back for you and, after your indiscretion, they'll put you somewhere no one will ever find you. You'll never see him again."

Chapter 18

Ērtsi Kalaola

Lindenlatha was a day of rest for the *Alle'oss*. Tye wouldn't be traveling to the Desulti village, so Tove had to walk to Ka'tan. She was making her way to the road that led to the village when she rounded a corner and almost collided with Danu.

"Oh!" Danu said and stepped back. She stared at Tove, her hand coming up and brushing at her forehead. "Sorry."

"My fault," Tove said. She hadn't seen Danu since the embarrassing encounter on the road to the fulling hut.

"I haven't seen you around," Danu said.

"I've been up in the mountains," Tove said, gesturing uselessly to the mountains north of the village.

Danu's eyes widened slightly. Her hand hovered partway to her forehead.

"Hunting."

"Oh."

Tove's face broke spontaneously into a smile in response to the smile that transformed Danu's face.

They gazed at one another long enough that Tove began to feel uncomfortable, then Danu's expression shifted into a curious frown. "Where are you going?"

"Ka'tan."

Danu's eyes widened again. "Why?"

"There's a tavern there I like."

Danu considered this. "There's a tavern here." She gestured in the general direction of the Elkhorn tavern.

"I feel…" Tove's voice trailed away, and she shrugged.

"More comfortable with the *Alle'oss?*"

Tove nodded, relieved. They stood, looking at one another awkwardly, then Tove gestured and said, "Well, I'm —"

"Can I come?" Danu blurted.

Realizing her mouth was still open, Tove snapped it shut. "You want to come to Ka'tan?" Remembering the hostile reaction she received the first time she was there, she said, "They don't… They might not…"

"Want a Desulti in their tavern?" Danu asked.

"Well, yes."

"You've been there?"

"Well… yes."

"You're Desulti."

"Yes… but —"

"You're also *Alle'oss.*"

"Right!" Tove said. "So, you see —"

"Can I come?"

Tove sighed, taking in her hopeful expression. Knowing she would probably regret it, she said, "Sure."

They walked in silence, Tove feeling awkward until Danu said, "I've never been to Ka'tan."

Tove glanced at her. Danu was gazing at the mountain peaks. "How long have you been in the Order?" A small frown appeared on Danu's face and Tove caught herself staring.

"Four years."

"And you've been working at the fulling hut all this time?"

"It's not so bad," Danu said. A smile appeared when she glanced at Tove. "Once you get used to the smell."

"What do you like about it?"

Danu shrugged. "It's usually just me and Fella and the work is easy." She peeked at Tove. "And I like the *Alle'oss* who work there. Or most of them. You all seem… so…" She gestured with one hand. "Happy." She grinned at Tove. "Even when you're walking in… you know?"

"I'm not sure we're always so happy."

Danu shrugged again. "Maybe happy isn't the right word. You don't seem to let bad things bring you down. You get on with things. Walking in pee doesn't make you…" Her face screwed up, but she didn't continue.

They walked in silence for a few minutes. Tove found herself stealing glances at Danu. "Why did you join the Order?" she asked finally.

Danu's frowned deepened. "My sister brought me."

"Who's your sister?"

"Brie," Danu said and smiled. "She told me about you. That's why…"

Tove watched her, fascinated at the blush that climbed her cheeks.

"Anyway," Danu continued. "There were these boys in the town where we lived. They…" She seemed to shrink within herself, shoulders hunching, arms crossing her chest.

"Why didn't someone call the gendarmes? Or, I don't know —"

"Their father was very powerful. No one would help me."

Tove was startled at the anger in her usually soft voice. "Your parents?"

"I think…" She looked down at her feet.

Watching Danu struggle with painful memories, Tove felt guilty for bringing up a difficult topic. But wanting to know more about this woman, she said, "So, Brie brought you to the Desulti to save you."

"Yeah," Danu said. "She didn't have to. No one messes with Brie." She took two more steps, then said, "She didn't have to stay, but she likes it here."

Tove watched emotions playing out on her face. "Do you like it here?"

Danu shrugged and glanced at Tove. "I like feeling safe."

"I know what you mean," Tove said, surprised how happy she was that Danu's small smile made an appearance.

***

They stopped on the wooden walkway before entering the Boar's Head. "There will be people in there who won't be happy you're here." When Danu nodded solemnly, Tove asked, "Are you sure you want to do this?"

Danu nodded again.

"Okay. I'll introduce you to the owner, Shia. What she says goes, so if she likes you, people will leave you alone. I hope."

When Danu nodded again, Tove pulled the door open and led Danu through the tables toward the far end of the bar where Shia watched them approach. It was early, so the crowd was light, but that only made it easier for everyone to notice Danu. Conversations died, and the tavern grew quiet.

"You got a way of looking for trouble," Shia said.

Ignoring her comment, Tove gestured to Danu and said, "This is Danu. She's my friend." She raised her voice and half turned to face the room. "She's a friend to the *Alle'oss.*" When she turned back to Shia, the woman peered at the fading bruise below her eye.

"Tripped," Tove said. "I've always been clumsy."

Shia sniffed. "Tripped." She studied Danu, who returned her gaze solemnly. When she looked back at Tove, she said, "You remember the rules?"

"No fighting."

"Right." She gestured to a nearby table. "I'd prefer if you stayed close."

Tove nodded, took Danu's arm, and led her to the table.

Feeling awkward, Tove focused on Shia motioning to a server and sending her over to their table. After she ordered bowls of stew and ales for both of them, she surveyed the room, noting how many people were casting open glances their way. That was okay, as long as they kept their disapproval to themselves.

After reassuring herself they were safe, Tove peeked at Danu. She had no idea what to say to this woman. Danu gazed at other patrons, a soft grin on her face.

When she noticed Tove watching her, she said, "This is nice."

Tove looked again at some of the flat stares they were receiving. Not quite hostile, which she supposed was an improvement over her expectations. "You don't notice they don't want you here?"

Danu nodded slowly. "Yes," she said with a smirk. "I'm quiet. I'm not a simpleton."

"No," Tove said. "I didn't —"

"I know what you meant. I was just teasing. You're always so serious."

"Talk about the pot and the kettle," Tove said, returning Danu's smile.

"I'm not serious, just quiet."

They held each other's gazes for a moment, then the arrival of the server broke the connection. The eyes of the woman who brought the food narrowed when Tove looked up at her. Tove was watching her walking away when Danu spoke.

"What is this?" She peered down at the stew.

Tove started to answer, then noticed on Danu's face the same distracting frown she noticed earlier. She held still, studying the contours of Danu's delicate features, not wanting to disturb the moment. When Danu glanced at her, catching Tove staring, Tove slammed her mouth shut, picked up her spoon and said, "It's boar stew." She dipped up a spoonful and shoved it into her mouth, then had to suck in air until it cooled enough to swallow. To hide her embarrassment, she sipped her ale and said, "You know Tye? He drives the wagon that brings the *Alle'oss* to the fulling hut."

"I know *who* he is," Danu said.

"Shia is his wife. She owns the place. He's the cook. This is his special recipe." She leaned toward Danu, close enough to catch a whiff of her scent. "Very secret, apparently," she whispered, then straightened, gestured to the bowl, and said, "Try it."

Danu's lips twisted. She picked up her spoon and dipped it into the stew. After sniffing it carefully, she slipped it into her mouth. She chewed slowly, then her eyes widened, and a smile chased the frown from her face. When she swallowed, she said, "Dear Daga." After another spoonful, she said around the mouthful, "This is so good! What did you say it was?"

"Boar stew," Tove said, smiling at Danu's reaction.

They ate without speaking, each of them stealing glances at the other. When they finished, they sat back and nursed their ales, much more comfortable in their silence than before.

"I like the ale, too," Danu said out of the blue.

Tove grinned at her. "You want another one?"

Danu shook her head slowly. "I have to be up early tomorrow," she said. She was silent for a moment, then she said, "*Tok.*"

Tove's eyes widened.

"Is that right?" Danu frowned. "Brie told me that meant thank you."

"Yes," Tove said. "That's right. I would say *aurina sha*, which means you're welcome, but I should say *tok* as well. This is the most fun I've had in… well, a long time."

"But we didn't do anything."

"Still," Tove said. "It's been lovely."

Danu's brows quirked up, a smile playing at the corners of her lips. "Lovely?"

"What?"

"I don't know," Danu said. "It just doesn't sound like you. Lovely." When Tove frowned, Danu reached a hand across the table and said, "I'm just teasing. It *has* been lovely."

Tove looked at Danu's hand on the table. Not exactly sure what she was supposed to do with it, she sat up, rested her elbows on the table. Her hand crawled toward Danu's, stopping a few inches short. When she looked up, Danu was suppressing a smile. "What?" Tove asked.

Danu lost her battle and begin to giggle. A blush blossomed on her cheeks, and her hand covered her mouth.

Tove thought she should be offended, but then the ridiculousness of the situation won out. Her laughter gave Danu permission, and they were both laughing. When they settled down, they sat back, breathless, and gazed at one another.

Tove was trying to decide what to say when she caught motion out of the corner of her eye and a bundle of cloth dropped onto the table. She looked up to find Meya, her servant, staring coldly down at her.

"This is yours," she said, then turned away.

Tove was up in a flash and caught Meya's arm before she got away.

Meya spun around, anger hardening her expression. "What do you want?"

"They pay you to be my servant?" Tove asked in an even tone. "The Desulti."

Caught off guard, Meya's eyes flicked to Danu. "Yes," she said. There was less vehemence in her tone, but it was still edged.

"Then I expect you to make yourself available," Tove said. "You ain't been around in days. I have things I need. You don't want to be my servant, that's fine, but if they're paying you, I expect you to do your job."

Meya pressed her lips tight, then she said, "I'll be by tomorrow morning."

She started to turn away, but Tove stopped her. She gestured to the fabric on the table and asked, "What's this?"

"Your cloak," Meya said.

"*My* cloak?"

Meya nodded.

"How did you get this?"

"You left it with my father the other night," Meya said.

"Garth is your father?" Tove asked, surprised.

Shia appeared behind Meya. "Is there trouble here?"

"No. No trouble," Meya said.

She started to turn away, and Tove stopped her again. "Is Garth still banned from the Boar's Head?" she asked Shia. When Shia nodded, Tove said, "Me and him worked out our differences." Shia shook her head, but before she could speak, Tove said, "It would be a gesture everyone here would understand if you were to allow him back in. Might change some minds. I would consider it a favor if you did."

Shia gazed at her. "I'll consider it." Meya gave Tove a troubled look, then turned away and pushed her way past Shia.

Shia watched her go, then gazed speculatively at Tove.

"What?" Tove asked.

"Nothing." Shia nodded to Danu, who was watching the exchange. "You and your girlfriend going to make it a habit of coming?"

Tove's mouth worked, but nothing emerged until she blurted, "Girlfriend?" She glanced at Danu and said, "We're… I don't…"

Smirking, Shia turned and made her way back to her usual spot at the end of the bar.

Tove watched her go. "Girlfriend," she muttered to herself. She turned back toward Danu, ready to apologize, but when she saw Danu smiling at her, she forgot what she was going to say.

"You want to walk me home?" Danu asked.

"Of course."

Danu opened up on the return walk, telling Tove tales about her childhood. She briefly described the Volloch lord who dominated the small town where she grew up, but mostly she talked about the happy times before she came to the attention of the lord's sons.

With Danu's attention on her memories, Tove felt free to study her. She supposed some would say Danu wasn't as beautiful as her sister, but Tove found her more appealing. Unlike Brie, who presented a carefully composed mask to the world, now that they had broken down their barriers, Danu's emotions frolicked across her face, leaving nothing concealed. She was an entirely different person than the shy woman Tove thought she was. There was a refreshing awkwardness to her that set Tove at ease.

As they neared the Desulti village, Danu fell silent. After a few moments, she asked, "Do you like being a hunter?"

Tove told Danu about the trouble she had with the dining hall staff and how she was able to feed herself in the mountains. "Besides," she said, "I like the mountains. It's quiet. It feels… safe."

Danu stopped at the edge of the village. She gestured down a side street and said, "My place is down here."

Tove glanced down the street, wondering if that was supposed to be an invitation. Before she could decide what to say, Danu spoke.

"I'm sorry for what they did to you." A small furrow appeared between her brows. She reached out and brushed the downy hair above Tove's ear, her fingers cool and whisper soft.

Tove had to swallow before she could get enough breath to murmur, "*Ērtsi kalaola.*"

Danu's eyes widened, and the furrow disappeared. "*Alle'oss?*"

Tove nodded.

"What does it mean?"

It took Tove a long time to understand the phrase after an old man explained it to her and Alar. She and Alar argued often about what it meant, Alar's steadfast optimism prying at Tove's stubborn wariness. But in this moment, with Danu watching her, she thought she finally understood. She had experienced trauma that irrevocably changed her life, survived violence that would give most people nightmares even to hear about it, suffered wounds from which she knew she would never recover. She would never claim it was a good thing. But everything that happened in her life made her the woman she was and brought her to this moment. What she made of it was up to her. She could bemoan the hardships she endured, or she could be present in this moment with this wonderful woman.

"It means 'it's life's colors,'" she said. When Danu frowned, she said, "It means the things that happen to you in life, good or bad, give you a palette of colors. It's up to you to… paint each moment. To make each moment a masterpiece." Alar would say it better, but watching Danu's face, Tove thought she did well enough.

Danu's chin quivered, her wide eyes glistened in the light of a street lamp.

Tove opened her mouth and hesitated, not sure what to say. Before she knew what happened, Danu took a step and brushed Tove's lips with her own. Stepping back, she gave Tove a shy smile and said, "Good night."

Tove watched her go, only remembering to say, "*Jae lōrna*," when Danu had disappeared down the dark street.

Chapter 19

A Good Party

Siofra sat at the desk in the rooms Governor Adelbart provided for her when she arrived in Richeleau. The governor's mansion was relatively new, having been built when the emperor moved the seat of Imperial government in Argren from Kartok. Artisans associated with the Order were involved in many parts of its construction. But the interior decoration was entirely overseen by Adelbart himself. She was sure he gave her one of the best suites in the building, but even so, Siofra was impressed. The rooms weren't as lavish as her own in Téama, but it was clear the governor had expensive tastes.

She gazed out the window at the city skyline. Unlike Kartok, the Empire hadn't placed its stamp on Richeleau. It still had the feel of an *Alle'oss* city. Eclectic architecture, winding roads, extensive green spaces, and at ease with its cosmopolitan population.

She and Eirin, the murtair who accompanied her when she traveled, arrived earlier in the afternoon. She grinned to herself, remembering the governor's scandalized expression when she appeared on horseback with Eirin rather than in a carriage. Just before she left, Lyssa decided it was important that three members of the Ruling Council accompany her. The thought of spending eight excruciating hours a day locked in a small space with those women was too much. Siofra was willing to endure the agony of reacquainting herself with riding to avoid it. The first week in the saddle was difficult, but the riding muscles she developed as a child were reasserting themselves by the time they arrived.

She was sure Lyssa sent the women to keep an eye on her as a direct result of her vote on Tove's entry into the Order. It was annoying. Lyssa was sending a message that she didn't trust Siofra and doing it in the most petty way. The three women she chose were arrogant, bigoted and churlish. She was sure Lyssa chose them for that reason. Besides, they weren't invited to the wedding. Lord Bergamot, the bride's father, would have to find them accommodations in his manor house, which meant that someone would be told to find rooms at inns in Lachton. It was hard enough to win friends for the Order without such ham handed slights.

With a sigh, she leafed through her journal, reviewing the notes she made for her meeting with the governor the following morning.

The governor will have to see the Desulti are preferable to what the Alle'oss can offer. The Order can provide access to larger markets and has the experience to manage the logistics. Though I have to admit we may have underestimated the Alle'oss, they will not be able to exploit this opportunity to the fullest for some time. In the event the governor feels some loyalty to the Alle'oss, we'll offer to come in as partners. The relative advantage the Order offers will become apparent to all before long. As a final argument, we can play on the governor's fears and inform him that the Alle'oss can't protect him in the event Imperial authorities discover the scheme.

"It's almost time, Mistress."

Siofra looked up to find Eirin standing in the doorway between the sitting room and her bedroom. The murtair always accompanied her when she traveled. The Order was not well liked in many circles. No one had ever accosted her, but it was always a possibility. Siofra assumed Eirin's menacing presence might be the reason she had been so lucky.

"Eirin." Siofra rose and held her journal to her chest. "What are your impressions of Adelbart?"

"He has expensive tastes. Tastes beyond his means," she said in a typically clinical murtair tone. "Despite the deal he made with the *Alle'oss*, his debts are considerable. That is a weakness easy to exploit. He has neither the competence, nor the intellect to rule Argren. The only reason he's governor is his mother is the emperor's older sister, and the emperor has always been terrified of her. So, the administration of the Imperial District of Argren falls to his assistant, Gerold, who is as competent as Adelbart isn't. Gerold is likely the one you will have to convince. Adelbart admires Argren and the *Alle'oss* in a patronizing way. I doubt he would ever allow his daughter, Elois, to marry an *Alle'oss*." She gazed at Siofra, considering, then gave a small shrug. "However, the governor is known for throwing a good party."

Siofra laughed. Murtair humor. The rare breaks in her murtair demeanor was why she always brought Eirin with her. She went to return her journal to her locked satchel, then stopped to check her appearance in the mirror and set her journal on her bedside table. She turned to the murtair, who waited patiently. "Okay, Eirin, let us go find out if the governor's reputation is true."

An hour later, Siofra had to admit, Eirin's assessment of the governor's parties was correct. She paid her respects to him when she arrived in the ballroom. He greeted her warmly, making her feel as if he gave the party just for her. He introduced her to the more prominent people in attendance, whispering intimate tidbits about each person in her ear. Her overall impression of him was that he was a charming buffoon. An entertaining conversationalist and a warm host, but a buffoon all the same. He was also obviously terrified of Eirin, who loomed nearby in her murtair blacks. Her inscrutable mask never cracked, but Siofra knew her well enough to know she rather enjoyed his unease.

Having extracted herself from the crowd gathered around Adelbart, she strolled through the ballroom, a glass of *Alle'oss* white in her hand. There were as many of Richeleau's wealthy *Alle'oss* as Imperials in attendance. *Alle'oss* servers circulated, offering a variety of canapes featuring *Alle'oss* flavors. And best of all, despite Brie losing the art the governor intended to use to pay his debt to the Order, the governor still retained a number of masterpieces of the *Alle'oss* new school. She briefly considered demanding he relinquish them to the Order, but the payment plan Brie arranged was a good deal for the Order. They got to keep the governor on the hook and the payments didn't depend on the governor's competence. They came from the sale of the *Alle'oss* pigments produced in the Ishien River Valley.

She stopped beside a painting by Omar, one of the new school artists the Inquisition forced into hiding. She didn't know what he painted they objected to, but it certainly wasn't this work of a mother at a spinning wheel and her curious child.

Someone beside her cleared her throat. When she turned her head, she found the three Desulti who rode in the carriage standing against the wall beside the painting. "You made it in time for the party, I see," she said.

They looked across the room and one of them said, "Yes, we endured two weeks bouncing up and down on that hard bench for this." She lifted a hand and gestured gracefully toward the gathering. "Cheap wine and *Alle'oss* food. Lucky us."

"I hope Lord Bergamot has better tastes," one of the other women said. "In wine, food *and* guests." That produced a twitter from all three women.

"I don't know," Siofra said. "If the wine and food aren't to your tastes, you could spend your time enjoying some of the greatest art that has ever been produced." She gestured to the Omar.

The three women turned and looked at the painting as if just noticing it. "What's so special about it?"

Siofra swept a hand across the canvas, palm toward the painting, fingers splayed. "The new school artists discovered how to add perspective in a way that almost makes their paintings seem real. And of course, the colors are to be found nowhere else in the Empire."

One of the women shrugged. "But it's just a picture of a woman and baby. What's the point?"

Siofra returned their frowns with a soft smile, sipped her wine, then turned her back on them and strolled away.

Hours later, Siofra decided the party would continue far beyond her endurance. Two weeks in the saddle left her sore and exhausted. So, at midnight, she made her excuses to a very inebriated governor and followed Eirin down to her room on the second floor.

Eirin handed her the key, but when Siofra inserted it into the lock, it wouldn't turn. She tried again, then extracted the key and turned the knob. It wasn't locked. "Didn't we lock this?"

"Yes, we did," the murtair said. She took Siofra's arm and pulled her gently, but firmly, away from the door. A knife appeared in her hand and she eased the door open.

Siofra watched Eirin exploring the empty sitting room from the doorway. When the murtair turned her attention to the bedroom, Siofra stepped into the room in time to see Eirin tense and lower into a crouch. After a moment, she rose and entered the bedroom. Siofra closed the door and walked further into the room, peering around. Nothing seemed out of place.

Eirin returned, her body language tense. Siofra watched her prowl around the dim sitting room again, peering into every corner. "What is the matter, Eirin?"

"I'm not sure." She came to a stop in front of the fireplace and turned in place, surveying the room. She pointed to the bedroom and said in a firm voice. "I saw someone in there, an *Alle'oss* man, and then… he was gone."

"You saw a man?" Siofra crossed the room and entered the bedroom. Eirin followed and stood in the doorway. The first thing Siofra noticed was her satchel on the desk. She was sure she left it on the bed.

She checked the lock on the satchel. Finding it locked, she turned and scanned the rest of the room. Crossing to her bedside table, she stared down at her journal. Didn't she leave it the other way around? She picked it up and leafed through it. She should have replaced it in her satchel. Returning it to the bedside table, she turned toward a waiting Eirin.

"Someone has been here," Siofra said.

Eirin glanced over her shoulder, then shrugged. "I saw someone. I'm sure of it. What does it mean?"

Siofra's lips twisted. Her fingers came up and rested on her cheek. "Whoever it was, they unlocked the door."

"The governor?"

"Maybe," Siofra said. "Though he doesn't seem the type. Maybe his assistant, Harold."

"Gerold."

Siofra nodded absently.

"Someone might have picked the lock," Eirin said. "The *Alle'oss*, maybe."

Siofra focused on her. "You are sure you saw someone? It wasn't just a trick of the light?"

"I'm sure."

Siofra gazed uneasily around the room, a shiver running up her spine. "So, it's someone who can disappear," she mumbled, "but they had to unlock the door so they can't walk through walls, obviously." She knew who it was. It was Alar, the leader of *Oss'stera*. It must be, unless the *Alle'oss* had more than one realm walker. She gazed down at her journal. Was there anything that could damage the Order? It was only her personal journal, but a clever person could do much with the smallest secrets. Was Alar a clever man? She grinned and muttered, "We shall see."

"Mistress?"

"Brie reported there is an *Alle'oss* man with this capability. It's called realm walking, apparently."

"Realm walking, Mistress?"

"Yes, he can enter the Otherworld, move about and return. While he's in the Otherworld, he's invisible to our sight."

"That sounds like what I saw." Eirin glanced over her shoulder. "So, he could be watching us as we speak."

"Yes," Siofra said uneasily. "Though I suspect if he meant us harm, he would have acted already. I hope. However, it appears we must assume nothing is secret," Siofra said. "Now, we have a big day tomorrow and I'm exhausted."

"You want me to sleep in here?"

Siofra chuckled. "No, that won't be necessary," she said with a grin. "I doubt very much if there is anything you can do to protect me if our mystery man can appear out of nowhere." And based on what Brie told her about Alar, she doubted she had anything to fear from him. Not yet, anyway.

***

Siofra and Eirin set out for Lachton the next morning after their meeting with the governor. Getting such a late start meant another night sleeping on the ground beneath the stars, but the warmer temperatures at lower altitudes made the evenings pleasant. She waited until they were on the open road before she asked, "What is your opinion of our meeting with the governor?" She often asked the murtair her opinion because her training taught her to be observant and she often saw to the heart of things.

Eirin considered for a moment, then said, "He surprised me."

"How so?" Siofra felt the same way, but she wanted to see if Eirin's opinion matched her own.

"He's as slippery as an eel," Eirin said. "Even now, I'm not sure exactly what he agreed to and what he didn't." She looked at Siofra. "That suggests he isn't as stupid as his reputation suggests."

"Yes," Siofra said with a satisfied grin. "I agree."

"The one thing you said that hit the mark was when you told him making deals with rebels could get him in hot water with the Inquisition."

That was what Siofra thought as well. She also told him if he were in business with the Desulti, the Order could protect him. All in all, she was satisfied with the meeting. She would give him some time to think, then she would return and expose more of the iron in her silk glove.

"There was one other thing," Eirin said.

"Someone was listening in from the other room," Siofra said. After she mentioned rebels, the governor's eyes kept darting to the door.

Eirin looked at her again. "Alar?"

"That would be my guess," Siofra said. "Let us see how they respond."

Chapter 20

Uncomfortable Truths

Despite her promise, Meya didn't appear the day after Tove confronted her at the Boar's Head. So, when she opened the door to a knock the next day, it came as a surprise to find her servant waiting for her. Her churlish expression wasn't a surprise.

"You said you have things you need," Meya said.

Tove glanced down the hall and said, "Come in."

Meya hesitated, then slipped past Tove and entered the small room.

"Have a seat," Tove said and gestured to the desk chair.

Meya glanced at the chair but remained standing.

"You obviously don't like me much," Tove said. When Meya didn't respond, she said, "Not sure why, since you don't know me."

"Why does it matter if I like you?"

"It would make this easier," Tove said. "For both of us." Before Meya could respond, she said, "Plus, it hurts my feelings."

Meya stared at her. "Hurts your feelings?!"

Tove watched the surprise on her face shift to anger. "The Inquisition arrested your brother," she said.

Meya froze. Closing her mouth, she dropped her chin, rolled her shoulders slightly forward and hooked a thumb in her belt. "What would someone like *you* care about my brother?"

"Someone like me?"

"A traitor to her people," Meya said, pulling her shoulders back and glaring at Tove.

Tove put her finger to the scar on her face. "Do you know where I got this?"

Meya hesitated, then nodded reluctantly.

"I know what the Inquisition is capable of, more than anyone you'll ever know," Tove said, taking a step forward. She turned her head to put her scarred face inches from Meya's nose. "This is the least of what they did to me." Meya slumped in on herself again. "You have no right to call me a traitor. You haven't earned that right. Maybe your brother has, but not you."

Meya's lips pursed. She forced her eyes to meet Tove's and asked, "Then why did you join the Desulti?"

"The Desulti are not the Empire."

"Might as well be." Meya threw a hand out. "The way they treat us. Tell me you didn't notice that."

"Oh, I noticed. It's no worse than they treat me."

"Then why?"

"It's… complicated," Tove said. "I thought…" She took a step back and half turned away. "It's not what I thought it would be."

Meya hesitated. When she spoke, the hard edge in her voice had softened. "What did you think it would be?" She gestured again and said, "They're Imperials."

"They're women who fled the Empire. Some of them have been horribly abused. Some of them want to be more than they could be in the Empire." Tove glanced at Meya. "I wanted to feel safe."

"So, you thought joining them would make you safe?" Meya asked, the edge returning. "Becoming an Imp?"

"No!" Tove said. "I didn't want that. I thought these women ran away from the Empire. They would have left all that behind."

"But they didn't."

"No," Tove said. "Not all of them, anyway. Some of them have. Or they want to." She turned to face Meya. "We just need to show them how."

"We?"

"Most people get angry at the way the Imps treat us, but they're too afraid to actually do anything about it. That's why nothing ever changes. You want to make things better, you have to be willing to do something other than play childish tricks." She was referring to the first morning when Meya took her to the dining hall for breakfast and she could see in Meya's expression she hit the mark.

"What could we possibly do to change the Desulti?"

"I don't know yet," Tove said. "But for starters, we can stop making enemies of people who should be allies. That's part of what the Imps do to make themselves stronger. They turn us against each other." When Meya hesitated, Tove stuck out her arm. It hung there until Tove began to feel awkward, but then Meya reached out hesitantly and grasped her forearm.

"I don't think you can change anything," Meya said. "But no more childish tricks."

"Good enough."

***

Tove told herself Ragan's business was her own, and she didn't want any part of it. But the appearance of Hoerst in Téama wouldn't leave her alone. So, having a rare free day after talking to Meya, she found herself loitering on the street, where she saw the inquisitor. She told herself she only wanted to find out who he visited, then she'd be satisfied.

The house, the largest on the block, was of an imposing Imperial style she was familiar with from Kartok. Remembering what Frey told her about the *Alle'oss* servants working for Desulti, she parked herself on a bench in a park across the street, and waited. Two hours later, she was still waiting. She'd seen plenty of her countrymen, but no one entered or left the large house. She was about to the give up for the day, when she noticed an *Alle'oss* man passing on the street.

When she approached him, his eyes went to her short hair before they flicked to her scar.

"You're Tove," he said, coming to a stop. To her surprise, he extended a hand and said, "Name's Balder."

She grasped his forearm briefly and said, "*Lehasa*, Balder." Taking in his grass stained pants, straw hat and the dirt under his nails, she said, "You're a gardener."

"That I am," he said and gestured over his shoulder. "I take care of Nessa's grounds." He peered at her. "What can I do for you?"

Tove gestured to the large house and asked, "Can you tell me who lives there?"

He shifted around so they were standing beside one another, looking across the street at the house. "I can. That's the home of the Chief Executive. Lyssa."

"Lyssa?!"

"Yup," he said. Noticing her stunned expression, he asked, "Why?"

Tove composed her face and said, "Oh, nothing. Just… She have any *Alle'oss* servants?"

He chuckled.

"What's so funny?"

"Lyssa's a bit weird about her servants."

"Why's that?"

Gesturing to the other houses on the street, he said, "She's the only one who won't have *Alle'oss* servants. She only lets Desulti work for her. And the rumor is she fired them all a while back."

Tove looked at him. "She takes care of that big house all by herself?"

"Like I said, a bit weird."

"*Tok*, Balder," Tove said. "Nice to have met you."

"Likewise," he said and continued on his way.

Tove gazed at the house. What was going on in there that Lyssa had to get rid of her servants? She looked up at the top floor and was sure she saw movement in one of the dark windows. "You do not need to be getting involved with Lyssa," she murmured to herself. Glancing both ways, she set off.

****

Brie stared at the book lying open on the table before her, but she wasn't seeing the words. Elois had given it to her. But try as she might, Brie couldn't get into the treacly romance. Giving up, she let her gaze drift across Old Jep's comfortable home. What would it be like to come home to a place like this every night? It was more modest than the house she grew up in, but it had the same homey feel. In moments like this, she allowed herself to imagine making a home like this with Elois. Maybe someday. Assuming she lived long enough.

Dismissing maudlin thoughts, she brought herself back to her current assignment. She didn't expect to win the *Alle'oss* over her first trip to Lirantok. Small-town people were suspicious of outsiders and didn't take easily to change. She expected to plant the seed of working with the Order, dangle potential riches in front of them, then leave and allow them to come to terms with the idea. But she was pleasantly surprised by the progress she made in a short time. Jep arranged meetings with many of the decision makers in the valley and allowed her to make her case. Ukrit and Scilla, Alar's fellow rebels, had already done half her job, introducing the idea of selling their goods to the outside world. Brie only needed to reinforce their doubts about the young rebels' ability to handle the business end of things. Though the merchants in the valley sent a small shipment to *Oss'stera* as a test, none of them expected the rebels to make a profit on it. Neither did Brie.

She was confident she almost had them convinced. Siofra would be happy with her progress.

A knock on the door drew her from her thoughts. When she opened it, she was surprised to find three young *Alle'oss* looking back at her.

"I know you." The boy in front said. He lifted his hand to his head. "You got hair now."

She studied his face, trying to place his name. "Lief," she said finally. He was one of the *Oss'stera* rebels she met in Richeleau. She looked past Lief and pointed at a younger boy. "I remember the boy, but I don't know her."

"Zaina," Zaina said. "And the *boy* is Keth."

"You're… Brie," Lief said, pointing at her. When she nodded, he asked, "Where's Old Jep?"

"He's in town."

Lief took a step toward the door and said, "We'll wait inside."

Brie hesitated, then shrugged and retreated into the interior.

She returned to her seat and Lief took the opposite seat. Zaina and Keth groaned like old people as they settled into rocking chairs in front of the cold hearth.

Lief settled an intense gaze on Brie. She ignored him, pretending to be interested in the book. When she glanced up at him, he asked, "Why are you here?"

"Jep offered me his guest room."

"Great," Zaina said under her breath for some reason.

"I mean," Lief said, "why are you in Lirantok?"

Brie closed the book and leveled a gaze at him. "I had business to discuss with Old Jep."

Lief glanced at her hair again. "What kind of business?"

"That's between Jep and me."

Lief rose, scanned the room, then checked the other rooms.

Brie watched him, amused. "Jep's in town."

"Alar said you're an assassin," Lief said as he took his seat. "Why'd they send an assassin to see Jep?"

The Order would eventually have to confront *Oss'stera* with what they intended, but Brie didn't want to get into it with this boy, so she remained silent.

When it was obvious she wouldn't respond, he said, "That Ragan woman told me women ran away from the Empire to become Desulti. That right?"

Brie's eyes narrowed slightly. She didn't know much about Ragan, but what she heard suggested she wasn't to be trusted. "Mostly."

"So, you have no reason to love the Empire," Lief said.

"What's your point?"

"You live up in Ka'tan so you've seen the slaves that work the mines."

For the first time, Brie felt uncomfortable. Like many of the women in the Order, she found the Empire's use of Brochen slaves in the mines deeply troubling. But what could they do about it? "Again, what's your point?"

"Do you know why Alar made that deal with the governor? The black market deal?"

"The same reason *we* would make that deal."

"That's right. He made it for the same reason the Desulti would. To become rich enough to protect ourselves from the Empire. So we can stop the slavers condemning our people to death in the mines, stop the inquisitors kidnapping little girls as witches, stop the Imps riding into a village, killing people just so the governor can take what he wants."

Brie gazed at him, as unsettled by the quiet boy's intensity as what he was saying.

"That's why you make yourselves rich, isn't it?" Lief asked. "To protect yourselves from the Imps. But maybe you left the Empire, and you're still Imps. Don't care about anyone but yourselves, especially us Brochen." He paused and said. "You've been living in *our* land for years. No one's complained. What have you done for the *Alle'oss?*"

The door opened, startling everyone in the room.

"Bless the Mother," Zaina mumbled and settled back into her chair.

Jep stood in the door, taking in the scene. "Lief," he said finally. He stepped into the room, closed the door, and looked Keth and Zaina over. "Don't know these two."

Zaina stood and extended an arm. "Zaina," she said. She hooked a thumb at Keth, who remained seated. "Keth."

Jep took her arm, an amused smile on his face. "You two with this *Oss'stera?*"

Zaina nodded and said, "I have twelve summers." She released his forearm and returned to her seat. "In case you're wondering."

Jep smiled at her, then turned a speculative gaze on Lief and Brie. "You two getting acquainted?"

Lief stood and fished a pouch from his pack. He shook it, producing the jingle of coin, then handed it to Jep, undoing all of Brie's good work. "From the first shipment," he said. "Alar wanted you to have it."

Jep stared at the pouch, then looked up at Lief's face. He took it, worked it open, and peered inside. "Looks to be more than we agreed to," he muttered.

"Alar says it's a show of good faith," Lief said, putting some emphasis on the last two words. His eyes cut to Brie, then he said to Jep, "We're ready for another shipment."

"Well, now," Jep said. "This might change some minds."

Tama led Brie's horse into the square, smiling from ear to ear. When he stopped, Brie patted the horse's neck and examined the braids the boy made of her mane.

"Didn't have the beads for Ka'tan," he said. "That's where Old Jep said you were from. So I used beads for the villages in the valley."

Brie took one of the braids in her hand and examined the beads. "She's never looked so good," she said and grinned. "*Tok.*" Fishing another coin from her pocket, she tossed it to him and mounted.

"*Andsutra!*" he called happily, heading off across the square at a jog as she urged the horse into motion.

She climbed the pass on the northern end of the valley, then turned her horse back to look out over the beautiful vista. The taciturn *Alle'oss* boy, Lief, surprised her. She met him briefly in Richeleau the previous winter and dismissed him as a simpleton. That he put his finger on the similarities between the goals of *Oss'stera* and the Desulti caught her off guard. And it unearthed troubling questions.

Did the *Alle'oss* have less right to exploit the fruits of their own land to protect themselves than the Desulti? Did the Order owe anything to the *Alle'oss*? The Order had taken refuge in Argren for decades and the *Alle'oss* had never asked anything in return. That was all the more remarkable when you considered how poorly many in the Order treated their *Alle'oss* servants. Her initial response when Lief pointed out the contradictions was anger. But she was honest enough with herself to know that anger had its roots in shame.

It never occurred to her before, but how different was the Order's treatment of the *Alle'oss* than the way the Gabra boys in her village treated her sister? They were the reason she brought Danu to the Desulti. They abused her because they believed she was beneath them and not deserving of respect. She was a woman of the Burne caste. They would never treat a woman of their own caste so poorly. The Gabra would never allow it. At least not until the woman married and became her husband's property to do with as he pleased.

And Lief's truths had done one other thing as well. It solidified her doubts about Nessa. She didn't appreciate the head of the Murtair's casual disdain for people she considered lower than herself, including lower caste Volloch. Brie dismissed it before because Nessa was like so many others in the Order. But Brie handed Nessa an opportunity to change the Order, and after pondering Lief's penetrating questions, Brie decided if change was coming, it had to be to something better than what Nessa envisioned. She worried about what was happening in Téama, but she had something to do in Lachton before returning.

Chapter 21

Negotiations

Siofra and Eirin arrived in the Imperial city of Lachton a day early. The bride's father, Lord Bergamot, was gracious enough to receive them anyway, and it wasn't because Eirin stared balefully down at him from atop of her horse. He was one of the few Volloch lords who openly acknowledged how profitable his dealings with the Order were for him.

The wedding was being held on the lord's immense estate. Siofra had to admit, even by the standards of the wealthiest Volloch, Lord Bergamot's property was impressive. Besides a manor house that would rival the emperor's summer palace, the grounds included a kitchen capable of feeding hundreds of guests for a week, extensive stables, an infirmary, gardens, a blacksmith, wide expanses of well-manicured lawn and shady stands of evergreens, oaks and elms traversed by well-groomed walking paths. An army of servants scurried about the property, preparing for the guests to arrive, and it was all overseen by a security detail that outnumbered the gendarmery in Téama.

The wedding was a weeklong affair, with luncheons and entertainment during the day and balls every night. But the most intriguing part of the festivities for Siofra was the art show. Bergamot enlisted artists from across the Empire to create exclusive works for the event. They had been at work for a week in a pavilion erected near the kitchens. When she heard there were two new school *Alle'oss* artists, she was tempted to preview their works. In the end, she decided to wait for the showing, which would be held in conjunction with the opening ball.

After a quiet first night with Eirin, Siofra spent the next morning wandering the gardens with the bride. It was nice to finally hear from Violette's own lips the story behind her marriage. Her parents tried for years to find a match for her, but Violette successfully fended them off. She was smarter than they were and wasn't afraid to show them. Siofra and Violette joked about her running away and joining the Order, but Violette loved everything about her life except the suitors her parents found for her. She would miss her friends, the parties, the gossip.

So, when the current groom approached her with what amounted to a business arrangement, she finally agreed to marry. They would take the enormous dowry Lord Bergamot was forced to pay and make parallel lives together. Linked by marriage, but independent by choice. Violette laughed at the arrangement, but Siofra wasn't fooled. Her laughter masked a deep sadness.

Guests arrived as the morning wore on. Among them were many of the most influential lords in the eastern Empire, as well as brothers of the Inquisition, and two Imperial governors. The emperor, embroiled in a war which recently took a bad turn, didn't come, but he sent his oldest son, the heir apparent. It was a fete that promised to provide grist for the Volloch gossip mill for years to come. More importantly, alcohol and good cheer would provide plenty of opportunities for Siofra to exploit.

In the afternoon, Siofra wandered the grounds, enjoying the attention Eirin's brooding presence attracted. Many of the lords knew Siofra by name, though they wouldn't recognize her. But a murtair was instantly recognizable and universally feared.

When they retired to their rooms to prepare for the evening's festivities, she and Eirin had a comprehensive understanding of the lay of the land, including potential threats and opportunities.

***

Her Desulti companions, Lyssa's watchdogs, were waiting in the manor house's immense entrance hall when Siofra and Eirin descended the stairs from their rooms that evening for the opening ball. She acknowledged their frosty greetings, then entered the reception hall where the art was displayed. Pausing just inside the entrance, she surveyed the crowded room. The artists' works were presented on easels around the perimeter of the room. A buffet table and bar occupied the center of the room. She considered getting a glass of wine, but a glance at the long line at the bar dissuaded her.

The other Desulti followed her into the reception hall, but Siofra ignored them and approached the first painting. The artist, seeing her coming, brushed off the elderly couple he was talking to and took a position beside his easel, watching her with hopeful eyes. Siofra glanced at his work, a portrait of the bride and groom in a staid Imperial style, and kept walking.

Bergamot had the wealth and influence in the art world to attract the very best artists in the Empire, and it was clear the artists had outdone themselves, hoping to find patrons in the elite crowd. Siofra made her way along the line of easels, sparing a smile for the eager artists. Some of their works were quite good, but she only had eyes for the works of the two *Alle'oss* artists.

She was beginning to think the rumor wasn't true, but when a crowd gathered around one of the easels scattered, driven away by Eirin's approach, their parting revealed a stunning painting. She pivoted around, looking for the absent artist, then approached the easel. It was unlike anything she saw before. Its roots were firmly in the *Alle'oss* new school. She could see the ghost of Valdemar, the brilliant new school artist the Inquisition executed. It had his bold use of vivid *Alle'oss* pigments and his grasp of perspective. But it was something entirely new.

It depicted the bride and groom standing on a small bridge Siofra stood on with the bride in Violette's gardens that morning. Not only had the artist depicted an idealized garden in all its complex beauty, but she managed to capture the sad truth at the heart of the couple's joining so subtly that anyone who didn't know would miss it.

And yet, it was all accomplished using technique Siofra never saw before. The artist applied the paint with bold brush strokes that almost appeared rushed, the paint applied in thick dabs. Up close, she couldn't see how the details were rendered, but standing back and gazing at the whole… The subtle interplay of light among the lily pads on the surface of the water, the delicately rendered blossoms, the movements of plants in a light breeze, the subtle signs of despair in the couple's expressions. It was stunning. In a room filled with the best the Imperial artistic community could offer, it rendered them all into insignificance.

Siofra stared dreamily at the painting, twisting slowly back and forth.

"Wine?"

Immersed in her own thoughts, she hadn't noticed anyone approach. She glanced at the man, dismissed him, then froze. He was *Alle'oss.* The only *Alle'oss* she'd seen at the wedding not wearing a servant's livery. Pivoting smoothly to face him, her eyes roved his face, lingering on his blond hair and braid. One bead showed he was from Richeleau. She didn't know the significance of the feather, but the blue bead meant he was promised. When she found his eyes, she expected him to look away, as most men did, but he held her gaze. After a long moment, she allowed him a half smile and took the offered wineglass by the stem. Her eyes on his, she sipped the wine, then her nose wrinkled. She held the glass up and peered at the golden liquid.

"Not to your liking?" he asked.

Arching one delicate eyebrow, she asked, "The wine or the painting?"

"Either, both."

Her eyes flicked to the painting, then she held up the glass. "The wine is serviceable. It's just that being offered wine by an *Alle'oss* man, I was expecting *Alle'oss* wine."

He gave her a small smile. "I agree with your assessment of the wine. However, as we are only guests, we have little say in the menu." He turned to face the painting. "And the painting? Is it serviceable?"

She sipped her wine and studied his profile. When she turned to face the painting, she shifted her weight, putting her bare shoulder close enough to his arm that she felt his heat.

"Unlike the wine, the painting is exquisite." She paused, then asked, "Are you the artist?"

"No, I am but the artist's manager."

"Manager," she murmured. She met his eyes when he looked at her, then turned back to the painting. "I've never seen the like. The technique is revolutionary. Not even Valdemar or Omar produced such… emotion. Even in their best works."

"You're an aficionado of the new school?"

Siofra nodded slowly, but didn't speak.

He leaned close and said, "I heard the Inquisition destroyed Valdemar's works."

"I heard that as well," Siofra said, matching his confidential tone. "But I know for a fact, some survived."

Eirin leaned closed and whispered in her other ear, "This is the man I saw in your room in Richeleau. The realm walker."

Siofra fought to remain calm. This was Alar. The leader of *Oss'stera.* The young man who conceived of the deals with the citizens of the Ishien River Valley and Adelbart. The man who must know where the priceless paintings Brie lost were hidden. After a pause, she turned, inviting him to face her.

"And you?" she asked. "An *Alle'oss.* A manager of artists. You must have seen Valdemar's works."

Alar glanced at Eirin, then gave Siofra a secret grin and said, "I have indeed. Including his greatest work, which I won't name. The one for which he was executed."

"So, the rumors are true. It survived."

Alar's grin widened. He lifted his glass in a toast.

"Where do you suppose such masterpieces are hidden?" Siofra asked. "Surely, whoever possesses them understands interested parties would go to any length to find them."

"I assume, wherever they are, they are with the rightful owners and are safe from… Imperial depredations."

Siofra's lips twisted. She swirled her wine and said, "It's a pity someone hid them away where they can't be appreciated."

"Appreciated by whom?"

She cocked her head, pursed her lips and gave a small shrug with one shoulder. Then she faced the painting again. "I wish to purchase this painting."

"You are free to make an offer," Alar said.

Was that an opening? "Then perhaps we should wait a week. After the wedding, when all the offers are on the table. Then we can meet. You and I, away from all these distractions." She turned back to face him, grinned, and cocked her head slightly. "To negotiate."

Alar gave her a shallow bow and said, "I look forward to it." He returned her smile and said, "I'm sure we can come to a *mutually* beneficial arrangement."

"Hmmm," she said, then she turned and made her way down the line of easels, the eager artists watching her approach.

Replaying the conversation, Siofra barely acknowledged the rest of the artists until she glanced to the side and found herself standing next to another *Alle'oss* man. He gave her a lazy grin and lifted a tankard in toast. "Siofra," he said.

She glanced at his braid and noticed he was also from Richeleau. "Do we know one another?"

He shook his head. "Only by reputation. I'm Ukrit Woodsmith," he said and gestured to a bronze sculpture on a pedestal. "This is mine."

She studied the two-foot-tall sculpture, the only one in the hall. "It's unusual," she said. It was a horse, but unlike most such sculptures by Imperial artists, it depicted an animal which was clearly unbroken. A wild stallion caught in a natural pose. And the artist hadn't polished the bronze to a high sheen, enhancing the untamed aspect. When he didn't respond, she looked up.

He shrugged. "Wanted to show him free."

She studied him for a moment. "I met your manager."

"Oh, yeah?" Ukit asked, his brows rising. "Didn't make a pest of himself, did he?"

"He was the perfect gentleman. A bit mysterious, perhaps."

"Yeah," Ukrit said. "He has that way. Don't let it put you off. He's as honorable a man as any that lived." He paused and met Siofra's eyes for a long moment, then shrugged and sipped his ale. "He better be, he's marrying my sister."

"The blue bead."

Ukrit's brows shot up.

"What does the feather mean?" Siofra asked, before he could say anything.

"Oh, uh…" He paled and his eyes shifted away.

His awkwardness suggested her guess was correct; the feather meant they were in *Oss'stera.* "Do you know the artist of the painting? The *Alle'oss* painting?" Siofra asked, rescuing him.

"My sister, Scilla," Ukrit said, looking relieved. He cleared his throat, sipped his ale and said, "It's incredible, isn't it?"

The only female artist at the wedding. "You come from a very artistic family."

Ukrit only shrugged, fidgety feet showing he was looking for a way to escape the conversation.

Siofra stepped back and gestured to the horse. "This is quite extraordinary as well," Siofra said. "I wish to buy it." Before he could respond, she quoted an extravagant figure.

His face froze. His eyes rotated toward Eirin, then he stuck out a hand and said, "You just bought yourself a horse."

The rest of the evening was much less interesting. She made pleasantries with men and women, who clearly despised her. The men because either they lost someone to the Order or because the Murtair forced them to treat women fairly in business, the women because they either felt Siofra got above her raising by joining the Order or because they longed to have the courage to follow her example. She was used to it and was unfazed by it.

In the back of her mind, she replayed her conversations with Alar and Ukrit. It wasn't until she was ascending the stairs with Eirin at the end of an exhausting day that it came to her why it wouldn't let her go.

The two conversations were the first normal conversations she had with anyone outside the Order since the night she ran away from home. Despite Eirin's intimidating presence and their knowledge of who she was, neither man showed the least fear or deference to her. It was refreshing. The more she learned about Alar and *Oss'stera*, the more intrigued she was by the possibilities they represented.

***

Despite the large security force, it was frighteningly easy for Brie to enter Bergamot's estate. To be fair, there was an immense perimeter to guard and with so many people wandering drunkenly around the grounds, it was virtually impossible to spot one uninvited guest. Especially one who knew how to stay unseen. She had changed from her blacks to the type of loose-fitting garments laborers wore. She didn't fit in with the well-heeled crowd, but she could easily be mistaken for one of the many workers brought in for the wedding. Still, she kept to the shadows, intending to wait until the ball was over before finding a way to Siofra's room.

She was watching people coming and going from the manor house, hoping to get lucky, when three Desulti exited. They were all Lyssa's creatures on the Ruling Council. They weren't invited to the wedding, so they must have been sent by Lyssa to keep an eye on Siofra. She watched them descend the steps from the wide veranda and set off across the lawn toward an elaborate garden. She was considering following them to listen in on their conversation when a familiar figure appeared at the top of the steps. It was Alar.

She set off across the lawn and managed to intercept him as he descended the steps. "Alar," she said. Before he could answer, she took his arm and pulled him into motion past the watchful gaze of the guards at the entrance to the manor house. "Should I ask why you're attending an event like this?"

"I wouldn't advise it," he said, shaking her grip off. They stopped at the corner of the veranda in the shadow of a large arborvitae. "How about you —" Glancing over his shoulder, he turned a worried frown on her and asked, "Someone here in trouble?"

"Not that kind of visit. I'm here to speak to another Desulti."

"Siofra?"

Brie, who was looking toward the three women who were ducking beneath the drooping branches of a large willow tree, looked back at Alar. "You know Siofra?"

"We've met."

"She know who you are?"

"I suspect she was aware," Alar said with a grin. "She invited me to *negotiate.*" His brows waggled.

"You should take that invitation," Brie said. "She is fair and a woman of her word." Before he could reply, she pointed to the willow tree. "In the meantime, I very much want to know what those three women are talking about."

"I had the same thought," Alar said. "Why don't you use your mysterious Murtair skills and sneak over there for us?"

She narrowed her eyes at his teasing tone. "Because I have a friend who can literally disappear."

"A friend?" he asked, one brow rising.

"Yes. A friend. For my part."

Alar's smile widened and an instant later, he vanished.

Brie watched the willow tree, but it was too dark to see either the women or Alar. She judged twenty minutes had passed when the three Desulti emerged. They strolled across the lawn toward the manor house. Even though Brie prepared herself, it still startled her when Alar appeared suddenly in front of her. At least, she managed not to cry out. She eyed him while he studied her speculatively. "Well?"

"We need to talk to Siofra," he said.

***

Siofra reread her notes on the ball in her journal, lingering over her conversation with Alar.

"Mistress," Eirin said.

"Yes," Siofra said vaguely.

"It's the third bell."

"Really?"

"You… I need some sleep before tomorrow," Eirin said, allowing an edge of irritation into her voice.

Siofra grinned, closed her journal, and wiped the nib of her quill. "Yes, of course —"

A soft knock at the door brought her around in her chair. She nodded to Eirin's unasked question.

Eirin opened the door a crack, hesitated, then stepped back and pulled it open.

Siofra came to her feet, astonished, when Brie entered, followed by Alar. "Brie," she said. "What has happened? Why is Alar here?"

"I have a confession," Brie said. "And Alar has information for you."

"Is this in regards to what you and Nessa are up to?"

Brie nodded, apparently unsurprised that Siofra discerned their conspiracy. "Many feel the Order is no longer the refuge it once was. Not for women of the lower castes. Lyssa is making the Order everything we wanted to escape."

Brie started to continue, but Siofra held up a hand to forestall her. "I had no idea the discontent ran so deep." She gave her head a hard shake. "Nessa discovered Lyssa has been amending Murtair contracts." She looked to Brie for confirmation. "She would never stand for that. So, she brings Tove into the Order and takes advantage of the unrest to create a crisis which will allow her to invoke article fifteen."

"That is the plan," Brie said.

"Article fifteen?" Alar asked, but Siofra ignored him.

"How does Nessa expect to maintain control if she invokes the article? The gendarmes are in Lyssa's pocket."

"She's recalled the murtair," Brie said.

"And why have you come to me?"

"My trust in Nessa was misplaced," Brie said. "I doubt she will hold a fair election, and she has little concern for the lower castes. The Order won't be any better off with her in charge. I want *you* to invoke the article." She looked at Eirin, who nodded. "The murtair would support you."

Siofra held her gaze, then looked at Alar, who was watching the exchange with interest. "And what information do you have for me?"

"I saw those other Desulti who came to the wedding heading out to the garden, so I decided to eavesdrop."

"And?"

"They said something about Lyssa moving the Council to Kartok."

Siofra gaped at him. "You must have misheard."

"No, I'm quite sure I heard them clearly. They said the Volloch were taking over Kartok and that the Desulti could be part of *polite society* there. They're tired of being outsiders."

"The Order would never stand for that," Eirin said.

"They said there's no one left to oppose it," Alar said. "Except Nessa and Siofra. Or something like that." He caught Brie's eye and said, "They also said Lyssa would take care of the *l'oss,* so they wouldn't have to see her scarred face anymore."

Ignoring his last comment, Eirin asked Siofra, "What does it mean?"

"Lyssa and the Ruling Council want to bring the Desulti into the Empire. It will destroy the Order," Siofra said. "Eirin, saddle our horses. We leave immediately."

Eirin nodded, retrieved a pack from the corner and left.

"Alar, I appreciate what you have done for us. I won't forget it."

"Just take care of Tove," Alar said.

"We will," Siofra said. "Brie, I have a task for you."

Chapter 22

They Call me Brochen

Hela had taken to escorting Tove to and from her rooms when they ventured into the mountains. She protested at first, but it was half-hearted. They had grown comfortable with one another, and it was a relief not having to sneak through the village. She didn't know if it was his presence, but there were no further incidents since her encounter with the two women.

They were returning from two days in the mountains, walking through nearly deserted streets. Hela was telling an amusing story about two of Ka'tan's prominent citizens, but Tove was lost in her own thoughts.

As it had every quiet moment since her evening with Danu, the woman's fascinating frown came into her mind. At first, she tried to understand why she found it so compelling. Was it the way her delicate eyebrows drew together, cradling a small crease? The slight pout to her lips? Maybe the furrowed brow below her awkwardly sheared bangs? Or was it what it revealed about the woman within? Eventually, she just decided she kept thinking about it because she wanted to and it didn't need analyzing.

She laughed when Hela appeared to expect it, then returned to her thoughts. Should she wait for Danu to look for her? Maybe she should just pass the spot she ran into her repeatedly until she accidentally encountered her again. She chuckled, feeling her face warm. That was stupid. Was she a child? Still, even if she worked up the courage to go looking for Danu, she only had a vague idea where she lived. She *did* know where she worked. She blew a breath out. If she didn't encounter her in the next couple of days, she would go looking for her at the fulling hut.

But if she went to the fulling hut, Danu would know she was looking for her. What if she had second thoughts after that brief kiss? With images of an awkward meeting in mind, Tove decided to give it another week. She'd take another trip, or a few trips, to Ka'tan. Could be she ran into her again.

They were entering the plaza when Tove spotted Danu. She was standing near the fountain talking to two other women. Though she couldn't see Danu's face, she recognized her from the slight stoop to her shoulders, her unruly hair, and her nervous habit of swiping at her forehead. In the middle of his story, Hela took two more steps before he noticed Tove stopped. Because of the other two women, Tove's first impulse was to retreat and find another way home. But hadn't she been imagining ridiculous schemes to meet this woman for days?

Hela looked back at her, then pivoted around and looked toward the three women. "Which one?"

Then Danu turned around and spotted her. Tove couldn't help returning Danu's delighted smile and enthusiastic wave.

"Brie's sister?" Hela asked, a knowing smile growing on his face.

"Shut up," Tove said under her breath. "I'll see you tomorrow." Hela nodded, waved to Danu, then winked at Tove and strolled back the way they came. Tove took a breath, blew it out, and set off across the plaza. When she drew near, she glanced at the other women over Danu's shoulder and did a double-take. "Gwynna?"

Gwynna nodded stiffly, looking embarrassed for some reason.

Danu looked down at Tove's bow and said, "We were hoping you could take us to that tavern in Ka'tan."

"Now? All of you?"

"Well… yes," Danu said with a worried smile. She half turned and gestured to the unfamiliar woman. "This is my friend Brigid. She works in the dining hall."

Brigid eyed Tove speculatively. She wasn't one of the women Tove encountered in the dining hall before.

"She wants to taste the stew," Danu said.

Tove looked up at the sun. It was late afternoon. She was exhausted and grimy with dried sweat.

"Is it not a good time?" Danu asked, hesitantly, her hand swiping her forehead again.

Tove took in her worried frown and smiled. "No, of course not," she said. "Let me drop off my bow and freshen up."

***

They walked in a silence that threatened to become awkward. After the quick kiss Danu gave Tove at their last parting, it would have been complicated enough with just the two of them. Gwynna's brooding silence didn't help, and the furtive glances Brigid kept throwing at her made Tove nervous. She could tell Danu was searching for a way to ease the tension, but every time she opened her mouth to speak, she hesitated and pressed her lips closed.

Finally, Tove decided she couldn't stand it anymore. She dropped back to walk next to Gwynna, who had fallen behind the others. "Gwynna," she said.

Gwynna was looking at her feet. Her head pivoted toward Tove and her lips twisted, but she didn't respond.

Tove pressed on. "I never got a chance to thank you." She glanced ahead and found Danu and Brigid looking back at them curiously. Tove focused on Gwynna to avoid their scrutiny. "For what you did after the initiation."

Gwynna glanced at the others, then looked down again. "It was nothing."

"No, it wasn't," Tove said, her voice firming. "It was everything to me. I'll never forget it."

Gwynna looked directly at Tove for the first time. She didn't speak, but the hard defensiveness in her expression shifted.

"Let's catch up," Tove said. She gave her head a small shake to Danu's questioning look when they drew near.

Though they continued to walk in silence, it was much less awkward. When they arrived at the tavern, Tove stopped them on the walkway as she had done with Danu. But before she could speak, Danu said, "Tove will introduce you to Shia. She owns the tavern. If she likes you, no one will bother us." Danu nodded to Tove. "Right?"

Tove couldn't help grinning. "Right."

It was later than when she came with Danu, and the tavern was busier. Though their presence was noted, and the volume of the conversations decreased when they entered, there weren't as many hostile glares as the time Tove came with Danu.

"I remember Danu," Shia said.

"This is Gwynna and Brigid," Tove said. "We won't start any fights."

Shia gestured to a nearby table. "Ales and stew?"

"Please," Tove said and ushered the other women to the table.

Once they were seated, Tove studied the other women. Danu smiled shyly at her. Gwynna frowned at the fiddler on the small stage, who was playing a slow reel. Brigid stared curiously around at the festive atmosphere.

Following her gaze, Tove realized with a start that it must be almost time for the early summer festival. Having grown up an orphan, festivals for Tove were mainly an opportunity to steal food in the few *Alle'oss* neighborhoods that remained in Kartok. Her memories were starkly different from the ones Alar described.

One of her happiest memories was when she had seven summers. She managed to filch two hand pies and lead the baker on a merry chase through the crowd. She thought herself remarkably clever at the time. It took her years to recognize what really happened. This was long before the Inquisition marred her, but the world had already left its mark on her. She was tiny from malnutrition, hollow-eyed, and filthy. The baker saw her coming. He made sure she was looking when he put the pies on the counter of his stall, then deliberately turned his back. He allowed her to steal the pies and his chase was just for show.

She smiled, remembering squatting in an alley, relishing a mouthful of venison pie, marveling at her good fortune. It was a joyful memory, and all the more precious because it was one of very few. Until Alar found her, anyway. Movement at her elbow drew her eye. When she looked up and saw Garth standing next to the table, she rose abruptly and faced him.

Garth glanced at the other Desulti, then gave Tove an unreadable look. One shoulder dropped, and he hitched a thumb in a pocket. "I want to apologize," he said and gestured toward the far side of the tavern where their confrontation occurred on Tove's first night. "It was wrong, what I said." He swallowed. "And what I tried to do. Later." His eyes came up and met Tove's briefly.

"Just a misunderstanding," Tove said. "You got a right to be angry with the Empire." She gestured to the other women who were watching, alarmed. "But we aren't the enemy. These women got as much beef with the Empire as you and I." She didn't *know* that was true, but she doubted they would contradict her.

Garth glanced at the women and nodded.

"Did Meya make you apologize?" Tove asked, letting one corner of her mouth rise.

He looked up sharply, but when he saw her half grin, he chuckled and nodded. "Thank you for asking Shia to let me back in."

Tove extended her hand and waited until Garth took her forearm. "All's forgotten," she said. "I'll buy you an ale." She glanced at Shia, who was watching closely. Shia nodded and signaled to the barman.

"*Tok,*" Garth said. He gave a slight bow to the other Desulti, said, "Ladies," and turned away.

The volume of conversations rose as everyone discussed this development. Tove sat, breathing a sigh of relief.

"What was that about?" Brigid asked.

"He and I didn't see eye to eye the first time I came in here," Tove said. Taking in their uncertain frowns, she added, "There's some here who think I'm a traitor for joining the Order."

"A traitor?" Brigid asked. "To who?"

Tove frowned at her. "To the *Alle'oss*. Who else?"

"Why would they think you're a traitor?"

Tove didn't answer right away. She thought about what Cianna told her about the Volloch castes. "What caste are you?" Tove asked. All the women at the table looked away from her, giving one another embarrassed glances. "What?" Tove asked.

Danu lay her hand on the table between them and said, "We don't talk about that sort of thing."

Tove stared at her. "How many times have I been reminded I'm not Volloch since I got here?" She took in their uncomfortable expressions and said, "Why is that different?"

Danu looked at the others, but it was Gwynna who responded. "It *is* different."

"Why?"

"Because you're *Alle'oss*," Brigid said, as if she were speaking to a child.

"And you're Vollen," Tove said.

"No," Gwynna said. "We're Volloch."

Tove didn't have the advantage of a formal education, but Alar insisted she learn to read and forced her to read *The History of the Empire*, despite her bitter complaints. Dense prose and a tendency to glorify the Empire's crimes made it torturous. But she learned more than she would admit to Alar. One part that interested her was the author's convoluted justifications for the caste system. She read it multiple times, but in the end she decided it was *sheoda*. After talking to Cianna, she recalled that passage and was surprised it never mentioned the divisions within the Volloch caste. But Cianna called it a dirty little secret. It was obviously something the author didn't want to stain his white washing of the Empire.

"Volloch is your caste," Tove said. "Your people, Abria's people, are Vollen." She waved a hand. "Just like we're all *Alle'oss*. The Vollen people created the castes — Volloch, Brochen and Volbroch, and the rest — to separate people. To make sure people know their place."

"Tove —" Danu said.

Tove gestured to the people in the tavern. "We don't call ourselves Brochen — broken. It's you who call us that." She leaned forward, tapped the table with her finger and said, "But we don't accept it. You can call us all the names you want, it doesn't make us think less of ourselves." When the women cast glances at the people at nearby tables who were listening to the conversation, Tove said, "Why would you let people like Lyssa tell you that you're less than her because of who your parents were?" She sat back and met their eyes. "That doesn't make any sense to us. You shouldn't let these Gabra and Angus people do that to you."

Silence fell until servers arrived, bringing bowls of stew and tankards of ale. Once they were gone, Tove said, "We're all women. We have our own stories, but we're all here because we were looking for a place to feel safe. We should be on each other's side. Right?" She lifted her tankard. "They call me Brochen, but I'm *Alle'oss* and I'm proud."

Danu lifted her tankard and smiled. "They call me Burne, but I'm… Vollen and I'm proud, too."

Looking as if she was being dragged against her will, Brigid lifted her tankard and said, "They call me Burne, but I'm Vollen." She hesitated, then said, "I'm proud."

Gwynna stared fixedly at her tankard.

"Come on, Gwynna," Danu said. "We're proud of you."

Brigid's expression softened as she gazed at Gwynna. "Yeah, Gwynna. You have more right to be proud than any of us. Look what you went through to get here. I couldn't have done it."

Danu put a hand on Gwynna's arm.

Gwynna's eyes flicked up to Tove and Tove saw something hidden there. But she smiled and said, "Come on, Gwynna."

Gwynna reached out and lifted her tankard. "I'm…" She squeezed her eyes shut. "They call me Baird… But I'm Vollen."

"And you're proud," Danu said.

"And I'm proud," Gwynna mumbled.

"There you go," Tove said. She took a swallow of her ale and banged her tankard down on the table. "Let's eat." Only Gwynna had not sipped her ale with the others.

The awkwardness didn't disappear all at once, but the familiar ritual of food and drink brought with it a shared sense of relief.

Brigid peered at her bowl, then she glanced at Danu.

"Try it," Danu said.

"It just looks like stew," Brigid said.

"What was it supposed to look like?" Tove asked with a grin.

Brigid shrugged. "The way Danu described it, I was expecting something… I don't know. Different."

"Try it," Danu said.

Brigid picked up her spoon, ladled up a small spoonful. She held it under her nose and her eyes widened slightly. When she put it in her mouth, she broke into a smile. "Dear Daga," she said. "This is good."

"Would any of you like to dance?"

Tove looked up at a young *Alle'oss* man smiling down at them. His long auburn hair was pulled back in a tail and he wore clothes suitable for a merchant. He scanned all their faces, then focused on Brigid and extended his hand.

"Me?" Brigid asked. When his smile widened, she glanced at the couples dancing to a lively jig on the small dance floor and said, "But I don't know how to dance."

"Beginners are welcome," he said. "We'll start slow." When she hesitated and threw a glance at Danu, he said, "Sorry, my name is Jens." He gave her a shallow bow and left his hand extended.

"Go on," Danu said.

Brigid looked at Tove, her brows rising slightly. Tove leaned in and said, "He just wants to dance. He doesn't expect anything more than that."

"Are you sure?" Brigid whispered, her eyes flicking up at him.

"Yes," Tove said firmly. When Brigid looked at her, she said, "If he tries anything, I'll kick his ass."

Brigid's eyes widened, then she burst out laughing.

Tove sat back and watched Brigid rise. She took Jens's hand, a smile slowly illuminating her face. They made their way through the tables to the dance floor. Jens took her around to the side, where there was some space, then leaned in and spoke to her while Brigid watched the dancers, an uncertain frown on her face. She glanced at Jens and shook her head, but he smiled, took her hand, and pulled her onto the dance floor.

It was a simple dance, perfect for tipsy evenings in a tavern, and Jens led Brigid confidently. Tove watched them for a few minutes, then Danu got her attention.

"You want to dance?" she asked.

Tove wasn't sure she heard right, but once she reassured herself she had, she blurted, "Dance!? You and me?" Danu nodded. Tove glanced at the dance floor, then shook her head and said, "I didn't… I never…"

Danu rose, took Tove's arm and tugged her to her feet. The next thing she knew, she was standing at the edge of the dance floor, frantically studying the dancers.

Danu leaned in and said, "You lead."

Distracted by the sensation of Danu's lips brushing her hair, Tove turned to her and asked, "What?"

"You lead."

"Lead?" Tove said and started to back away. "Where?"

Danu pulled her onto the dance floor, and before Tove knew it, they were dancing. It wasn't the same dance everyone else was doing, but with Danu's soft hands in hers, her face radiant, Tove didn't care.

When the music stopped, Danu pulled her hands free of Tove's. A blush darkened her cheeks. She smiled shyly, the fingers of one hand brushing her forehead. They were jostled by couples returning to their seats, but Tove could only stare at Danu.

"I thought you were shy," she said, returning Danu's smile.

Danu stepped close and spoke into Tove's ear. "I'm not shy. I'm just quiet. Guess I got a little of Brie in me."

Tove breathed in Danu's scent and let her eyes close. When she opened them, Danu was grinning at her.

"Come on," Danu said. "We're the only one's on the dance floor."

She took Tove's arm and pulled her toward their table. When Tove turned around, a sea of faces were turned their way. She felt her face warm. She was used to being the topic of conversation among the patrons of this tavern. Knew her presence sparked debates. But somehow, the knowing smiles on many of the faces were harder to face than their hostility. She avoided meeting anyone's eyes as they made their way to the back of the tavern, where Gwynna waited alone.

"You should dance, Gwynna," Danu said.

"I don't like to dance."

Brigid appeared and whispered something to Danu. Danu said, "We'll be back," to Tove, then rose and led Brigid to the privies.

Tove watched her until she disappeared.

"It's not right," Gwynna said. "What you said."

Tove, focused on the door where Danu disappeared, almost didn't respond, but then the words penetrated her thoughts. She looked at Gwynna and asked, "What wasn't right?"

"We aren't all the same," Gwynna said. "*L'oss*, Baird, Burne…" She waved a hand and said, "We're just who we are. We can't change that."

Tove stared at her. "Do you think Lyssa is better than you?" Gwynna bit her lip, but she didn't answer. "Do you think you're better than me?"

Gwynna's head tipped to the side and her lips twisted.

"Ah," Tove said. "I get it. You don't think you're good enough for people like Lyssa, but at least you're better than us *l'oss*."

Gwynna, who had been looking everywhere but at Tove, met Tove's eyes.

Before Tove could think of what to say, Danu and Brigid arrived. They dropped into their seats, giggling like young girls. Not wanting to spoil their mood, Tove forced a smile onto her face and ladled up a spoonful of stew.

Chapter 23

She's Not Murtair

Tove edged along the cliff face, careful how she placed her feet on the narrow ledge. She stopped at the spot she and Hela decided would give her the best view of potential prey and surveyed the scene. It was on the southern face of a ridge, close to where the rocky outcrop ended. She had a good view to the south and west. The ledge on which she stood rose from ground level in the south and wrapped around the end of the ridge. Ten paces below her, the stream she and Hela spotted elk frequenting burbled. Hela was concealed thirty paces east of her position. She leaned her bow against the face of the ridge, sank to sit and extracted a pouch full of blueberries from her pack.

Munching the berries, she lifted her gaze to an eagle riding a column of air thrust up by the ridge and replayed her last trip to Ka'tan with Danu. The kiss they shared at the end of the night was much more intentional this time and left Tove feeling warm and drifty. Returning the pouch to her pack, she scanned the treeline on the opposite bank of the stream. It was still a little early for the elk to arrive if they kept to their usual routine.

The woman wearing Murtair blacks rounded the end of the ridge so silently, Tove didn't notice her until she was only a pace away. She looked up and had a glimpse of a linen wrapped face against the blue sky and a heavy truncheon. Tove fell onto her side. The truncheon clipped her head above her ear, then smacked against the stone. Tove ended up between her attacker's feet, which were spaced as wide as the narrow ledge allowed.

Before her assailant could readjust and swing again, Tove struck her ankle with the heel of her palm. The woman's foot slipped off the edge of the ledge. The truncheon went flying, as she scrabbled for a hold on the face of the ridge, to no avail. With a sharp yelp, she fell, her knee driving the side of Tove's face against the rough granite as she dropped out of sight.

Tove clenched her teeth and squeezed her eyes shut. When the pain subsided somewhat, she cracked her eyes open and pushed herself up to sit. Leaning out, she looked down. The woman was lying face down on the bank of the stream, her legs in the water. Carefully, Tove explored the side of her face and above her ear with her fingertips. "Bless the Father," she mumbled, "that hurt."

"Hey!" Hela shouted from below her. "You okay up there?!"

Tove leaned out and looked down.

"Thank the Mother!" Hela exclaimed, his hand going to his chest.

"That the murtair?" Tove called and winced at the resulting throb in her head. Since noticing the murtair following them, they made it a game to make it as difficult as possible for her, laughing when they tricked her into revealing herself. Tove suspected she was aware of what they were up to. Twice, Tove backtracked to confront her, but evading pursuit was much easier than following someone in the mountains. Eventually, she and Hela decided if she had bad intentions, she would have made them known already, so they decided not to worry about it. But maybe they should have.

Hela knelt beside the woman and rolled her onto her back. Linen strips wrapped her head, but there was something off about her. She didn't have the lean, powerful build as other murtair Tove had seen. She climbed down, arriving as Hela was removing the last of the wraps. Standing, he dropped the linen to the ground and he and Tove studied the woman's face.

"Hair's pretty long for a murtair," Tove said.

"Some keep it," Hela said with a nod. "But it's always short." He shook a finger at the woman. "I've seen this one. Don't remember who she is, but she's not Murtair. Seen her around the village."

They fell silent, Tove exploring the growing knot above her ear with her fingertips. "She dead?"

Hela knelt and pressed his fingers to her throat. "Nope," he said and stood. He turned toward Tove, lifted her chin, and turned the side of her face to the sun.

"Am I going to have matching scars on that side?" she asked with a weak grin.

"Superficial," he said. "We should clean it, but you'll be as pretty as usual in no time." He grinned at her frown and looked down at her assailant.

"You think this is the woman been following us?" Tove asked.

Hela shook his head. "Unlikely. That other one is definitely Murtair." He scanned the nearby forest. "Which begs the question, if she's not following you to protect you, what's she doing out here?"

"Hey you, out there?" Tove shouted and winced. "This one with you?" There was no answer.

"You think we gave her the slip?" Hela asked.

"Not likely." Tove looked down at the woman. "What do we do with her? Leave her?"

Hela smiled widely. "Was going to wait until we bagged an elk to teach you how to build a travois. Now's as good a time as ever."

***

Tove couldn't decide which hurt worse; her throbbing head, Hela cleaning her scrapes or the sweat that dripped into them as they pulled the travois through the rugged terrain toward the village.

"This is hard with two people," she said when they paused to catch their breath. She looked at the woman trussed up and lashed to the frame made of saplings. "And she ain't that heavy."

"No doubt," Hela said and took a swallow from his waterskin.

"How am I supposed to bring in an elk stag all by myself?"

He nodded and pushed the cork into the neck of his waterskin. "That's why it's best to hunt with someone else. *If* you are with someone, you could lash it to a sapling and carry the load on your shoulders. But, if you *are* alone…" He tucked his waterskin into his pack. "This is the best way. You have to process the game. Bring back the good parts. Course, whatever you leave behind will be scavenged." He shrugged. "But it's better than losing it all."

"Was what I thought," Tove said. "Just wanted to make sure I wasn't missing something."

"You ready?"

Tove nodded and knelt to take the handle of the travois.

The woman woke up not long after they started. At first, all she did was moan, but when she realized her predicament, she started complaining. Loudly. Tove put up with until they reached the relatively flat terrain that surrounded the village.

"Hold on," she said. They set the travois down and Tove bent over the woman. "Shut up, *nā minu*\!" she shouted. "You're lucky we didn't leave you out there. Was what you deserved. You keep your mouth shut, I won't leave you out here trussed up and gagged for the bears to find."

When she returned to the front and bent to lift the travois, Hela mumbled, "Bears? Be more likely wolves this low."

Tove narrowed her eyes at him.

"Right," he mumbled. "One's as good as another for the purpose."

"How you think they're going to react?" she asked when the outer buildings of the village came into view.

"I saw the whole thing," Hela said. They exchanged a look, and he shrugged. "We *could* have left her out there. That's got to be worth something."

As they made their way through the streets toward the Gendarmery, people noticed them and word spread. A crowd gathered and trailed behind them. As soon as people worked out what was happening, arguments broke out. Tove wasn't surprised to hear angry retorts directed at her, but she was shocked when others responded on her behalf.

"She's Murtair!" someone said. "The *l'oss* attacked a murtair!" Someone else called for freeing the woman. Scuffles broke out.

"Are you stupid? How could she capture a murtair?" someone asked, and the scuffles stopped as people took a closer look.

The trussed-up woman called out to people in the crowd she recognized.

"She's not Murtair. It's Tish."

"Why is Tish wearing blacks?"

On and on it went. Tove expected someone to turn their ire on her and Hela, but there was just enough doubt about what happened and enough people defending her that no one interfered with them. News raced ahead, so when they made it to their destination, a group of gendarmes was waiting for them. The crowd had grown to nearly two hundred, and there was a violent undercurrent in the air.

Tove and Hela stood in a small space in the middle of the crowd, pressed up against the steps to the Gendarmery. They dropped the handles of the travois, eliciting a yelp from their passenger.

"What's this?" the woman, whom Tove assumed was the commander of the Gendarmery, asked. The crowd grew silent.

"I'd press charges for assault," Tove said, lifting her chin to show the side of her face. "But I reckon she suffered enough for the harm she done."

She turned to walk away, but the gendarme said, "Hold on there! Suppose you tell us what happened?"

"She attacked a murtair!" a recent arrival in the crowd shouted. Others shouted her down, pointing out what many had already concluded; the woman wasn't murtair.

"This woman," Hela said, gesturing to the woman lashed to the travois, "is not Murtair, though she wore the blacks and wraps to impersonate one." He held up the end of the linen and dropped it. "She attacked Tove unprovoked. I would have left her, but Tove insisted we bring her back."

The crowd responded to this news with angry shouts. "They're both *l'oss!*" someone shouted over the clamor. "Of course they're going to tell the same lies!"

A woman leaning over the prisoner said, "Why is Tish wearing blacks?" The crowd quieted as the woman straightened. "What exactly are you saying they did? Attack Tish, then dress her in blacks?"

The woman who called Tove and Hela liars shoved her. But before the fight could escalate, people pressed in closer, trying to get a better view of Tish.

Tove had never been involved in a riot, but she was well acquainted with the frisson of impending violence. She glanced at the small group of gendarmes. The normally peaceful Desulti village didn't need a large force, so the few women charged with keeping the peace looked pitifully small in the middle of the throng. Jostled by the crowd, Tove saw fear in their expressions. The head gendarme lifted her arms and called for calm. When she came down the steps, she revealed a familiar face standing behind her. It was the short woman who attacked Tove earlier. Their eyes met for a moment, then the crowd grew suddenly quiet.

Tove looked back and found a tall murtair pushing through the crowd. It was the same woman she saw the day she arrived in Téama. Her face wasn't wrapped, and her head was covered in short hair, but she wore blacks, and she moved with the coiled grace of a murtair. She peered down at the prisoner, then looked around at the crowd.

"It is as Hela said," she said and pointed down at the prisoner. "Tish attacked Tove without provocation."

Angry murmurs rose, but no one contradicted her. The head gendarme asked, "And you witnessed this, Laoise?"

"Yes."

"You just happened to be up in the mountains?"

"Didn't say it was up in the mountains," Tove said before the murtair could respond.

The gendarme gaped at her, then she gestured to the woman still lashed to the travois. "I just assumed! Where else *would* it be?" Face red, she gestured to her comrades and said, "Get her untied."

Tove met Laoise's eyes, but before she could say anything, the murtair turned and disappeared through the crowd. Tove watched her go, nodded to Hela, said, "*Tok*," then turned and pushed her way through the crowd.

Chapter 24

Cianna Lies

"A riot?" Nessa asked Laoise. "Are you sure?"

Laoise stared calmly at the head of the Murtair. "The situation was getting out of control. There was the *potential* for a situation the gendarmes couldn't control."

Nessa sat back and gazed out the window. It was too soon. When Brie told her about the unrest among the lower castes Lyssa's reforms were causing, Nessa had been skeptical. But it appeared Brie was right. That or Shailey had been more successful stoking unrest than her reports suggested.

"You told me to intervene if I judged Tove was in imminent danger," Laoise said. She paused, one brow rising slightly, and asked, "Have your instructions changed?"

Instead of answering, Nessa asked, "Why is it this attacker was able to get so close to her?"

"I saw her too late to intervene. The mountains are not an ideal setting to provide protection unseen." Laoise eyed Nessa. "She wore blacks."

Nessa stared at her. "Blacks?"

Laoise nodded. "Yes, Mistress. She also wore wraps."

"Not Murtair?"

"No," Laoise said. "It was Tish."

"Tish?!" Nessa gaped at her. Tish attempted the Murtair training and failed. She was Angus, closely allied with Lyssa. Everyone would know who orchestrated the attack on Tove. Shailey could use this. Noticing Laoise watching her, she asked, "How did Tove survive the attack?"

Laoise explained she arrived on the top of the ridge in time to witness the encounter from above. When she finished, Nessa studied her placid face. She was the only murtair in Ka'tan at the moment. The Order didn't have as many murtair as it required because it was hard to find women capable of surviving the intensive training. When Nessa decided Tove was what she was waiting for, she recalled as many murtair as possible, but after receiving the recall, they would have to extract themselves from their current contracts and make the trek back to Téama. They would not begin arriving for another few weeks. If a riot had broken out today, Nessa would have had a hard time controlling the situation. It would be the gendarmes who attempted to impose order, and the gendarmes were loyal to Lyssa. Lyssa could use the riot as an excuse to do the same as Nessa intended. Laoise may have averted a disaster today.

"You did the right thing by intervening," Nessa said. Laoise's only acknowledgment was a barely perceptible nod. Nessa gazed at her. How much was she willing to tell this woman?

"Laoise," she said. "How long has it been since you returned to Téama?" Nessa was aware of the movements of all her murtair, but she wasn't exactly sure how to start this conversation. Laoise was Baird. She didn't suffer the same discrimination as others of her caste because she was Murtair, but bringing up another person's caste was such an ingrained taboo, Nessa found it difficult to broach a subject which highlighted the differences in their caste.

"Three months, Mistress."

"Have you noticed… unrest…" Nessa glanced away from Laoise's face, unsure how to continue.

"Among the Burne and Baird?" Laoise asked.

"Yes," Nessa said, relieved.

Laoise hesitated, her face uncharacteristically revealing an internal calculation. Finally, she said, "Many women are unhappy with the changes in the Order. Some of them are more willing to express their displeasure since Tove was admitted. The Gabra and Angus have responded to protect their position. There are increasing instances of violence. My partner has received threats because of her association with Tove." She paused. "I assumed that was why you have me tracking this woman."

"Threats?!" This sort of thing was unheard of in the Order. And it was partially Nessa's fault. She had been working for months to fan these flames. But she didn't rise to lead the Murtair by being squeamish. It was Lyssa who introduced disharmony into the Order. Not her. Casualties were unavoidable, even necessary. She would regret it if something happened to Cianna, but if a woman as popular among the lower castes as her were harmed, it could only help Nessa's cause. Protecting the institution of the Murtair was paramount.

Laoise was watching her closely when Nessa focused on her. The tiniest narrowing of the murtair's eyes was the only indication she guessed Nessa's thoughts. The two women watched one another. Nessa could order Laoise to do what she needed her to, but it would be better if she were on Nessa's side.

"I have watched with concern what is happening in the Order since the fire," she said carefully. "I've also become increasingly worried about the unrest among the lower castes." She flinched inwardly as Laoise's face tightened, but she continued. "I've recalled as many murtair as is possible to ensure *we...*" She paused and met Laoise's eyes. "To ensure we can maintain order *if* it becomes necessary."

Laoise rarely revealed her inner thoughts, but her complete lack of reaction to this news was startling. All she said was, "I understand. Is there anything else, Mistress?"

"No. Continue watching Tove."

Laoise hesitated, then nodded and left.

Nessa stared at the door. She couldn't help thinking Laoise guessed what she and Brie intended. Did Brie tell her? No, she trusted Brie. It was Brie's plan, a plan she concocted for her sister's sake. She wouldn't do anything to jeopardize it.

She stood and paced her office. The near riot proved the situation was much less predictable than she believed. She stopped and gazed out the window, fighting a sinking sensation that events were spinning out of her control. If Laoise guessed what they intended, she would tell Cianna, and there was no telling what Cianna would do. As a Burne, there was little she could do by herself, but she had a lot of influence among the lower castes. Nessa wasn't worried about having the votes she needed, because she didn't intend there to be a fair election. But it was hard enough when all she had to do was keep track of what Lyssa was up to. She had no idea how Cianna would react if she knew Nessa was intentionally stirring the unrest roiling the Order. Would she understand it was for the greater good? If she informed Lyssa or Siofra what Nessa intended, all would be lost.

***

Lyssa's assistant, Cara, burst into her office and blurted, "Tish failed."

The Chief Executive looked at the ink blot spreading on the letter she was writing when Cara's appearance startled her. She placed the quill in the stand, sat back, and asked, "What happened?"

Lyssa listened calmly as Cara gave a disjointed description of the near riot outside the Gendarmery, but when she mentioned Laoise's appearance, Lyssa sat forward and put up a hand to stop her.

"Laoise?" she asked. "Are you sure?"

"Yes, Mistress. She should have left days ago, which means she ignored the contract."

Lyssa stood, came around her desk and went to stare out her windows. Cara waited until Lyssa turned toward her.

"Tove was unharmed?" she asked.

"Superficial scrapes."

"Tish?"

"Unharmed beyond a concussion," Cara said. "The gendarmes arrested her." When she saw Lyssa's reaction, she said, "They had no choice. Laoise accused her of an unprovoked attack on the *l'oss* and she…" Her lips twisted.

"She was wearing blacks," Lyssa said.

Cara nodded.

"Daga! Could this get any worse?"

"They can't trace it back to you," Cara said. "I had the gendarmes give Tish instructions."

"As long as *they* don't talk."

"Who would they talk to?"

"Nessa," Lyssa said.

"What should we do?"

Lyssa gazed up at the ceiling, thinking. Laoise likely wouldn't be easy to find, but… "Send gendarmes to track down Cianna. Let's find out why Laoise ignored the contract."

"Yes, Mistress," Cara said.

***

Cianna entered Lyssa's office and found the Chief Executive staring out her window. She didn't move until Cianna spoke.

"Mistress," Cianna said. "You wished to see me?"

Lyssa turned and said, "When was the last time you saw Laoise?"

Cianna smiled inwardly. No preliminaries. Lyssa usually hid her contempt for the Baird and Burne behind a polite formality. She must be worried. "A week ago. She had a contract that would take her to Lubern." She held her face steady while Lyssa studied her.

"That's curious. Laoise was seen in Téama today," Lyssa said.

Cianna and Laoise discussed what Cianna's reaction should be to this revelation, and Cianna insisted she practice her facial expressions, much to Laoise's amusement.

Cianna's face froze. She held it for the amount of time she guessed it would take the revelation to sink in if she hadn't seen Laoise earlier that day, then she furrowed her brow and cocked her head. "I'm sure you're mistaken. I watched Laoise leave."

Lyssa glanced at Cara and said, "Check with the quartermaster. See if Laoise requisitioned a horse."

"Yes, Mistress," Cara said and left.

"Are you calling me a liar?" Cianna asked, letting a hint of offense into her voice.

"*Someone* is lying," Lyssa snapped. "Laoise was seen. There are many witnesses."

Cianna stared at her, then let her face crumple and fell into one of the chairs arranged in front of the windows. "That can't be," she said. "Why would she lie to me?"

She didn't dare look up to gauge Lyssa's reaction.

Lyssa took the opposite chair. "Did Laoise tell you what she was doing before she left?"

Cianna looked at her and shook her head. "She was gone most of the day, but she wouldn't talk about it. That wasn't unusual. She rarely talks about her assignments."

Lyssa gazed at her long enough that Cianna wondered if her expression revealed something, then she looked away, obviously frustrated. When she looked back, she said, "You may go. Inform me if you hear from Laoise."

Cianna nodded vaguely, then got unsteadily to her feet and shuffled out of the office. Cara was not in the outer office, so she hurried to leave.

Standing atop the steps to the Great Hall, Cianna gazed pensively across the plaza. Two women appeared on the far side. Even from a distance, she could tell they were having a heated argument. It wasn't necessarily about Tove, but she couldn't help thinking it was another sign events were getting out of hand.

She watched the two women part and stalk off in opposite directions. When Brie brought Tove to Téama, Cianna and Laoise guessed what would happen and vowed to keep her safe. Laoise was hiding outside the village. She would try to protect Tove when she ventured into the mountains, but Tove would be vulnerable when she was in public places. Cianna considered, then set off across the plaza.

***

While she waited for her assistant to return, Lyssa settled into a chair by the fire and gazed out the window. Until today, the *l'oss* had only been an irritant, but the near riot frightened her. She had to come to grips with the rising unrest before it boiled over. But how? It was clear she didn't understand the situation in the Order as well as she assumed. She was aware of simmering anger among the lower castes. Knew it was because of the changes she was imposing on the Order. But she couldn't believe the lower castes were capable of such sustained agitation on their own. Especially in support of a Brochen woman. There had to be someone behind the scenes, someone capable of organizing and focusing their anger.

Between Siofra and Nessa, it was most likely Nessa. Siofra didn't have that level of cunning. She would be out front, making speeches, eager to negotiate what she thought was a just settlement among the castes. Besides, if it was her, why would she leave Téama for the wedding?

But Nessa was perfectly capable of such subterfuge. The problem was the head of the Murtair hadn't interfered with Lyssa's initiatives before now. If anything, she signaled tacit approval. So why would she act now?

Lyssa gave her head a frustrated shake. It was nearly impossible to gain any useful intelligence on Nessa. She lived alone with her housekeeper, never employing servants in her home. And getting useful information out of her murtair was next to impossible. There was no way to know what she was thinki —

Lyssa's eyes focused. She shook her head slowly, not wanting to believe it. But it would explain everything. Nessa must have caught wind of Lyssa's intention to eliminate the Murtair. She intended to use the same provision of the Charter that Lyssa did to gain control of the Council. It all made sense now. All of this was an attempt to create the conditions that would justify invoking article fifteen of the Charter. Lyssa should have seen it before.

She stood abruptly, hesitated, then fell into the chair again and forced herself to think. Article fifteen was included in the Order's Charter when it was written not long after the Order was founded. It provided a means for handling unforeseen emergencies. The article could be invoked by a member of the Inner Council. Once invoked, it contained many provisions for addressing the emergency. Among them were the ability for the one who invoked it to declare martial law, recall members of the Order from across the world to Téama, take temporary control of the Order's commercial interests… And call for a new election and appoint anyone they wished to oversee the election.

It was that provision that Lyssa used to take control of the Council. The people she appointed to oversee the election never told Lyssa what they did to dispose of the actual ballots, but she didn't need to know.

Nessa intended to use this *l'oss* to inflame the anger of the lower castes, goad them into a riot, then invoke the article. The near riot today suggested it was working. Lyssa could only guess Nessa was waiting for her murtair to return so she could impose martial law. She must have issued a recall, but it would take weeks for them to return.

So she knew Nessa's game. The question was what to do about it.

She could preempt Nessa and invoke the article, but without a suitable emergency, everyone would interpret that for the naked power grab it was. The village would erupt, and the gendarmes wouldn't be enough to squash the riot. It was likely she wouldn't survive the subsequent turmoil.

She could wait until the inevitable riot erupted and beat Nessa to the punch. She dismissed that as ridiculous. The article was invoked by lighting a brazier outside the Great Hall. The image of her and

Nessa hovering outside the Great Hall, both hoping to be the first to light the fire, brought a sour smile to her face.

As part of her deal with the emperor, she exacted from Hoerst a commitment that she could call on the soldiers in the Imperial fortress north of Ka'tan. She intended to have a century of soldiers standing by when she announced she was disbanding the Murtair. They would impose order and deal with any murtair who happened to be in Téama. It would be traumatic for the Order, but by the time news spread beyond the Order's home village, it would all be over. To most Desulti, it would be business as usual.

However, the timing was delicate. If she were to simply declare the elimination of the Murtair, the existing murtair wouldn't take it well. She shuddered at the thought of a dozen angry murtair with her head in their sights. So, she agreed to provide the details of their contracts to Hoerst so the Inquisition could arrest them. If she were to bring in the soldiers now, before the Inquisition put their forces in place, some of the murtair might evade capture.

She needed to delay, to quell the unrest and delay the riot Nessa was counting on. The Baird and Burne weren't capable of organizing themselves, so Nessa must be relying on a few agitators to organize and direct the anger. She just needed to identify and neutralize those women. If she could put the emergency off long enough for Hoerst to put his people in place, she would accuse Nessa of sedition and use it as an excuse to invoke the article herself. It would prove the perfect subtext to impose martial law and announce the end of the Murtair.

Cara entered the office, breathless from running to the quartermaster. "Laoise did requisition a horse and the supplies she would require for a journey to Lubern," she said.

"So, Cianna was telling the truth." Lyssa looked out the window. "Probably."

"Do you think Laoise was acting on Nessa's orders?"

"Undoubtedly." Before Cara could respond, Lyssa stood and said, "It was a mistake to allow this unrest to go unanswered."

"If we start making arrests, it might only inflame the situation," Cara said. "Expressing an opinion is specifically protected in the Charter."

"Not all speech is protected. If we could prove incitement to violence or sedition… There would still be anger, but there's no way to avoid it at this point. If Nessa is behind this, then she'll have recruited people to stir things up. We need informants. Get me a list of women among the Baird or Burne we can rely on."

***

Lyssa had just poured herself a cup of tea when a voice startled her, causing her to spill her tea.

"Mistress?"

Lyssa looked up and found a woman with a familiar face standing in her office door. Cara was out and apparently hadn't locked her door.

"Yes?" Lyssa asked, not trying to hide her annoyance.

The woman flinched at her tone, but she took a small step into the office. "I was wondering if you talked to the counselor's office yet."

Lyssa stared at her, a tea towel hovering in one hand, but the mention of the counselor brought the woman's name to mind. Gwynna. She almost told her to come back and make an appointment with Cara, then remembered she needed people to spy for her. What better spy than this mouse of a woman? She stood and pasted her warmest smile on her face.

"Gwynna, so good to see you." She put her hands on Gwynna's arms and gave her an awkward hug. When she pulled away, and glimpsed the terror in Gwynna's expression, she had to turn away to hide her contempt. Gesturing to a chair, she said, "Have a seat, Gwynna."

Gwynna perched stiffly on the edge of the chair, hands twisting in her lap.

Lyssa poured Gwynna a cup of tea and was surprised when the timid woman spoke again.

"The counselor, Mistress?"

Lyssa paused and looked up. The tea overflowed. "Oh, zut!" She set the teapot down and dabbed at the wayward liquid with the towel. While she tipped the tea in the saucer into the teapot, she tried to recall her previous conversation with this woman.

"Yes, of course," she said. She handed the teacup to Gwynna. "The counselor's office is, unfortunately, short staffed at the moment. Cianna, quite inexplicably, disobeyed a direct order and took the *l'oss* on as a client. We were forced to reassign her, of course. I'm sure you agree, you can't have people disobeying orders."

Gwynna stared at Lyssa, the tea cradled in her lap, disappointment in every part of her expression.

Perfect. "I remember how anxious you were to get out of the…"

"The laundry, Mistress."

"Ah, yes. I knew it was a disagreeable job." She sipped her tea. "It's really a shame what is happening in the Order." She shook her head and set the cup down. "It has always been so peaceful here, a place where women could find like-minded women. Hasn't it?"

Gwynna, startled at being asked her opinion, blurted, "Oh, yes, Mistress."

"It's a shame some malcontents have used this woman's presence, this Tove, to stir up trouble. I'm sure it is only a few, but they have managed to disrupt our peaceful community." She fixed Gwynna with a stare and waited until Gwynna realized she expected a response.

"I agree," Gwynna said and took a nervous sip of her tea.

"We could, of course, arrest the troublemakers," Lyssa said. "But we would have to have a good *reason*. We would need to know who they are, what they are saying, and we would have to have evidence they are inciting others to violence."

Gwynna's eyes took on a distant look.

"You know, Gwynna," Lyssa said. "I just had a thought. What if we hired *you* as a sort of covert gendarme?" She smiled at Gwynna, who frowned in confusion.

"What does that mean? Mistress."

"You would listen to what people are saying and report to us. We would need to know who they are and what they say."

"And you would pay me?"

The hope in her voice was pitiful. "Of course," Lyssa said.

Chapter 25

Festival

Tove and Hela emerged from the trees lugging the travois laden with Tove's first elk. "Hold it," she said. They set their burden down, and Tove gestured to a woman loitering at the edge of the village. "What do you think that's about?" she asked. When the woman saw them, she turned and jogged deeper into the village.

Hela followed her pointing finger and shrugged. "She waiting for you?"

Tove nodded. "Just the one this time. There's usually more."

Hela grinned and said, "You got friends now, apparently. You complaining?"

"I ain't gonna complain about having friends. But I can't go anywhere without them now. Most of them hardly say a word to me, and I don't even know their names. They're just, sort of, nearby, hovering."

Hela's grin fell away, and he looked at his feet. When he looked up, he said, "You must have noticed how tense the atmosphere is around here." She nodded. "Someone's looking out for you."

"That include you?" she asked. "Notice you don't go very far, even when we're high up in the mountains."

"Worried about you."

Tove gazed at him, then looked down the street where several women were approaching. "So, not necessarily friends. More like bodyguards." But they weren't *all* there on someone else's orders. Tove's heart skipped a beat when she recognized Danu. One of the other women spotted Tove and got Danu's attention. When she waved, Tove couldn't help smile and return her wave.

"Not so bad, is it?" Hela asked.

"Could be worse," Tove said, returning his smile. "Let's get this done," she said as she bent and took hold of the travois.

They had discussed what to do with an elk given Tove's issues with the dining hall staff. Hela suggested they try to sell it to the Elkhorn Tavern. They pulled the travois through the streets, the women trailing behind them, until they were in the alley behind the tavern.

Tove glanced behind her to Danu, watching as Hela pounded on the back door. The door opened and a Volloch man stepped out onto the single step.

He glanced at the travois and said, "Hela, you got something for me?"

Hela shook the man's hand and gestured to Tove. "Actually, Tove got this one. I just helped her bring it in."

The man's smile fell away as he studied Tove. "This the *Alle'oss* Desulti, then?"

Taking it as a good sign he didn't use a slur, Tove stepped forward and extended her hand. "Tove."

He glanced at her hand, then took it and gave it a firm shake, but he spoke to Hela, "How come you to bring the elk to me, rather than the Order's dining hall?"

"Because some in the Order won't do business with me," Tove said.

The man nodded as if this wasn't surprising.

"So, you want it?" Tove asked.

The man stepped down into the alley and examined the elk. He glanced at Tove, then Hela. "Taking into consideration, you got no one else to sell it —"

"That's not true," Tove said. When his eyebrows lifted, she said, "Could take it to Ka'tan." She shrugged.

The man gazed at her, then wiped his mouth with his hand. "That's true. Course you have to get it there."

"The wagon that brings the workers to the fulling hut heads back empty," Tove said. "And the driver is the cook at the Boar's Head."

"Then why are you bringing it to me?"

"Want to be part of the community," Tove said, ignoring his obvious irritation. "Just want to be treated fairly."

Hela laughed. "She knows what she's about. You treat her right, she'll be a reliable source."

He eyed Hela, then asked Tove, "What would you think is fair?"

"Heard what you're paying the *Alle'oss* hunters," she said, then quoted a lower price. It was Hela who suggested the price.

He grinned and stuck out his hand. "Deal."

***

The sun was behind the mountains to the west when they concluded their business. Hela nodded to the women still waiting for Tove and said, "I'll take care of this." He lifted the empty travois and winked, but before he could go, Tove caught his arm.

"Here," she said and held out two coins.

"What's this?"

"Your share. For helping me bring the elk."

"I didn't do it to get paid," Hela said.

"I know. But I'll feel better. Besides, we're partners."

He gazed at Tove, considering, then nodded and took the coins.

Tove watched him go, then turned to find Danu and the others approaching. Now that she saw them up close, she recognized some of the women. Brigid apparently spread the word after their first trip to the Boar's Head and a week later, Danu showed up with Brigid and six other women, all claiming they wanted to try the stew. The *Alle'oss* patrons hardly blinked at her bringing eight Desulti.

"Jens told Brigid there's a festival in Ka'tan," Danu said, a small smile curling her lips. Her hand swiped her bangs.

Tove looked over Danu's shoulder to find Brigid grinning at her. "Yeah," she said. "It's the early summer festival."

"Jens invited us," Brigid asked. "He said we could bring friends."

"I don't see why not," Tove said. "As long as you're respectful and don't go around calling people *l'oss.*" She focused on Gwynna, standing behind Brigid. Gwynna looked away. Danu's frown appeared briefly, but before she could speak, Tove asked, "You've lived here for years and never went to a festival in Ka'tan?"

"We didn't think we would be welcome," Danu said.

"Most of the *Alle'oss* who work in Téama don't like us very much," Brigid said.

"I suspect they act that way because of how they're treated," Tove said.

"Which is why we need to go to the festival," Danu said hurriedly. "We haven't gone before, but now that we have an *Alle'oss* woman in the Order, we can break down barriers."

"What do they do at the festival?" Brigid asked, a smile smoothing the lines of her frown. "Jens said there would be dancing."

"There's music, dancing, games," Tove said. "Food. A lot of food. And stories."

"Will they have Tye's boar stew?" Brigid asked.

"Can't say, but the taverns usually have stalls."

"So, it's settled. We're all going to the festival," Danu said. She took Tove's arm and pulled her into motion. "Come on, we'll walk you home."

***

You must have a date," Meya said.

Tove felt her cheeks warm. "What makes you say that?" After they came to an understanding, Tove spent more time with Meya and decided she liked her. Though she wouldn't call them friends yet, it was nice to have another *Alle'oss* woman to talk to. Tove had even started teaching Meya some *Alle'oss* phrases.

Meya gestured to Tove's new clothes. "You took a bath with that lavender soap you made me get, and those new clothes are a lot nicer than what you usually wear." She glanced down. "Except the boots. You're not wearing the new boots."

"They hurt my feet," Tove grumbled. When she noticed Meya's knowing smile, she dropped her eyes to her old boots.

"You look fine," Meya said. "*Danu* will be very impressed."

"You think so?" Tove asked, her blush deepening.

"Of course," Meya said. "Now I have to go. I'll see you in Ka'tan."

***

The early summer festival lasted two days, starting in the morning of Lindenlatha and lasting until the evening of Elinalatha. The sun hovered above the mountain peaks to the east, chasing the usual mountain chill, when Tove entered the plaza. She stopped and stared at the large group of women gathered around the fountain in the center of the plaza. There must have been twenty. They stood in small groups, many of them laughing and talking excitedly. Anticipating the festival. The Volloch had a few annual events they called festivals, but as far as Tove knew, they weren't anything like the celebratory affairs *Alle'oss* festivals were.

Glancing down at her boots, she set off across the plaza. Danu saw her coming and jogged over to greet her. "You got new clothes," she said. She kissed Tove's cheek, brushed her forehead, and blushed. "And you smell really nice."

Tove gestured to the women watching them. "Who is this?"

"Well, when people found out about the festival, they wanted to go. Is it okay?"

"I don't know," Tove said. "I'm not from Ka'tan." Tove had seen festivals in the small villages in the hills above Richeleau. Those events would be overwhelmed by a large influx of Volloch. But Ka'tan was the third largest city in Argren. Twenty Volloch women shouldn't be a big deal. She hoped.

It didn't take her long to relax as they walked to Ka'tan. Everyone broke into groups, leaving Tove alone with Danu, Brigid and Gwynna. Danu and Brigid peppered her with questions about *Alle'oss* festivals. She answered as best she could, leaving out the fact festivals for her growing up were mostly a time when stealing food was easier. Still, their enthusiasm was hard to ignore, and by the time they neared Ka'tan, she was sharing their excitement.

"You said this is the early summer festival," Brigid said. "What are you celebrating?"

"It's the traditional festival from which the *Alle'oss* mark their ages." When they looked at her confused, she said, "In the old days, getting through the mountain winters was a big deal, so when people asked your age, you told them how many summers you had. It says how many winters you survived."

"Everyone has the same birthday?" Brigid asked, aghast.

"No. Everyone, or most everyone, knows their actual birth dates," Tove said. "Families celebrate them, but a person's age in the community is measured by how many winters they survived."

"How many winters have you survived?" Danu asked with a grin.

"You say how many summers you have," Tove said. She had no idea when she was born, but she was ashamed to tell them that. Alar guessed she had seventeen summers last year, so today marked her eighteenth summer. "I have eighteen summers," she said, returning Danu's grin. "Today."

Danu's face screwup and she looked up at the sky. "I was born in Lianapok, so today I have… seventeen summers." She looked back at Brigid and Gwynna. "How about you two?"

"Nineteen summers," Brigid said.

"Gwynna?" Danu asked.

"I'm not *Alle'oss.* Why would I care?"

Danu started to protest, but Tove said, "Listen."

The rhythmic beat of a bodhrain was the first thing they heard, but as they drew even with the Boar's Head tavern, a fiddle joined the drum. Wood smoke and the tantalizing aromas of *Alle'oss* festival foods drifted on the wind before the festival in the center of the city came into view. Tove had never been farther into Ka'tan than Shia's tavern, so she didn't know what the rest of the city was like. It was more like Richeleau than Kartok. Most of the buildings were of *Alle'oss* design. The buildings leading up to the town square and the buildings lining the square were decorated for the festival with streamers and bunting in the traditional Argren blue and green. The festive scene was only marred by the twin towers of the Vollen cathedral visible above the rooftops to the north.

Tove pulled Danu to the side of the road and watched nervously as the Desulti filtered into the festival crowd. They were noticed right away, but their presence only spurred conversations. No one approached them or appeared hostile. The women broke into small groups and spread out.

Tove looked down and found her fingers entwined with Danu's. When she looked at the other woman's face, Danu was smiling at her.

"You, uh… Are you hungry?" Tove asked. Danu nodded. Tove tried to pull her hand free, but Danu wouldn't let her go.

"What should we eat?" Danu asked.

"I know exactly what I want," Tove said. She pulled Danu into the crowd, skirting the square, looking for a stall that sold *Alle'oss* hand pies. As a child, these were the treats she most coveted. Sweet or savory in a flaky pastry and easily carried in one hand. She found what she was looking for and they joined the line.

The man in line ahead of her glanced back, then did a double take. His eyes went to her scar, then to her hair. A small smile appeared, then he turned around and got the attention of the woman ahead of him. He whispered to her, then the woman looked at Tove over his shoulder.

Suppressing her scowl, Tove turned around to face Danu.

"What are we having?" Danu asked.

"Hand pies."

"Hand pies?"

"Trust me," Tove said and grinned.

After acquiring two pies and a tankard of mead, they found seats at a table beside the space reserved for dancing. Brigid and Jens were already among the dancers and several Desulti were standing at the edge, studying the steps. While Tove watched, two of the women joined hands and mimicked the steps slowly.

"Mmmm."

Tove turned back to Danu, who held the tankard in both hands. "Have you had mead before?" Tove asked.

Danu nodded. "My father made mead. Brie and I would sneak some when my parents had parties."

Tove took the tankard from her and handed her the venison pie. "This one first."

Danu took the pie in both hands, studying the browned pastry with the serious frown Tove found so fascinating. When she lifted it to her nose, a grin grew on her face.

"Go ahead," Tove said and sipped the mead.

Danu nibbled the crust, then took a bigger bite. She chewed, her eyes rolling up. "You grew up eating these?"

"Sort of," Tove said, swapping the tankard for the pie.

They passed the pie and mead back and forth until they were licking their fingers and pleasantly mellow.

"What about that one?" Danu asked, pointing to the smaller pie.

"That's for later," Tove said, She tucked it into the pouch on her belt.

"You want to dance?" Danu asked.

"Yes."

They joined other members of the Order, watching the dancers. One of the women Tove didn't know saw her and asked, "Do you know this dance?"

Tove shook her head. She was surprised when the woman took her hand.

"I think I have it," she said. She took Danu's hand in her other hand and they plunged into the maelstrom.

She didn't have it. But it didn't matter. They did their best, inventing their own dance out of the way of the other dancers. When they finished, smiling and breathless, people sitting at the tables cheered them. The woman who dragged them onto the dance floor took a bow and set off laughing with other Desulti.

Tove slipped her arm around Danu's waist and pulled her close. Danu startled, then gave her a small smile. Tove kissed her. Conscious of their audience, she made it a quick kiss, but it left her breathless.

At an age when most people were beginning to think about sex and relationships, Tove was occupied with her fight for survival. It wasn't that she didn't feel the stirrings other people felt. But those feelings were unwelcome. She'd seen the lust in men's eyes and she knew what drove it. Their unwanted attention suppressed and cauterized her nascent longings. Forever, she thought.

Alar rescued her from a short, hopeless life. Through his irrepressible optimism and gentle prodding, he showed her life didn't have to be a brutish struggle. He couldn't erase her scars. But she began to believe as long as she was careful, as long as she walled off the feelings that made her vulnerable, she might have a life worth living.

Then she saw Brie and Elois in Adelbart's dungeon. The sight of the two women kissing tore a hole in her barriers and released feelings she thought had been stolen from her. She looked into Danu's smiling eyes. That kiss, as simple and brief as it was, was monumental. They kissed before. But that was always Danu's idea. This time, Tove kissed Danu. Out of her own desire. And it wasn't ugly or dirty. It was pure and joyful. And it could only have been possible with this gentle woman.

"You want to go hear a story?" Danu asked.

Chapter 26

I Chose to Fight

"They found the bodies."

Tove spun around to find Seele, her fellow fulling worker, standing behind her.

"Bodies?" she asked warily.

Seele glanced at Danu, then motioned for Tove to follow. He led her into a tree-lined street that lead from the square. While they walked, Tove watched Seele's back, mind racing. The only bodies that might be connected to her were the Imperial Rangers *Oss'stera* battled when they captured the Imperial supply caravan to Ka'tan the previous winter. They hid the bodies afterward to prevent anyone from finding them until summer. But how would Seele know she was connected with them?

When they were far enough from the festival to be alone, Seele turned around. When he saw Danu accompanied Tove, he nodded at her and said, "You sure you want her to hear this?"

"Danu," she said. "Maybe you should wait back at the square."

Danu's frown had hurt in it. She hesitated, then she said, "No, I'm staying."

Tove lifted a hand in supplication, but before she could speak, Danu interrupted her.

"Brie told me you had a past." She waved a hand at Seele. "I don't know the details, but I'm not afraid to hear them."

Tove took her hand and squeezed, thinking it may be the last innocent moment they shared. But she knew Danu would have to know the truth, eventually. "Okay." She leaned forward and murmured, "But whatever you think about this, give me a chance to explain." When Danu gave Tove a determined nod, Tove asked Seele, "Bodies?"

"Imperial Rangers. A whole company of rangers."

"Why would I care about that?" Tove asked.

"You let it slip at the fulling hut, about the supply caravan to Ka'tan," Seele said. "So, I asked around about this *Oss'stera.* You are rebels."

Tove squinted at the leafy branches of an elm behind Seele, trying to bring her conversations with her coworkers to mind. She didn't remember mentioning the supply caravan, and she was sure she denied *Oss'stera* were rebels. "Never said we were rebels."

"No, but there are whispers in Richeleau. People said *Oss'stera* was involved in a battle with some mercenaries at the fort." He paused. "I put two and two together. Everyone in Ka'tan knows the supply caravan last winter never arrived at the fort. It was you attacked it, wasn't it? Who else could it be?"

Tove glanced at Danu to gauge her reaction. She was staring intensely at Seele.

"How do you know?" Tove asked him. "About the bodies?"

"Overheard a couple of drunk Imps from the fort."

When the Empire discovered coal and other minerals in the mountains surrounding Ka'tan, they built a fortress north of the city. The Imps that garrisoned the fortress were there to oversee the slaves that worked the mines. Although people of all the Brochen castes might find themselves working the mines, most of the slaves were *Alle'oss.* Ka'tan owed much of their prosperity to the Imps in the fortress. Whether this sullied the citizens of Ka'tan or not was a topic of heated debate elsewhere in Argren, but Tove and her fellow rebels had very clear views on the matter. Tove hadn't made an issue of it because she had enough to deal with without alienating her few friends among the *Alle'oss* here. But the idea of Seele socializing with Imps set her on edge.

"From the fort?" Tove asked. Seele's eyes grew furtive, noticing the edge in her voice, but he nodded. "The Imps come into Ka'tan?"

"Not usually," Seele said slowly. "There's businesses up north, outside the city, that serve Imps."

"You frequent Imp taverns?"

Seele eyed her. "You…" He planted his hands on his hips and let his gaze drop. When he looked up, his face had hardened. "It's a complicated situation in Ka'tan. We didn't ask the Imps to put their fort here. But they're here. We've figured out how to live with that. You told me we don't know anything about you, so we don't have a right to judge. You should heed your own words."

Tove chewed her lips and lifted her gaze over his head. Despite his initial hostility, Seele had been her most steadfast companion in Ka'tan. Besides Hela. "You're right," she said and met his eyes. He opened his mouth, but Tove lifted a hand to forestall him. "These bodies… They know who's responsible?"

"No," Seele said. "You did a good job covering your tracks."

There was a question in his expression, but Tove only asked, "Why are you telling me this?"

"I've been thinking about what you said. About not being able to hide by staying meek. Wasn't right, what happened to my daughter's husband. I'm not… I want to contribute if I can. As long as it doesn't endanger my family."

Tove eyed him, remembering what Alar had always told her and her fellow rebels; you have to let people resist in any way they were comfortable. "They say what they're going to do? About the bodies?"

"They're appealing to the governor. Want him to investigate."

"That's good news," Tove said.

"It is?" Seele asked, surprised.

"Yeah." Alar told her he and the governor's assistant, Gerold, decided the best thing to do was to implicate the Union mercenaries for the death of the rangers. After the battle with the mercenaries at the fort in Richeleau, it was a plausible lie. "Hey, Seele. *Tok.*" She stuck out her arm.

"You're welcome," he said, grasping her forearm, sounding relieved. "I hear anything else, I'll let you know."

She watched him retreating down the street, then turned and froze. She had forgotten Danu was listening.

Danu was frowning at Seele with an intensity Tove hadn't seen on her face before. She looked at Tove and said, "Were you involved in that? Killing those rangers?"

Tove was about to offer an explanation, but she could see in Danu's expression, no words would suffice. Instead, she took Danu's hand and pulled her into motion. "Come with me," she said when Danu resisted. "I want to show you something. Afterwards, I'll explain."

Danu relented and allowed Tove to lead her away from the square. She remained silent as they headed north, crossing the plaza in front of the cathedral. A priest of the Vollen Church watched them from the open doors. They walked along the side of the cathedral, past the flying buttresses, then took the road that led north to the fort.

When they left the city limits, Danu asked, "Where are we going?" She pulled her hand free, but kept walking.

"I want to show you why we fight the Imps."

"Tove, I know why you would want to fight."

"But have you *seen* it?" Tove looked at Danu. "For yourself?"

Danu only hurried to keep up with Tove's pace.

A collection of buildings came into view, the businesses that catered to the Imps in the fort. Tove led Danu into the forest. They climbed the shoulder of a low mountain, then headed north, skirting the buildings.

"Where are we going?" Danu asked, her frustration coming through.

"Up here," Tove said and pointed north. She had seen the fort from the top of the pass when Brie brought her to Ka'tan. If she was right, their route would take them close enough that they would have a view of the fort and the slave camps.

Before they reached the plain on which the fort sat, they encountered a rocky promontory that jutted out over the road. "Let's try this," Tove said. She led Danu out until their view was no longer obstructed by trees. They had come farther than Tove thought. The stone walls of the fort were visible less than a league away on the floor of a wide valley. They were above the walls and could see guards patrolling along the top of the wall.

"That's the fort," Tove said. She pointed to the wooden stockade west of the fort. "That's where they keep the slaves."

They couldn't see much of the inside of the stockade, but as they watched, a line of men and women exited the gate and shuffled toward the mines in the mountains behind the fort. From the red and blond hues of their hair, Tove could tell most of them were *Alle'oss*, but there were also what Tove guessed were Styrians and a surprising number with the dark skin of Tituuns from the far north. Imps on horses rode alongside them. Even from a distance, the pitiable condition of the slaves was evident. Their clothes were little better than rags, and they shuffled slowly. One of the men stumbled. While others helped him to his feet, an Imp on horseback flogged them with a carriage whip.

"Dear Daga," Danu breathed.

"You didn't know they used slaves in the mines?"

"I… I heard they were criminals," Danu said, her head shaking slowly.

"The only crime these people are guilty of is being Brochen. But even if they are criminals, no one deserves to be treated like this." Tove turned to face Danu.

Tears beaded in Danu's lashes. "I didn't know," she said. Before Tove could respond, she said, "But I should have."

"Most people don't want to know. Not really," Tove said. "Knowing means you have to make a choice. Fight this evil or look the other way." Danu opened her mouth, but Tove put her fingers on her lips and looked into her eyes. "I understand why most people look the other way. It's safe and they don't want to risk what they have. The people they love. I don't know what I would have done if I had anything in my life worth protecting. But I didn't, and I chose to fight."

She pulled Danu close and spoke into her hair. "I belong to a rebel group called *Oss'stera*. It means our struggle in our language. I've done things I don't want to talk about. But I don't regret them."

"The rangers," Danu mumbled.

"We captured the supply caravan heading to this fort so we would have enough to eat in the winter."

"Did you kill anyone?"

"Yes." She squeezed her eyes shut against the memories. Not of the rangers she killed during the battle, but of the faces of the wounded rangers *Oss'stera* killed afterwards.

Danu pulled back and looked up at Tove. Her tears had overflowed her eyes and moistened her cheeks. She reached up and gently touched the scar on Tove's face. "You have someone who loves you now. Will you still fight?"

"Yes. But maybe not in the same way. The leader of our group, a man named Alar, wants to make *Oss'stera* like the Desulti. The Order protects themselves by being wealthy and powerful, not by killing. Not often, anyway. That's what we want. I can't say I'll never have to kill again, but Alar says killing Imps won't be enough to win our freedom, and I want to believe him."

Danu molded herself to Tove's body and whispered, "Thank you for showing me this."

***

Danu and Tove returned to Ka'tan in silence, their mood subdued. But as they sat, shoulder to shoulder, at a table, sharing the strawberry hand pie Tove saved, the festive mood and the effects of a mead slowly lifted their spirits. Tove watched Danu laughing at Brigid and Jens dancing.

"She's getting good," Danu said.

Tove brushed a pastry flake from Danu's lips and licked it from her finger.

Danu grinned and held up the last morsel of pie. "You want the last bite?"

"No, it's your first. You can have it."

"*Tok,*" Danu said, popped it into her mouth and grinned impishly.

Tove leaned back and scanned the crowd, searching out the black hair of the Desulti. Many of the women who accompanied them to Ka'tan were still at the festival, and they all seemed to be having a good time. Some of them were even mixing with *Alle'oss.*

"You're worried," Danu said.

"I *was* worried while we were away," Tove said. "But it looks like it's going to be okay. No fights. No arguments. Not so far, anyway."

"Not with the *Alle'oss* anyway," Danu said.

Tove followed her gaze. Gwynna and two other Desulti stood at the edge of the square near the road to Téama. Gwynna was scowling, gesturing, and speaking heatedly. The other two women turned away. Putting their heads together and giggling, they walked away, arm in arm. Gwynna watched them go, looking near tears, then she noticed Tove watching her. Her gaze lingered for a moment, then she turned away and disappeared down the road to Téama.

Before Tove could speculate about what that was about, Danu leaned in and whispered. "You ready to go home?"

Her breath in her ear sent a shiver down Tove's back.

***

They took their time, strolling, coming together, their shoulders brushing, then parting. Excited, Danu relived her first festival and pressed Tove about other festivals the *Alle'oss* celebrated. Tove answered vaguely, too enthralled by Danu to focus on the conversation. She was fascinated by the way Danu walked, by the way her small hands punctuated her words, by her face, an ever changing window into her thoughts. Gone was the timid woman who seemed to sink in on herself when other people were around. Feeling Danu had granted her a rare privilege, Tove felt a deep affection growing inside her.

By the time they passed the outskirts of Téama, the sun was dipping toward the horizon. Tove stopped at the spot where Danu usually left when they went to Ka'tan. She waited awkwardly, unsure what Danu expected. Should she kiss her goodnight?

"Why are we stopping?" Danu asked.

Tove pointed down the street. "Don't you live down there?"

"I do," Danu said, nodding. "But my roommate is probably home."

Tove stared at her, sure she was missing something.

"*You* don't have a roommate," Danu said.

"Oh! Oh! Right. You, uh, want to go to my room?"

***

Tove opened the door and hurried over to light the lamp before Danu closed the door. The dark safely at bay, she turned to face Danu. She watched her removing her boots and staring curiously around the room. Tove hopped on one foot, hurrying to remove her boots. When she had two bare feet safely on the floor, Danu startled her by stepping closer.

"I've never…" Tove hesitated, her breath coming too fast to allow her to speak properly.

"I have," Danu murmured, moving close enough that Tove breathed her intoxicating scent. Danu gazed into Tove's eyes, then her lips gave a small twist and she glanced to the side. "Once." Her lips quirked up, and her eyes opened wide. "It was exciting. Awkward. Embarrassing." The frown Tove found so intriguing flickered across her face, then she grew solemn. "You don't have to feel embarrassed with me. We can go slow." She leaned in and brushed Tove's lips with her own. "I just want to feel your skin next to mine."

Tove took the tail of Danu's shirt between her fingertips and searched Danu's face.

Danu smiled and lifted her arms, allowing Tove to lift her shirt over her head and drop it to the floor.

Tove pushed gently, urging Danu back so she could see her.

Danu let her look. Clasping her hands behind her back, she grinned and twisted slowly back and forth. "Now you."

Tove removed the belt that held her shirt tight, then helped Danu lift her shirt over her head. She went to pull Danu close, but Danu put her hands on Tove's shoulders and held her off.

"Wait," she whispered. Tove watched, fascinated, as Danu's fingers hovered just above her shoulders. Feather light brushes sent a shiver through Tove's body, then the feathery touches trailed down her arms, leaving goosebumps in their wake. When her fingers reached Tove's elbows, Danu bent forward and planted small kisses across Tove's chest.

Tove wanted to return Danu's attention, to make her feel what Danu was making her feel, but she was frozen, unsure what to do. Danu pulled back and gazed solemnly at her. Her hand pulled at the laces of Tove's pants.

Tove's hand clamped on Danu's wrist. Her muscles locked protectively, lest she embarrass herself by backing away. She gasped, but couldn't draw breath into her lungs. Unable to take Danu's alarmed expression, she squeezed her eyes shut. "I'm sor —"

"Sssh," Danu whispered. Her other hand caressed Tove's cheek, cool against Tove's flush.

Tove forced her eyes open and focused on Danu's serene eyes to find an anchor amidst the turmoil swirling her thoughts.

"You're safe," Danu whispered. "Only when you're ready." She pulled gently to release her hand from Tove's grip, then stepped close to nuzzle Tove's neck, her breasts brushing Tove's.

"Can… can we lie down?" Tove whispered between pants. "In the bed."

Danu grinned and lay down, edging over to the wall to make room.

Tove gazed down at her, the sight of her gentle smile nudging the fear aside and unlocking her clenched body. Setting aside a burden she became so used to, she no longer noticed it, she sighed and lowered herself onto her side, facing Danu.

"Oh," Danu said with a small frown. "What's wrong?" She touched Tove's cheek.

"Nothing is wrong," Tove said. "Not anymore."

Danu placed her hand on the side of Tove's head and kissed the scar on her cheek. She pulled back, her lips wet with Tove's tears. When she saw Tove's smile, she grinned.

Chapter 27

Gwynna Tattles

Tove's eyes opened to the lamp on the table beside her bed. The wick was turned down, but there was enough light to keep the darkness away. "I need to get a room with a window," she murmured. Rolling onto her back, she put her hand on the empty space Danu occupied the night before. It wasn't warm. Without sunlight, she had no way to know what time it was.

She lifted the blanket and looked at herself. She was naked. Letting the blanket fall, she stretched lazily, letting her eyes slide shut and replaying the previous night. It was a night for many firsts, most importantly the awakening of emotions she thought amputated by men's brutality. Tenderness, vulnerability, desire. She gazed up at the ceiling, hands behind her head, letting her mind drift.

The door opening brought her to sit upright. Danu entered, a plate piled with breakfast. She grinned when she saw Tove awake. Tove pulled the blanket around her waist as Danu sat cross-legged on the bed and placed the plate between them.

"Good morning, sleepyhead," Danu said and bit down on a slice of buttered toast.

"What time is it?" Tove asked and picked up an unfamiliar wedge of yellow fruit.

"Just after the eighth bell."

"I'm late," Tove said. She held up the fruit between two fingers. "What is this?"

Danu grinned around a mouthful of bread. "Pineapple. It comes from some islands in the middle of the Eastern Sea. We almost never get it, but it's sooo good." She put her hand to her mouth and giggled at Tove's expression. "Try it. It won't bite you."

Tove put the fruit into her mouth, chewed and grinned. "That is good," she said and took another piece.

"Brigid saved some for us."

Tove watched Danu chewing, feeling her face warm. When Danu noticed her grin, she swallowed and said, "Your first time."

"Your second," Tove said.

"Sooo much better than the first time," Danu said, and blushed.

"I…" Tove had always admired Alar's way of putting his feelings into words. In this moment, maybe one of the most important of her life, she had no words for what she felt. But it didn't matter. Danu understood.

"Me too," Danu said. She got to her knees, leaned over the plate and kissed Tove, her lips lingering, then she sat back and grinned mischievously.

Stuffing a third piece of pineapple into her mouth, Tove rose and rummaged around on the floor for her clothes. "I was supposed to meet Hela at the eighth bell."

"How long are you going to be gone?" Danu asked and bit down on a piece of pineapple.

"Three days at the most," Tove said and sat to pull on her boots. "If we get lucky, we'll be back sooner."

"That reminds me. Brigid told me to tell you she wants a boar."

Buckling her belt over her shirt, Tove asked, "A boar? What for?"

"Um," Danu said with a silly grin. "Brigid *does* work in the dining hall."

"I know, but they never buy anything from me."

"She said bring it by after the sixteenth bell. That's when her shift starts."

"A boar it is. I've been meaning to bug Hela about them," Tove said, gathering up some breakfast to take with her. She bent over and kissed Danu's lips, sticky from pineapple juice. "Take care."

"You take care," Danu said. "Out there with all the wild beasts."

"I'll tell Hela what you called him," Tove said as she left.

***

"A boar, huh?" Hela asked. "Okay." He looked away, considering. "We'll head west to lower altitudes." He hefted his pack and bow, but before he started walking, Tove stopped him.

"That murtair been following us," she said. "What was her name?"

"Laoise."

"Hey, Laoise," Tove shouted. "Come on out."

A moment later, the murtair appeared from behind a tangled juniper. When she neared, she said, "Thank Daga."

"Not easy to stay close and unseen in the mountains, is it?" Hela asked with a grin.

"You've no idea."

"Nessa got you following me?" Tove asked.

Laoise shrugged. "Why do I have to be doing it for someone else? Can't I have my own reasons?"

"You watchin over me out of the goodness of your heart?"

"A murtair can't have a heart?"

Tove met Hela's eye. "Fair enough," she said. "For now. In the meantime, if you can keep up and stay quiet, there's no reason for you to be sneaking around after us."

***

Tove studied Laoise through a curtain of smoke, while Hela pinched the meat on the legs of the turkey hanging above the fire.

"Not yet," he said and returned his attention to honing his knife.

Noticing Tove watching her, Laoise said, "Go ahead."

"What?"

"You obviously have something on your mind," the murtair said. "Spit it out."

Tove stretched a leg out and shrugged. "You and Cianna. You're together."

Laoise gaped at Tove, then laughed.

"What?"

"Nothing. Just… that wasn't what I was expecting."

"So?" Tove asked. "You and Cianna."

Laoise nodded.

"It's Cianna's got you keeping an eye on me," Tove said, narrowing her eyes and pointing her knife at the murtair.

Laoise's grin softened. "Why would you say that?"

"She went out of her way to help me when I got here. She said they couldn't hurt her because her partner was Murtair. You following me around." Tove shrugged. "Not hard putting it together."

Laoise shook her head and worked the straps that held her shirt tight.

"Was her who organized all my bodyguards, too," Tove said.

"That's Danu's doing."

"Danu?" When Laoise gave her a knowing grin, Tove glanced at Hela and said, "How did that quiet woman make so many friends?"

Hela and Laoise both laughed.

"You have any idea why Nessa and Siofra voted to allow me into the Order?" Tove asked.

If Laoise hadn't relaxed over the course of the day, Tove wouldn't have known she was hiding something, but it was the only conclusion she could draw when the impassive Murtair mask wiped her smile away. "I don't," was all she said.

Tove caught Hela's eye and let it go. Later, as they satisfied their hunger, the relaxed feeling returned. It was clear that people in the Order were using her presence for their own ends, but it wasn't so obvious that all of them meant her harm. That would have to be good enough for now.

Tove opened her door and found Danu and Meya standing in the hall, grinning from ear to ear. "What?" Tove asked and looked down the hall in both directions. It was a day after she returned with Hela, a large boar on a travois.

"You have to come with us," Danu said.

"I just woke up," Tove said.

"Sorry," Danu said, taking Tove by the arm and pulling her into the hall. "Refusal is not allowed."

Sighing, Tove reached back and pulled the door closed.

Danu looped her arm in Tove's and they followed Meya down the hall.

"What's going on?"

"You'll see," Danu said. "Don't worry. It's a good thing."

Meya led them at an angle across the plaza. Lost in thoughts about her most recent trip into the mountains, Tove hadn't noticed how deserted the plaza was until familiar music drifted from the street that led to the dining hall.

"What's going on?" Tove asked.

"So distrustful," Meya said.

The merry clamor of a festival was identifiable before it came into view. When they rounded a corner and she saw the crowd, she stopped. Meya threw her a smile, but kept walking. Danu took her hand.

"What's this?" Tove asked.

"It's our first festival. A Desulti festival," Danu said with a smile. "In Téama." She leaned in close and took Tove's hand in both of hers. "Look. Some *Alle'oss* came from Ka'tan to help us celebrate."

It was true. Among the mostly black haired women were flashes of blond and red hair. "Why?" was all Tove managed to say.

"Come on," Danu said and pulled Tove into motion.

The tables had been removed from the dining hall and arranged in rows in the middle of the street. As she neared, a familiar aroma reached her.

"Is that…"

"Yes," Danu said. They edged over to the side of the street. Among some of the women who waved, she recognized some who accompanied them to the festival in Ka'tan. Seele was sitting at a table with her other fulling coworkers. They waved to her, but they also called Danu's name.

"Things are much friendlier at the fulling hut," Danu said as she returned their waves. "We talked things over."

Tove turned and looked toward the entrance of the dining hall and saw a familiar figure toiling over a large kettle.

"Tye," Tove said.

The big man looked up. When he saw who it was, his scowl disappeared. He ladled some of the contents of the kettle into two bowls and handed them to Tove and Danu.

Tove held it under her nose and returned his grin. "Boar stew."

"Ayuh," he said. He leaned in and said, "Brigid's and Meya's doing. They came to me with the idea for this festival. Wanted me to share the recipe." He straightened and scoffed. "Told them I couldn't do that, but I'd come cook up a batch." He gestured to the mixed crowd. "Sort of grew from there." He leaned in again. "This is all your doing. Got people talking. Broke down some barriers. Course, you'll remember it was my idea, the first day we met." He winked, straightened, and looked out over the crowd. "It's a start, anyway."

As Tove and Danu found a table, musicians took up their instruments and began a lively jig. Tove and Danu were sitting when people rose, as if they had been waiting, and made their way to the open space in front of the musicians. They watched the mixed group of Desulti and *Alle'oss* dancing while enjoying their stew.

"I think they're finally getting it," Tove said and gestured to the dancers.

"Brigid and Jens have been teaching them," Danu said.

"Hello Tove."

Tove looked up to find Cianna standing with a familiar figure. Elois only nodded a greeting, but the smile she gave Tove was the friendliest gesture she ever showed her.

"It makes me happy to see you doing so well," Cianna said. "Hela tells me very good things about you." She gestured around to the festival. "In fact, there are many who have good things to say."

"*Tok*," Tove said.

"*Aurina sha.*"

"Shame Laoise can't enjoy the festival," Tove said, adding a small smirk.

"Yes, well, crowds, even festive crowds, aren't much to Laoise's liking," Cianna said. She leaned over close enough she could speak quietly. "She is rather tired of the mountains, though."

"Tell her to come back into town," Tove said. "Don't need a bodyguard in the mountains. Besides, I have Hela hovering over me like a mother hen."

"Ah, well, my partner has other reasons for avoiding Téama at the moment," Cianna said, and straightened. "Won't be long now, I suspect." She waved to Danu, and she and Elois made their way down the aisle between the tables.

Tove watched Cianna greeting people, stopping to whisper to some.

"She's very popular," Danu said.

"Yeah," Tove said, tearing her eyes away from Cianna. "You want to dance?"

"Think you can keep up?"

A half-hour later, faces flushed, they left the dance floor. After purchasing ales, they found a table with seats available. When Tove looked to the person sitting beside her, she found Gwynna looking back at her. Before an impassive mask wiped it away, Tove was sure she saw anger in her expression.

"Hello, Gwynna," Tove said.

Gwynna glanced past Tove to Danu then said, "Hello."

Ever since Gwynna accompanied her to Ka'tan, the riddle of this woman had come into Tove's mind often. When she came to Tove after the humiliating initiation ceremony, she showed her such tenderness. But her reactions to Tove since ranged from indifference to hatred. It was like she was two people. Danu was involved in another conversation, so when Gwynna looked away, Tove cast about for some way to get her to open up.

"Brigid said you had it tough. Before you came," Tove said and winced inwardly when Gwynna's face froze. "I mean, it's none of my business, but —"

"It *is* none of your business," Gwynna snapped.

But she didn't leave, so Tove tried again. "Where are you from?"

Gwynna's lips pursed. Her eyes cut to Tove, then away. "West of Maintz. On a farm near a village called Hammon."

Encouraged, Tove asked, "You're a farm girl. What sort of farm?"

"Pigs, chickens," Gwynna said. Her body relaxed the smallest amount. "We had cows for a time." A small smile hovered at the edge of her expression. "I had to help birth a calf once. Pa and my brother were too drunk…" The smile fled before it could take root. "But then my Pa…"

Desperate to retrieve the connection that was just out of reach, Tove asked, "Did you like it, taking care of the animals?"

Gwynna nodded absently. Her face crumpled, the tears pooling in her eyes overflowing.

Tove touched her shoulder. It was the lightest of caresses. A reaching out to someone in obvious pain. But the effect was shocking.

Gwynna jerked away. The stricken expression she turned on Tove pushed Tove back.

"What —" Tove started. Gwynna lurched up and fought to free herself from the bench. She took a step backward, eyes wild, a hand up as if warding Tove off. Then awareness of her surroundings came into her eyes. She glanced around at the people watching her and seemed to settle in on herself. Her shoulders rounded and her arms crossed over her chest..

Then Danu appeared at her side. She put her arm around Gwynna's shoulders and whispered to her as she led her away. When they neared the edge of the crowd, Danu threw Tove an apologetic smile over her shoulder.

Tove watched them retreating, heart racing. When she lost sight of them, she faced forward and noticed her untouched ale. Taking a sip, she tried to ignore the stares.

"She had a very difficult childhood," Brigid said as she took Danu's place.

"Didn't we all," Tove said and immediately felt ashamed.

"Yes," Brigid said. "Many of us did. But some of us are more sensitive than others. Gwynna is a gentle soul."

Tove sighed. "I'm sorry. I was just trying to understand her. All I did was touch her shoulder."

"It's not your fault, Tove," Brigid said, laying a hand on Tove's shoulder. "It's a simple gesture. You didn't know. It's not the first time Gwynna reacted like that and, unfortunately, it won't be the last. Just give her time and don't push it. Don't let it spoil the festival for you."

Tove looked at her.

Brigid smiled and gestured. "We thought about naming the festival after you." She leaned in and said, "But Danu said you would hate that."

"Hate what?" Danu asked as she dropped into the seat previously occupied by Gwynna. She reached across Tove and said, "Give me my ale."

"Is she okay?" Tove asked.

"No," Danu said. "But it's not because of anything you did. She's had a hard time making any sort of connections."

"I feel so bad," Tove said.

"She'll be okay," Danu said. "Just give her some time and be gentle."

***

Lyssa looked up when Cara opened her office door and leaned in.

"Gwynna wishes to speak to you," Cara said.

"Gwynna?"

Cara glanced over her shoulder, then whispered, "The laundry woman. She's crying her eyes out here in my office." Speaking in a normal voice, she said, "She says she has something to tell you about Tove."

Lyssa tensed. None of the Baird and Burne women she and Cara enlisted to gather dirt on women agitating for the *l'oss* reported anything of consequence. At least nothing the gendarmes could act on. It was as if whoever was causing the trouble knew what Lyssa's spies were up to.

Then the laundry woman shows up. It was probably nothing, a cry for attention, but she hadn't had any luck with others, so with a sigh, she set her quill aside. "Send her in."

Gwynna followed Cara into the office. She was indeed crying. Tears streaked her face, but she had a determined set to her jaw. She wiped her nose with the back of her hand and came to a stop in front of Lyssa's desk.

"Oh, dear," Lyssa said, pasting a concerned frown on her face. "What is this?"

"They're having a festival," Gwynna blurted.

Lyssa threw a questioning glance at Cara, but only received a shrug. "The... *Alle'oss?*"

"No!" Gwynna said. "Desulti and *l'oss*, all mixed together." She pointed. "Over in front of the dining hall." When Lyssa didn't react right away, Gwynna added, "Right now!"

"A festival in Téama? With *l'oss* and Desulti together?" Lyssa asked.

"Yes!" Gwynna said. She threw a hand out. "They — Danu, Brigid, and... others — went to a festival in Ka'tan with Tove a few weeks ago. They decided to have a Desulti festival, and they invited *l'oss* to it." She stopped, her breath coming fast and shallow. "It was Tove. She didn't do the festival, but they did it *for* her."

It finally sank in. "Cara," Lyssa said. "Have Gwynna take you to see this festival. Make a list of everyone in attendance."

"Yes, Mistress."

Before Gwynna turned away, she asked with a hopeful expression, "Is this what you wanted?" When Lyssa looked blankly at her, she said, "You said you would help me if I told you who was helping Tove."

"Oh," Lyssa said. She stood and came around the desk. As she ushered Gwynna toward the door, she said, "Yes, you did well. As soon as we take care of this little matter, we will see that you are… helped."

Gwynna frowned, but Lyssa gave her a small shove through the door, then closed it after her. A festival with *I'oss* and Desulti together? She had seen what the *I'oss* called festivals and dismissed them as rustic bacchanalia. She knew the lower castes couldn't be expected to have the same refined tastes as proper Volloch, but that they would stoop to eating hand pies and dancing like Brochen… She gave her head a hard shake. What was happening to the Order? Standing, frozen, in the middle of her office, images of Desulti women brazenly cavorting with *Alle'oss* wouldn't leave her head.

Slowly, she regained control of her thoughts. Returning to her desk, she dropped into her chair. Once again, she misread the situation. As ludicrous as it seemed, it appeared many of the lower castes accepted the *I'oss.* Tove was like an infection, spreading to the Baird and Burne and making them *I'oss* like her.

It had gone too far. Regardless of the risks, Tove had to go. She would deal with the rest of the traitors after she was gone.

Chapter 28

Ragan Keeps Her Secrets

"You sure about this?" Hela asked Tove.

"No," Tove said. "But something is going on in there. Something I want to know about." She and Hela were among the trees that pressed up against the back of the park, across from Lyssa's manor.

"What is it you saw again?" Hela asked.

"Lyssa fired all her servants months ago, but I saw someone up there when Lyssa wasn't home." She pointed to the window on the top floor. "She's hiding someone. Someone the Inquisition is interested in." She didn't mention the baby because she wasn't in the mood to explain Ragan.

"You saw brothers? In Téama?"

Tove nodded. "In the middle of the night." Before Hela could continue, Tove cut him off. "And yes, I'm sure they were brothers. I recognized one of them." She held Hela's gaze until he looked away.

"Right," he said. "Sorry."

They watched Lyssa enter her house for her midday meal. An hour later, the sun was past its zenith when Hela said, "She'll be leaving soon. You have any idea how you're getting in?"

"Thought I'd try the door," Tove said and shrugged. "Might get lucky."

"Worth a try, I guess. You realize if she's holding someone prisoner, someone is in there guarding them," Hela said, sounding skeptical. Before Tove could respond, he pointed to the street. "There she is."

They watched Lyssa exit the gate and set off down the street. When she turned down a side street, Tove said, "Keep watch."

As she left their cover and crossed the park, Hela called, "For what? What do I do if I see someone?"

Ignoring him, Tove glanced both ways on the street. Seeing only a few *Alle'oss* servants not paying attention, she hurried across the street to the gate, pulled it open and slipped through the narrow gap. Worried someone was watching from inside the house, she sprinted to the front door. It was locked, so she ran in a crouch toward the side of the house. Slowing in the narrow space between the house and the wall, she made her way toward the back of the house, peeking in windows blocked by curtains.

In the backyard, a brick patio pressed up against the back of the house. Debris from a garden, which hadn't seen the attention of a gardener in a long time, littered the bricks. She crept along the back of the house, peeking into windows, until she reached the door and tried the knob. It was locked. "Couldn't be that lucky," she murmured. She stared at the lock, then gave her head a shake. There was no help for it. Casting about, she found a loose brick and worked it free. She pressed her ear to a pane of glass in the door. Hearing nothing, she hefted the brick and struck the pane just above the lock. The glass shattered, the brick slipped out of her grasp, fell through the window and thunked on the floor.

Wincing, she reached in, twisted the lock, and pulled the door open. She crossed a pantry and entered a kitchen. Hurried footsteps came from what looked like a servant's staircase that entered the room next to a hearth. Dashing around a table in the center of the room, her hand hovered over the fireplace poker for a moment, then she snatched up the lighter ash shovel and pressed herself against the wall beside the door to the stairs, just in time.

She had half a moment to recognize the white uniform before she swung the shovel at the side of the man's head. He fell to his knees. She drew the shovel back and swung again. It hit the back of his head with a dull clunk, dropping him onto his stomach.

She raised the shovel again and stood above him, watching for movement and listening. The house was silent. Lowering the shovel, she bent down and peered at the man's face hopefully, but she didn't recognize him. Pressing her fingers to his neck, she felt a strong, steady pulse. "Oh, well."

She tied his hands and feet with strips of cloth ripped from a curtain. Then, with the shovel resting on her shoulder, she crept up the servant's stairs. She had seen motion in the window on the top floor, so she continued past the second floor landing without stopping. Encountering no more brothers, she arrived at the top floor and paused, twisting sweaty hands on the shovel. When she was ready, she eased the door open a crack and peeked in.

The room took up nearly the entire top floor of the house. Dormers defined the space, creating nooks on three walls. A large four-poster bed sat in the center of the room. Seeing no one, she eased the door open and entered silently. At first, she was disappointed to find the room deserted, but then she noticed a woman rising from a rocking chair tucked away in the dormer at the front of the house.

The woman barely reacted to Tove's appearance. "You're *Alle'oss*," she said.

Tove studied her as she approached. There didn't appear to be anything special about her. Her long black hair looked as if she barely ran a brush through it after rising. She was pale and wore a simple dress and slippers. "You're Volloch," she said.

"What are you doing here?" the woman asked.

"Is there more than one brother in the house?" Tove asked.

"No," the woman said, eying the shovel on Tove's shoulder. "Did you kill him?"

"No," Tove said. "He's tied up in the kitchen."

The woman sank into the chair. "Good. He's a good man." Smiling at Tove's snort, she said, "People are often more complicated than they appear. Not all brothers are evil."

"Maybe not, but they got to prove it if they aren't." Tove sat in the chair across from the woman and let the business end of the shovel rest on the floor. "Who are you?"

"It would be best if that remained a secret." She let her head fall back and looked out the window.

"Okay," Tove said. "Lyssa is keeping you prisoner for the Inquisition. Why?"

"I'm an embarrassment," the woman said with a soft chuckle that contained more melancholy than humor.

Tove watched her gazing out the window, trying to put the pieces of the riddle together. "It was your baby," she said. "The one Ragan had."

The woman's head snapped around. "You saw my son?"

"I did," Tove said. She watched her face closely when she said, "With Ragan." The woman's face relaxed, and her head returned to rest on the back of the chair. "She's taking him somewhere to keep him safe for you."

"Did she tell you where?" the woman asked, suddenly tense again.

"Ragan keeps her secrets."

The woman relaxed. "Yes. She's keeping him safe."

"From the Inquisition," Tove said. The woman didn't respond. "So, why is the Inquisition interested in him?"

"I can't tell you that," she said. "Another secret Ragan asked me to keep."

"You don't seem too sussed that I broke into Lyssa's house," Tove said.

The woman's chuckle held some humor this time. "You're Tove." When she saw Tove's surprise, she said, "Ragan told me to expect you."

"She tell you why I came?"

The woman's smile softened. "She said the riddle of the Inquisition visiting Lyssa would be too much for you to resist."

"And she told you to keep it all a secret."

"Oh, no. Not all of it," the woman said. "The Inquisition does want my son. The why isn't any of your business." She looked away again and spoke softly. "Fortunately, Ragan beat them to it."

Tove looked out the window, pressing her lips in a tight line. Why did that witch always make things so complicated? She was right there in Tove's room. She could have told her whatever she wanted Tove to know. Tove eyed the woman and tried again. "So, Lyssa was supposed to keep you here until your son is born, then hand him over to the Inquisition. But your son is someone Ragan wants to protect."

The woman gazed out the window without responding.

"You're a woman who obviously needs sanctuary. Lyssa has violated everything the Order stands for. Why would she do that?"

The woman smiled and looked at Tove, settling herself, as if she were waiting for Tove to ask that question. "She wanted something from them. Something only the emperor can grant. She plans to bring the Desulti back into the Empire."

Tove stared at her. "How?"

"The Order will be registered as a merchant's guild. The Murtair will be disbanded. The Council will be moved to Kartok," she said. "It's all in the works. They've already broken ground on the new compound in Kartok."

"The Order would never stand for that."

"What can anyone do to stop it?" the woman said. "Lyssa owns the Ruling Council. She's banished most of her opposition from Téama. She plans to bring soldiers from the fort to keep order when she makes the announcement. Some women out in the world doing the Order's business may object, but for most of them, it will be business as usual. Their lives won't change. At first, anyway. Eventually, they'll get used to the idea." She sighed. "At least, that's what Lyssa expects to happen."

"How can she trust men like Hoerst and the emperor?"

"She doesn't. Lyssa isn't a stupid woman." She gazed out the window again. "The emperor's coffers are nearly empty and his war with the Kaileuk is not going well. Lyssa has promised to finance his war." Tove stared at her, stunned. "It's not as farfetched as it sounds. The Order will be the wealthiest guild in the Empire. She's counting on the fact the war won't drag on too long. A vain hope, I fear."

Tove couldn't think of a response. Though she had given up her initial dream of a safe utopia as naïve, the life she was building with Danu, Brigid, Meya and others was something she never imagined she would have. And Lyssa was going to throw all that away. Ragan's last words to her came back to her. "Besides, you have enough to be about here." Those words took on an altogether different meaning now. Tove smirked and shook her head. The witch had her fingers in everything. "Ragan tell you to tell me this?"

The woman smiled.

"Why?" Tove asked. "What does she expect me to do about it?"

"Like you said, the woman has her secrets." The woman nodded to the window. "He with you?"

Tove stood and looked out the window. Hela was standing next to a massive spruce, waving his arms frantically. She had taken two steps toward the servant's stairs when she stopped and turned back. "I can take you with me."

"If I leave, I'll never see my son again," she said.

"How do you know you'll see him again if you stay?"

"Ragan assured me it's the only way I *will* see him." They heard the front door open, followed by a man's shouts from the kitchen. "You better go."

Tove hesitated, then crossed the room and listened at the door to the servant's stairs. When she heard footsteps on the stairs, she hurried across the room to another door, yanked it open, and found the main staircase. With one more glance at the woman, she hurried down the stairs, grateful for the soft soles of her moccasin boots. She was crossing the second floor landing when she heard the door from the servant's stairs in the attic room open. She flew down the stairs.

Crossing the foyer on the main floor, she caught motion out of the corner of her eye. Ducking her head, she burst through the front door, which Lyssa left ajar. She sprinted toward the gate, then crossed the street and entered the park. Hela saw her coming and led her deeper into the park, then into the forest.

"What happened?" Hela asked when they finally came to a stop.

Too winded to speak, she rested her hands on her hips, put her head back and concentrated on pulling air into her lungs.

"What happened?" Hela asked again.

"Found her," she said. "She wouldn't tell me who she was, but she's someone important enough the Inquisition hid here to have her baby."

"Baby?"

Tove told him everything, leaving out as much about Ragan as she could.

When she was done, he stared at her for a long moment, then gazed back toward the street.

"Who do we tell?" Tove asked. "Nessa?"

He seemed to come back from his thoughts. "Nessa. No. I wouldn't trust her."

"Then who?"

He shrugged. "Siofra, maybe, but she's not in Téama." He met her eyes. "She say when this is all supposed to happen?"

Tove shook her head. "But Lyssa'll know someone was in her house. Whatever she was planning, it might change now."

"If Lyssa brings soldiers from the fort, the situation could get out of control." He eyed her. "You think this woman would give you away?"

"Maybe."

"Right," he said. "You go collect your things. I'll gather provisions. We'll head up into the mountains. Get you out of harm's way and find Laoise. She'll know better than we do who to talk to."

***

Hela left Tove just before they entered the plaza. She took side streets to skirt the plaza and approached her building from an unusual direction. Stopping on a street corner a block away, she watched the door for a half hour, but saw no one enter or leave. No one was waiting in the hall, either. In her room, she lit the lamp, then closed the door, stood in the center of the room and gazed at the familiar space. It wasn't much, but it had become a home with Danu's help. She didn't know what Lyssa would do, but she had a feeling she wouldn't be returning.

She gathered her few belongings and was stuffing everything into her pack when someone knocked. She whirled around and stared at the door. She wouldn't expect the gendarmes to knock. Danu just entered without knocking. It could be Hela.

She drew her knife and held it behind her back, then eased the door open a crack. It was Gwynna. Pulling the door open, Tove glanced to the sides but found no one else with her.

"Gwynna," she said.

"I'm supposed to get you," Gwynna said. The flat tone didn't match the pained smile on her face.

Tove hesitated, trying to meet Gwynna's eyes, but she looked away. "Did Hela send you?"

There was the slightest hesitation before Gwynna's smile widened and she said, "Yeah, Hela sent me." Her eyes flicked to Tove's pack and bow on her bed. "He said you're going hunting."

"Why did he send you?"

"I don't know, do I?" she said, a flash of irritation in her eyes. "He said he was busy. He was… meeting someone."

Tove returned the knife to its sheath. Gwynna's eyes widened when she saw it.

"Hold on," Tove said and retrieved her belongings.

"Why do you need that?" Gwynna asked, eying the bow in Tove's hand.

"We're going hunting, right?"

Gwynna hesitated, then nodded and walked down the hall. Tove caught up with her as they exited the building. "I'm sorry about the other day. At the festival," she said.

"No, it was my fault," Gwynna said brusquely.

"I don't know if fault has anything to do with it," Tove said, trying not to let her frustration show. She had no idea how to talk to this woman. They entered the plaza and Gwynna led them to the left. "Where are we going?"

"The quartermaster's," Gwynna said. "That's where Hela said to meet."

Just before they left the plaza, Tove looked toward the street she usually took to meet Hela. She stopped. She should just go. Find Laoise if Hela wasn't there.

"Are you coming?" Gwynna had stopped and was looking back at her, a deep frown on her face. "Hela said you would want to talk to the person he's meeting. He said it was very important."

"Who is it?"

Gwynna shrugged. "I don't know. He just said it was important."

Maybe Hela had decided who they could talk to about Lyssa's plans. When Tove started walking again, Gwynna turned and strode away.

Chapter 29

Lyssa Acts

"Are you sure she will come this way?" Lyssa asked. They chose the street because it was lined with rarely used warehouses and old offices. The sun was approaching the tops of the buildings, leaving the treelined street in premature dusk. Lyssa, Tish and three gendarmes hid out of sight in the narrow space between two buildings.

"No," Tish said. "But this is the way I told that simpleton, Gwynna, to bring her."

Lyssa had only gotten a glimpse of the woman who broke into her house, but it was enough to see the auburn hair. It had to be Tove. It was the final straw. The unmitigated gall of the *l'oss*, breaking into her house. Lyssa had stormed up to the attic and confronted her prisoner. The woman denied telling Tove anything, but her smug grin revealed her lie. Only the brother's intervention prevented Lyssa from slapping the grin from her face.

She didn't know for sure what the woman told Tove, but she couldn't take any chances. If Tove knew her plan and told anyone, the village would explode. She already sent Cara to alert the commander of the garrison at the fort. In a few hours, a century of Imperial infantry would be waiting outside Téama. Just in case.

"Shhh," Tish said. "They're coming."

A moment later, Lyssa heard the scuff of two pairs of feet on the cobbles. There were no voices. Tish put a hand on Lyssa's arm and eased her backward, behind the gendarmes. They pressed themselves against the wall of the building and waited, tense.

Tove and Gwynna came into view. Before they reached the ideal spot for their ambush the idiot, Gwynna looked in their direction. Tove glanced at Gwynna, then followed her gaze and caught sight of them. Too late.

Tish and the gendarmes burst out of the shadows. Tove ran, but Tish was on her before she could gain any speed. The big woman kicked Tove's trailing foot, sending her sprawling. Before she could rise, the others were on her, pinning her arms behind her back. They lifted her onto her feet and set to tying her hands.

Lyssa hoped to see her cower, but when Tove spotted Lyssa, she barely reacted. Lyssa approached her, fighting to match the *l'oss's* calm, but unable to keep her glee at bay.

"Laoise will know what you're doing," Tove said and nodded back the way she came.

Lyssa hesitated. She managed to stop herself from looking over her shoulder, but a sneer betrayed her, before she pulled a haughty mask across it. "Laoise doesn't keep watch over you in the village." She took a step forward until she was towering over the shorter woman. "You broke into my house. What did —" Sudden, searing pain ripped an undignified screech from her and sent her stumbling backwards.

Tove had kicked her in the shin. The *l'oss* grinned before Tish's fist spun her head around. When she turned back, blood from her nose tinted the teeth in her smile pink. She spat and said, "Amateurs."

Lyssa took a limping step toward her, before she reined in her temper. Keeping out of range of Tove's feet, she threw a hand toward Gwynna and said, "You think you're tough, little *l'oss*, but thanks to your friend, we know what will soften you up. You'll tell me everything I want to know after a week or two in the dark."

For the first time, Tove's bravado wavered. But the expression she threw at Gwynna was more disappointed than fearful. "What's your plan?" she asked when she looked at Lyssa. "I go missing, a lot of people are going to ask questions."

"Let them," Lyssa said. "After a couple of weeks, they'll find your body up in the mountains. Another tragic hunting accident." Lyssa chuckled. "People can ask all the questions they like. They can't prove anything." She allowed herself a smug smile when Tove didn't come back with a clever quip. "Take her to Building B," she said to Tish.

Dismissing the troublesome *I'oss*, Lyssa spun around to find Gwynna standing in her way.

"We got her," Gwynna said.

"Excuse me?"

"We got her," Gwynna said again. "Tove."

"Oh," Lyssa said. "Indeed, we did. You were a big help, Gwynna. Thank you." She stepped sideways to get around the woman, but Gwynna spoke again.

"You're going to see I get a better job, right?"

"Yes, of course."

"Of course. You say that every time, but you never do anything."

Lyssa couldn't say whether it was the words or the insolent expression on her face, but the anger she'd been holding at bay surged, taking her by surprise. "How dare you question me, you little Baird," she snarled. "You'll do the job we give you and be happy. You're lucky we gave you a place to escape your pathetic little life." She drew herself up and took a deep breath. It was beneath her to allow this woman to draw her into such a display. She looked down at Gwynna and said, "Now, run along and let your betters do their jobs."

Without a glance back, she strode off, fighting to avoid limping. Before she was halfway to her office, she dismissed the laundry woman from her mind, allowing the elation at her triumph over the *I'oss* to come to the fore again. Perhaps it would be best to preempt any disorder that might arise from her disappearance. When Cara returned, she would send a message to the soldiers' commander to have them take control of the village. It was time to make her plans known.

***

Gwynna watched Lyssa limp away. The sky had faded to a deep blue and there were no streetlights on this street, so she lost the older woman in the shadows before her footsteps faded away.

When she could no longer hear her, Gwynna sank to her knees, the sobs hope kept at bay, clawing their way past her clenched teeth. Hope that Lyssa would realize she made a mistake. Hope that she would return and apologize. Hope that the older woman would put an arm around her and comfort her.

Like her father always did.

When her sobs subsided, she rolled onto her side on the dusty cobbles and hugged herself. It was clear to her now. Why she always debased herself to please Lyssa, despite how dirty she felt afterward. And it wasn't for a better job. It was when Lyssa said, "Run along and let your betters do their jobs," that she understood. The words weren't exactly what her father always said to her after he apologized, but they were near enough.

She climbed to her feet, let her head fall back and looked up at the stars that emerged while she wept. When her father told her to 'run along,' she counted herself lucky. She was still alive, and she knew his guilt would protect her. For a time. Lyssa never hit her, but in some ways she was worse than her father. The physical blows were never the worst part with her father. It was the contempt in his eyes when she cowered. The same contempt Lyssa showed her just now. And Lyssa would never feel guilty. Never reveal the moments of compassion which allowed Gwynna to forgive her father time and again.

What hurt most about the way Lyssa treated her was what it said about Gwynna. She escaped her father that rainy day long ago, but she hadn't escaped that meek girl who allowed herself to be abused repeatedly. She squeezed her eyes shut, searching inside herself for the courage that girl found crouching outside her father's bedroom door.

"No more," she whispered. "She calls me Baird, but I'm not what she calls me. I'm Desulti, a woman who escaped on her own." She looked down the street and wiped the dust from her hands on her blouse.

It was her fault they caught Tove. Even after Tove showed her nothing but kindness. Had gone out of her way to try to be friends. Tears leaked once more from her eyes. "Stop it!" she said, squeezing her hands into fists.

She took a step. Then another. Then she was striding down the street. She would go for help. No! She stopped and turned around. She needed to apologize to Tove for what she did before anyone else found out. Lyssa told the gendarmes to take Tove to Building B. She could guess why. The building once housed the Order's legal department. It was a warren of small, windowless offices and storage rooms. Now it was a warehouse where broken and disused items were thrown and forgotten. No one would think to look for Tove there. No one would hear her if she were in one of the interior rooms. Rooms with no windows. Rooms that would be pitch black.

She started walking, then broke into a jog. Building B was next to the Laundry. She knew how to get into the building unseen.

✳✳✳

Siofra and Eirin paused at the top of the pass that overlooked the valley containing Téama. Only the mountains on the far side of the valley were still in sunlight. She looked back at the riders which had been gaining on them as they climbed the pass.

Brie reined her horse to a stop when they caught up and said to Siofra, "We were lucky." She nodded at the three murtair sitting quietly on their horses behind her. "I found Tara and Aedion where you said I would. Caedan was staying at the Order's house in Richeleau."

"Thank you, Brie," Siofra said, then she addressed the other murtair. "Has Brie told you what is happening in Téama?" When she received confirmations, she said, "We don't know what is happening right now. Hopefully, we are in time to prevent any problems. But we must be ready for anything." When they nodded, she wheeled her horse around and set off down the other side of the pass.

***

When they ambushed her, Tove assumed they intended to kill her. But Lyssa obviously wanted to know what the woman she was hiding told Tove. They were going to put her some place dark. Someplace no one would hear her scream. She tried to steel herself, but the thought of two weeks in the dark was almost too much for her the bear. She was so frightened, she couldn't fight or scream into the gag they tied across her mouth while they dragged her through the deserted streets. Her heart thudded so hard, she was sure it would give out. Hoped it would give out.

When they approached a two-story brick building, she started to pant through her nose. Dark windows watched them approach in the gathering gloom. *Oss'stera* had a tradition of telling stories around the fire at night. Her favorite stories were the ghost stories. For Tove, who had witnessed more horrors than most people could imagine, the stories were amusing. But Alar's story about the Vollen god, Daga, had truly frightened her. She laughed it off, along with the other rebels. But his lurid description of the Imperial god's gaping maw and black eyes terrified her. These black, yawning windows saw into the dark places in her mind and unearthed the image that had terrified her.

Tish retrieved a set of keys and unlocked the door. After pausing to light a lamp, they tossed Tove's bow and pack to the floor and dragged her down a black hallway. The dark danced and clutched at her with the lamp swaying with Tish's steps. Deep inside the building, in a hall sunlight never touched, Tish stopped and handed the lamp to another woman.

She faced Tove and sneered. "I've been waiting for this," she said, then before Tove could brace herself, Tish punched her in the face. The shock hadn't subsided when she punched her again in the stomach. Before Tove could retreat to the part of her mind she used to hide from the inquisitors, another blow to her jaw dragged a grunt from her.

Gasping for air, only upright because of the women holding her up, she was barely aware of Tish pulling an iron bolt that barred a heavy door. After pulling the door open, she turned a wide leer on Tove.

"Welcome to the last room you'll ever see."

They threw her into the tiny room. She landed hard on her knees, then collapsed forward, unable to break her fall with her hands tied behind her back. She glimpsed four blank walls in the lamplight before the door slammed shut, leaving her in total darkness.

She told herself to resist the terror, but the darkness clung to her, worming its way past her defenses. As soon as the door slammed shut, she fainted. It was a blessing. She dreamed terrible dreams. Dreams of leering inquisitors, of stark rooms full of frightening devices, of tables with straps. But the images had the gauzy quality of dreams. Though they terrified her, a part of her knew they couldn't hurt her.

Then she woke up and found herself in the dark, blood pooling beneath her cheek. And the horrors locked in buried memories emerged and frolicked, the images startlingly vivid on the black canvas.

***

Hela paced back and forth across the street near the spot where he and Tove agreed to meet. She was an hour late. He was on the verge of going to look for her when Laoise appeared from the forest at the edge of the village.

"What's happening?" the murtair asked.

"Tove was supposed to meet me here an hour ago."

"It's almost dark. Why are you leaving so late?"

Hela told her about Tove breaking into Lyssa's house, about Lyssa's prisoner, and what Tove learned from the woman.

Laoise listened without reacting until Hela finished, then she said, "Come on," and set off toward the village.

Hela retrieved his pack and bow and followed. They left the main road and skirted the center of the village, lest someone see Laoise and report her presence to Lyssa. Hela followed silently.

Laoise stopped outside the home she shared with Cianna and faced him. "If you come in, you agree to do exactly what we tell you to until this is all over."

"All over?" he asked. "Is making sure Tove is okay part of the all over?" When she nodded, he said, "Okay."

Laoise pulled the door open to reveal Cianna, looking as if she were about to open the door.

"What's happened?" Cianna asked.

"It's time," Laoise said. "Whether we're ready or not."

Cianna's face took on a determined set. She nodded and stepped back to allow them to enter.

Chapter 30

You Can Hate Me All You Want

Gwynna peeked around the corner of the laundry. Seeing no one guarding the entrance to Building B, she tried the door. It was locked. Retreating, she entered the laundry, stole past the vast vats she tended every day and entered the backyard. She found what she was looking for in the storage shed beside the pile of firewood used to heat the vats. Hefting the axe with two hands, she returned to the laundry. After retrieving a lantern from the office, she crept up the stairs, the axe bumping each step behind her. She had to rest the axe on the landing in order to heave on the sticky door that let out onto the roof. She made her way through the maze of clothes lines where they hung the wet laundry to dry in the sun to the north side of the building. The second floor of Building B was across a narrow gap.

The glass from the last window broke long ago and the boards that were installed to keep out the weather warped. She set the axe and lantern down, took hold of the bottom edge of one of the boards and jerked with all her strength.

The board came free easily, sending Gwynna sprawling on her back. Climbing to her feet, she brushed grit from her hands and set to removing the rest of the boards. After dropping the axe and lantern through the window, she felt along the windowsill until she found spots free of broken glass. It was awkward, climbing through the window, but she managed it with only a few scrapes.

She paused to light the lantern, then exited the room and stood in the hall, peering in both directions, taking shallow breaths through parted lips. It was a big building. Where to start?

"There's no reason they would carry her up the stairs," she whispered to the watchful silence.

She found the stairwell in the corner of the building and descended to the first floor, careful to keep the axe from thumping behind her. It took her a moment to get the basic layout of the building, but then she started searching methodically through the halls, the axe balanced on her shoulder. Most of the doors were open. The few that were closed were not locked.

She peered around a corner into a long hallway and her breath caught. A lamp glowed around the far corner. She doused her lantern, crept along the hall, stopping a dozen paces from the end, and listened. Footsteps. Someone pacing slowly and humming tunelessly. Creeping forward, the axe in both hands, she stopped at the corner, trying to read the footsteps. When they started to recede, she peeked around the corner. Even from the back, she recognized Tish. She was only ten paces away, so she would be within a couple of paces of the corner when she turned around on her next pass.

Gwynna ducked behind the corner and peered at the axe. Giving her head a shake, she retrieved the lantern and waited, gripping the lantern handle in sweaty hands. When she heard Tish turn on her next lap, she stepped around the corner and swung the lantern at the back of Tish's head. Heavy with oil, the lantern made a hollow thunk when it made contact. Tish collapsed in a heap and lay still.

Gwynna stared at her, heart thumping painfully. Coming to herself, she jumped back, then crouched and peered at Tish's face. She was out or dead. Putting her ear near Tish's mouth, she caught the faint whisper of her breath. Relief weakening her legs, she hurried to retrieve the axe, then returned and examined the door that was at the center of Tish's pacing. It was oak and barred with a heavy bolt, but there was no lock.

Dropping the axe, she heaved on the bolt until it came free. She lifted Tish's lamp, then eased the door open and peered into the room.

Tove huddled in the back corner, head down, hands still tied behind her back. She didn't react when Gwynna whispered her name, so she crossed the space and knelt beside her.

"Tove," she murmured.

Tove's head jerked up so fast, Gwynna fell back, startled, the lamp held safely above the floor. She lifted the lamp up where Tove's wide eyes could focus on the light, then knelt beside her and pulled the cloth from her mouth. Tove glanced at her for the first time.

"You!" she spat.

Gwynna froze. Her first reaction was to leave the lamp and flee. But there was something at the edges of Tove's angry grimace that stopped her. A need. A pleading that tugged at Gwynna's heart.

"Shhh," she said. "Let's get you out of here. Then you can hate me all you want." For a frightening moment, she thought Tove wouldn't relent, but then her grimace softened, her gritted teeth parted and she sucked in a ragged breath.

Gwynna helped her onto her knees and placed the lamp on the floor where she could see it. "Stay here. We have to get your hands untied." When Tove nodded, she retrieved the axe and sawed awkwardly at the ropes. Tove was so focused on the light, she barely flinched when Gwynna nicked her wrist.

When the ropes fell away, Tove groaned, brought her arms around and gingerly hugged her abdomen.

Gwynna pulled Tove to her feet and retrieved the lamp. "We have to go up to get out," she said.

Tove didn't speak until they were standing on the roof of the laundry, then she jerked her arm free of Gwynna's grip, shoved her away, and took a stumbling step backwards.

"You turned me over to them!"

Gwynna had no response.

"After I showed you nothing but friendship," Tove said, lowering her voice.

Gwynna lifted the hand that held the lamp and gestured to the window they emerged from, but all she managed to say was, "I made a mistake."

"A mistake?!" Tove asked incredulously. "That what you call it?"

"I'm sorry. I won't… I know…" She gave Tove a pleading look, but when she found no encouragement, she slumped and said, "The stairs are over here."

On the way through the laundry, Tove picked one of the heavy paddles used to agitate the laundry from a rack on the wall. Gwynna watched mutely. They didn't speak again until they emerged onto the street. After they made sure they were alone, Gwynna stopped and turned toward Tove, steeling herself for the condemnation Tove had a right to make.

"You got to pick a side," Tove said.

Confused, Gwynna looked up and found Tove's expression contained no anger. "Side?"

"You treat me like you hate me most of the time. Betrayed me to Lyssa and her goons," Tove said. She gestured toward the center of town. "But you done that thing after the initiation and then you come rescue me."

Gwynna stared at her, too surprised to think of a response.

"Which is it going to be?" Tove asked.

"I… I want to be friends."

Tove gazed at her for a long moment, then nodded and turned to looked down the street.

Gwynna watched her, unsure what just happened. Was Tove capable of forgiving her just like that? She was still trying to decide what to say when Tove spoke.

"Come on. We got to figure out what to do about Lyssa."

***

Laoise heard the tramp of the soldier's feet before they came into view. "You best hide," she said to Hela.

"Hide?"

"If this doesn't go well, someone needs to let Cianna know."

"Right," Hela said, unable to keep the relief from his voice.

He disappeared into the underbrush and Laoise moved into the middle of the road that led to Ka'tan and the Imperial fort. A century of Imperial infantry, one hundred men, came into view around a curve in the road. The soldiers were on foot, but two officers rode horses at the head of the column.

She recognized one of the mounted men as the colonel, who was the garrison commander. When he saw her blocking their path, he put up a hand to halt the column. He leaned forward and peered at her. "What is it you want, Murtair?" he asked, contempt or fear coloring his voice.

"You have no business in Téama," Laoise said. "Turn around and return to the fort."

He stared at her for a moment, as if he weren't sure he understood. Then he laughed with disbelief. "My orders say I do have business in Téama. I'm to keep order."

"You have no authority over the Order. You aren't welcome."

He hesitated, his face blank, then he sat back and glanced over his shoulder. "I have one hundred men with me who say I have the authority to go where I wish."

Laoise rolled her neck. "Your soldiers answer to you, so *you* will bear the consequences of their actions."

He stared at her, mouth hanging open. He looked as if he were going to speak, then he closed his mouth and licked his lips.

"Tell your superiors you spoke to a representative of the Murtair and were told we can manage our own affairs," Laoise said.

A calculating expression came over his face. He grinned at her. "That is good news. We, of course, will stand at the ready should you need us." When Laoise didn't respond, the colonel said to the other mounted man, "Captain, we're returning to the fort." The captain gave the orders, and the men turned about. The colonel nodded to Laoise, then wheeled his horse around and made his way to the head of the column, now headed in the opposite direction.

As the soldiers receded into the darkness, Hela appeared. "Bless the Father. That was the bravest thing I've ever seen."

Laoise turned and started walking back toward the village. "The man is commanding a garrison of slave drivers. He's not interested in a fair fight and he definitely isn't interested in dying." She shrugged. "He's a coward. I just needed to give him a plausible way out."

"Still…" They walked in silence until the edge of the village came into view. "Now what?"

"Now we let Cianna know the soldiers aren't on their way."

***

"Why are we meeting here?" Shailey asked, peering around at the council room.

Nessa rose from her spot at the conference table, crossed to a cabinet, extracted a chest, and placed it on the table.

"What's this?" Shailey asked.

"In your last report, you suggested the time was right. Is that still true?"

"Yeah. Just need the smallest spark. Lyssa taking names at the festival nearly done the trick without our help."

Nessa lifted the lid.

Shailey squinted at the contents in the low light, then grinned. "Ballots," she said. "Didn't think you would leave it to a fair vote."

"All filled out and ready to count," Nessa said, closing the lid. She returned the chest to the cabinet and locked it.

"Who you going to get to oversee the election?"

"People who will be above reproach," Nessa said. "You, of course. The lower castes trust you. You don't need to know the others."

"What do you want me to do with the real ballots?"

As Nessa headed to the exit, she gestured to the hearth. "Burn them. Just make sure you don't leave any trace."

"Just say the word when you're ready."

Nessa headed across the reception hall. After peering into the shadows cast by the columns to be sure they were alone, she spoke in a low voice. "We need an inciting incident. Something to spark the riot."

"Huh," Shailey said. "Have some ideas along those lines."

"Make it soon, but be sure to warn me," Nessa said and paused at the wicket door.

"Right."

Nessa pulled the door open and stepped through to find a throng gathering in the plaza.

"What is going on here?" Shailey asked.

Many of the women carried torches and lanterns. It was impossible to discern individual voices, but there was a dangerous edge to the crowd's murmur. Seeing Tilla, the Chair of the Ruling Council, at the edge of the crowd with a group of other upper caste women, a lantern in her hand, Nessa called to her. When she climbed the steps, Nessa asked, "What is going on?"

"We're not really sure. There is a rumor that someone killed Tove."

Nessa gaped at her.

"Killed her?" Shailey asked. "Someone in Téama?"

Tilla shrugged. "No one really knows anything."

Nessa looked out at the gathering in the plaza. Was this enough? No. There was an angry undertone, but nothing that suggested violence. She needed a spark. She caught Shailey's eye and gave her a nod. The woman descended the steps and disappeared into the crowd.

***

Captain Palmer reined up his horse when the colonel halted the column on the outskirts of Téama. Gazing at the peaceful village, the growing disquiet that he'd felt since the colonel informed him of this expedition surged. "It's awfully quiet," he said. "And you told the murtair we were returning to the fort." They had only returned a hundred paces before the colonel reversed course again. The only concession the colonel made to the murtair's threats was to reorganize the column, so he and Palmer were in the center, surrounded by their soldiers. From the stories he had heard, Palmer doubted that would make a difference to a murtair.

"Captain, we have been tasked with maintaining order in Téama," the colonel said. "And that is what I intend to do, murtair be damned."

Palmer gazed at the colonel's face, locked in a resolute frown, wondering what kind of insanity led one to defy a murtair. "Yes, Colonel. But, as I said, the village looks quiet."

"Nevertheless," the colonel said. "We are tasked with maintaining order, and that's what I intend to do." He grinned at Palmer and spoke as if he were instructing Palmer on a point of military tactics. "It is far better to *interdict* trouble before it starts."

The captain glanced back at the men waiting impatiently behind them. He was a recent arrival to Ka'tan. Six months ago, he was a lieutenant in the Ninth Legion, heroically defending the Empire from the Kaileuk. When the Kaileuk took his hand, the powers that be promoted him to captain for this service and relegated him to watching over slaves for his infirmity. He was having a hard time adjusting.

There was much to lament about his current posting, but one of the most distressing things was having to command what amounted to a gang of thugs rather than professional soldiers. He lay most of the responsibility for that on the colonel. The man announced he was Gabra in their first meeting. For a Baird like Palmer, it was a startling breach in social protocol that explained a lot about the man. The colonel was obviously a third son of a wealthy Volloch lord who purchased his commission. That he was in command of the fort in Ka'tan when the Empire was desperate for competent officers suggested a staggering level of incompetence.

He glanced at the older man, still staring resolutely ahead. Palmer would have resigned his commission rather than serve under this man, if he had any other options. But he didn't, so like it or not, whatever was about to happen was partially his responsibility.

The colonel announced their current mission as if it was a grand campaign against the Empire's foes. Many in the Empire would agree. The prevailing opinion in the Empire was that the Desulti were a threat to the proper social order. But while it was a question of out of sight, out of mind for most Imperial citizens, for men isolated in the northern reaches of Argren, the proximity of a village populated almost entirely by lawless women was a dangerous fascination. It had been a shocking revelation for Palmer the first time he heard their lecherous speculations about the Desulti village. Anyone could see unleashing these undisciplined men on Téama, for whatever reason, could only end in disaster.

Looking back at the soldier's eager faces, he made one last ditch effort to avoid catastrophe. "Colonel, Téama is obviously quiet. Perhaps the men can wait here while you and I enter the village with your guard and meet with whoever is in charge."

"We must take control of the streets," Palmer said with a brisk nod.

"The streets? Sir? What does that entail? Exactly?"

"Take the initiative. Ensure that we don't allow things to get out of hand. We'll start by confining everyone to their abodes. Declare martial law." He paused, then nodded to himself. "Once we are in control, we can meet with the… women in charge."

Palmer glanced back at the men again. He opened his mouth to protest once more, but nothing that would penetrate this man's affronted prejudice against the Desulti came to mind.

The colonel twisted in his saddle to face him. "Captain, if you are unwilling to accomplish this task, I will find someone who will."

Palmer stared at him. The colonel was offering him a chance to avoid responsibility for what was to come. But he couldn't walk away. That it would be a disaster was a certainty, but perhaps he could mitigate it in some small way.

Wheeling his horse around, he addressed the lieutenants under his command. They studied a map of Téama before they left the fort. After reminding each man of their areas of responsibility, he explained the rules of engagement. They were there to maintain order. They should avoid conflict unless absolutely necessary. Halfway through the long list of instructions he had been pondering ever since the colonel informed him of the mission, the colonel interrupted him.

"Palmer," he said, "the longer we wait, the more likely the situation will get out of hand."

Palmer glanced at the still quiet village, then said to the impatient lieutenants, "These women are not slaves. They are Volloch. I will hold you personally responsible for the actions of the men under your command."

The colonel nodded, pointed toward the village, and said, "Take the village."

The men raised their truncheons, cheered and surged forward.

Chapter 31

Protect Our Sisters

The wicket door opened behind Nessa, and a moment later, Lyssa and Cara stepped up beside her.

"What is this?" Lyssa asked.

"Someone killed Tove," Nessa said and turned to face Lyssa.

Lyssa glanced at Nessa. Seeing her expression, she turned to face her. "What? You think it was me?"

"You aren't seriously going to claim Tish acted on her own. Up in the mountains?" Nessa asked. "Everyone in Téama knows she acted on your behalf."

"That is a lie!"

A scream interrupted Nessa's response. Nessa whirled around and found women fleeing toward the far side of the plaza. Looking to the right to see what frightened them, she found Imperial soldiers streaming into the plaza, heavy truncheons raised above their heads. At the sight of the fleeing women, the soldiers whooped and jeered. Stunned, Nessa almost didn't hear Lyssa laughing behind her. When she turned and gaped at her, Lyssa smiled triumphantly.

"Light the brazier, Tilla," Lyssa said.

Tilla didn't move.

"Tilla," Nessa said, with a wide smile. "Light the brazier."

Tilla climbed onto the pedestal on which the brazier was mounted.

"Tilla!" Lyssa screamed.

Tilla extracted the stopper in her lantern and dribbled oil on the logs in the dish of the brazier, then swung the lantern, smashing the glass and igniting the logs. When she jumped to the ground, she smiled at Lyssa and said, "I'm done being your toady, you sanctimonious bigot."

Lyssa and Cara stared in horror at her, then looked out at the soldiers pursuing women further into the village. A group of soldiers smashed the windows on the building which housed the Order's legal apparatus across the plaza and threw a torch through the window.

Nessa grabbed Lyssa's arm and pulled her around. "You did this."

"I —" Lyssa looked away from Nessa at the sound of distant screams and stared openmouthed at the chaos erupting in the plaza.

***

Brie pulled her horse to a stop and put up a hand. "Quiet," she said. The streets in the residential district on the western edge of the village were ominously deserted. "What is that?"

"That was a scream," Eirin said.

Siofra threw caution to the wind on the cobbled streets and urged her horse into a gallop. When they neared the plaza, they met women fleeing in the opposite direction, fear distorting their features. Catching sight of Danu, Brie leapt from her horse and grabbed her arm as she passed. "What's going on?"

Hearing Brie's voice, Danu stopped fighting to free herself. "Thank Daga," she said and threw a frightened look back the way she came. "There are soldiers in the plaza."

"Soldiers?!" Siofra asked from atop her horse.

Danu nodded frantically. "Tove is missing. We were organizing to search for her, then the soldiers —" She pointed up the street and fought to free herself from Brie's grip.

A half dozen soldiers were sprinting toward them, laughing and taking swipes with truncheons at women scattering to get out of their way. "Get Siofra to the Great Hall," Brie said to Eirin. "Light the brazier."

Eirin nodded, took hold of Siofra's reins and led her away from the soldiers.

"Get indoors," Brie told Danu, then caught the eyes of Tara, Aedion, and Caedan. She returned their nods, then the murtair turned to meet the soldiers.

***

Tove clutched the heavy laundry paddle as they made their way through the quiet streets toward the center of the village. She didn't expect to encounter Lyssa's thugs, but she wanted to be ready. She had decided the best course of action was to find Hela and Laoise. When they were a block from the plaza, a familiar sound emerged from the ominous silence; the low murmur of many voices. A crowd. A sound she was used to in larger cities, but not in Téama. Already wary, she stopped and put an arm out to bring Gwynna to a halt. Then someone screamed.

Gwynna's hand wrapped around Tove's arm. "What was that?"

"Something's not right," Tove said. She hefted the paddle and scanned the buildings on each side of the street. "Let's get out of sight." She led Gwynna to the side of the street where a row of oak trees cast the walkway into shadow. Other screams split the night and were followed by a sound far more frightening; the bestial bellows of men.

"Men!" Gwynna said and pulled Tove close.

Before Tove could think of what to do, several women appeared at a run at the end of the block. They crossed the street and disappeared. Tove set off to follow, but before she made it to the intersection, men wearing the blue uniforms of Imperial infantry appeared in pursuit. They brandished heavy truncheons and were laughing and flinging taunts after their quarry. "Imps!" she whispered. She took off after them.

"Where are you going?!" Gwynna called after her.

Tove stopped, crept into the intersection, and peered down the street. Halfway down the block, three soldiers had two women cornered on the stoop of a building. One of the women was frantically pounding on the door, while the other held her hands up, warding the men off. The men were laughing and brandishing their clubs.

Noticing Gwynna had followed her, Tove said, "Wait here." She jogged in the shadows on the opposite side of the street from the confrontation. Once she was even with them, she sprinted across the street, raising the paddle in two hands over her shoulder.

Tove's moccasin boots made barely a whisper on the cobbles. Too amused by the cowering women, the men didn't hear her until the last moment. As the one she was targeting turned, Tove swung with all her might. She was aiming for the side of his head, but when he turned, he put his face into the paddle's path. His nose splatted in a splash of blood and he dropped.

Tove swung at the man on her left, but he lifted his club to deflect the blow. She pulled her paddle back, ready for another go at him, but the third man swung his club at her head, forcing her to duck.

She held the paddle out, warding them off.

"You little bitch," one of the men said, glancing at his comrade writhing at his feet.

"I'm looking forward to this," the third man said, extending his club like a sword.

They had started to spread out and advance, when one of the women on the stoop launched herself from the top step onto one of the men's backs. She wrapped her legs around his waist, her arms around his neck, and sunk her teeth into his ear.

His shriek startled his companion. Distracted, he didn't see Gwynna until she hit him at a full sprint from the side. Stumbling, he dropped to a knee and struck out, striking Gwynna's cheek. Tove swung the paddle with all her strength. It hit his head with a sharp crack.

She was pulling the paddle back to take care of the third man, who was struggling with the assailant attached to his back and ear when the other woman they cornered on the stoop kicked him between the legs from behind. He squealed, his hands went to his groin, he fell to his knees and flopped forward.

The woman who jumped onto his back rolled off and spit his ear onto his back. It was Orla. She grinned at Tove and wiped blood from her chin with the back of her hand.

Chest expanding and contracting, Gwynna looked at Tove with wild eyes. She scooped up one of the men's truncheons, gave it an awkward swing and asked Tove, "What do we do?"

"You okay?" Tove asked.

Gwynna touched the side of her face and grinned. "Great!"

The village was alive with screams, raucous laughter, and voices raised in anger. "Get their clubs," Tove said. The women retrieved them and hefted them, feeling their weight. "Let's go," Tove said and led them down the street.

***

Captain Palmer watched in horror as the men under his command raged across the plaza, pursuing their prey. He cast about for his lieutenants, but they had joined their men. "Colonel!" he shouted. "You must get control of this situation."

The colonel let a small smile fall from his face and scowled at Palmer. "The operation is in the early stages. We must give them time to accomplish the objectives."

"What are you talking about? The men are out of control."

"They dispersed what was obviously a riot in the making and they are pursuing the miscreants." The colonel cocked his head and gave Palmer a disgusted look. "I would think a veteran of the Empire's wars would understand the need for the men to enjoy the fruits of victory."

Palmer stared at him, aghast. "Victory? What victory?"

The colonel looked past Palmer and said, "Ah, there is the woman in charge of this village."

He set his horse in motion and rode to the base of the steps in front of the massive building on the northern edge of the plaza. The ten men in his personal guard followed. Four women watched as he approached, their expressions reflecting their horror at the unfolding disaster.

"Lyssa, I presume," the colonel said.

"Colonel!" the woman snapped. "You were supposed to maintain order, not run amok."

"I assure you, we will put things in order. You are only witnessing a necessary —"

A scream interrupted him. Two women appeared at a run on the far end of the plaza and disappeared into the burning building. A moment later, four soldiers appeared, cast about for their quarry, then disappeared down another street.

"Colonel!" Palmer growled. The colonel turned a blank expression on him, but before Palmer could continue, the woman named Lyssa spoke.

"Colonel, rest assured I will give a detailed report of this night and your conduct to Inquisitor Hoerst."

The colonel's face went rigid. Glancing across the plaza, he said, "Perhaps... perhaps you women should retreat inside while the captain and I gain control of the situation." He gave a brisk nod. "What matters is the end result. It may appear as if things have gotten out of hand... to the untrained eye. But it is the end result that must be considered."

Lyssa spun on her heel and disappeared into the building. Two other women followed her. The last woman watched them go, then frowned out at the plaza and said, "But..." She looked from the colonel to the door where the other women disappeared, then followed them.

The colonel dismounted, removed his gloves, and climbed the steps. Palmer and the lieutenant in command of the colonel's guard followed. The men set up a cordon at the base of the steps.

"What did she mean she would give a report to an inquisitor?" Palmer asked the colonel. "Why would the Inquisition be interested in this fiasco?"

"An empty threat," the colonel muttered. But the tick that had started in the colonel's cheek put the lie to his words. He looked out over the plaza, one eye winking spasmodically, his resolute frown replaced by a panicky furtiveness.

"Colonel?" Movement at the edge of Palmer's vision was the only warning he had before someone separated themselves from the shadows beneath the brazier. She crossed the distance to the colonel so fast, Palmer barely reacted before she reached around and put a blade to the colonel's throat. It was the murtair. Terrified at a ghost story come to life, Palmer's instinct was to flee, but his muscles locked, freezing him in place.

"Colonel," the woman said, just loud enough for Palmer to hear. "I told you there would be consequences." Her eyes flicked to Palmer, to the insignia on his collar, then she dragged the blade across the colonel's throat. She shoved the dying man, so he tumbled down the steps, then turned toward Palmer, the blade in her hand dribbling blood onto the stone pavers.

The colonel's guard were facing into the plaza, but when the body flopped onto the ground at their feet, they spun around. Seeing a murtair, they hesitated. The woman brought the blade up until the tip pressed into the soft flesh below Palmer's chin. Palmer put his hand up to keep the soldiers at bay. "Lieutenant," he said to their commander, who had only gaped at the murtair since she appeared. "Lieutenant!" Palmer repeated, pricking his skin against the knife tip. When the man's head snapped around, Palmer said, "Sound the assembly."

The young man hesitated, then nodded to one of his soldiers, who licked his lips and put a bugle to his lips. On his second try, he managed to play the notes that would call the men to assemble.

"Continue, until the men respond," Palmer told him, then he focused on the murtair. Unlike the murtair in all the stories, she didn't hide her face, and she had hair like a man. Palmer swallowed. "I'm afraid the men are beyond reasonable thought," he said. "They probably won't respond."

"Then they will die." She scanned the men of the colonel's guard. The anger in their expressions couldn't quite hide their fear. One of them took a step backward when she looked at him.

"You must do what you have to, to defend your people," Palmer said. "But murder is murder." His eyes flicked to the colonel's body. "If no one is left to explain this disaster, the Empire will investigate. A cohort of the Empire's finest would be an altogether different thing than these men."

"Get control of your men, Captain," the murtair said. "Or we will." She turned and made her way along the front of the building, then disappeared around the corner.

Palmer watched the spot where she disappeared on watery legs.

"Captain?" the lieutenant asked.

Palmer looked down at the colonel's body. It was likely only his mother and father would lament his loss. Wiping blood from beneath his chin, he looked out at the village, echoing with the chaos his men had unleashed. "Lieutenant, our task now is to save as many of our men as we can."

"But they're only women," the young man said with a scowl.

Palmer barked a laugh and pointed after the murtair. "You mean like her?"

***

Brie stepped back and let the soldier's body fall, then crouched and spun around, scanning the street. Only her three murtair companions were still standing. Four soldiers' bodies lay on the cobbles. The other two fled as soon as the murtair appeared.

"Protect our sisters," Brie said. The other murtair nodded, turned, and headed off into the night.

Brie ran to the plaza and looked across to the Great Hall. The brazier was lit. She didn't know how long they were involved with the soldiers, but it wasn't long enough for Siofra to make her way through the chaos to the brazier. Nessa or Lyssa must have lit it. A group of about ten soldiers were gathered around the body of another soldier on the steps to the Great Hall. What looked like an officer was speaking stridently to them.

She considered finding a way across the plaza to take out the officer, but that probably would have little affect on the beasts the soldiers had become. The best thing she could do was follow the instructions she gave her sisters; protect the women of the village. She retreated to the first intersection and set off at a jog down the street. The village had descended into a nightmare. Screams drifted in the night, both male and female. No one lit the street lamps and men and women appeared out of the shadows and disappeared before she could reach them.

Coming upon two soldiers standing over an unconscious woman in a small park, Brie drew a pair of push daggers, slipped into the park and approached the men from behind. While one of the men lowered himself on top of the woman, Brie drove a blade into the back of the other man's neck and gave it a twist, killing him instantly. She dispatched the other before he was aware his companion was dead, then hauled his body to the side and examined the woman.

It was Brigid, a woman who worked in the dining hall. Pressing her fingers to her throat, she was relieved to feel a steady pulse. Hearing people approaching on the street, she rose and found a familiar figure at the head of a dozen women. "Tove!" she shouted.

Tove stopped and turned, raising what looked like an oar in her hands. "Brie?" She relaxed and let the oar drop to her side.

Brie stepped onto the street. "Someone needs to take care of Brigid," she said, and pointed at the fallen woman. Half the women who had been following Tove responded.

"She okay?" Tove asked.

"She's alive." Brie eyed the women behind Tove, armed with a variety of weapons. "What are you doing?"

"Hunting," Tove said with a straight face.

Brie was surprised to find Gwynna standing next to Tove, a large welt below her eye. "Gwynna?"

Gwynna nodded enthusiastically.

"Let's go," Brie said and led them down the street. She glanced at Tove's battered face. "The soldiers do that to your face?"

"Lyssa's goons," Tove said. She gave Brie a grim look. "You and me need to talk."

Brie knew that day was inevitable when she chose Tove for her and Nessa's scheme. She wasn't afraid of it. But something else terrified her. "Have you seen Elois?"

Tove shook her head. "You seen your sister?"

Brie nodded. "Told her to get inside."

They rounded a corner and found four soldiers attacking the door to a dormitory with a crowbar.

"Come on," Brie said.

***

Siofra sat on her horse and gazed at the flame in the brazier across the plaza. A group of soldiers, an officer in the lead, were walking away from the Great Hall, leaving the body of another soldier at the bottom of the steps.

"Too late," Eirin said, reining her horse up beside Siofra. "Now what?"

"Now we defend our village," Siofra said, turning her horse away from the plaza. A group of women carrying clubs and other weapons appeared two blocks away. Siofra called to them, then walked her horse to meet them. She recognized Elois at the head of the five women. Some of them were bruised and cut, but their expressions were full of fire.

Before Siofra could speak, soldiers appeared in the street two blocks away. Siofra leaned down and spoke to Elois. "Draw them this way. Look weak and frightened, then lead them that way." She pointed toward the plaza. When Elois nodded, Siofra led Eirin down a cross street and hid in the shadows.

Elois and the other women put on a show, hiding their weapons, wailing, crying, and clutching one another. Moments later, they fled up the street with a half dozen laughing men in pursuit. Siofra and Eirin followed at a gallop. The thunder of the horses' hooves warned the men, but they had no time to evade them. Siofra trampled a soldier, then wheeled her horse around and made another pass.

Elois and the other women returned and set on the men who had been scattered by the horses.

When it was over, Siofra looked down at the triumphant women. She gave them a moment to catch their breath, then said, "Let's go."

***

Nessa followed Lyssa across the reception hall, Tilla in her wake. Cara headed off to the wing that housed Lyssa's offices. When Lyssa disappeared through the door that led to the council room, Nessa turned and held a hand up toward Tilla. "Wait here."

"What are we going to do?"

"About?"

Tilla threw her hand toward the front of the building. "About those men rampaging through Téama!"

"What do you propose I do?"

"I... There must be something we can do."

"There is nothing. But I *can* do something to ensure the future of the Order. Now, wait here." Nessa turned and followed Lyssa.

Lyssa was sitting in her usual chair at the conference table, legs crossed. When Nessa entered, Lyssa stared coolly at her, but didn't speak.

"You brought those men into Téama," Nessa said, her voice controlled.

"Don't play the innocent with me!" Lyssa spat. "You've been stoking the unrest the *l'oss* caused for weeks. Don't lie and say you haven't. I called the soldiers because I was worried about what might happen. This is as much your fault as mine."

Nessa gaped at her, too stunned by Lyssa's audacity to think of a response.

"What are you going to do?" Lyssa asked, ignoring Nessa's shock.

Nessa, unsure how she lost control of the conversation, stammered, "What do you —".

"Don't be obtuse," Lyssa said with a scowl. "You lit the brazier. With the help of a traitor, apparently. Tilla," she said under her breath. "How did I not see that?" She shook her head and gave Nessa a speculative look. "So. What are your plans?"

"How dare you accuse me of being responsible for this disaster!" Nessa said, a step behind. But anger was finally focusing her mind. "It was you who made the deal with the emperor. I had no choice. Do you have any idea what the Volloch will do to the Order if they don't have to worry about the Murtair?"

Lyssa scoffed and gestured dismissively. "The emperor won't let anyone take advantage of the Order."

"What are you talking about?"

Lyssa smiled indulgently. "Your spy apparently didn't tell you everything." She let her smile fall away and lifted her chin. "I've promised to finance his war. He's desperate. He'll protect us because he needs us."

"His… war?" Nessa asked. "That will break us."

"We'll feel it," Lyssa said with a sniff. "At first. But we'll gain so many efficiencies being integrated into the Empire, it won't take long to make up the difference."

"As long as the war doesn't last too long."

Lyssa barked a laugh. "It's the Kaileuk! The Empire gets their nose bloodied by the Kaileuk every hundred years. Like his predecessors, the emperor will declare victory and find a way out. The Kaileuk will let him go. They always do."

"And you're willing to gamble the future of the Order on that?" Nessa asked.

"A small gamble for a guaranteed reward." Lyssa eyed Nessa. "But *you* lit the brazier. You have all the power. I'm assuming you have no intention of holding a fair election."

Nessa's eyes flicked to the cabinet where the ballots she prepared were hidden. She didn't answer, but the truth must have been evident on her face.

"Perhaps we could make a deal," Lyssa said.

"Why would I make any deal with you?" Nessa asked. "As you said, I have all the power. What do I need you for?"

Lyssa pursed her lips. "Because I have the ear of the emperor and powerful men in the Inquisition. Something the Order has never had." She paused. "This is my offer. We keep the deal with the emperor and open the compound in Kartok. I'll run that operation, put up a good front. The Order will keep its shadow existence headquartered in Téama, run by you."

"In exchange for what?"

"We keep the Murtair. A more circumspect Murtair. One which leaves no trace of its existence." Lyssa let her head tilt to the side. "And as I said, I have the ear of the emperor. If I go, that goes with me."

"I could keep the Murtair without you?"

Lyssa smiled a cat's grin. "I've provided details on the murtairs' movements to the Inquisition. They will be arrested and I don't imagine the inquisitors will treat them with kid gloves." She eyed Nessa. "Oh, you'll have Laoise, wherever she's hiding. How long do you think she'll last with the entire Inquisition searching for her?" She paused and lifted her chin. "It's not too late. I say the word, I can prevent the Inquisition from getting what they need."

"You couldn't have given away the location of the murtair. I've recalled them. They are on their way to Téama."

"Yes, you have. Quite convenient, as they will have to travel the long lonely road from Richeleau to get here." Lyssa shrugged. "Of course, we will have to sacrifice a few to the Inquisition. For show." She smiled widely. "I'll even allow you to choose who."

"Why should I trust you?"

"Why would I betray you? I have no interest in waking up in the middle of the night to find a murtair standing over me." She shrugged. "This works out better, anyway. We don't even have to make the big announcement the Council is moving. We only need to announce an expanded presence in Kartok. No one will complain about that."

Nessa gazed at her, considering. Was she lying about the Inquisition arresting the murtair? It was possible Lyssa found out she recalled the murtair. Nessa had to send messages to the Order's houses in many cities. She marked them as secret, but a leak was possible. And there was something to what Lyssa said. Having access to the highest levels of power in the Empire would be something the Order never had before. Who knew, maybe this was the beginning of a new era for women in the Empire. "I will consider your offer," she said after a long pause.

Chapter 32

Aftermath

Tove, Gwynna and Brie walked down the middle of a quiet street toward the plaza. Torrential rains began around the third bell, but by dawn, only remnants of the clouds troubled a clear sky. In the bright morning light, with the birds singing their morning songs, the scenes of depravity Tove witnessed during the night were obscured by the veil of fatigue.

But brutal reality insisted on pulling the veil aside. The scent of wood smoke wasn't unusual in the crisp early summer mornings, but the pall of gray smoke that hung above the trees was a reminder the fire brigade was still at work. Violence's banal litter — broken glass, charred wood, torn clothing, blood–tinged puddles — was scattered randomly around the village. *Alle'oss* servants appearing as dawn approached gazed around, baffled to find the village seemingly deserted. They were directed to the quartermaster, where recovery efforts were being coordinated.

Brie held up a hand to stop them when two unfamiliar murtair appeared. When she went to meet them, Tove glanced at Gwynna, who hadn't left her side throughout the night. Finding her staring into space, Tove nudged her and nodded to the curb. Tossing the laundry paddle to clatter on the walkway's stone pavers, she dropped limply to sit. Gwynna sat beside her and dropped her club at her feet.

The adrenaline that kept Tove going through the night had ebbed, leaving her exhausted and sore. Her stomach gave up reminding her she hadn't eaten since the previous morning and had hardened into a sullen knot. She needed food, water, and sleep. But what she needed before any of that was to find Danu. She looked up at the trees. Alar once told her the birds sang in the morning to let their mates know they made it through the night. If only Danu could sing a morning song to let Tove know she was okay.

They hadn't seen a soldier for hours. As dawn approached, they reverted to coaxing women out of hiding and sending them to the plaza where Siofra and Laoise had taken charge. They helped the injured and took the worst cases to the infirmary, where Tove searched the beds for Danu. She wasn't sure whether she was relieved or not that she didn't find her. Brie told her she told her sister to get inside, but Tove couldn't help picturing her lying injured in some hidden spot. She let her gaze fall to Brie and the other murtair. Finding nothing in their quiet conversation to keep her attention, she let her eyes unfocus and let her thoughts drift on waves of fatigue.

****

Gwynna sank to sit beside Tove and dropped her club on the street at her feet. She was ashamed to admit it, but a part of her was sorry to see the long night end. She couldn't honestly say how much help she was fighting the soldiers, but at least she was part of things. A Desulti defending their village. Now she was just Gwynna again.

When she first joined the Order, her euphoria at being free, and the Order's experience at taking in traumatized women masked her awkwardness. It didn't take long after her initiation for her to discover navigating social situations was entirely beyond her. Her father kept her isolated her entire life, never allowing her to have friends. She tried to fit in, but people found her awkward, and not knowing how to respond, they kept their distance. She knew it, but was powerless to do anything about it. The harder she tried, the more off-putting she became. No one abused her here. She didn't want for any physical need. But she was desperately lonely. In her darker moments, she even missed her father and her brother.

Perhaps it was exhaustion or hunger. Or perhaps it was the fact that Tove looked after her during the night, even after Gwynna's betrayal. Whatever the reason, she heard herself saying the things that festered inside her. "I thought it would be different here. I thought I would feel safe. That I would find other women who…" She gestured vaguely. She risked a glance at Tove, but she only stared absently at the murtair. Gwynna pressed her eyes closed and fought the urge to slink away. She had confessed, and no one heard.

"Who understood what you been through?"

Gwynna startled. She opened her eyes and found Tove gazing at her. Dark circles cradled her blue eyes and the bruises and cuts from Tish's beating stood out on her pale face. But beneath that was a genuine concern.

Gwynna looked away and whispered, "I can't make friends." She hunched her shoulders, waiting for Tove to laugh at her.

"Me and you got a lot in common."

Gwynna peeked at her, expecting the awkward smile people often gave her, but Tove merely gazed solemnly at her. "You and me? Everyone likes you."

Tove snorted. "That's obviously not true."

A grin stole onto Gwynna's face. "Well, maybe not Lyssa." The grin fled. "But everyone goes to Ka'tan with you, then they did that festival here. People didn't like you when you got here, but now, a lot of people are saying you being here is good for the Order."

"You came to the tavern with us. The festival in Ka'tan and the festival here," Tove said. "I see you with other people."

"Yeah, but…" Gwynna paused and gazed across the street. "Even when I'm with people, I feel all alone. I don't understand what I'm supposed to feel." She dropped her head and peered at a scrape that appeared on her palm sometime during the night. "And I *never* know what to say."

"*We* could be friends. If you let us." When Gwynna saw Tove's easy grin, she stopped herself from dropping her eyes. "You can be as awkward as you want to be. You don't have to say anything. In fact, that's the way I prefer it, to be honest. You can feel anyway you want. All I ask is you let me trust you. Don't turn me over the Lyssa again."

Gwynna returned her smile, feeling something she hadn't since shortly after she arrived. Relief. Relief and genuine happiness. "Deal."

They looked up as Brie approached. "They're holding the last of the soldiers prisoner in the plaza," Brie said. "Let's go."

Tove stood and offered a hand to help Gwynna rise. "Seriously, you need to tell someone this stuff. Maybe not all the time, cause it could get tiresome. But when you need it. You might find out you're not as weird as you thought."

"Maybe," Gwynna said, doubtfully.

They started walking. "Or maybe not," Tove said with a shrug. "But I'd prefer your weirdness over a lot of people's normal."

***

Tove, Gwynna and Brie paused at the edge of the plaza. Gwynna lifted a hand to shade her eyes and pointed to the blackened remains of the legal building. Smoke drifted from broken windows, but the downpour had confined the fire to the one building.

"We were lucky it rained," Tove said.

They set off across the plaza toward the Great Hall, where a group of perhaps twenty soldiers were huddled together on the porch, surrounded by hundreds of angry Desulti and three dour murtair. Brie angled them to intercept Siofra, Laoise, and an unfamiliar murtair. When they neared the trio, Siofra noticed them and waited for them to catch up.

"I'm happy to see all of you relatively well," Siofra said, eying Tove's and Gwynna's bruised faces.

"You didn't light the brazier," Brie said.

"No," Siofra said. "I've been too occupied to find out who did. I haven't seen Lyssa or Nessa. But before we can deal with that issue, we must deal with this situation." She gestured toward the Great Hall, turned and headed toward the back of the crowd who were keeping watch on the soldiers.

Laoise and Brie made a path for Siofra, then preceded her up the stairs. Tove and Gwynna waited at the bottom of the steps. Tove glanced down at the body of an Imperial colonel, then returned her attention to Siofra.

One of the soldiers, a captain if Tove remembered the insignia on his collar right, stepped forward to greet Siofra. Laoise leaned in and whispered to Siofra. When she finished, Siofra said to the captain, "Explain."

The captain looked as exhausted as Tove felt, but he spoke without hesitation. He gestured to the body of the colonel. "The colonel received a request to send soldiers to suppress unrest in Téama."

"Who sent this request?" Siofra asked.

"That would be speculation on my part."

Siofra gestured to the gathered women, many of whom had injuries. "Was this what you would call suppressing unrest?"

"No, Ma'am, I would not," the captain said, then hesitated. "The colonel… lacked the training for such a delicate operation —"

"He was incompetent."

"I would not like to cast aspersions on the dead," the captain said, but his expression said otherwise.

"And your soldiers are thugs," Siofra said. This caused some murmurs among the soldiers.

"Many of the men behaved abominably," the captain said.

"Captain, I'm placing them under arrest. They will be tried and, if found guilty, they will be sentenced."

The captain looked uncomfortable. "I'm afraid that is unacceptable. For better or worse, they are Imperial soldiers and are subject to the Imperial military code of conduct. I can assure you, they will be tried by military courts for their actions."

"Captain, you know who we are. How likely do you think Imperial courts, military or otherwise, will take our concerns seriously?"

The captain cleared his throat. "I understand your need to see justice done. However, regardless of what actions we take here, the Empire *will* investigate. You are correct that these men are not the finest examples of the Empire's soldiers. They are not representative of the kind of force the Empire can bring to bear. If the Imperial high command feels someone has usurped their authority, they will seek… retribution."

"Is that a threat?"

"No, Ma'am. It's a warning."

"Do you think these men should escape justice?" Siofra asked.

"I'm afraid it's not what I think that matters."

Siofra hesitated, then motioned for the captain to follow and retreated down the steps. They were standing right in front of Tove and out of earshot of the other soldiers when Siofra spoke quietly. "Captain, Laoise tells me, and your actions suggest you are not entirely to blame for this catastrophe." The captain only gazed at her. "I assume you are no more interested in attracting undo Imperial attention to this disaster than we are?"

The captain hesitated, then said, "An Imperial colonel is dead, as well as many men under his command. It will be next to impossible to avoid Imperial attention."

"Captain, my primary concern is that Imperial authorities don't take this unprovoked attack by your men as an excuse to settle old grudges."

"As the highest ranking officer remaining at the fort, I can assure you I will provide an honest account of the events of the previous evening." He shrugged. "That is all that I can do."

"I'm afraid that will not do," Siofra said. "I'm afraid the manner of the colonel's death would provoke… an emotional response, if it were known."

The captain glanced at the body, then gazed at Siofra. "The colonel died at the hands of women who were defending themselves from an unprovoked attack." He cocked his head. "Such losses are an inevitable consequence of conflict."

Siofra smiled grimly. "I think we understand one another. As for the rest of your men… We have witnesses that say you, and a small group of your soldiers, attempted to gain control of the situation. You may take those men and return to the fort. We will keep the rest of your men in custody. For now. When tempers have moderated, we will decide what is to be done about them. If we need to, we will wait until we can speak to someone whose opinion *does* matter."

The captain glanced at the murtair watching from the top step, then nodded.

"We also have a number of your men in our infirmary, and we don't have the staff or the supplies to manage under these conditions."

"We have a very good medic," the captain said. "I'll send him and all the supplies we can spare to assist your staff."

As Siofra was responding, someone tapped on Tove's shoulder. Tove turned and found it was Cianna.

"Come with me, Tove," she said. "I have someone who is desperate to find you."

Danu! Tove followed Cianna, ignoring the drama playing out behind her. She emerged out of the crowd and was nearly bowled over by a weeping Danu. She threw her arms around Tove's neck and pressed her lips to Tove's.

"Thank Daga!" she said after breaking the kiss. "I was so worried. You went missing, then the soldiers attacked. Someone told me they saw you fighting. I didn't know what to think." She went on like this for a full minute, then ran out of steam. Stepping back, she swiped at her bangs and peeked up at Tove. "I was worried."

Tove laughed and pulled her into a hug.

Danu fought free. "What happened to you?" She leaned in and examined Tove's battered face.

Before Tove could answer, Cianna said, "Tove, I hate to interrupt, but I have an urgent matter we need to discuss." She apologized to Danu, then pulled Tove away. She put an arm around her shoulders and spoke quietly as she led her toward the front of the Great Hall. "This is going to be confusing, but I need you to trust me. Remember when we met in the park and I told you I was going to look for a way to change the Order?"

"Maybe," Tove said.

"Nessa has invoked an article in the Charter, which will allow her to hold a new election."

"Like Lyssa did."

Cianna's smile lit her face. "You do remember!" She grew serious again. "I need you to tell everyone what you learned from the woman in Lyssa's house."

They worked their way through the crowd at the base of the steps to the Great Hall. "How did you know about that?" Tove asked.

"Hela was quite worried when you didn't meet him. Laoise brought him to me."

"How is that going to help?" Tove asked. "Nessa doesn't intend to have a fair election. She'll do what Lyssa did."

"Trust me," Cianna said.

A commotion pulled Tove's attention away from Cianna. Gwynna was pushing people aside, forcing her way through the crowd. Head down, arms held in front of her to shove people aside, Gwynna didn't notice Tove until she stepped in front of her to block her path. Gwynna looked up, her expression stricken. When she saw it was Tove, she gave her a head small shake and tried to pull away. Tove caught her arms to hold her in place and looked over her shoulder to see what she was fleeing. The soldiers were gone, and Lyssa and Nessa had appeared to join Siofra. The three appeared to be arguing.

Tove leaned close and murmured, "You have to show bullies you're not afraid of them."

"I can't," Gwynna whispered.

Tove turned her around and pulled her through the crowd. They were climbing the steps, trailing Cianna, when Tove heard Siofra's angry words.

"This is not the time to hold a new election," Siofra said.

"The brazier has been lit," Lyssa said coolly. "The Order has no Council." She gestured to the women watching the argument. "The sooner we hold the election, the sooner there will be someone with the authority to organize —" She froze, hand outstretched, and gaped at Tove and Gwynna.

Tove squeezed Gwynna's arm until she lifted her chin with an obvious effort.

Noticing Lyssa's response, Siofra glanced at Tove and Gwynna, then said, "The infirmary is full!"

"Someone can bring them ballots," Nessa said.

"And those who are too injured to vote?" Siofra asked.

"Their votes would make little difference," Nessa said. Glancing at Lyssa, she interrupted Siofra's response. "Perhaps we should retire to chambers to discuss this."

Before Siofra could respond, Lyssa fled into the Great Hall, followed by Nessa. Cianna stopped Siofra before she followed and held a whispered conversation with her. Siofra stared at her, a shocked expression on her face. Tove heard her ask, "Are you sure?"

When Cianna nodded, Siofra's expression became grim. "Follow me, Tove," she said and entered the Great Hall.

Tove grinned at Gwynna. "See? You scared the *sheoda* out of her."

"Yeah," Gwynna said, panting, disbelief in her smile.

Tove left Gwynna with Danu and followed Cianna and Siofra. When they entered the council room, Lyssa stood abruptly. "What are they doing here?"

"Nessa has invoked article fifteen," Siofra said. "According to the article, any surviving member of the Inner Council has the right to address the women of the Order before an election."

"Fine," Nessa said. "But what does that have to do with these two?"

"The article allows a member of the Inner Council to have someone speak on their behalf." Siofra paused, then said, "Tove will speak on my behalf."

Tove would have taken a step back if Cianna didn't have her hand on her back. She looked doubtfully at Cianna, who gave her a confident nod.

Lyssa erupted. "You will not have this *l'oss*, the cause of this disaster, speak to the Order. It's lies. All of it."

"I'm curious how you know she will lie when you don't know what she is going to say," Siofra said.

"She —" Lyssa's mouth worked, her eyes casting about. "She's *l'oss*."

Siofra hesitated, frowning at Lyssa as if she were expecting more. But when Lyssa didn't continue, Siofra looked at Nessa and said, "The Charter is clear. Tove is a member of the Order and has as much right to speak as anyone. You or Lyssa are free to speak for yourself if you feel she hasn't been truthful."

Lyssa's pale face went livid, but before she could respond, Nessa cut her off. "Fine. Let her speak."

"According to the Charter," Cianna said. "You must name the three people who oversee the election prior to the statements of the Inner Council."

"I'm aware what the Charter says," Nessa said impatiently. "I name Tilla, Shailey, and…" She smiled widely. "Lyssa."

"Lyssa?" Siofra said with a scowl. She hesitated and looked to Cianna. "Can she do that?"

"She can appoint anyone in the Order."

"A night's sleep," Siofra said. "That is not too much to ask."

"Let's get this over with," Nessa said and stood.

Chapter 33

We Are All Desulti

Tove stepped onto the dais in the Great Hall. Lyssa was doing her best to maintain her usual cool demeanor, but the slight stoop to her shoulders gave her away. After Siofra announced Tove would speak for her, Nessa cornered Lyssa in the council room alone. Nessa emerged, looking even more smug than she had before. Siofra gave Tove a small nod, but otherwise gave her no indication what she was thinking. Tove turned to look out at the women of the Order. It looked as if every person in Téama who wasn't in the infirmary was packed into the room or spilled out onto the porch of the Great Hall.

To her surprise, though there were some murmurs when Siofra announced Tove would speak for her, there were no jeers. Now the room was silent. With sunlight from the open doors casting the faces in the back into silhouettes, Tove could only see the expressions of the nearest women in the light of the braziers. She saw sympathy, speculation, and contempt, but none of the anger and hatred she saw her first day. News of her fighting the soldiers had spread and Siofra ceding her time to Tove had them curious. They wanted to hear what she had to say.

When she asked Cianna what she should say, Cianna only told her to speak from her heart and tell everyone what she learned from the woman in Lyssa's home. Tove could have talked about what Lyssa and Tish did to her. The evidence was clear on her face. But she didn't want to make it about her. In recent weeks, she had seen glimpses of the Order she imagined before she arrived. This was her chance to reach those people she told Meya about. To give courage to the women who wanted change. Clearing her throat, she started to speak, then was interrupted.

"Louder!"

She cleared her throat again, lifted her chin and spoke in a loud, clear voice. "When I heard there was an Order that gave sanctuary to women… well, I couldn't believe it. I imagined a place where being *Alle'oss*, Brochen, Baird, Burne, Gabra or Angus didn't matter. Where what mattered was we were women who needed the support of other women." She gestured to Brie, who stood at the foot of the dais. "Brie told me I wouldn't be accepted. But I guess I didn't want to hear that."

She chuckled and lifted her hands to take in the room. "That first day, in this room, I found out she was telling the truth. Then the initiation, the women in the dining hall, the prank at the fulling hut… Some of you made it clear you didn't want me here." She paused, scanning their faces and letting people repeat her words to the women outside the Great Hall. "Seemed like everyone hated me for daring to want what I did. Even the *Alle'oss* in Ka'tan called me a traitor." She raised her gaze above their heads. "But I've experienced far worse in my life. All that stuff only made me mad." She chuckled again. "I wanted to get even." She lowered her gaze and paused again.

"But it's funny how things work out. Despite it all, I found what I was looking for. I found women who didn't call me *l'oss*, who didn't care who my parents were. People who were willing to learn what kind of *person* I was." She tapped her fist to her chest and paused, allowing her words to be repeated. "And I found out what the Order *used* to be. A place where women *could* come and find support, could control their own destiny, no matter who they were." She decided not to mention that these women all had to be Volloch. "All that mattered was they contribute in whatever way they could. It was a place of safety, harmony and strength." She paused again, then said, "Some of you may remember that." There were glances exchanged and nods from the older women.

She pointed at Lyssa and said, "But that all changed because of people like Lyssa." Lyssa scoffed, but Tove ignored her. "It was when she fixed the vote after the fire to put her people on the Ruling Council that things really changed."

"Liar!" Lyssa spat, but there was an uneasy note to the murmurs that arose in the crowd.

"But what Lyssa has done that you don't know about is far worse," Tove said. "Lyssa is keeping a woman prisoner in her house for the Inquisition." The murmurs in the crowd grew louder. "I've seen Inquisition brothers visiting Lyssa in the middle of the night." Tove had to raise her voice to be heard. "The brothers hid the woman in Téama to have her baby because it was embarrassing to some Imperial men." The murmurs gave way to shouts. Many of them calling her a liar. "In exchange for keeping this woman hidden, Lyssa made a deal with the emperor. She's moving the Council to Kartok, getting rid of the Murtair. And she promised to finance his war." Shouting now, she said, "It was her who brought the soldiers to Téama because she knew what would happen when you found out what she planned."

The shouts drowned her out and scuffles broke out.

Elois and three murtair stepped up onto the dais and the volume diminished.

"There's nothing in the Charter that allows them to speak!" Lyssa said.

"Actually," Cianna said, from the audience, raising her voice so most in the Great Hall could hear. "If there is a question of fact, the speaker can call witnesses to corroborate their story." She looked at Tove. "Do you wish Elois to speak on your behalf?"

"Um… sure."

Elois smiled at Cianna, then gazed out at the women in the Great Hall, as comfortable addressing such a large crowd as Tove wasn't. When she spoke, her voice rang out. "When Tove told Cianna Lyssa was holding a woman prisoner, Cianna couldn't believe it. How could a Desulti violate the principles of the Order so completely? But it is a serious accusation, so she came to me and asked me to go to Lyssa's house and speak to the woman."

"You broke into my house?!" Lyssa asked. "I would expect that kind of behavior from the *Voss*, but —"

"As a matter of fact," Elois said, her voice rising to cut Lyssa off. "A very nice Inquisition brother invited me in."

Lyssa gaped at her and silence spread like a wave toward the back of the room as her words were repeated.

When Elois turned back to face the crowd, she only needed to speak in a normal voice when she said, "Cianna asked me to speak to this woman because the nature of her imprisonment suggested she was a woman of high standing. As it turns out, I know her personally. We've been friends for many years. She wishes to keep her identity secret, and I will honor her request. But I can assure you everything Tove said is true."

In the stunned silence that followed, Tove said, "I'm not sure who you should vote for in this election. But when you vote, remember last night. We weren't Gabra, Angus, Baird, Burne or Brochen. We were all Desulti. We survived because we supported one another. That's how it should be."

"They call me Baird, but I'm Desulti and I'm proud!"

Startled, Tove looked down and found Gwynna, equal parts surprise that she spoke and mortification at the twitters that greeted her pronouncement on her face.

Danu, standing beside her, rested a hand on her shoulder and shouted, "They call me Burne, but I'm Desulti and I'm proud!"

There was an awkward silence, then Elois, still standing next to Tove, said, "They call me Gabra, but I'm Desulti and I'm proud."

Others, mostly the women who went with Tove to Ka'tan or attended the Desulti festival, answered. Then a chorus of declarations joined them. Not everyone spoke, but many did, and the mood in the room shifted subtly. Easy laughter and quiet conversations broke out.

"Are you done?"

Tove turned and found Nessa standing next to her, a stiff smile pasted on her face. Tove looked at Cianna, who nodded. "Yeah, I'm done," she said. She stepped off the dais and allowed Nessa to explain the procedures for the election. Lyssa had disappeared.

Moments later, as the crowd headed toward the exit. Cianna found Tove. "That was well done. Brie was right to choose you."

"You and Brie and whoever else been using me," Tove said.

"Yes," Cianna said brightly, then she cocked her head and let a small frown wipe away her smile. "Let me amend that. I guessed what Nessa planned for you and used it against her."

Tove studied her, then looked at Danu, who took her hand and said, "It was Cianna who had me organize people to keep you safe, and she had Laoise watch over you."

"You could have told me," Tove said to Cianna.

Cianna's smile returned. "Tove, I may be wrong, but I'm guessing guile is not one of your strengths."

"Guile?"

"You are who you appear to be. A good person. And that is why so many people grow to like you when they know you." Cianna winked and said, "I wouldn't risk changing that for anything."

Tove wasn't sure what that meant, but she didn't feel like pursuing it. She nodded to Elois, who was talking to Siofra on the dais. "Elois knew everything I did. Why didn't you just have her speak instead of me?"

"Because now everyone will remember, *you* were the hero." Cianna patted Tove's shoulder, then turned to join a waiting Laoise. The two of them joined the crowd, heading toward the exit.

"Not sure what I think of that." Tove said.

Danu pressed herself against Tove's side and grinned. "Let's go get something to eat while you think about it."

"In the dining hall?"

"I think after last night and today, you may find you are more welcome," Danu said.

***

It took four days to hold an election that should have taken one. Between the trauma of the attack on the village and the inclusion of Lyssa on the election panel, many women were reluctant to participate. But the Charter was clear. Only Nessa could remove Lyssa, and she had complete control of the timing of the election. Intense lobbying by Cianna and Elois finally convinced enough women to vote.

Shailey carried the chest containing the ballots into the council room. Lyssa followed and fell into a chair at the conference table. She had hidden in her bedroom in her house since her crimes came to light and had nothing to do with the election. It had taken Shailey and Laoise to make her emerge so the ballots could be counted. Tilla closed the door and came to stand beside Shailey, who set the chest on the table.

Lyssa wasn't sure what her future held. Nessa made it clear she didn't feel obligated to honor their agreement. Lyssa held out hope Nessa would be content to allow her to preside over a smaller Desulti operation in Kartok. That would put Lyssa close enough to powerful people in the Empire. People she could use to resurrect her fortunes. And eventually take her revenge.

"How long should we wait to make it look good?" she asked.

Shailey crossed to the cabinet and extracted an identical-looking chest with the ballots Nessa prepared. She carried it to the hearth, knelt and started tossing the ballots into the fire.

"What?!" Lyssa leapt to her feet.

Tilla moved to insert herself between Shailey and Shailey. She pointed to the seat Lyssa vacated and said, "Sit down."

Lyssa's mouth worked, but no sound emerged. She looked past Tilla to Shailey, who was tossing the last ballots into the fire.

When Shailey finished, she rose and said, "You two have been making a mess of things long enough. You and Nessa." She returned the empty chest to the cabinet and locked it.

"What about the vote?" Lyssa asked.

Shailey unlocked the chest she placed on the conference table and lifted the lid. She pointed to the far end of the conference table and said, "You are excused from counting votes. Sit, so I don't have to make you. And keep quiet."

"You think you can keep me quiet about this?" Lyssa asked.

"Absolutely not," Tilla said with a chuckle, pulling a handful of ballots from the chest. "Feel free to tell *everyone* how we made sure the election was fair."

"But…" Lyssa's eyes roamed the room. "How…" She focused on Tilla. "You were Nessa's spy."

Shailey and Tilla laughed as they lowered themselves into chairs and arranged themselves to count. "I stopped working for you or Nessa when I saw what you were doing to the Order," Tilla said.

"But…"

"Sit. Down," Shailey said.

After Lyssa returned to her seat, Tilla said, "Cianna has been trying to come up with a way to get rid of you for a long time. When Brie showed up with Tove, she guessed Nessa was plotting."

"She didn't know what, so she came to us to find out what Nessa had in mind," Shailey said.

"It was a risk, coming to us, but she knew we were as dissatisfied as many others," Tilla said. "Once she knew what Nessa was up to, she let you two play your games. It was a gamble that Nessa would choose Shailey or me to oversee the election, but…" Tilla lifted her hands, palms up, and shrugged.

"Cianna is often right," Shailey said.

"It was dangerous for Tove, but Cianna did what she could to keep her safe."

Lyssa gaped at them. "You're fixing the election."

"No, we're ensuring a *fair* election. I imagine that's what has you confused. We don't know the outcome, but we assumed it couldn't be worse than what you and Nessa were cooking up," Shailey said. "For me, wasn't sure it was the right way to go. Too risky." She shook her head and chuckled. "But I feel better about it after your bungling. Bringing Imperial soldiers to attack a village of women who fled the Empire because of men. Not your smartest move."

"And holding a woman prisoner and giving her baby away to the Inquisition," Tilla said. "It's like you have no idea why the Order exists."

"Now, sit there and keep your mouth shut," Shailey said.

***

Tove and Gwynna sat on a bench at the edge of the plaza, enjoying the warm day as they waited for the results of the election. Tove glanced at Gwynna and said, "You're awfully quiet today."

Gwynna let a dreamy smile grow on her face. "I'm just happy, is all." She started to say something else, but then gave her head a shake and fell silent.

Tove looked across the crowded plaza and spotted a familiar face among three people entering the plaza on horseback. Seele, her fulling coworker, reined up and searched the plaza. When he saw Tove waving, he reached out and tapped the shoulder of one of the women with him and pointed. They dismounted and led their horses toward Tove and Gwynna. A furtive looking dog accompanying them weaved in and out of the crowd.

"Who is that?" Gwynna asked.

"A friend," Tove said. She took in Gwynna's worried frown and said, "Gwynna, you told me you liked taking care of the animals on your farm back home."

After a moment, a small smile appeared on Gwynna's face and she nodded.

"I may have found a job for you. Well, more than a job, really."

Seele stopped twenty paces away and said something to the two women, then took their reins. The two women and the dog approached.

Tove stood and grasped the older woman's offered forearm. "You must be Eula. I see the resemblance," she said and gestured to Seele.

"Yep," she said. She put her hand on the shoulder of the younger woman. "This is my daughter, Hallie. And Inga," she said, gesturing to the dog who sat beside Hallie, tongue lolling.

Tove thought Hallie might have fifteen summers. She gestured to Gwynna, who was watching warily. "This is Gwynna."

"Hello Gwynna," Eula and Hallie said at the same time.

"Hello," Gwynna said in a small voice.

Tove sat beside Gwynna and got her attention. "Eula owns a sheep farm."

Gwynna frowned at Tove, lifting a hand to shade her eyes from the sun.

"Her husband was arrested by the Empire, so she and her daughter are running the farm by themselves." Tove pointed to Seele. "That's Eula's father. He isn't able to work very much anymore."

Gwynna glanced at Seele, then returned her gaze to Tove.

"He's a *good* man," Tove said. "Very kind."

"We were wondering if you would want to come live with us. Help us run the farm," Eula said.

Gwynna looked at her, her lips parted. "Sheep?" When Eula nodded, she said, "I don't know anything about sheep."

"But you know about animals," Tove said. "You'll learn."

"We have goats, chickens, ducks and horses, too," Hallie said brightly. "Sheep are easy." She stooped and scratched behind the dog's ears. "Inga is one of our sheepdogs. We have livestock dogs too. They keep the sheep safe from predators." She stood. "The dogs do most of the work. Until the spring. That's when we shear the sheep." She rolled her eyes. "That's a lot of —"

Her mother put a hand on her shoulder again and gave her a smile.

"I talk a lot," Hallie said, a smile lighting up her face.

Gwynna gave her a tentative smile, then she looked at Tove and the smile fell away.

"Siofra says wool is important enough to the Order, she wants someone to learn about sheep. It's a job. Siofra says she'll pay you to go learn." Tove watched a smile trying to find a place on Gwynna's face. "It's a lot better than the laundry, right? And it's really important for the Order."

The smile almost blossomed, then faltered. "I'll have to live there?"

"Yes," Tove said. "But you'll be nearby. You can visit and we'll come visit you. There will be festivals. We'll see each other at the Boar's Head." She glanced at Eula, who nodded. Tove had seen her and her daughter on previous visits to the tavern.

"Can you ride?" Eula asked.

Gwynna shook her head.

"You'll learn," Eula said. "You can come and visit with all your friends one night every week. I'm sure Hallie would enjoy that as well."

Hallie's head bobbed.

"My friends?" Gwynna asked, her brow furrowing. She looked at Tove.

"Yes," Tove said. "You're still Desulti. Like other women out doing the Order's business. You'll just be closer." She gestured to the women in the plaza. "We'll get everyone together, one day each week, and have a party. You can tell us about the farm."

"It's really pretty!" Hallie blurted. "And we have a room for you all ready. It's warm and cozy, especially when you have a dog to sleep with —"

"Hallie," her mother said. She looked at Gwynna and said, "You can come for a month. If it doesn't work out, no hard feelings."

Gwynna gazed at her, then frowned at Tove.

Tove nodded. "Give it a try. You might find you like sheep."

Gwynna looked at Eula, then Hallie, and tried another smile. "Okay."

"Come on," Hallie said. "We can go get your things. You can show me around. I've never been in Téama."

After Tove gave Gwynna an encouraging nod, she rose and fell in beside Hallie. Tove stood, joined Eula, and watched Gwynna patting one of the horse's necks, listening to a constant stream from Hallie.

"She'll be fine," Eula said.

Tove watched them set off across the plaza, Gwynna pointing out various sights in the plaza, Inga at their heels. "Yeah."

A bell rang, the signal that the election results were about to be announced. Tove took Eula's forearm again and said, "I'll come check on her in a week." Waving to Seele, she joined the crowd streaming toward the Great Hall.

Danu was waiting for her just inside the entrance. She gave Tove a quick kiss and asked, "How did it go?"

"Hard to tell with Gwynna, but I think she's going to love it there," Tove said.

The murmur of the crowd quieted as Tilla and Shailey appeared on the dais on the far side of the reception hall. They were joined by Nessa, who stood confidently beside Tilla, and Lyssa, who slouched, arms across her stomach at the back of the platform.

Tilla waited until she had everyone's attention, then she said, "The members of the Ruling Council, in alphabetical order, are Cianna —"

"What?!"

It was Nessa. Nessa turned a shocked frown on Lyssa, who shook her head.

Smiling, Tilla resumed reading the results.

"She doesn't look happy," Tove said to Danu.

"Not what she expected, apparently," Danu said as Nessa exited through a door at the back of the platform. Lyssa hesitated, then followed.

"What do you suppose will happen to Lyssa?" Tove asked.

"She could always go home," Danu said.

"Would her family take her back? I know she came with her sister, but she's been here a long time. She could have gone home before."

Danu shrugged. "I don't care, as long as she can't cause any more harm."

As the last name was read a ragged cheer rose. Soon, others joined in and the mood was very light as women filed out of the Great Hall. "I don't know most of those names," Tove said. "Except for Cianna and Elois."

"It's mixed." When Tove raised a brow, Danu said, "Different castes." She grinned. "You want to go for a walk?"

"A walk?"

"Yeah. We can walk over to your room."

Chapter 34

Murtair

"We need to get you a better place," Danu said. "You need a window, at least." Tove and Danu were in Tove's room, getting acquainted after Tove returned from a three-day hunting trip.

"I don't know," Tove said with an uncharacteristically impish grin. "It's private. No one around to hear anything."

"You'll just have to learn to be quieter," Danu said, nibbling Tove's chin.

Before Tove could respond, someone knocked on her door.

"Who could that be?" Tove mumbled as she rose from the bed. She opened the door to find Brie waiting. When Brie spotted Danu sitting on the bed, a brow lifted. Feeling her cheeks warm, Tove said, "Brie."

"The Inner Council wants to see you," Brie said.

"Now?"

Brie only gave her a quizzical frown.

"Right," Tove said. "Now." She waited until Danu joined her, then the three women made their way out onto the plaza.

Before they climbed the steps to the Great Hall, Danu gave Tove a quick kiss and said, "Come find me at home." Then she waved to Brie and headed to her apartment.

Brie watched her go, then turned to face Tove, her feelings hidden by a familiar mask. Before Tove could say anything, Brie held up a hand to stop her. "I used you. Put you in a dangerous situation. I trusted that Nessa had your welfare at heart. I was wrong about that. But I did it for the Order and, more importantly, for my sister. And it worked. I would do it again." She paused. "Plus, I approve of you and my sister."

Tove studied her. It was pretty much what she worked out for herself, and she appreciated the honesty more than she would an apology. She nodded to the Great Hall and asked, "What do they want?"

"Let's go see."

They headed up the steps, through the open doors, and across the reception hall to the door that led to the council room. When Tove entered, the new members of the Inner Council were sitting in the same places as the old Inner Council. They all rose when Tove and Brie appeared.

Cianna, the new Chief Executive, came around the table. She took Tove's hand in both of hers and smiled. "Tove, it's good to see you. I apologize that we have taken so long to have this meeting, but we've been very busy, as you can imagine."

"It's okay," Tove said. She nodded to Laoise, the new head of the Murtair and Siofra. "I've been hunting, anyway."

"And quite successfully," Cianna said with a bright smile, "if the reports from the dining hall are to be believed."

Tove wasn't sure what to say, so she only smiled and nodded.

Cianna gestured to chairs at the table near the end where the Inner Council sat. "Please, have a seat. Both of you." When they were all seated, Cianna cupped her hands on the table and smiled at Tove. "We called you here for two reasons. We have a proposal for you, but before we get to that, I imagine you have questions for us."

Tove glanced at Brie, then sifted through the many questions that had occupied her over the past couple of weeks. Most of them Danu was able to answer, but there were a few she wanted to ask these women. "Were you in on it from the beginning?" Tove asked Cianna. "When you assigned yourself as my counselor?"

Cianna smiled and tipped her head, as if she expected this question. "No. I became suspicious when Brie brought you to Téama. But when I heard Nessa supported your petition, I knew she and Brie were planning something." She paused and pursed her lips disapprovingly. "Nessa has no love for those she deems lower than herself and would have been little better for the Order than Lyssa." She smiled. "It was only after I learned from Tilla and Shailey what Nessa had in mind that I decided to use her plans against her. I assigned myself as your counselor to find out what kind of woman you were and put myself in a position to protect you."

"Hela," Tove said.

"Yes, among other ways. Please, don't hold it against him."

Tove looked at Siofra.

"I suspected what Nessa intended," Siofra said. "But I wasn't sure until Brie confirmed it when she came to me in Lachton."

Tove glanced at Brie, then said to Cianna, "You said you wanted to use Nessa's plans against her." When Cianna nodded, Tove asked, "How?"

"Remember, I told you how Lyssa used the fire that killed many on the Council to hold a new election?"

"And fixed the election," Tove said.

"That was what Nessa planned," Laoise said. "She wanted to stoke the unrest Lyssa's reforms started. When the anger erupted, she planned to declare an emergency and call for a new election."

"We assumed she wouldn't hold a fair election," Cianna said. "But there *would* be an election. All we wanted to do was make sure it was a fair election."

"How were you sure who would win the election?"

"We weren't," Cianna said. "But then you discovered Lyssa's crimes, and she was foolish enough to invite the soldiers from the fort in Téama."

"All our efforts were in reducing the damage Nessa's efforts caused," Laoise said.

"We were not always successful, unfortunately," Cianna said. "It was a fine line we walked. When we discovered Nessa recalled the murtair, we decided a *staged* riot would give Nessa the emergency she needed, while minimizing the potential for uncontrolled violence. We didn't want anyone to be hurt."

"The problem was there were only a few people we could let in on the plan," Laoise said. "We didn't want it getting back to Lyssa or Nessa."

"We were about to start the show when the soldiers appeared," Cianna said.

"You were playing a dangerous game," Tove said, remembering the near riot in the aftermath of Tish's attack on her.

"Yes," Cianna said. "But what alternative did we have? Some people already suspected what Lyssa did with the fire, but we had no proof. Nessa might have been a better option than Lyssa, but she would not have returned the Order to what it once was. My only doubt was whether we should tell you what was happening. If we told you, what would you have done?"

Tove stared at her, then let her gaze drift as she considered. She had known from the beginning Nessa had something in mind. Would knowing the details have changed anything? She thought of Danu, the Desulti festival, and the women who waved and greeted her with smiles now. Despite everything, she found what she came to Téama to find. And the truth was, she lived in the shadow of violence her entire life. Not once had she felt as unsafe here as she had every day in Kartok.

"I couldn't honestly say. It doesn't sit right with me that everyone had plans for me I didn't know about, but I can't argue with the outcome." Before anyone could prolong the discussion, Tove asked, "You said something about a proposal?"

Cianna gave her a bright smile. "Of course, but if any other questions occur to you, we are at your disposal anytime. We owe you a great deal." When Tove nodded, Cianna gestured to Laoise.

"Cianna mentioned you were interested in becoming Murtair."

Tove stared at her, reassuring herself she heard right. This was why she came to the Order. To give herself time to organize her thoughts and catch her breath, she glanced at Brie, who nodded.

"I know the dining hall will be sorry to see you go," Cianna said. "But Brie and Laoise both recommended you for the program and we always need Murtair."

"There's no guarantee," Laoise said. "Few women complete the program."

"And of those who do, most don't remain Murtair for long," Brie said. "The physical demands require a young person's body." She paused, then said, "And it's very dangerous."

"Yes," Laoise said. "Think, very carefully, whether this is really something you want."

"When do I have to decide?"

"There is no deadline," Cianna said. "However, the sooner you start, the sooner the Order will have a new Murtair."

The conversation continued for another half hour, then Brie and Tove left. On the steps of the Great Hall, Tove asked Brie, "Is it worth it?"

"Only you can answer that for yourself," Brie said. "It's a solitary existence while you're on a contract. You need to be self-reliant, physically tough and disciplined." She paused. "And you will have to leave loved ones for weeks at a time. It can be a hard life." She held Tove's gaze for a moment, then shrugged. "For me..." The mask slipped. "I like the power. I like knowing there is no one in the Empire I need fear. I like knowing women have a safe refuge because of my sacrifices."

"Do you think I can do it?"

Brie didn't hesitate. "Yes."

***

"A murtair?!" Danu asked.

They were walking the road to Ka'tan to meet Gwynna and Hailey at the Boar's Head. "Yes," Tove said. Her initial excitement had slowly diminished as she contemplated Brie's warning about having to leave loved ones.

"No," Danu said. "I'm afraid every time Brie leaves. If something were to happen to her… or you, I may never know what."

"Becoming Murtair was the reason I came to the Order," Tove said.

"But that was before you had what you have now. You have hunting. You said how much you love the mountains. There's Hela, Gwynna, Brigid and all the others." She stopped, forcing Tove to stop and face her. "You have me."

"I'll still have you," Tove said.

Danu shook her head. "I won't wait. I'm not going to go through that with you."

"Danu —"

"No!" She made a cutting gesture with her hand. "I won't talk about it anymore."

Tove sighed, taking in her bleak expression. "We're going to be late. Let's go have dinner with Gwynna. We can talk about this later."

Danu hesitated, then started walking without responding.

Tove took Danu's hand and tried a grin. Danu tried to pull away, but when Tove held her fast, Danu leaned into her.

When they entered the Boar's Head, no one paid them any attention. Tove wasn't surprised to find a dozen or so Desulti among the patrons, some of them sitting at tables with *Alle'oss.* She scanned the room and found Gwynna sitting with Hallie, the farmer's daughter, near the wall. They were frowning up at Seele, who stood next to the table, gesticulating with his arms as he talked. When he threw his arms above his head and bent slightly forward, Hallie burst out laughing. Seele walked away with a smile on his face. Gwynna frowned, perplexed, until Hallie whispered something to her. Surprise wiped Gwynna's frown away, then a smile blossomed, transforming her entire demeanor. She laughed, a hand covering her mouth.

"What is going on there?" Tove asked.

"She's happy," Danu said, amazed. She gripped Tove's arm. "Don't let Gwynna know we were arguing. She'll feel bad about it."

Tove studied her worried face. "We're not fighting. We're working through a decision that affects us both." She hesitated, then said, "But you're right. Let's not spoil the night."

***

Tove and Danu returned to Téama in silence. Only when they reached the outskirts of the village did Tove speak. "I think Gwynna said more words tonight than in all the time I've known her."

"It still wasn't a lot, but with Hallie sitting next to her, she couldn't get a word in edge wise." Danu met Tove's eyes. "That girl can talk." She looked ahead. "Still, I've never seen Gwynna smile so much. The farm has been good for her."

"I think Brigid and Jens are getting serious. It's good she doesn't remember what happened," Tove said, trying to keep the conversation going. Danu only nodded. They fell silent again until they were crossing the plaza when Danu pulled Tove to a stop. Following her gaze, Tove found a familiar boy loitering at the entrance to the street that passed in front of her dormitory.

"Who is he?" Danu asked.

Tove stopped and stared at him. He grinned when he noticed her. "Aron," Tove said.

"Who?"

Tove took Danu's hand and started walking without answering. When they neared him, Tove glanced around and asked, "Ragan around?"

"She's waiting in your room." He nodded at Danu. "Danu."

They left him and made their way to her room. Before she opened the door, Tove whispered, "Whatever you hear in here…" She stared open-mouthed at Danu, not sure how to end the sentence. After a moment, she gave her head a shake and said, "Just listen. I'll try to explain later." Opening the door, she mumbled, "If I can."

Ragan was sitting on Tove's bed, gazing around at the small space. Alone.

"Where's Lika?" Tove asked, pushing the door closed.

Ignoring the question, Ragan greeted Danu, then said to Tove, "Tove, you single-handedly changed the Order. For the better. You should be proud."

"Not taking all the credit," Tove said, taking Danu's hand. When Ragan only smiled, she said, "But, yes, I'm proud of what happened here. This what you saw would happen?"

Ragan didn't answer. Her head tilted to the side, and she gazed at Tove speculatively. "What will you do, Tove? Are you going to become Murtair?"

"You mean you don't know?"

"Danu doesn't want you to," Ragan said, giving Danu a sad smile. "And I can understand why."

"But?"

"I'm sorry, Danu, but…" Ragan fixed Tove with a stare. "I need you to. All of Argren needs you to."

Tove rolled her eyes. Always the dire pronouncements with this woman. "So I have to choose; Danu or all of Argren? That what you're putting on me?"

Ragan sighed and gazed at the wall behind Tove. "The future is always in flux. Nothing is ever certain. That is why I never tell anyone what I see in their futures. There are no guarantees." She paused and focused on Tove, a question in the lift of her brows.

"I understand." Tove's heart sped. She glanced at Danu and squeezed her hand.

The witch's gaze returned to the wall behind Tove and Tove felt the twist in her mind that meant the witch was opening herself to the spirits. Danu let out a small gasp, but Tove held her hand firmly.

"Some currents in time are stronger than others, some visions are more… likely to come true," Ragan murmured. She lifted a hand and stared at something Tove couldn't see. "I see you and Danu walking, hand in hand, your hair gone to gray." She focused on Danu, then on Tove. The twisting sensation diminished.

"Why would you tell me this?" Tove asked.

"Because family and friends are more important to you than anything," Ragan said. "If I asked you to choose between Danu and Argren, you will always choose Danu." She gave her head a shake. "I'm telling you, so you know that's not a choice you have to make."

Tove could only stare at her.

"Neither of you must tell anyone what I've told you," Ragan said. "The cause and effect of time is fragile. I could not predict what would happen if you told anyone." She rose and gave them both a sad smile, then headed to the door.

"Is the boy okay?" Tove asked as she opened the door. "Lika?"

Ragan looked back and smiled. "Oh, yes. He is safe and happy."

When she was gone, Tove sat on the bed.

Danu hesitated, then sat beside her. "What was that about? Who is she?"

"She is… was a Seidi novice," Tove said.

"I know. I saw the tattoo," Danu said, exasperated.

"She can see the future," Tove said. "She helped us rescue someone from an Inquisition prison in Kartok last year."

"The future…" Danu said. "I don't understand. How is that possible?"

"It's complicated," Tove said. "It's her gift. Her magic. But it's not like everything she sees comes true. Some do and some don't. I don't know how she can tell which ones."

"But she said we grow old together. You and I. And it sounded like she was sure of it."

Tove gazed into Danu's worried eyes, then rested her elbows on her knees, let her hands dangle, and focused on the floor. Despite what the witch said, Tove still had to make a choice. Was Ragan telling the truth? Would she survive being Murtair and have a long, happy life with Danu? Or was Ragan just giving Tove the excuse she needed to make the choice Ragan wanted her to make?

"What does she want?" Danu asked. "Why does she say Argren needs you to be Murtair?"

"She trying to get rid of the Empire. That's the future she's trying to bring to pass."

"Get rid… Is that possible?"

"I don't know," Tove said, sat up and turned toward Danu. "Alar thinks so."

The uncertainty on Danu's face disappeared, replaced by a determined frown. "Promise me."

"Promise what?"

"Promise me you will always come home," Danu said. "Promise me I will *always* be more important than any contract. If you have to fail at your mission so you can come home, that's what you will do."

"What are you saying?"

"You told me once you chose to fight. That you would continue to fight. If you are going to fight, this is the best way because the witch said you'll always come back to me. She may be lying, but she might not be. It's more than we would have any other way." She paused, gave Tove a determined nod and said, "If this witch believes you being Murtair will help end the Empire, then that's what you should do."

Tove stared at her, suddenly aware of her scent. She cradled Danu's cheek with her hand, brushed her lips with her own and whispered, "I promise." She kissed her neck. "I promise." She ran the tip of her tongue along Danu's jaw, sucked on her earlobe and whispered, "I promise." She eased Danu onto her back, lowered herself down on top of the woman she loved, gazed into her eyes and whispered, "I promise, I will always come home to you."

***

"It's time." Danu said.

Tove nodded and asked, "Are you sure about this?"

"Are you?"

"Yes," Tove said with a firm nod.

Danu started to turn away, then Tove caught her arm. "I have a surprise." Faced with Danu's wide, curious eyes, Tove had to drop her gaze. Forcing herself to look up, she said, "I got an apartment. It's… uh, down the street from yours. It has a window. Windows. More than one…" For the Mother's sake, she was about to become Murtair. Why was this so hard? She grinned. "Anyway, It's big enough for two. I thought we… I mean, you could move in with me." She looked away. "If that's okay."

She nearly fell over backward when Danu leapt onto her, wrapping her arms around her neck and planting kisses all over her face. Then she stepped back, a shy smile on her face. Her fingers swiped at her forehead. "We'll be late if I show you how happy I am."

Laughing, Tove wrapped her arms around Danu and kissed her. When they separated, she said, "You can show me later." She took Danu's hand. "Come on."

As they crossed the plaza, the few people who were out waved. "A lot different than the first time," Tove said.

"A lot has changed since then," Danu said. "Not you. You're the same. They've changed."

Tove grinned at her. When she looked toward the Great Hall, she stopped. A man stood on the porch of the Great Hall with Siofra. An *Alle'oss* man. When he saw her looking, a smile broke out on his face. He ran down the steps, leaving a confused Siofra behind. Tove ran to meet him. She threw her arms around him and pressed her face into his chest, then fought free and pushed him with both hands.

"What was that for?" Alar asked, his smile widening.

The old ritual instantly brought back the warm feelings of the home and family she found when Alar brought her into *Oss'stera*. She thumped him on his chest. "That's for not telling me you were in Téama," she said, matching his smile.

"Had to find out where you lived, didn't I?" Alar pulled Tove into a hug, squeezing her, then letting her go. He noticed Danu and said, "Heard you were making friends. Is this Danu?" He let Tove go, then extended a hand to Danu. She took his forearm in the *Alle'oss* fashion.

"You're late."

Tove turned to find Siofra waiting nearby. "Right!" She took Alar's arm and said, "I have something to do right now, but we're going to the tavern in Ka'tan after. You're coming."

"Of course." He said to Siofra, "You want to come?"

Tove wasn't sure Siofra was a tavern kind of woman, but she smiled and said, "I wouldn't miss it. It's time I start making connections in Ka'tan." She grinned at Tove. "Plus, I've heard rumors about a stew that are difficult to believe."

"You're late." Brie had appeared on the top step of the Great Hall. She wasn't smiling when she said, "Not a good start."

"Wait here," Tove said to Danu, then jogged up the steps. Brie led her through a familiar path to the room where her humiliating initiation took place a few short months ago.

"Ready?" Brie said. When Tove nodded, Brie opened the door.

The room looked the same as the last time. It was illuminated by lamps on the walls, dozens of candles on tall stands and two braziers near the dais on the far side. However, instead of dozens of women in white robes, ten murtair in their blacks stood in an arc centered on Laoise who stood on the spot where Lyssa stood before.

"There usually aren't so many murtair in Téama," Brie said. "But Nessa recalled them weeks ago. Now, if you are finally ready." Her words were softened by a slight curve of her lips.

Tove took a breath, stepped across the threshold and let it sigh out between parted lips. After a brief pause, she approached Laoise. Noting the small cushion on the floor, she grinned.

She stopped, scanned the faces of the silent murtair, then focused on Laoise. She was surprised when Laoise smiled at her.

"Welcome, Tove," she said and the other women intoned their welcome. "Your journey begins today. It will be more difficult than anything you've ever done. Few women reach the destination and become Murtair. But being here is a great accomplishment. It symbolizes our belief in you." She lifted her arms toward the other murtair. "You are among women who will be your sisters for life."

"Kneel," she said. After Tove had settled onto the cushion, she said, "You shed your hair as you shed your previous life." She nodded to someone behind Tove.

Tove heard a footstep on the stone floor and braced herself, but the hands that took hold her hair were gentle. The sheers cut easily, and the hair wasn't dropped into her face. The murtair watched in silence as her hair was shorn. When the sheers disappeared, strong, calloused hands applied a cream to her scalp. The razor that removed the stubble had been whetted and left her skin smooth in a single swipe. After the soothing salve was massaged into her scalp, Tove looked up at a smiling Laoise.

Brie appeared to block her view, looking down at Tove, but she heard Laoise speak. "Because we are not all the same, our journeys to becoming Murtair are our own. You will need a guide to help you along the way. Brie has asked to be your guide. She will be your teacher, mentor, counselor, taskmaster, and your advocate. Being Murtair means you keep our secrets. It means you will adhere to our standards and rules, the first of which is that you must obey your guide in all things. Failure to do any of these will result in your immediate dismissal." When she paused, Tove looked up at Brie's face and saw no sympathy there.

"Do you agree to these terms?" Brie asked in a loud, clear voice.

Tove had to swallow to moisten her mouth before she could speak, but when she did, her voice was steady. "Yes."

Brie smiled.

"Now we are all sisters for life," Laoise said. "Rise and begin your new life."

Brie reached down, took her arms and helped her to her feet. As soon as she was upright, she was engulfed by smiling murtair.

Chapter 35

Reunion

Lyssa gazed out the window at the trees in the park across the street from her house. Ironically, the Order had imprisoned her in the same attic room where she held the woman for months. Part of her knew it could have been worse. They could have confined her to a small cell in the Gendarmery. But she wasn't in the mood to concede anything to the women who made a ruin of her life.

The door that led to the main staircase opened and the murtair, Caedon, entered. One of the many petty slights they forced her to endure was that no one bothered knocking when they entered. Lyssa watched the murtair scanning the room until she found Lyssa sitting in the alcove created by the dormer at the front of the house.

"You have a visitor," the murtair said. "You have ten minutes."

Lyssa's heart thumped, and she sat up. She didn't really care who the visitor was. Anything to interrupt the monotony was welcome. When the murtair stepped aside, revealing Nessa, Lyssa sighed and settled back. Nessa had been about to abandon Lyssa and their deal after the *l'oss's* speech. She couldn't forgive that. Worse, she had escaped punishment despite her crimes against the Order.

Nessa moved further into the room, her eyes lingering on the unmade bed and the discarded clothes littering the floor. She eased herself into the chair across from Lyssa and glanced at the murtair who stood beside the door.

"You lied about the murtair," Nessa said, when her gaze returned to Lyssa. When Lyssa frowned, Nessa said, "About the Inquisition waiting for them on the road from Richeleau. You didn't know I recalled them. All of them returned safely."

Lyssa didn't respond.

"You were lucky," Nessa said. "If it were me, after the debacle with the soldiers, I would have thrown you into a dark cell and forgotten about you."

Lyssa snorted. "Lucky," she mumbled. "They're sending me to Hautten. You know what Hautten is known for?" When Nessa didn't respond, Lyssa looked out the window and said, "Fish. Fog. Rain. A lot of rain."

Nessa chuckled. "Oh, come on. You'll be the only Gabra in Hautten. I'm sure they will show you all the deference you expect."

Lyssa's head rotated until she was looking at Nessa. "And what about you? How did you escape their retribution?"

A frown chased Nessa's mocking grin, and she gazed across the room. "I wouldn't say I escaped entirely. They returned me to my old job. Intelligence analyst." She looked at Lyssa. "I suppose I should be glad the Murtair are so desperate for skilled people." Lyssa looked out the window, and Nessa followed her gaze. "Not like I'll be entirely free. They'll keep a close eye on me."

Lyssa didn't answer. When she learned she would be exiled to Hautten, she began spinning elaborate escape plans. Once free, she would find Hoerst and plot her revenge on the Order. Hoerst was a man who held grudges and after the fiasco with the boy, he would be motivated. He would be angry with her, but he needed her. As the former Chief Executive of the Order, Lyssa knew enough to take the Order apart, piece by piece. That was why they didn't simply expel her from the Order. She knew too much.

Nessa let out a low hiss, bringing Lyssa's gaze back to her face. A quiet intensity on her face caught Lyssa's attention.

"As long as you are alive, there is hope," Nessa said.

"Hope?"

"Revenge." Nessa didn't say the word out aloud. She mouthed it very deliberately, so that Lyssa was sure to understand. Hope, like a sunbeam on a rainy day, swept Lyssa's gloom away. She returned Nessa's smile.

***

Kari and Eirin had been climbing the pass most of the morning over trails that bent back on themselves to make the steep climb manageable. The Northern Mountains dwarfed the mountains of Argren. It had taken them weeks to make their way north from Téama, then west to their destination, but the arduous journey was necessary to avoid the Inquisition brothers who were scouring Argren for Kari and her son.

Eirin had arrived in Lyssa's house not long after Elois visited. The murtair made it crystal clear to Brother Joseph, her guard, that he was no longer in charge. It was a tense moment, but what Kari told Tove was true. The young brother was a good man. Kari thought he even looked relieved when the Desulti arranged for her to disappear. She hoped the Inquisition didn't punish him too harshly for allowing her to escape.

Lyssa was tried by the Desulti and found guilty of subverting the Order's Charter among other crimes. Her sentence, banishment to a remote fishing village on the Empire's western coast, was too lenient in Kari's mind. But the Order wasn't in the habit of imposing harsh penalties and couldn't very well allow her to leave. As the former Chief Executive, she knew too many of the Order's secrets. Lyssa tried to maintain the same haughty superiority as Kari bid her farewell, but Kari could tell it was a facade.

When they finally reached the top of the pass, they paused and looked across the valley to the ancient monastery carved into the slopes of a towering mountain. It was high summer, during the brief period when the sun held sway in the mountains and the temperatures moderated. One grew so accustomed to the wind that it was indistinguishable from silence.

"That the place?" the murtair asked.

"Yes," Kari said, with a wistful note in her voice. "I spent many summers of my childhood among the Eidolon monks in this remote retreat." It was the peacefulness that drew her here. The quiet acceptance of the monks was a balm for the trauma inflicted by the invasive court politics of the Imperial capital in Brennan. It was risky for her to hide here. Ragan had argued against it. The Inquisition was sure to look for her here. But she was confident the monks would keep her secrets.

"It's beautiful," Eirin said, her gaze sweeping the snow-capped mountains that ringed the valley. "I imagine winter is rough, though."

"The winter is challenging, but it will keep the Inquisition away," Kari said. "At least until next summer." She put her hand up to shade her eyes when she twisted in her saddle to look at the murtair. "But you shouldn't linger."

"Well, then," Eirin said, urging her mount into motion. "Let's get you home."

✳✳✳

They left their horses in a stable in the small Tituun village on the valley floor, then mounted the two thousand steps that climbed to the monastery. Altitude and a lack of physical activity since the Inquisition arrested her months before had taken its toll on Kari. They were forced to stop at waystations to allow Kari to catch her breath. Each time she said her devotions to the shrine to Eidolon, Daga's youngest son. Not that she was devout, but Eidolon represented virtues she held dear; virtues like charity, justice, honesty, and wisdom. Virtues the Empire had forgotten long ago.

She was exhausted when they finally arrived at the top, but the familiar sight of the gates and anticipation revived her. With a spring in her step, she crossed the cobbled square in front of the entrance to the monastery and rang the bell. Moments later, the gates creaked open. Three monks Kari had known since she was seven years old appeared, one of them holding a baby boy.

Kari felt her breath catch. When Ragan came to her and told her she would take her son to keep him safe, hope blossomed where she thought none could. She didn't believe Ragan when the witch told her they would be reunited, but the thought that her son would live was enough. Still, she nearly broke down as Ragan carried her son away, his solemn gaze on Kari over the witch's shoulder. When Tove arrived, just as Ragan said she would, she allowed herself a small hope that she might escape the Inquisition and see her son again. But it wasn't until Eirin showed up that she believed. Since then, she fought to tamp down the anxiety about this moment. Would her son remember her?

He gazed placidly at her, a handful of the monk's habit in one fist. "Remember me?" she asked, smiling and reaching tentatively for him. He let her take him, then pulled back and studied her face. For a moment, she feared he wouldn't remember, but then a rare smile appeared and laughter burbled up out of him. He buried his face against her neck, then looked up at her face, reached up and touched her nose. Kari hugged him to her, unashamed of her tears.

She looked up at the smiling monks. "It's nice to see you, Brother Xander. Thank you for looking after my son."

Xander's laughter brought Kari's own childhood back to her. "It's been a long time since we had a child to dote on. Not since you were a little girl. Though your son is much younger, we managed." He winked. "I'm afraid we have spoiled him shamelessly."

"I'm sure. I remember that well," Kari said, burying her nose in her son's mussy hair.

Xander greeted Eirin, then said, "Now come on, let's get you all settled."

About the Author

Ross Hightower and Deb Heim have been partners in crime for nearly forty years. While Ross built a career as a professor and Deb worked on four advanced degrees, they managed to raise two wonderful people and launch them into the world. When Ross started writing his first novel, *Spirit Sight*, they never dreamed they would work together, but after a rocky beginning, they discovered they loved writing together. It took a few beers, many intense conversations, and a few arguments to produce *Desulti*, the second prequel novel in the Spirit Song series. There will be many more to come.

Other Titles by Ross Hightower and Deb Heim

Note from Ross Hightower and Deb Heim

Word-of-mouth is crucial for any author to succeed. If you enjoyed *Desulti,* please leave a review online—anywhere you are able. Even if it's just a sentence or two. It would make all the difference and would be very much appreciated.

And if you would like to read a bonus chapter from *Desulti,* let me know at author@rosshightower.com.

Thanks!
Ross Hightower and Deb Heim

We hope you enjoyed reading this title from:

www.blackrosewriting.com

Subscribe to our mailing list – *The Rosevine* – and receive **FREE** books, daily deals, and stay current with news about upcoming releases and our hottest authors.
Scan the QR code below to sign up.

Already a subscriber? Please accept a sincere thank you for being a fan of Black Rose Writing authors.

View other Black Rose Writing titles at www.blackrosewriting.com/books and use promo code **PRINT** to receive a **20% discount** when purchasing.